Reviews on *THE P...*

FIVE STARS (highest ... exquisite tale of English and Japanese society . . . showing us there is balance in everything, including love."
—*Affaire de Coeur*

"Mary Burkhardt writes a vibrant and original love story that touches your funny bone and your heart."
—Kathe Robin, *Romantic Times*

"Burkhardt is a master at plotting. She has created a heroine who is strong despite her illness and a hero every woman dreams of. THE PANTHER AND THE ROSE is a tale of high adventure, with sexual tension that is bow string tight. Excellent reading!" —*Rendezvous*

Raves on Mary Burkhardt's earlier book,
HIGHLAND ECSTASY:

"Delightful, utterly refreshing. HIGHLAND ECSTASY is a real treasure of a read. Mary Burkhardt's writing has great vitality and exuberance."
—Kathe Robin, *Romantic Times*

"Mary Burkhardt has given us a very endearing love story which will last in readers' minds and hearts. [HIGHLAND ECSTASY] will move you to tears and the story, like a haunting bagpipe melody, will touch your soul."
—*Affaire de Coeur*

"An exciting book . . . Mary Burkhardt has achieved a fine balance of humor and taut suspense . . ."
—*Rendezvous*

MEETING IN THE MIDDLE

Amy sighed, then rested her head on the backs of her arms. "I wasn't trying to kill myself," she admitted. "I was just trying to get away from you."

Slowly, Toshiro lifted her up to cradle her on his lap. "How relieved I am to hear it," he bit out, but his touch was comforting.

Dizzy, Amy had to rest her head against his bare chest. "I've never seen you this way before. It frightened me."

He cupped her chin in his fingers. "Truly, *koneko*, I've never felt this way before. No woman I have ever known has been able to get under my skin the way you do. One minute I want to spank you, the next I want to smother your face with kisses."

She swallowed, then reached up to trace the familiar line of his jaw. When she viewed the cut on his face, she winced. "I'm sorry I hit you with a rock." She reached down to tear away a square of the thin nightgown and used it to blot his face. "I do not understand myself tonight. I'm usually quite deferential. Just ask anyone in Bristol—"

He took her ministering hand and kissed her fingers. "Everyone doesn't know you as I do, fiery lotus."

Lost in the look from his green eyes, Amy could only stare transfixed as he continued holding her in his arms.

"Marry me," Toshiro whispered. He kissed her eyes, her nose, the planes of her cheeks. All the while his hands stroked her body. His lips and tongue savored the salty taste of her skin.

"I . . . I can't, my darling," she answered. "It's impossible . . ."

MARY BURKHARDT
THE PANTHER AND THE ROSE

ZEBRA BOOKS
KENSINGTON PUBLISHING CORP.

ZEBRA BOOKS are published by

Kensington Publishing Corp.
475 Park Avenue South
New York, NY 10016

Copyright © 1993 by Mary Burkhardt

All rights reserved. No part of this book may be reproduced in any form or by any means without the prior written consent of the Publisher, excepting brief quotes used in reviews.

If you purchased this book without a cover you should be aware that this book is stolen property. It was reported as "unsold and destroyed" to the Publisher and neither the Author nor the Publisher has received any payment for this "stripped book."

Zebra and the Z logo Reg. U.S. Pat. & TM Off. Heartfire Romance and the Heartfire Romance logo are trademarks of Kensington Publishing Corp.

First Printing: December, 1993

Printed in the United States of America

To my mother, Mary Donovan of Oswego, New York, who continues to show me how important laughter is to the quality of life. Hi, Mom. It's me, Buster.

and

With special gratitude to Donald McCann—journalist, actor, delightful member of my Oswego family. My first introduction to the magical world of theater came from watching your wonderful performances with the Oswego Players.

One

Bristol, England, April 1768.

"Well, I don't like it. Very odd behavior." Simon Townsend's jowls moved in agitation. "He may be a Dutch count, but what the devil do we know about the fellow? Two years ago the estate next to ours is purchased in his name, all that renovating, then today the man sails into Bristol for the first time to move in. And what in thunderation is in that East Wing of his? Inside shutters across the three windows—even my barber couldn't find out what's hidden in that room, and he knew Queen Charlotte was pregnant again long before the king did. All very bizarre if you ask me."

"No one did ask you." Though less corpulent than his older brother, Henry Townsend had to unfasten one of the silver buttons on his coat to bend his right elbow more easily when he took a pinch of snuff from the back of his hand. A portion of the powdered tobacco landed on the dingy lace at his cuff. "Besides, what would you know about anything bizarre? Greatest problem ever taxes your brain is whether to have nine bottles of claret or Madeira before you devour a side of mutton."

The ripples of skin across Simon's face resembled a ripe tomato. "And I suppose you find time to think while you're mounting those doxies along the harbor. Your burly wife still believes those evenings out are business meetings, does she?"

Henry sneezed into his pocket handkerchief. "I'll thank you to leave Penelope out of this discussion. And she's a more pleasant armful than that pasty-faced barber pole you married."

During their altercation a blond-haired woman sat silently readjusting her fawn-colored gloves. She fidgeted on the cushioned seat of her wooden wheelchair. Telling herself she should be used to her uncles quarreling, Amy Stockwell still experienced that familiar knotting in her stomach. She looked up and sent a silent message to Uncle Giles, who stood closest to her.

Giles Townsend smiled down at his niece. "Gentlemen, it won't do to have the servants hear us. Please, a little less brawling on such a lovely morning." Unlike his two older brothers, fifty-six-year-old Giles did not have the Townsend dark eyes nor their large frame. His voice was much softer, too. "Since Amy is now legally the head of Stockwell Enterprises, the decision is hers."

Amy clenched and unclenched her gloved fingers across the leather covered arms of her wheelchair. The strained silence continued among the three similarly dressed brothers.

"Where the deuce is Clarice?" Simon asked no one in particular.

"You know she never rises before noon," Henry answered. He gave a wicked chuckle. "Wonder if getting up this early will show?"

Amy's features relaxed. She was certain Clarice would look stunning as always. The thought of her devoted aunt comforted her. "I do appreciate your concern about this new business venture, Uncles. However, I believe it is a splendid opportunity for Stockwell Enterprises. Both our colonial and English clientele have been clamoring for more silks, ceramics, and lacquer ware. Since we cannot deal directly with Japan, we're fortunate Count Valerius has contacted our Mr. Rigby, else we might never have had first chance to buy the entire cargo. After I meet the man, I'll . . . we can decide if we wish to enter into the more formal written contract I drew up with Joshua Rigby, and—"

Her words were interrupted when Clarice entered Amy's sitting room, followed by a tall gentleman dressed in coat and breeches, with recently polished riding boots. Sunlight from the window sparked off the dress sword on his hip, and Amy had to turn her gaze from the glare that hurt her eyes.

"David!" Amy greeted in surprise. "You are back from London. How wonderful."

For the first time in weeks, Amy's pale face took on a pinkish hue when the young man gave her an engaging smile, then bent down to take her hand in his. He lowered his head to place a brief kiss across the back of her gloved fingers. Though tempted, the Englishwoman did not reach out to touch his light brown hair with her free hand. Joviality always radiated from him. When he moved away from her wheelchair, Amy knew again how lucky she was to have David Saunders, Earl of Woodcroft, come into her life four years ago, just when she most needed a special friend.

"Now, Amy, are you sure you feel up to this?" Clarice asked. Dressed in lavender gown and traveling cloak, matching felt hat perched at a saucy angle over her black curls, Clarice bent down to tuck the wool lap rug more securely about her niece's cloak-covered legs. "Remember to put your hood up before we leave. Dear me, I know your doctor would not approve."

At the mention of Norbert Wakefield, Amy bit her lower lip. The spindly-legged physician in his mid-sixties would probably raise a raucous if he knew she was leaving the house for a few hours today. But the winter had been so long this year, and though she derived satisfaction from running her late father's business from her sitting room, spring was in the air and she wanted to feel the sun on her face. "Please don't worry, Aunt Clarice. I will be fine. Papa always said first impressions are important. I want to see the ship as she arrives."

"Where are we headed? Can I come, too?"

Amy could not suppress a giggle. For a man of twenty-eight, David still retained a boyish eagerness to be included. "Of course, my Lord, you are most welcome. We are headed to the edge of my property where I can get a first glance at that Dutch ship. Mr. Rigby will meet us there."

David went behind Amy's chair and proceeded to push it slowly out of the room. "I can tell when Amy has made up her mind," he told the others. "Let's get moving. Dash it all, my Dutch is limited to what I picked up on my Grand Tour five years ago. Clean place Holland, lot of canals, friendly people, red-cheeked, smiling girls with large—"

10

"My Lord, really." Giles glanced first at Amy, then his sister. "I hardly think you are sauntering toward a topic suitable for the ladies."

For some unexplained reason, Amy felt David's puckish ways might be catching this morning. "Large what?" she asked with deliberate innocence. From her seated position, the Englishwoman craned her neck to glance over her shoulder. Amy caught a look pass between David and Clarice.

For an instant David's attention went to the area of Clarice's well-formed bosom, where her cape was unfastened. "I'll tell you when you're older, Miss Stockwell," he said to the top of Amy's head.

"Love a duck," muttered Amy. "I'm twenty-five years old; I know you are talking about well-endowed forward keels."

Clarice's brown eyes mirrored her shock. "Amy, I do think you are spending far too much time with those British sea captains who come to Stockwell Hall with their logbooks.

"Oh, David," Clarice added, as he continued wheeling her out of the room, "don't forget my spyglass on the desk."

"You'll see better, Amy, if you're over here." David Saunders began pushing Amy's chair up toward the right, past the cedar tree.

"No, David, stop!" Clarice called, rushing over to them.

Amy had to shut her eyes as panic seized her. She was on that spot near the edge of the cliff. Unconsciously, she gripped the arms of her wheelchair so hard, the muscles cramped in her fingers. When she opened her eyes,

Amy saw the worried features of her aunt. Clarice was pulling the wool hood of her niece's cape more securely over her blond hair. What was wrong with her to be so skittish about the spot after all these years? Amy chided herself. Bless Aunt Clarice for understanding. How much her mother's younger, beautiful sister had given up to take care of her. She could have been happily married, raising children of her own by now. Forcing a half-smile, Amy said, "David is right, this will give me a better view. Not to worry, Clari." Yet, she was grateful when Clarice went to stand protectively behind her chair after David moved away to talk with her uncles.

"I'm cold standing up here," Simon grumbled. "Should have brought a flask of brandy. Anyone think to bring a pork pie?" When no one responded, Simon squinted his left eye and raised Amy's spyglass to his other eye. "About time. There's Rigby. And that must be Count Valerius behind him."

"Valerius?" echoed the Earl of Woodcroft. "May I take a look, Mr. Townsend?"

Seeming not to hear the request, Simon continued peering through the circular eyepiece. "Hold on." He glanced away, frowned, then looked back through the lens.

"What's the matter?" Henry and Giles asked in unison.

Simon swore. "Gad, Rigby should have told us." He thrust the spyglass at Henry, who took a look, then added his expletive to Simon's.

"Good Lord," exclaimed Giles, the third Townsend brother to peer at the gangway below. "What will our neighbors say?"

From Amy's vantage point, all she could make out was the profile of a man dressed in black coat and breeches, dark hair tied neatly at the back of the neck, a hat under his arm. He stood conversing with the shorter Mr. Rigby. What was going on?

"We can't be expected to work with that heathen," Simon went on. "The Townsends have a position to maintain in Bristol."

David was speaking in hushed tones to Amy's three uncles, while her aunt stood with a firm hold on the back of her chair.

"No," answered Simon to a whispered question from the earl. Simon's irritated voice carried some distance. "Rigby never gave us the count's first name. Just said it was T. Valerius. Thought it was probably a long winded Dutch handle, like Toofgekookte or something."

"Henry, what is amiss?"

Scowling, Henry walked over and handed the spyglass to his sister. "Have a gander, Clarice, and see if you're not as disgusted with this trickery as we are."

Before Amy could demand to know the problem, the wooden wheels on her chair lurched forward. She tried to push backward, but it was too late. Crying out in alarm, she gripped the arms of her wheelchair as it pitched down the steep hill with sickening speed. A scream tore from her throat when the sting of cold air and budding branches swiped against her face, yet she dared not raise a hand to shield herself.

The man conversing with Mr. Rigby glanced up immediately at the sound of a woman's outcry, followed by shouts from above. Tossing his three-cornered hat to the ground, he leapt off the side of the gangway.

Before Joshua Rigby barely blinked, the count was racing up the escarpment toward the careening wheelchair.

There wasn't time for Amy to do anything but shut her eyes when she saw the huge jagged boulder ahead. Strange, it was almost comforting to think she would be with her parents now, there wouldn't be any more nightmares about the dragon and . . . instantly, two strong arms scooped her upward. Sky, the shoreline of the Avon River, then the rocky ground spun about her as the rolling motion continued. The tossing stopped when she landed hard across a muscular body.

"Amy?"

She heard the masculine voice, but it seemed so far away. At first, she didn't have enough strength to answer, even when her upper body was moved gently to be cradled in the warm, comforting arms of a stranger. Puffing indignities about being placed on an unknown man's lap seemed illogical at the moment. The faint, pleasant scent of spicy soap assailed her nostrils. Her lashes fluttered open.

"That's right, Amy. Take another deep breath for me. There's a good girl."

Automatically, the Englishwoman complied with the directive. She found herself gazing into the concerned features of her rescuer. Strands of straight black hair had come undone from the leather thong that held his unpowdered locks away from his face. High cheekbones, straight nose, angular jaw line. The earlier scent of soap must have come from his recently shaved face. Her breath caught in her throat when she looked into his green eyes. Then she understood why her relatives had been so upset earlier. The features were unmistakable—

slanting at the corners of his eyes, the texture of the blue-black hair—Count Valerius was part Japanese.

Yet, a more disturbing thought suddenly occurred to her. "Ho . . . how did you know my name?" To Amy, a brief disappointment etched across his face, then it was gone.

"Later, we will talk. Rest for now." He placed a fingertip on her left cheek. Her slender face was red from the biting air and her quick descent down the shrub-covered hill.

His fingers were gentle on her face, but it surprised Amy to realize the small callouses on his palm showed the count did a laborer's work of some sort.

The hood of her cloak had fallen back, followed by assorted pins, which left her blond curls in disarray about her shoulders. "Enchanting," the Eurasian whispered aloud. Then he checked this train of thought and began a more clinical examination of the rest of her.

"Here, stop that," Amy protested. Even through the cloak and gown she could feel his warm hands on her stocking-covered limbs. "Sir, you forget yourself." Amy struggled to move away, only to see her determined rescuer shake his head, before he placed her right back across his outstretched legs.

"I must be sure nothing is broken."

"Dr. Wakefield, my family physician, will see to me, thank you very much. There is no need for you to. . . . Love a duck . . . I mean, I'm quite unharmed," she added, the Stockwell reserve in place. She was relieved when he dropped his hands to his sides at her tone.

"Again, my Lord, I wish to learn how you know my identity when we have never met?"

No answer.

His features became unreadable. Irritating man, Amy thought, rebuttoning the cape about her shoulders. She looked ahead quickly to her right, then blanched when she saw her wheelchair against the gray boulder a few feet away. One of the wooden wheels lay splintered in pieces next to the overturned chair.

Amy clamped a hand to her mouth, fighting the nausea that threatened. "Please, I think I'm . . ." she tried to push away from the count, but his strong hands held her arms again. Humiliated at the thought of losing control, she cried, "Let me go before I puke all ov. . . ."

"Close your eyes," came the soothing voice once more. He pressed her head against his shoulder. "Do not look down there. Just breathe in and out. Listen to the gulls overhead, the peaceful lapping of water against the shore. The sun feels good, does it not? There is nothing to fear. You are safe. Gently, Amy. I am here with you."

As his mesmerizing voice continued, almost like an invisible caress against her senses, Amy found herself relaxing against the strength and warmth of him. Unlike Mr. Rigby or her uncles who clipped out their words and often left their sentences incomplete, this gentleman spoke English with the unhurried preciseness of an educated foreigner. "I do feel better," she admitted.

When she moved back and opened her eyes, the count's expression showed relief. "Thank you for your gallant rescue." She noticed his torn right sleeve and his once fastidious attire covered with dirt and debris. She realized this man had protected her from serious injury with his own body. He'd taken the brunt of their descent to the hard, rocky ground. "Oh, my Lord, were you hurt? I'm so sorry I did not make sure you . . . I mean the rocks, we tumbled down that embankment for what seemed like forever, and . . ."

"I am unharmed, Amy." His sensual mouth turned up at the corners at her quick change back to anxious fluster. "You do not let tranquility stay within your inner place for long, do you, *koneko?*"

Before she could inquire what the foreign word meant, she found herself surrounded by people. David reached them first. The earl bent down and pulled her out of Toshiro's arms, cloak and all. Later this would strike Amy as uncharacteristically impolite.

"Oh, Amy, you gave me such a fright," he said, holding her high against his chest.

When the count stood up, she noticed he was a few inches shorter than David's over-six-foot frame.

"Valerius," David said.

The count returned the earl's nod. "It has been a long time, Woodcroft." Then he went back to brushing some of the landscape off his well-tailored black coat.

"You know each other?" Amy asked. Though David occasionally waved away a servant at home to lift her into the Stockwell carriage, Amy felt embarrassed to be carried by David in front of this man. But since her wheelchair was inoperable, she realized there was little choice.

The Eurasian's features were inscrutable this time as he looked at Amy. "David and I first met years ago at yo—"

"At Eton," David completed.

Aunt Clarice looked ashen-faced when she reached them, with her three brothers and Mr. Rigby puffing behind her. "Poor lamb, are you all right?"

Amy reassured them quickly. "I am unharmed, thanks

to this gentleman's courage. I'll have James Conroy ride back here to retrieve my broken chair. Perhaps he can mend it. From what I could see, the main damage is just to the left wheel."

"Of course, dear. Whatever you wish will be fine, as always." Clarice looked as uneasy as Amy's uncles.

"Is it too late for introductions, Mr. Rigby?" Amy asked in an attempt to relieve the uncomfortable atmosphere for everyone.

"Quite so," said Joshua Rigby. With the barrel chest and meaty hands of a laborer, he possessed the booming voice of a town crier. "Miss Amy Stockwell, I would like you to meet Count Toshiro Valerius, sole owner of Valerius Shipping."

Amy nodded and Toshiro bowed from the waist. "I am honored to meet you, Miss Stockwell."

"Toshiro?" muttered Simon. "Sounds like a sneeze."

The rest of the introductions proceeded with more awkwardness. When Mr. Rigby finished, Amy gave the stranger a wan smile. "Thank you again, Count Valerius, for rescuing me." She saw something soften in the depths of his arresting green eyes.

"The title has only been with me a few months, since my honorable father passed away. Please, Miss Stockwell, my friends call me Toshiro."

Amy felt David's arms tighten around her. Suddenly ashamed at the way the others, save Mr. Rigby, were treating him with such glacial reserve, she added, "Only if you call me Amy, as my friends do, Toshiro."

"Come along," said the Englishman holding her in his arms. "I'd best get you back to the house. You're in no condition to go aboard that ship now. Enough nonsense for one day."

"Pray, just a moment more, David." Amy saw something change in Toshiro's eyes, but his strong face remained impassive. The image of a sleek panther ready to pounce flashed across her mind, but she dismissed it as only her imagination after such a harrowing fright. At the moment David's unusual lack of courtesy began to irritate her. Why was everyone being so discourteous? Clarice and her uncles stood gazing stonily ahead, not an ounce of welcome on their faces.

When two worried-looking Japanese scurried over, followed by a much taller Dutchman, Amy was relieved to see at least someone was acting concerned for Toshiro's welfare in this mishap. The Japanese man was dressed in the gray livery of a European servant. His left shoulder drooped a little when he walked. The lady wore a dark wool kimono, with straw sandals over her sock-covered feet. They looked to be in their fifties, with touches of gray in their black hair, a few lines about the eyes.

After both bowed to Toshiro, the man asked something rapidly in their native tongue. Toshiro answered.

The count turned to the English people about him. "I would like to introduce my two unworthy servants, Iwao." He nodded to the man. "And his wife, Sumi."

Aghast at the derogatory adjective, Amy could only nod after their deep bows. She was brought up short by a man's loud laughter behind the two servants.

"Toshiro, lad, you best explain about Japanese, for I can see Miss Stockwell now thinks you are *een* . . . ogre with your servants."

Amy felt her cheeks warm. Why did she show her feelings so openly?

The count blinked, then caught the merriment in his

19

companion's eyes. "This rambunctious fellow is Jan Roonhuysen, my second in command."

Jan was dressed a bit more casually than his employer, with opened shirt, no outer coat, his brown hair flowing freely about his broad shoulders. Without hesitation he stalked over to Amy, who was still being held in David's arms. He gave her shoulder a pat, much to David's obvious displeasure. "Please to meet you, little lady."

Amy could not help smiling at the Dutchman's open friendliness. "Mr. Roonhuysen, I am happy to meet you also. Did the count's servants understand his English just now?"

Jan looked nonchalant. "*Ja*, that is why Toshiro had to use the term. Sumi and Iwao speak English." He looked back at Toshiro. "Told you she probably thinks you're *onbeleefd*." At the puzzled English faces about him, Jan translated the Dutch. "Rude."

Amy heard David's sound of impatience. "My Lord, I own you must be frightfully tired of holding me. Please put me down against that rock next to you."

David's expression changed instantly. "You're light as a slender reed, Amy. I've sent one of your servants for the carriage, and when it arrives, home you go."

Normally, she accepted David's habit of taking charge like this, but today it ruffled her. She turned her attention back to the count. "I admit, sir, I was taken aback to hear you call your servants 'unworthy' when you introduced them."

"Here you would call Iwao my equerry. In Japan," Toshiro said with patience, "it would be considered bad manners to introduce one's family, including servants, with outward praise. It is seen as a lack of humility. If a father presents his son in Japan as 'My untrained son,' he really means 'I would like you to meet my son,' nothing more. Indeed, he might be glowing with pride inside."

"How odd," Simon pointed out. "Confounded waste of time. Man ought to say what he means."

Henry laughed at his brother. "Mutton face, you ought to try introducing Mabel as your unworthy wife, and see if she bows like they did; probably give you a boot up the bum for it."

"You wouldn't try it either," countered Simon. "When she goes shopping with Mabel, I've seen Penelope lug crates of marzipan in one hand with two hat cases in the other. Isn't it true she used to box at Gentleman Jack's in London?"

Entering into the spirit, Henry added, "Course she did. It's where we met. Had our first romantic tryst in the ring."

Horrified at her uncles' remarks, Amy felt even worse when Simon, Henry, and David burst out laughing. Giles and Clarice smirked. Toshiro and his two servants maintained a mask of polite restraint. God, how could she hope to do business with the Japanese when things were going so awry in only a few moments?

Not sure of what to say, the blond-haired woman sighed with relief when she glanced over David's shoulder and caught sight of the name across the bow just ahead. *"Nightingale*. What a lovely name for a ship." It encouraged her when Toshiro gave her just the hint of a smile. Did he guess how nervous she felt? She giggled aloud, then saw his puzzlement. "My Lord, it just occurred to me how pompous I sounded a few hours earlier when I lectured my uncles on the importance of first impressions. Lord only knows what you must think of me after nearly running you down with my wheelchair." She heard the carriage arriving in the distance. "It appears I'll have to up anchor for the present."

Amy came to a decision. "Count Valerius . . . I mean, Toshiro, if I confess I have another wheelchair at home, based on your first impression of me, will you now feel in peril of your life if I ask you to dine with me at Stockwell Hall tonight?"

She heard David's indrawn breath next to her ear, saw her relatives frown. However, when Toshiro appeared pleased, for once Amy ignored them.

"With my uncles and Mr. Rigby, we can then go over business matters after supper," the Englishwoman added. After all, she didn't want him to think her lacking in decorum or too forward with her invitation.

Again the formal Oriental bow, yet this time he seemed more Dutch with his open smile that reached those piercing green eyes. "I shall be most honored to dine with you this evening . . . Amy."

When her landau arrived, David wasted little time bustling her into the leather enclosure next to him. Her three uncles wedged themselves on the seat across from them. Aunt Clarice said she would stay behind to give the count the directions to Stockwell Hall. Mr. Rigby would see her home. Jan, the solicitor, and Toshiro's two servants went back to the ship to oversee the unloading of the cargo.

Toshiro watched the carriage drive away. He allowed his feelings to show on his sculptured features. While he could brush aside his disappointment Amy did not remember having met him before, he was appalled at the change in the once energetic, laughing little girl. He winced even now recalling that fragile body in his arms as he tried to keep her from harm during the accident. And why did David Saunders, who'd been present at that meeting years ago, deliberately seek to cover it up?

Two

"My Lord?" Clarice Townsend called again.

Toshiro turned and faced the woman standing behind him.

Amy's aunt was dressed more fashionably than her niece, he noted. The lavender cloak and bonnet had a Paris look to them, along with the rich embroidery on the bodice of the gown where her cape now opened. Apparently caring for Amy had not worn this beauty into a decline. At forty-three, Clarice still had the rich dark hair and eyes, the bloom of health on her cheeks he remembered. He gave her a polite bow. "Your servant, Miss Townsend."

As if she guessed the direction of his thoughts, Clarice's appearance changed almost to flirtatiousness. "No doubt, my Lord, you are wondering why the earl and I did not acknowledge meeting you fifteen years ago."

For a reason Toshiro could not explain, the back hairs on his neck prickled in wariness. "I am more concerned to learn what happened to Amy," he stated with uncharacteristic bluntness.

Clarice's expression became less congenial. "Miss Stockwell's personal life is none of your affair. All you need know is that Dav . . . the Earl of Woodcroft and I have been advised by her physician against any attempt to remind her of what occurred the tragic night her parents died. Dr. Wakefield says remembering might result in my niece's complete collapse, both mentally and physically. That she met you earlier on that horrid day cannot be helped. She remembers little of it. The poor child has been through enough, therefore, I must insist you promise never to remind Miss Stockwell," she emphasized again, clearly to censure his earlier familiarity, "of the day you and your late father came to Stockwell Manor."

And that second time he'd come alone to call on Amy months later, Clarice had sent him away. Giving nothing away, Toshiro said, "You guard the English rose well, I see. Please be assured I would never do anything to hurt your niece, Miss Townsend. You have my solemn promise if ever I speak of our first meeting, it must be Amy herself who asks me."

If the woman desired more than this concession, she did not show her displeasure. "Thank you, Count Valerius. Dinner is promptly at six. I will tell Mr. Rigby to accompany you. Good day, sir." With those clipped words, so like her brothers, Clarice turned her back on the count to proceed over to Mr. Rigby, who now waited near his carriage several feet ahead.

Hands behind his back, Toshiro stared down at his now scuffed boots. Cool and dark, beautiful yet forbidding— that was the way he'd remembered Clarice years ago. And he knew already what David thought of him, that first year at Eton gnawing at him once more. He looked ahead toward the sun on the bow of his ship, then began walking back to the gangway. He needed to speak with Mr. Rigby before dinner tonight.

Joshua Rigby raised his hand near the bulbous crystal goblet. "That's fine, Sumi. Though I enjoy his Lordship's brandy, it wouldn't do to have Amy Stockwell's solicitor foxed before we haggle over contracts this evening."

There was a slight smile on the Japanese woman's lips when she bowed, before quietly going out of the room.

Not joining his guest, for he disliked the taste of brandy, Toshiro sat in a similar overstuffed chair across from the Englishman.

After taking a generous swallow of the amber liquid, the older man replaced his glass on the mahogany table to his right. He looked about the tastefully furnished parlor. Gold brocade-covered chairs and sofa, beige and red Chinese carpet over the hardwood floor, which still smelled pleasantly new and recently polished. "I see the window tax doesn't bother you," commented Rigby, observing the number of views he had through the many panes of glass.

The young man smiled. "I enjoy light, airy rooms."

Rigby frowned suddenly. "I should be cross with you for not telling me you knew Miss Amy. Don't forget, I'm still her solicitor. Some people might say you are taking a chance not having separate representation of your own in this business venture."

"I trust you, Joshua."

"But not enough to confide in me." Leaning a strong elbow on the arm of the chair he occupied, Joshua gave the younger man a measured look. "Ah, that inscrutable Oriental mask is up again, I see. Just what the devil are you up to, Valerius? You could have easily sold your cargo in Amsterdam or London for more money. Why come out of your way to Bristol?"

Dressed in black evening clothes in preparation for dining at Stockwell Hall that evening, Toshiro stretched his legs out in front of him and folded his arms across his chest. For a moment he seemed interested in his white stockings and diamond buckles on his black dress pumps. "I have told you, Joshua, I need an English merchant to act as mediator for selling my cargo. Stockwell Enterprises is one of the most successful businesses in England. And you tell me the lady even takes a hand in the business? I am intrigued."

"Harrumph. Intrigued, are you? Well, let me tell you one thing, my Lord, since the day Amy reached her majority four years ago, she's run the business from her rooms downstairs at Stockwell Hall. Others do the legwork, but the decision making is completely hers. One of the few times her late father showed good sense was arranging it in his will. Amy even has meetings with her various employees—heads of departments in her store and certain rough-speaking captains—much to the horror of her lovely aunt." Rigby took another sip of brandy, then he looked straight at Toshiro. "I've known Miss Stockwell for only four years, but I would not take kindly to anyone who sought to harm her. The powerful connections I still maintain in London could prove detrimental to a certain count if he failed to honor the business contract we sign tonight."

When Rigby's host remained silent, the man in his fifties blustered, "Look here, Valerius, I won't have that girl upset. If you plan to dig up past events, I'll end our brief—"

"Clarice Townsend read me the riot act this morning," Toshiro interrupted, raising his hands. "I give you my word you have no cause for alarm on that level."

"Well, at least that's settled." Joshua shifted his frame in the overstuffed chair. "I went along with the logic of your request to keep your first name from them for as long as possible. The Townsends looked ready to hang me when they discovered you are part Japanese, but you tell me you're used to that reaction from Europeans. But if I'm going to represent both your and Amy's interests in this mutual venture, I think I have a right to learn how you know the lady."

Toshiro sat straighter in his chair. "I agree, but first I want you to see one of my prized possessions." He clapped his hands. His aide, Iwao, came in carrying a cloth-covered painting. After handing it to his employer, he bowed and left.

The count rose and carried the picture to the carved wooden sideboard on the other side of the spacious room. "This lady's portrait has traveled with me on every voyage during the past four years. See if you are not as captivated as I have been." Carefully, he untied the outer wrappings.

Rigby got up and walked over to him. "Ah, now I am interested. A picture of risque beauty from your travels, minimal draping, I'll wager, as she languishes on a Turkish sofa."

Giving nothing away, Toshiro held up the carved wooden frame. "I purchased it from a private London dealer four years ago, before it was to be placed on the market for auction. All I could find out was that the lady herself owned the portrait and now wished to sell it. Gainsborough captured her vibrancy, do you not agree?"

Clearly, the oil painting was not what Joshua expected. Yet, he smiled at the captivating portrait of a young girl with riotous blond curls and mischievous blue eyes. Dressed in a pink gown, she was holding a round red ball over her head as a brown and white spaniel puppy romped at her dainty feet. The blue sash at her waist had come untied, no doubt from her boisterous play. "Enchanting child, who . . . ?" He looked closer at the engraved plate on the bottom of the frame. *"Miss Amy Stockwell, age ten,"* Joshua read aloud.

The dark-haired man understood his companion's surprise. "We met only once as children when Amy was ten. Apparently, the lady has no recollection. I saw no point in mentioning it. Just as you saw no reason to inform me of the lady's present condition."

Rigby looked defensive. "Amy's always been intrigued by the Far East. Used to badger her late father into letting her sit in his study while he talked business with his ship captains. Though her mother and aunt didn't approve, George gave in to Amy's pleading to be taken with him to the Bristol docks to watch the ships come into port." His voice became gruffer. "The young woman appeared so excited about the prospect of Japanese goods when I told her of your letter, someone who actually traveled there, I . . . Lord love me, I thought the diversion would do her good. Besides, intolerance isn't confined just to different races, you know. There are a lot of Englishmen I know who wouldn't even consider entering into commerce with a woman . . . and, well, a handicapped one at that."

"Yes," Toshiro answered quietly, "I know about such things." He placed the portrait on the sideboard, then walked across the room to stand near the marble fireplace. How many times, he thought, had he lost business when a prospective buyer found out he was part Japanese? Stretching out his hands near the welcoming flames, he tried to take the chill from his fingers. "God, Joshua, what happened to her? Her aunt would tell me nothing. Please, I need to know. What changed that happy, energetic little girl into such a fragile rose?"

Rigby heard the genuine concern behind the count's request. He walked over to stand next to him. "It was before I closed my London practice to come here. Dare say, I don't know all the details, but it appears Jane Townsend's family pressured her to marry George Stockwell. Her father, a lesser baronet, had drunk and gambled away the family fortune, including what is now Stockwell Hall. George bought the place when it went on the market for unpaid taxes. The three brothers were forced to marry wealthy wives, but that still left the family in dire straits. And the youngest, eighteen-year-old Clarice, needed to be launched properly into society, not to mention a dowry provided. It is still a sore point with the genteel but financially strapped Townsends to be reminded of how George Stockwell first made his fortune. Oh, I can see by your smile you know the truth. Well, George did have many rough edges, a bit blind in some areas, but he seemed pleased enough with Jane in the beginning. When she became pregnant with Amy, their life was complete. Jane asked Clarice to visit during her confinement. The girls were inseparable, shopping, going to parties with George in attendance. All the eligible bachelors in Bristol flocked about Clarice, for she was considered one of the beauties of the Ton—witty, outgoing, unlike Jane, who appeared shy, some now say too high-strung. Amy's a bit like Jane in other ways, too, not just her blond features.

Well, Jane was only too happy to take her beautiful sister under her wing, provide for her, see that she moved in the best circles. George gave in to Jane's pleading that the three Townsend brothers be brought into Stockwell Enterprises. All went well for a year or so. Then strange things began happening at Stockwell Hall. Jane's pregnancy proved difficult. They say childbearing can offset a woman's mind. At least that is Dr. Wakefield's theory. George was beside himself. With the birth of Amy, everyone hoped Jane would get better. When Amy was about seven, Jane began acting even more peculiar. Reclusive, frail, she ate little, fits of crying, appeared dazed, often found by the servants wandering about the grounds of the estate at night. Three years later Jane hurled herself off the cliff at the edge of Stockwell's property. George dove in the water to save her, but he drowned with her in the process. Poor little Amy, orphaned so young."

Toshiro looked puzzled. "Yes, it was a terrible tragedy, but they say Amy's heart suffered. I do not see how—"

"Amy saw the whole thing happen," Joshua pointed out. "Poor mite. It was past midnight before Clarice finally found her sitting on the edge of that cliff, her dead spaniel puppy right next to her. Dog's neck was broken. Never did find out how it happened. Amy was mute for months afterward. Seems she remembers nothing of that day. The mind's protection, they say. Later on, with Clarice's devoted care, Amy started to get better. Her relatives thought she wasn't strong enough to be out in the world. Tutors were brought in. The Earl of Woodcroft's family home is in Clifton, so his parents allowed him to come over and play often, before he went away to Eton. Amy's mind is as sharp as a blade, though. You'll see that as you negotiate a business deal with her. Yet, after I became her solicitor near her twenty-first birthday, she had some spell or relapse. Norbert Wakefield, the Townsends' physician for years, was called to the house late one evening. Since then she has been as you see her, confined to that infernal wheelchair. All a sad business."

"Yes," agreed the younger man. "And left in that huge, empty house with just her aunt and servants. What a lonely existence."

Rigby failed to bite back a guffaw. "Lonely, empty? Lord bless you, Valerius, wait until dinner tonight before you talk of Miss Stockwell's solitude."

Dressed in one of her better gowns, Amy wondered if it needed a little tulle to brighten the tan color. Of course, Clarice had excellent taste. Amy would always be grateful for the way she refurnished her rooms downstairs four years ago, when it seemed more practical than making a servant haul her upstairs to her former rooms each night. Clari took care of running the house, hiring the servants, choosing Amy's clothes. Yes, Amy reminded herself, she had much to be thankful for. However, tonight she was more interested in her appearance than usual. "Do you think my hair should be pulled back this way, Aunt Clari? Cousin Susan says ringlets around the face are more fashionable this season."

Attired in a fetching gown of red silk, Clarice smiled at her niece. "You look lovely, my dear. With your golden hair pulled back from your face, we can see those lovely cheekbones and your expressive blue eyes. Don't you agree, David?"

From his seated position on a green brocade-covered chair, the earl glanced away from Clarice to look at the girl in the wheelchair. "Of course. Amy, you always look fine to me."

Amy gave him a shy smile. "Perhaps it is time to go out into the hallway. The count should be arriving with Mr. Rigby any moment." She could hear the voices of her three uncles, their wives, and fifteen children in the next room. "I'd better remind the others Count Valerius may not be used to our rather . . . informal family gatherings." She was thinking about their penchant for loud squabbles.

David took a deep breath. "Amy, before you and Clarice go in, I need to discuss something with you."

In light blue breeches and coat, his brown hair tied neatly at the back of his neck, the earl rose from his chair and came over to her. She noticed the concern on his usually congenial features. "David, what is troubling you? I know you favor my uncles' position against my decision to enter into this venture, but I assure you I have gone over the contract with Mr. Rigby many times. My company will make a sizeable profit in this exclusive business arrangement."

"It isn't the money I am worried about, Amy." David hunkered down to look directly into her eyes. "I know this fellow; you do not. I doubt he's changed much since our Eton days. You don't even know about his people. Yes, his father was a Dutch count, but his mother was some Jappo peasant born in a rice field, probably a whore from the pleasure houses."

Amy could not hide her shock. "David, you should not say those things. How can you be certain of such private details?"

"It is true. Dash it, Amy. With business matters you're coolheaded and sharp, but with people, you are too trusting. Valerius has roamed about the world with no base to call home. God only knows how many bastards he's likely fathered, with his dark good looks and unassuming manner. Never stays long enough in any port to take a count of them I'll wager. Until his father died less than a year ago, Valerius acted more like a sea captain than a count's son. He piloted many of their ships himself. Why does he choose to take a house in Bristol as his home base, a place where none of his parents have any kin? Strange is it not, the location being right next to your estate? Then he enters into a lucrative business agreement with the most successful merchant in Bristol." The tall Englishman stood up. "I just don't want to see you . . . talk at my club is that Valerius is strapped for money. It wouldn't be the first time a suave continental danced his way into an Englishwoman's heart merely to charm her out of her fortune and lands."

Amy looked down at the heavy material covering her legs. Something began to ache inside at David's last remark. She turned her chair away from the two people staring at her. It was only a business arrangement, she told herself. Yet, the Englishwoman suddenly remembered how wonderful it felt to be held in Toshiro's arms this morning. Never had she experienced this emotion, not even with David—comforted, yet. . . . Had that been attraction she'd seen in his green eyes? Why hadn't he kissed her, as she first thought he might?

Her face heated at the outrageous train of her thoughts. What was the matter with her? For an instant, she did not want to go in to dinner now. Her practical side forced her to see reality. Hadn't Dr. Wakefield told her she could never have a normal woman's life? David had been her friend since childhood. Many times she'd stayed with his parents to take the waters at Clifton Hotwells when David was called away on business in London. Amy knew he spoke out of concern for her. She chided herself for showing her mother's weakness in such romantic musings. Her father had never been hoodwinked in a business deal. George Stockwell's daughter squared her shoulders.

"Besides," David added, still watching her, "Toshiro is too secretive, always has been. Part of the race, I suppose. That damn mask they present to the world. Can never tell what they think or feel. One of the Dutch sailors from the *Nightingale* told me the Japanese call Valerius *Hyo,* the panther, because he's proven a fierce warrior to his enemies. Raised among heathens, his European manner and dress are just a facade, Amy. He has returned to Nagasaki many times. You cannot trust these people. They know nothing about English honor or our civilized way of life. Since our childhood days, I've known of your fascination with the Far East. I only wish to warn you because I see you in a vulnerable position right now. And it's not just because you're an invalid."

Inside, Amy winced at the last word. Running her hands over the round wooden wheels, she maneuvered her chair about to face her longtime friend. "I do appreciate your candor, David. You may take me into dinner now. I shall be on my guard."

As the elaborate meal of salmon and fowl progressed, Toshiro glanced across his side of the table to see the amused expression of Joshua Rigby. The two of them had been seated at the end of the long table, almost segregated from the rest of the family. Toshiro could tell the large man was reminding him of his remark about "Poor

Amy living in lonely solitude." The clamor at the table was almost deafening to Toshiro, who was more accustomed to a harmonious atmosphere when dining.

All the way down at the other end Amy Stockwell sat, looking small and quiet. Though polite when he arrived, the count noticed she spoke briefly to him and ate little. David Saunders sat to her right, his attention hardly wavering from her. The heavy dark furniture, olive green drapes, black and brown carpeting made the whole atmosphere somber. Assorted children sprang up from their seats at the table to race about and toss food at one another. The quarreling uncles and their wives took little notice. When one of the little hoydens missed his cousin, and a chicken bone hit Amy on the shoulder, Toshiro had to compress his lips to keep from bellowing out a naval command for order. He saw Amy merely smile, whisper something into her cousin's ear, whereupon the lad laughed, then went back to his chair.

"Joshua," Toshiro said in a low voice across his side of the table, where they were both almost ignored. "Is it usually like this?"

"In truth, it's one of the quieter evenings," chortled the Englishman. "You should have been here when that young man brought two small monkeys into the dining room. It took Amy's coaxing voice to get the animals to swing down from the chandelier. Almost had a fire from the lighted candles they pelted at us."

The other man shook his head. "But why does she allow such . . . ?" He let his words drift off when Henry called Simon "mutton face" again. They were arguing now about one of George III's recent appointments.

"Loyalty to the relatives," answered Joshua, after wiping his mouth on his linen napkin. "She feels beholden to all the Townsends for taking care of her and George's business when she was not able as a child. Of course, the Townsends owe their fortunes to Stockwell money. Yet, she's stubborn where blood ties are concerned. I'd be careful about criticizing the Townsends in front of her if I were you. The English rose, as you call her, is not as helpless as you seem to believe."

With dinner over, the adults piled into the music room for conversation but little peace. Much to Toshiro's irritation, David moved Amy's chair as far away from him as possible. The earl squeezed her between his chair and Clarice's, obviously eager to entertain both ladies with his sparkling conversation.

"Oh, such stories of my youth," David added, with a hearty laugh. For once everyone stopped talking and looked at their countryman.

"Boarding school exploits were always such fun," remarked Simon. "Nothing like a good English education. All the Townsend males went to Eton, too. Makes a boy into a man. Eton's produced more renowned Englishmen than the world has ever known."

David's pale blue eyes lighted on Toshiro. "Why, even the count did his share of pranks. Remember old Cranshaw, our housemaster?" Not waiting for a reply, the earl continued. "The other lads and I could never understand Toshiro's obsession with bathing everyday. Even in the cold of winter he'd strip off his clothes to wash from head to foot. When Valerius was late three nights in a row, Cranshaw found out who the culprit was who'd put sticking paste on his chair. The count took the caning of the century we found out later, yet never a whimper from him."

Despite his restrained expression, Amy sensed Toshiro's

discomfort with David's reminiscences about their Eton days. She tried to ease the conversation in another direction. "Well, I remember finding countless ways to get into mischief when I was young, too. I used to hide in cupboards so my nanny couldn't find me for hours."

David gave her an indulgent smile. "Amy, you were an angel next to the tricks we played on our foreign classmates. No comment, Toshiro? Just that inscrutable Eastern stoicism again?"

Toshiro's gaze bore across to the man sitting with his hand on the top of Amy's high-back wheelchair. His controlled voice belied his strong emotions. "In Japan where I lived until I was ten years old, I was taught that the more important the position in the society one held, the greater the responsibility to act with humility and honor. In your English boarding school I soon learned, such an advanced Eastern philosophy is not always found among Western aristocrats."

Amy saw the tension between the two men. Things hinted at but not spoken. Quickly, she glanced at her Uncle Giles, who was watching her.

Giles cleared his throat. "Count Valerius, can you explain to me why Japan will not trade with anyone but the Dutch and Chinese?"

"Yes, I should like to know that, too, my Lord." Amy gave her foreign guest an encouraging look. "I cannot tell you how frustrating it is not to be able to send my ships directly to Japan."

Toshiro felt his body relax. Everyone sat watching him. How marvelous the silence was, he mused. A smile tugged at the corners of his mouth before he began to enlighten them. "The Dutch and Chinese traders told the Shogun that the pope had promised Japan to the Portuguese and

Spanish. Rightly alarmed that he would lose power over Japan, in 1603 the Tokugawa Shogun closed Japan to all foreigners except the Dutch and Chinese, who are allowed to trade only from the man-made port of Dejima in Nagasaki. It is the law that if a Japanese is caught trying to leave Japan, he will be killed. Because of my Japanese uncle's intercession, I am allowed the privilege of trading in Nagasaki, as well as having Iwao and Sumi with me. It has not been an easy time for those Japanese scholars who wish knowledge of science and medicine, along with other advances made in the outside world."

"You sound as if you do not approve of the Shogun's ruling."

Toshiro was surprised at Amy's observation, for he had not intended to give himself away. Or was it just that they were more sensitive to each other's thoughts? he wondered. "You are right, Miss Stockwell. I suppose I lean more toward supporting the emperor as my Akashi family has done for generations, rather than blindly following the military dictatorship of the shogunate. Perhaps it is the mark of my more pleasant Oxford days, but I have never thought it harmful to learn new ideas, even when I do not always agree with them."

Amy could understand and admire his attitude. But when she remembered David's warning, she suppressed her comment of support.

Simon spoke up. "Yet, for a man who purports interest in new ideas, David tells me you never wear a dress sword, even when you go out after dark. Why, any Englishman would feel positively naked without a sword, not to mention the danger sauntering unarmed about these streets."

Looking politely along the row of Townsends to the eldest uncle, Toshiro answered, "I have never felt comfortable with the feel of a straight sword hanging down my leg. Maneuvering the clanking metal against the curved legs of your chairs still challenges me. And there are other forms of defense besides English swords."

"Harrumph," muttered Simon. "Do you ride to the hounds then or shoot in the fall?"

With unflappable good humor, Toshiro shook his head. "Alas, no, I do not care for blood sports. I prefer to observe nature."

"Cards, dice?" Simon tried again, only to be met with the count's same negative answer.

Appearing thoroughly disgusted, Simon leaned his beefy elbows on his side of the table. "What about women or are they against a Jappo's strange upbringing, too?"

Amy knew her face was crimson. Her older relatives laughed outright, making her want to apologize to her foreign guest immediately.

"Yes," Toshiro answered, "I have visited the Yoshiwara, the pleasure quarters of Edo. It is true that our geishas there are among the most beautiful women in the world. The sound of the samisen played by an accomplished geisha is a very pleasant experience."

"Samisen?" Amy repeated.

"Yes," her guest answered. "It is like a guitar but has an extremely long neck and three strings, plucked with a small piece of ivory. Sumi learned how to play in my mother's home. Perhaps one day you will allow me to have her play the samisen for you."

Remembering what David had said about the lowly birth of the count's mother, Amy shot her uncle a look of warning when he appeared ready to add another scathing comment.

Instead, Simon took a long swallow of wine. "Know

you didn't go there just for the acoustics, lad. Damn me, at least I found something to salvage you. Had me worried for a minute. Beginning to think you were a poof. Care to tell us more about those—what do you call them—gay what?"

"Ah . . . Uncle Simon," Amy interjected. "We must remember the count was raised in a culture different from ours. I am sure his Lordship has other hobbies that would meet with your approval," she added in a nervous rush. Anything to steer the conversation away from Uncle Simon's unsuitable topic in mixed company about the count's amorous conquests.

"Oh, yes," Toshiro said, warmed by Amy's attempt to help him just now. "My father taught me the joys of working with wood."

"Gad," Henry piped up, "you mean you actually muck about like a common cabinetmaker?" Even the wives tittered this time.

"Damn me," muttered Simon, "the count would have more in common dinin' with James Conroy, the footman."

"Carpentry can be very relaxing." Toshiro noted that the adult Townsends looked even more horrified to learn that a count worked with his hands. "I also enjoy gardening," he tossed out for free.

Though she was certain only she could detect it, Amy caught the brief spark of humor that glinted from Toshiro's eyes before he hid it.

Holding the quill pen in her slender fingers, Amy signed her name to the formal document. She then moved the parchment along her desk for Toshiro to sign. Mr. Rigby, her three uncles, and David Saunders were the only others in her study. "You have made a wise trade agreement, my Lord."

Toshiro looked up at the woman sitting on the other side of her late father's carved mahogany desk. At the moment she was every inch the owner of Stockwell Enterprises. Her blue eyes glittered in the candlelight. And he had to admit, never had he enjoyed negotiating more, even if he knew the shrewd woman had outmaneuvered him into conceding more than he'd intended. He had even agreed to sail the *Nightingale* to London in a few weeks when another of his ships arrived from China so he could bring the entire cargo back to Bristol for her, instead of selling it in London as he'd planned. Amy's uncles remained unusually silent, prompting the count to wonder if she had warned them to stay out of these talks. If he was irritated when she asked David to accompany them into her closed office a few hours ago, he was careful not to show it. He reached for the quill pen and signed his name below her bold signature. "Let us hope there are no more Anglo-Dutch wars in the future to put our mutual interests in jeopardy."

Amy smoothed the white lace where her right sleeve ended at the elbow. "I have always admired Holland lace. Unfortunately, monarchs make military strategy and foreign policy." Her cornflower blue eyes were bright with eagerness. "Perhaps it would be wiser if politicians allowed the merchants to make the policy, for I would rather Valerius Shipping continued."

As if they were the only two in the room, Toshiro studied her, his green eyes warming to her pale loveliness in the candlelight. "And you believe England does not wish the Dutch well?"

"I believe England intends to destroy Dutch trade," she said without hesitation.

Her new partner's dark brows rose at her direct grasp of the situation. It was another reason he'd wanted to enter into this trade agreement, for he saw on the horizon the English giant flexing his muscles against Holland. "Mr. Rigby," he said, turning to the amused Englishman. "You were right." He knew Joshua understood he spoke of having underestimated Amy's ability to run her company. "It is a mistake I shall not make again."

Before Amy could ask what Toshiro meant, her Aunt Clarice knocked at the door and entered.

Candlelight shimmered from the impressive brooch nestled against the silk across Clarice's breast. Toshiro recognized the pin as Chinese. The gold bird's feathers were embedded with diamonds, rubies, and other precious stones. She carried a glass filled with some murky liquid.

"I am sorry, my dear, but it is time for your tonic."

Amy wrinkled her nose but reached out to take the glass from her aunt. "You know, Clari, I'm glad you didn't come in earlier. Cosseting does take the edge off my efforts to appear ruthless," she commented with good-natured acceptance.

Toshiro watched her drink the contents of the crystal glass. The only indication of how vile the stuff must taste was when she pressed her lace pocket handkerchief to her pink lips and closed her eyes for a second. After her aunt left, the conversation resumed.

However, about forty minutes later, Toshiro was surprised to see the change in Amy. Appearing less alert, she stared ahead, often as though she weren't even listening. When she yawned behind her hand, she blushed, then tried to sit up straighter.

"Forgive me, gentlemen," she finally said. "I am usually in bed by eight. I believe I must ask your forgiveness if I retire now."

Toshiro rose, but before he could go over to say his goodbyes, David placed himself behind the lady's wheelchair to move her toward the door.

"No, Count Valerius, you need not leave," Amy said over her shoulder. "My family usually stays to enjoy the after-dinner festivities. I am quite used to this, my Lord," she added, seeing something in his green eyes she did not understand. "I should like to speak to you again about your travels, if ever you have the time."

The strain on his face eased. He bowed from the waist. "Nothing would please me more."

As David wheeled her into the next room, obviously her bedroom, a young servant girl came over to her mistress. The aunt hovered over Amy. When Clarice looked up to find Toshiro watching them, she walked over and closed the door.

The Eurasian left with Mr. Rigby shortly afterward. When a line of carriages pulled up, the Townsend uncles and their brood piled into them. He could hear the children tussling for positions within the conveyances. David Saunders was the only one left behind.

As Toshiro and Mr. Rigby rode home in silence, the younger man sat ruminating, looking out the closed window. Questions besieged him. From the brief glimpse at her bedroom, he noted only one small window to let in the morning sunlight. As they drove down the long gravel path that led away from Stockwell Manor, he could not help wondering, with all the tranquil beauty outside the house and grounds, what unsettled him about this place tonight?

"Joshua, is there a time one might chance to call at Stockwell Hall and find Miss Amy without her . . . entourage?"

Mr. Rigby leaned his large hands on the top of his gold-tipped walking stick. "The lady's Uncle Henry is a bit indiscreet. He complained once to me that Clarice usually sleeps until noon, while his niece is up at dawn working in her office."

"Thank you, Mr. Rigby." More relaxed, the count leaned back against the plush cushions of his coach. Yes, tonight had convinced him. He intended to learn more about Amy Stockwell.

Three

The young footman looked up at the fashionably dressed man with cool disdain. "Regrettably, my Lord, Miss Townsend is not receiving callers this early."

Removing his hat from his unpowdered hair, Count Toshiro Valerius handed it to the young man and walked purposely into the entryway. He kept a firm hold on the large package cradled under his left arm. "I am here to see Miss Stockwell, not her aunt. Kindly announce me."

Such was the tone from the man used to being obeyed that the irritated but wary servant walked down the hall to Amy's rooms at the back of the house. Toshiro hoped he hadn't played his hand too forcefully, but he knew from last evening Clarice ran the house, including all the servants. Strange all of them were so young.

He was relieved when the green-coated footman directed him to Amy's study. After the door was closed behind him, Toshiro saw Amy hunched over her desk where they had signed their trade agreement the evening before. There was a large wooden globe at the back of the room, next to a table strewn with maps. Bookshelves stuffed with leather-bound volumes lined one wall.

She was writing in a logbook. Her hair was again pulled back and up in an unflattering style, similar to last evening. She wore a morning gown that did nothing to show her blond beauty to advantage. Toshiro took a deep breath, then frowned. The stuffy room needed airing. Unlike her bedroom, at least this room had two windows on one side, yet the heavy velvet drapes were still drawn, keeping out the morning sun. Realizing she knew he was standing here, he wondered why she continued to work. He cleared his throat.

Amy glanced up. "Oh, Count Valerius, I did not see you."

"Because you did not look up," countered her visitor.

She looked amused. "Quite so, yet I did hear your directive to the servant who showed you in. You must forgive James Conroy. He hasn't been here long. Servants come and go quickly. It is not easy working for a woman in . . . ill health. Pray sit down," she added, indicating the comfortable chair next to her desk. "If I had refused to see you this morning, what would you have done, I wonder?"

Toshiro walked gracefully into the room, still holding his heavy package. "Why, I should have left quietly, of course."

"I doubt it," she added, secretly amazed at her directness, yet enjoying their light banter. "I thought cooling your heels for a few moments might give you a chance to remember you are not on the deck of one of your ships." When she saw his dark brows rise in surprise at her reprimand, she gave him an impudent smile. "However, I am happy to see you this morning."

Even in the dimly lighted room he could see a black smudge of ink on the tip of her upturned nose. He found the effect endearing but knew they were not acquainted well enough for him to mention it . . . yet. "I have brought you a small gift to mark the signing of our business agreement." He carried his present over to the other side of the desk for her to unwrap. "I hope it is acceptable."

Embarrassed, she said, "Oh, my Lord, you did not have to do this. I assure you, I am well pleased by our contract." When she saw how eagerly he waited for her to unwrap the colorful paper that encased the long gift, she set to the task.

"Here, let me turn it for you. It is heavy."

When it was unwrapped, Amy could not contain her delight. "Oh, Toshiro, it is beautiful. The deep aqua shimmers like the waters of Capri," she whispered, running her fingers across the bolt of fabric.

"So, you did travel farther than Rome when you visited Italy years ago? I too have enjoyed that lovely part of the world."

Amy looked puzzled. "One of the captains told me of the area. Someday, perhaps I shall travel. I would love to see Italy. In truth, my Lord," she added, making light of it, "the only time I have been out of Bristol is when I go two miles up to Clifton to visit David's parents and take the waters at Clifton Hotwells. Perhaps it is why I'm so boring," she added with a chuckle. "Limited horizon."

Toshiro stood looking down at her as she went back to admiring the Japanese silk. He was thinking of the second time he'd come to visit ten-year-old Amy Stockwell to offer his personal condolences on the recent death of her parents. Clarice had told him Amy was in Italy for an extended visit. Why had her aunt lied to him?

When he heard Amy's voice again, he tried to shake off his troubled thoughts.

"Thank you so much for this exquisite gift. I shall ask Clari's seamstress to make her a lovely gown. My aunt has a fondness for Chinese jewelry, and I recall one peacock brooch that will match this perfectly."

He frowned. His white neckband suddenly seemed too tight around his throat. Turning his burgundy-coated back on Amy, he went to the chair she'd offered him earlier. After he sat down, he said, "I hoped you would have a gown made for yourself, as I have given the silk to you, not your aunt."

Oh, dear, she had not meant to ruffle him. It was just that she had so few opportunities to socialize, especially during the last four years. It seemed more logical for Clarice to have the expensive material. "Forgive me, my Lord, I did not mean to offend you. Of course, I shall have a gown made for myself."

He had the distinct impression she was placating him as if he were one of her petulant young cousins; it did not sit well with him. Tempted to tell her Clarice probably had a wardrobe full of Paris frocks upstairs and needed no more, he clamped his lips together. He tried to remember Rigby's warning about criticizing the Townsends in front of her. The Eurasian searched for a change of subject. With a carpenter's eye for detail, he spotted the carved chest to his right. "I have often admired the skill of your English woodworkers. The shell pattern is one of my favorites. May I?"

Amy followed the direction of his gaze. "Of course."

Toshiro pulled out one of the drawers. "Excellent dovetailing," he remarked, as he studied the back of the drawer.

"I shall tell James Conroy you like his work."

Toshiro couldn't hide his amazement. "That young footman made this?"

Amy nodded. "Yes, he was an apprentice to a local cabinetmaker. Clari hired him on the spot when she first went to settle a bill with his master. He's proven handy for repairs about the place, including making me a new wheel for my old chair. His use of regular spoke wheels with iron rims makes my chair more sturdy, unlike most Bath chairs."

The oppressiveness of the gloomy room affected him. "It is a beautiful day and seems a shame not to let in the sun. Would you mind if I opened those drapes?"

Disconcerted by his quick change of topic, she peered at the windows as if noticing them for the first time. "No, please go ahead." Then she remembered about the tricky cord after he went over to the window farthest from her and began pushing back the heavy material. Getting to her feet with care, she walked silently over to the window closest to her, while he continued working on the other one without looking up. "I'll open this one. A few of the pins are missing from the rod, and if you don't move it carefully, the whole drape falls on you. I speak from experience, of course."

When he looked over his shoulder to acknowledge her playful warning, he wasn't able to hide his astonishment. She was standing! The morning sun poured into the gray-papered walls of her office, and he saw her face and slender neck clearly. Her skin was soft and pale, her hair hinted at thick curls held in too severe a style for her youth and fine-boned features. Shorter than Clarice, her head would just reach to the point under his chin, he mused. He walked over to her. "Amy, you can stand."

"Most humans do, I'm told." His reaction amused her. "I walk about, too. Only, please do not tell Clari or my doctor. They've warned me I am too weak for such strenuous exercise. The only thing I've gotten them used to so far is allowing me to get in and out of the bed and wheelchair on my own. I'm working them up to accepting this." She swayed, then reached for the chest. "Guess I'm still a bit wobbly on my pins."

Toshiro found he could not hold back from taking her gently by her slender arms. "Your secrets are safe with me," he whispered, overjoyed by this discovery.

She turned toward him, forced to press her palms against the soft material of his coat for support. "I beg your pardon, but I need the leverage." She felt the hard muscles of his chest through his white lawn shirt, embroidered waistcoat, and outer coat. Panther eyes, she thought when she looked up into the depths of his green eyes. Why did she feel so attracted to this man after such a brief acquaintance? she wondered. He did not have David's ready wit, but there was a gentle patience about him, as if he didn't mind if she could not rush about or ride or travel. At the moment, his arms reminded her how cherished she felt that time he'd rescued her.

With all that had happened to her, Toshiro marveled she could still have such a rich sense of humor and not be embittered. In the same circumstance he was not certain he would have been as even-tempered.

It was wonderful to rest just for a few moments in this man's arms. Again, she felt the hypnotic power of him as he encouraged her to relax, to let the tenseness leave her shoulders. Closing her eyes, she gave in to the enticing sound of his voice. When his warm fingers began to massage the stiffness from the muscles at the back of her neck, she tried to remind herself she should pull away. Yet, another side of her reasoned his gesture was one not of impropriety but giving, as one would offer solace to a dear friend. "Oh, that feels heavenly. Much better than Dr. Wakefield's leeches." Instantly, she regretted her jesting comment when she felt Toshiro's hands pull away from her.

"Good God, do you actually mean he bleeds you?"

Using the edge of her desk for support, she walked back to her wheelchair and slumped down. Her tone was dismissive. "My physician says it clears the sickly humors from my body . . . something about too much blood, and—"

"*Unko!* Never have I heard such . . . idiocy. You are clearly underweight and need uplifting—no, that is not the right word," he added, frustrated his emotion caused him to get the English words mixed up. "You need . . . building up. The last thing you require is to be weakened by bloodletting. Leeches have their place if there is bruising under the skin but this . . ." His masculine voice rose an octave. "It is . . . barbaric."

Amy's chin moved northward. "Bilge water. I hardly think you are in a position to know what is the best treatment for me. Dr. Norbert Wakefield has been my family's physician for years. He looked after my mother during her . . . long illness." She saw the slanting at the corners of his eyes become more pronounced, before he thrust his hands behind his back and walked to the other side of the room in silence. It surprised Amy to realize this usually calm man possessed a temper. "Incidentally, I meant to ask you what *koneko* and *unko* mean? I assume they are Japanese words. Languages have always fascinated me," she went on in a clear attempt to move to more neutral terrain.

Fists on either side of his waist, Toshiro's scowl from across the room showed he wasn't ready for bland conversation.

The count was trying to control his reaction to what he considered medieval medical practices, along with her blind defense of people taking care of her. *"Koneko* means 'kitten.' The other word is totally unsuitable for a lady's ears."

"Nevertheless, if I am to be growled at, I insist on knowing exactly what is being said. Now, translate the word for me."

He sucked in his breath at the arrogance in her tone. Never had a woman spoken to him in this manner. "The other word, stubborn one, is what an untrained *koneko* does on the carpet. Is that blunt enough for you?"

Despite her efforts, heat suffused her cheeks. "I see," she said, her eyes the shade of the Avon in winter. "Nothing like a foreign language to broaden one's mind, is there?"

Her mettle in refusing to flutter in maidenly shock, along with her English propensity for understatement, undid him. His shoulders shook as open laughter overtook him.

It was the first time Amy heard Toshiro laugh, and she found it a pleasant sound. It was rich and masculine unlike David's boyish giggles. She could almost see his Dutch heritage in that laughter. When her own lips twitched, her earlier umbrage departed. "I dare say, cultural exchanges are not always easy. A truce, my Lord?"

Still grinning, he walked back to her. Leaning over, he braced his hands on the edge of her massive desk.

"My Dutch relatives often chided me for being too restrained, whereas growing up in Nagasaki, I was criticized by my Japanese family for showing too much of my feelings. Instructed in Buddhism, baptized an Anglican, I have been raised a Protestant. The entire process has, I fear, unsettled me toward a rather quick temper on occasion. Of course, Jan Roonhuysen says it is because I am too used to bellowing orders to rough sailors on my ships." He held out his right hand. "A truce, Miss Stockwell."

Readily, she lifted her right hand to shake his but did not expect him to turn her hand over to place a feathery kiss on the sensitive skin of her knuckles. He gave her fingers a soft squeeze before releasing them. When their eyes met, she found the intensity of his gaze overpowering. She had to look down at the logbook on her desk. It took her a moment to think of something to say. "Please, Toshiro, won't you tell me about some of your travels?"

"Yes, I would like to talk with you, not about medicine or politics but of more pleasant things." He glanced at the overstuffed sofa in the space between the two windows. "With you on the other side of the desk, it reminds me of when I had to report to my headmaster at Eton."

After he shrugged and walked over to his chair next to her desk, Amy stopped him before he sat down. "I think we would be more comfortable on the sofa over there." Inside she was surprised at her forwardness. Yet, when he smiled, she rose again from her wheelchair and took the arm he offered for support. David would have insisted on carrying her over to the couch. She was grateful Toshiro did not fuss over her. He showed his attention by taking smaller steps to accommodate her slower gait, but he acted as if it were the most natural thing in the world for her to walk on her own.

For over an hour Amy's visitor intrigued her with tales of the foreign ports and different cultures of India, Canton, and the Caribbean. She sat spellbound, brushing aside his one comment that she must let him know if he tired her.

The man next to her was captivated by her animated expression as she sat with her body turned slightly toward his in eager anticipation of his next word. The questions she asked proved how much she'd read on a variety of topics. Certain she had no idea how intriguing he found her, it took much of his restraint not to lean over to kiss that adorable nose with the smudge of ink across it. Instead, he forced himself to concentrate on telling her about Amsterdam.

"Mr. Rigby informed me of the recent death of your father," she added with sympathy. "Was it a long illness?"

Memories crashed against him. While visiting his father in Amsterdam, Toshiro had found Pieter Valerius in his study late one evening—a five-pointed silver star embedded in his jugular, the sign of a Japanese assassin, blood all. . . . Toshiro caught himself, remembered where he was and who sat watching him with such perceptive blue eyes. He shook his head. "No, my father's death was sudden."

She sensed this was as disquieting a topic as her own parents' deaths; therefore, she quickly turned the subject back to his travels.

Toshiro answered her questions about the Akashi stables in Nagasaki, where his mother's family bred the wide-chested horses for their strength in carrying the weight of a samurai in armor. "I brought my own horse with me from Japan. Perhaps you would like to see him sometime."

"Oh, yes." Amy sighed. "One of the things I miss most is horseback riding. Though I might not look it now, until four years ago I used to ride every morning." She closed her eyes at the pleasant memories. "I can almost smell the wet grass and dewy wildflowers along the estate, feel the earth as I race along with my horse. In a trunk in the attic I still have the pair of breeches and white shirt I used to wear so I could ride astride." Realizing she'd probably just shocked the man next to her, Amy's lashes flashed open with a nervous start. "Of course I never went beyond Stockwell lands so attired."

She blushed charmingly, Toshiro thought. The sun on the back of her golden hair made it shine like polished coins. How he longed to see her hair unpinned, like that day she'd tumbled into his arms.

A little unsettled by his expression, Amy looked down at her hands. "Dr. Wakefield says I'm not well enough to ride. If I get stronger by the summer, David has promised to take me for a short ride one morning."

At the mention of the earl, both of them felt some of the magic dissipate between them.

When Amy turned her head to the right, the sun through the long windows glared into her eyes, and she quickly raised her right hand to shield them.

"The light bothers you?" He saw her change her position away from the direct sunlight.

She tried to brush it off. "Lately my eyes seem to prefer the drapes drawn. Probably just eyestrain. When I'm not fussing over ship's logs and invoices, I enjoy reading, especially sea stories and travel diaries. David teases me about being too bookish."

At the mention of David Saunders again, Toshiro came to a decision. "Amy, will you answer a personal question for me?"

Alarm gripped her, but she tried to hide it. Would he ask about that part of her she dreaded anyone discovering? "If I can," she finally answered, her throat suddenly dry.

"Are you and David Saunders engaged?"

She could have shouted with relief that this was all he wanted to know about her. "No, the earl and I are not betrothed. Why do you ask?"

He moved closer across the green satin cushion of the sofa. When she did not appear unsettled, he took her hand in his. "Because, Miss Amy Stockwell, I would like to know you better. I find your company most pleasing. Yet, I am aware of English protocol in these matters. Therefore, I had to ask. Any moment I half expect that Englishman to charge into the room, waving the Eton banner," he added, entertained by the picture it presented.

Not sure she should encourage such jocularity at David's expense, the young woman thought it disloyal to join the count's amusement. She reclaimed her hand. "You should know, my Lord, David and I have been friends since we were children. After he went away to school I saw little of him until four years ago when he returned from his Grand Tour. He entered my life when I needed a friend most."

Rebuked, Toshiro cursed himself for his clumsy misstep. "I . . . Amy, I apologize for the last remark. My intent was to make certain that you are. . . ." His words drifted off in his dilemma. Damn it, he thought, in Japan these things were handled more efficiently. A trusted person acted as intermediary with the parents of both parties. Yes, he'd been with women before, but never had he felt this way about anyone. Before he'd asked the question, she'd appeared ready to bolt in terror. No, he reminded himself, he would have to handle this carefully. And he was still waiting to hear from his uncle in Japan to straighten out the matter of his father's murder. At the moment his East and West upbringing were tripping over each other like lumbering oafs at a tea party.

"Pray continue, my Lord," she encouraged, though there was a cool reserve in her voice. Amy remembered David's warning. "You were speaking of your intent."

He stifled his impatient retort. Slowly, he told himself. "I only meant that I would like to see you again, and—"

"Oh, love a duck, is that all?" Then she giggled. "Of course, you may call here again. You must think of me as a friend. I shall make a point of introducing you to business people who can assist you in Bristol. I realize a foreign visitor might get lonely for a homey atmosphere. There are always people running in and out of this house. You will not be lonely."

Aware she still didn't understand what he meant, he knew it was wiser to leave things as they were for the present. Homey atmosphere? he thought with derision. When the Townsend horde descended, Stockwell Hall had all the peacefulness of a clan raid. "Thank you," he replied more formally than he intended.

"I confess now that David will be away for a few weeks again on business in London. If you have an occasional moment, I would look forward to talking with you further about your travels. The poor earl is so busy with handling his family's investments in London.

Though I know it sounds selfish, sometimes I wish the Woodcroft fortune was invested here in Bristol, then David would not have to go to London so often."

David was away? Delightful, thought the count. "Amy, I—"

His words were cut off when Clarice bustled in.

Obviously out of breath from hurrying, she took a moment before she could speak. "Amy, why didn't you have my maid send for me? I had no idea there was a caller so early this morning. James Conroy just informed me."

"I did not wish to disturb you, Clari." Amy looked up at the brass mantel clock on the fireplace ledge. "Heavens, I had no idea of the time." Chagrined, she said to the man next to her, "You must think me a poor hostess, for I did not even offer you tea."

"I shall ring for it now." Clarice reached for the brocade bell cord against the wall.

Toshiro raised his hand. "No need, Miss Townsend, I have taken up enough of Amy's morning."

As the count prepared to leave, he heard Clarice gasp. "Why, Amy, you are not in your chair!" Quickly, she rushed over to get the wheelchair behind the desk, then pushed it over to the woman seated on the sofa. "Come, give me your hands and I will help you up. I cannot think what Dr. Wakefield will say." She took firm hold of her niece's arms.

Amy rose and allowed her aunt to practically lift her into her wheelchair. The contacts with the straight-back chair, feel of the cushion on the hard wooden seat—all reminders that muted her earlier pleasure this morning.

"Really, my Lord," Clarice grated to the man with his hand on the brass knob that led out of Amy's study. "I must protest your encouraging Amy in such a dangerous practice as leaving her chair and opening the draperies." Without hesitation, Miss Townsend went over and roughly closed both sets of green velvet.

"Please, Aunt Clarice, it was not the count's fault. I . . . I asked him to join me on the sofa so I could hear about his travels."

"I am surprised at you, Amy." Clarice's lovely features took on a strained appearance when she went back to her niece. "Dr. Wakefield's instructions were clear to us both. It is not like you to be so foolish. I try to do what is best for you, and. . . ." She stopped to retrieve a lacy handkerchief from the small slit on the side of her pink and white striped gown. After dabbing at the corner of her right eye, she continued. "Of course, you are mistress here and must do as you please."

Amy experienced the knotting in her stomach again and unconsciously began rubbing her hands. She owed everything to Clarice. Dear Clarice protected her, guarded the secret they both knew could destroy Amy. "I'm truly sorry, Clari. I never meant to upset you. Please forgive me." Her vision suddenly wavered with the threat of tears. She kept her head lowered, trying to hide them.

Clarice bent down to her niece and kissed her cheek. "Of course, my dear. You know you mean everything to me." As if surprised Toshiro was still here, the older woman looked toward the man who continued to watch them from the half-opened door. Clarice walked gracefully over to him and whispered, "Kindly remember, my Lord, you are not a physician."

Green eyes locked with dark brown in a declaration of war. "And you are not God, Miss Townsend," he muttered before walking out the door.

Four

"When I received your note this morning, I wasn't sure I should accept." Amy looked over her shoulder and found Toshiro Valerius smiling down at her as he wheeled her chair slowly toward the door.

Yes, Toshiro mused, he'd been correct to send Iwao with his missive to see Miss Stockwell in person in her study. Would the footman have delivered the note to Clarice instead?

"Besides, I haven't had this riding skirt on in four years."

Despite her lighthearted words this morning, the count knew Amy Stockwell was nervous about riding again after four years. And though he tried to dismiss it, the Eurasian could not help wondering if she was also apprehensive to be seen in his company. As the Earl of Woodcroft and other Englishmen were so fond of pointing out, he was a foreigner. However, he could not forget their first discussion a few days earlier when her blue eyes had sparkled as she mentioned her hope to be taken riding again. He studied her velvet jacket and skirt. Though it hung on her willow-thin body, he took the color as a good omen. "You look like a lovely iris this morning."

Warmed by his remark, she looked back down at her gloved fingers. "Thank you. It's an outfit I purchased in London before the acci . . . before I became ill. Of course, I do not know what David will say if he ever finds out." Then she laughed outright at her own timidity. "Lord, I sound like a green cabin boy on his first voyage. I still remember what a horse looks like. Come on, let's weigh anchor and get to it."

For an instant she reminded him of that vibrant, happy ten-year-old he'd met fifteen years ago. And though it might unsettle his companion if she guessed it, her escort experienced a wicked delight in being the first to take her riding again, instead of the Earl of Woodcroft.

"Here, you can't take her out of here!" came a high-pitched voice behind them. As he bustled out toward the hallway, James Conroy apparently read the warning in the count's green eyes, for he cleared his throat and stepped back. Yet, the young lad looked down at Amy. "I mean . . . your aunt, miss. I'm sure she wouldn't want you to go out with that, ah. . . ." He peered up at the scowling count. "That is . . . especially so early in the mornin'."

Amy nibbled her lower lip. Of course, the last thing she intended was to worry her aunt. In a few hours when she awoke, Clari would come into her study as always to check on her. "Ah, yes, of course. Well, when my aunt comes downstairs, just tell her I went for a short ride with his Lordship. It is a mild spring day. I feel stronger today, and . . ." She stopped, scolding herself for feeling at such a disadvantage again with one of the ever-changing staff. She straightened against the wooden chair. "Just tell my aunt I shall return in one hour after I—"

"I'll see Miss Stockwell safely returned by two this afternoon," the count amended. "That is all her aunt needs to know. Now, please open the door, unless you wish to discuss varnishing techniques outside in private."

The former cabinetmaker's apprentice obviously realized the threat in Toshiro's last words, for Conroy nodded and quickly did as bidden.

"Will you permit me to lift you down the stairs?" asked Toshiro.

Amy was preoccupied with his comment about their return. Practical assumptions of her physical ability overshadowed her earlier exuberance. Ignoring his question, she couldn't help looking up at him hesitantly. "In truth, my Lord, I own I am certain I could not stay atop even the most cooperative horse for more than an hour. You wish to stay out riding about Bristol until two?"

"Oh, forgive my stupidity, Amy." Toshiro gave her a courtly bow of apology. "I should have explained. I meant only a short ride, then we shall have lunch. If you agree, I should like you to be the first visitor to see my garden."

Relief then interest showed on her pale features. Amy's uncles had been speculating for weeks about what was behind the former walled garden that had gone to ruination after the last occupant died two years ago. "Splendid. No apology necessary. I should have guessed you wouldn't plan a cavalry charge across the hills on my first day out. We'll save that for next week." Then the implication of her playful words hit her. "Oh, my Lord," she said in a fluster, "I did not mean that you have even the slightest obligation to entertain me in future, or that I would expect you to. . . ."

The black-haired man saw the smirk on Conroy's face as he stood in listening distance behind his employer's wheelchair. The youth was clearly amused by Amy's embarrassment. Toshiro wanted to be out of this house. "May I lift you down to the gravel path, Miss Stockwell?" he asked again, wishing to put an end to her discomfort in front of this servant with the insolent gray eyes.

He appeared irritated. Oh, dear, this part was always awkward for her, even with David. She couldn't blame Toshiro for probably finding the prospect distasteful. "Yes, thank you," Amy answered, her voice small. "But, of course, if you'd rather, James can carry me out—"

"No," Toshiro interjected. When he saw her shoulders slump, he regretted his curt tone, even though it was not directed at Amy. "That is, I would be honored to assist you." Without hesitation, he leaned down and slipped one of his arms about her narrow waist, the other under her legs. After a nod from the count, the footman pulled the wooden chair back into the hallway. As when he'd rescued her, it saddened him to feel how light she was. With her golden hair pinned high and back, it was like holding a wispy purple iris. He couldn't whisper the soothing words that hovered near his lips. Instinctively, he knew this Conroy fellow would report back to Clarice and her brothers verbatim what occurred here.

The faint scent of his clean-smelling soap tickled Amy's nostrils in a pleasant way. Without a hat on such a mild spring morning, the count's straight black hair was tied neatly back against the collar of his snugly fitting riding jacket. Below dark riding breeches, his black boots crunched on the small stones of the driveway as he carried her effortlessly toward the waiting—it was then she realized—"My Lord, you only brought one horse?"

An enigmatic smile played at the corners of his lips before he answered matter-of-factly, "I thought it more practical to have you ride up in front of me on our first outing." When he saw her open her mouth, obviously with words about "propriety," he quickly added, "You did say it had been four years. I would never forgive myself if you came to any harm, *koneko.*"

His voice was pleasant, especially when he called her that word in Japanese again. It did seem more logical, she told herself and looked at the lumbering horse. Then she recalled Toshiro's proud description of the Akashi stables. Not wishing to hurt his feelings, Amy said, "So, this is your Japanese horse you told me about. My, isn't he . . . gray," was all she could muster for praise.

Toshiro felt laughter well up in his chest. "No, Amy-san, my black stallion is in the stable at Valerius Hall. Here, I will put you down so you can get acquainted with Grog first." With care, he placed her brown riding boots on the ground, then offered his arm for support.

"Grog?" She giggled when the gelding's ears perked up. Her gloved fingers on Toshiro's firm arm, Amy walked slowly over to the wide, older horse. "How ever did he acquire such a name?"

With his free left hand, Toshiro reached into his coat pocket and pulled out two lumps of sugar. He handed them to Amy. "Jan Roonhuysen named him when I purchased him yesterday. Said anyone would have to be full of more rum than water to ever see this animal as a horse. But I know Grog has potential. There is the spirit of solid rock in those eyes." He watched as Amy held out the sugar in her gloved fingers. "He likes apples, too."

More confident, the young woman moved away from the support of Toshiro's arm. "Yes," she quipped, "I can see Grog and his feed bag are very close." After the good-tempered horse had his treat, Amy tentatively reached out to rub his soft gray nose. "Why, you're a gentle darling, aren't you, Grog?"

The horse nuzzled her hand, clearly content to be fussed over.

Amy continued cooing over him. "And you do have such warm brown eyes. We'll take a short canter with you, right across my property, then along the quay. Your owner and I will show Bristol what a gallant charger you are. Shall we be off, my Lord?" Amy turned to spot the count watching her intently. His almond-shaped eyes held an expression she did not recognize. "Well, here we go. Cast off, shall we?" she added, amused when he blinked, then appeared taken aback to discover he'd been caught, and she was hinting it was time to leave. "Do I board first?"

"Yes, yes, of course." Disconcerted to learn for the first time his years of cultivating self-discipline might not always apply when he was around Amy Stockwell, Toshiro came quickly over to her. He placed his hands on either side of her small waist and gently lifted her atop Grog's leather saddle. He took extra time to adjust her securely on the older horse's expansive back. "There, Grog hardly feels you."

Perhaps it was the sunny morning or the welcoming scents as the earth warmed to spring that caused Amy to lean over and say in Grog's ear, "When you feel who's climbing on deck next, Grog, you'll know you're carrying more than feathers."

Aware Amy meant him to hear, Toshiro's panther eyes lighted with amusement. A man used to the feel of a horse beneath his muscular legs, he swung up easily onto the saddle behind her.

The gelding grunted, then shifted automatically to accommodate the solid weight of his new owner.

"See," Amy piped up, "poor Grog just moaned that his legs are about to fold like the sides of a collapsing tent." She gave the gray beast a mewl of sympathy, then reached down to pat his wide neck. "There, there, dear Grog, picture yourself winning at Ascot."

"Spring air brings out the impudence in you, Amy-san."

"I guess it does," she admitted, not unhappy with the discovery.

Toshiro watched her. Without the familiar backrest of her wheelchair, she had to struggle to hold her spine straight as her legs dangled over Grog's back. The Eurasian leaned forward to sweep her up across his legs to hold her firmly in front of him. "That will help support your back more comfortably. Lean against me."

"Oh, I don't think this . . ." she blushed, squirmed, then stopped immediately when she felt the cords of his thighs even through the material of her heavy riding skirt. "Perhaps this isn't such a good idea. I don't wish to crowd you," she added, then felt the heat on her face once more. She turned her head slightly to look up into his face. Amy could see the gold flecks in his green eyes. There was something secure in those eyes, she thought. The arms surrounding her as he held Grog's reins were strong yet gentle.

"Amy, do you want me to take you back inside? It is for you to decide."

The voice was like a light through shadows. Not comprehending all of it, she knew right now she trusted him. "No, I had a moment of my usual hysteria," she said, then chuckled. "Part of being raised like a potted orchid. Left me with a terror of breaking easily. So silly. But you see, I've never been . . . well, I mean this is the first time I've sat in a man's lap," she blurted, then chided herself for acting like such a rube. What must he think of her? Toshiro's calm expression gave nothing away as he continued holding her. Grog went about munching the leaves from one of the early-blossoming shrubs near his head.

Amy sought to gain more control of the situation. "Of course, I realize this is nothing to you. You are just being efficient. Riding is probably something you've done hundreds of times with many women." When she saw his dark brows rise suddenly, the double entendre of her words struck her. Good God, she was making it worse. As her nervous chatter continued, she didn't come up for air. "That is, I didn't mean to imply that you are a libertine. Well, of course, your relations with women are none of my business. Last evening you said you had visited the Yoshiwara. I mean, a man of the world, ah. . . . Love a duck."

He caught the humiliation in her eyes before she clamped her lips together and turned her face away from his. Leaning closer, he spoke softly. "Amy, I would like us to be friends. And part of becoming friends is that you feel free to be yourself when we are together. Frankly, *koneko,* I like you the way you were just now: open, smiling, that hint of naughtiness lurking about your sky blue eyes. It does suit you well. Please do not shove her back into that lonely corner of reserve. A sea captain and the head of Stockwell Enterprises—wouldn't it be wonderful just to have a play day?"

His enticing words settled over her. This time when she tipped her face up to his, she smiled. "Oh, yes, my Lord, I should love to have a day with an adventure away from Stockwell Hall." It was then she realized he, too, probably needed a carefree day. *"Carpe diem!"* she shouted in Latin.

"Yes, Amy, let us 'seize the day.' " Her golden laugh was contagious. Touching his legs to Grog's haunches, Toshiro started them on their holiday.

They rode the length of Amy's property, and as she requested, Toshiro took her across the Bristol docks so she could watch the throng of ships and activity along the wharf. The count saw a few of Bristol's finest matrons come out of the myriad of shops only to look shocked to discover Miss Amy Stockwell trotting slowly around the harbor atop an overweight horse, nestled in the arms of a dark foreigner. Toshiro was pleased that the young woman in his arms was clearly too enraptured with being out in the spring air to notice anyone's censure this day. Indeed, her companion was amused at the sheer delight she took in recognizing one or two of the ships' captains. She called out to them and waved energetically. He realized she must be a favorite with them, too, for they dropped what they were doing and rushed over to tell her how happy they were to see her up and about. It was now clear to him that none of her relatives or David had thought to take her down here even in the carriage to give her an hour or two of diversion from Stockwell Hall.

"Oh, look, Toshiro," Amy shouted, then pointed to the right. "That's one of my ships, *Lady Jane,* the men are loading. She's taking tools and bolts of silk and wool to the colonies. I've managed to persuade a South Carolina planter to let me buy his tobacco. It was a long process, but I made a good deal."

"Yes, I am sure you did. Rigby tried to caution me, but I learned the hard way that you are a shrewd bargainer."

"Papa taught me. He used to let me sit in on his business discussions. I always stayed hidden behind a Chinese screen," she added in a conspiratorial whisper. "Picked up a lot of useful information, along with a few colorful nautical expressions that pop out once in a while."

The count was enthralled at the sparkle of excitement in her eyes and rosy hue on her smooth cheeks. In the open air, away from the stifling confines of Stockwell Hall, Amy came alive. Gone was the hesitant fluster that occurred when she was nervous.

"Let's race up to the ridge and see her mainmast as my ship pulls out of the harbor. Come on, can't we go any faster?"

This was hardly the timorous Miss Stockwell of a few days ago. His joy at her eagerness warred with his sense of responsibility not to overtire her this first day out. "As much as you would enjoy it," he said tactfully, "I do not think Grog is up to any faster clip than this. He looks a bit done in."

All contrite, Amy gave Grog's neck another affectionate pat. "Sorry, Grog, you sweet darling. Perhaps we should give you a rest. We'll leave this ride at just under an hour, shall we?"

They'd been out riding for over an hour and a half, but Toshiro wasn't going to tell her. She acted unconcerned that two of the pins had slipped from her hair, and strands of gold fell against her back to catch the morning light. He had to master the urge to touch those silky locks. When she rested her head on his shoulder for a few minutes, he could tell it was time to end the riding for today. Besides, he was becoming very aware of the soft feel of her, the subtle scent of an English garden that surrounded her. He turned Grog to the left and headed them slowly toward his own estate.

"I'll just close my eyes for a second." She stifled a yawn.

"Yes, just rest. You are safe, Amy-san. Nothing will harm you."

Similar to the first time when Toshiro had rescued then calmed her, his hypnotic voice had the same effect. "Mmm, I do . . . feel . . . just for a minute," she murmured, then drifted off to sleep with the warmth and security of Toshiro's arms about her.

When they arrived at the count's estate, Toshiro was hard-pressed not to kiss her warm, inviting lips as she came slowly awake. No, he reminded himself, their first kiss would be special and in a private place when they were completely alone.

Amy stretched her velvet-covered arms over her head. "Oh, that was a wonderful nap," she admitted. Sitting up, she gave Toshiro a rueful smile. "You have been most kind to give up your morning this way, my Lord. Thank you."

"Miss Stockwell, I have not enjoyed myself so much

in a long time. It was not a sacrifice nor an efficient duty," he added, thinking of her earlier remark. "And I intend, with your permission, to see you many more times."

"Oh, I should like that," the Englishwoman answered without guile. She watched Toshiro swing his leg over and jump down from Grog's back. A gray-haired man came out from one of the barns. It was then she realized how much renovating had been accomplished during the last year. "Why, you've rebuilt the barns, repaired the fences. How happy the late duchess would be with your efforts, my Lord."

The count nodded his thanks. "I should like you to meet my head groom, Dover Jenkins."

When he grinned, Dover showed a few missing teeth. "Please to meet ye, Miss Stockwell."

Amy gave him a friendly greeting.

The groom took Grog's bridle from his employer. "My Lord, Ethel 'as lunch ready in the garden as you instructed."

"Thank you, Dover." Toshiro then went around to assist Amy off Grog. "Just simple fare, but I thought I could show you the garden while we ate. Is that agreeable to you?"

His manner of asking her wishes touched Amy. Other than the business decisions she made, thanks to her father's will, often David and her uncles went ahead and took charge of her life in other areas. While they never said no if she disagreed, they rarely asked for her opinions. She held on to the count's arms as he lifted her to the ground. "Yes, that sounds lovely. I'm famished," she confessed, suddenly aware her appetite had returned.

"Good. Ethel is Dover's wife. I am pleased they came

up from the East End of London to work for me." As she took his arm, and he led them toward the back of the mansion, his words became more hesitant. "I hope you do not mind if we serve ourselves. I . . . ah . . . have not been as successful finding locals to enter into service here. Word seems to have spread throughout Bristol about my . . . unusual background."

Amy did not miss the abashment in Toshiro's voice that his house wasn't as staffed as other estates in the area. For an instant she caught a glimpse of the barriers the Eurasian must have faced when he first arrived as a teenager to enter the English boarding school system. Yet, she sensed they were still too new as friends for her to comment.

As they walked, Amy looked near the stables where Dover Jenkins was now leading Grog. She noticed the carriage outside the barn. Unlike the ornate gilding on the Earl of Woodcroft's coach, Amy was struck by the single sword-shaped leaf carved within a gold circle. Did it have any significance or was it just Toshiro's preference for simple elegance? Later, when they knew each other better, she would ask him. She listened as Dover talked to Grog.

"Come on, Grog, pick up those big feet, else it will be close to dark afore I get ye into the barn. Cor, what a slow one."

Ready to laugh, she stopped when she noticed the strain on her companion's face. Was he still embarrassed about having trouble hiring local servants to work for him? She tried to ease him back toward a lighter subject. "My Lord, I do like your horse Grog," she said truthfully. "He is relaxing to be around. Someone of my intense nature gravitates toward peaceful things. He really is a darling."

He understood her gesture. "You have a way with animals."

"Growing up I always had dogs, horses, rabbits, and cats about the house. Papa used to tease me about my zoo at Stockwell Hall."

"Yet, you do not have pets now," Toshiro observed aloud. He felt her hand slip away as she stopped walking. Automatically, he reached down and placed it back into the crook of his arm.

She straightened but resumed walking next to him. "No, I do not have pets now." Then she was silent for a few moments. "Clarice and the staff have enough to do looking after me, and I am occupied with running my business."

For an instant she reminded him of her aunt, the way she clipped out the words. However, the count hadn't missed the shadow that crossed her face, just before she attempted to hide it. This was definitely a topic Amy Stockwell wasn't willing to share with him yet. Yes, they both had much to learn about being friends first. For one thing, it was clear they each had painful memories of the past, and it would take time before they trusted enough to share them. And trust did not come easily to Toshiro Valerius, especially among these English.

Toshiro opened the wooden gate that led to his garden behind the house. He relaxed when he saw Amy's blue eyes return to their earlier luster.

Only from books and talking to the captains of her ships had she ever heard about Japanese gardens. "Oh, Toshiro, oh my!" The meticulous care taken to give maximum beauty and symmetry was evident. She inhaled the welcoming scent of purple and white hyacinths. There were small shrubs with yellow flowers and green leaves, a circular pond with a wide ledge surrounding it that welcomed a visitor to sit down. Even the gravel along the right side of the garden had been raked into even curves. There was only the sound of a bird overhead and the lapping water as one of the goldfish in the pond swam next to a white lotus with green leaves. Within this sheltered, sunny spot, his garden was somehow weeks ahead of Stockwell Hall only a few miles away. "Toshiro, it is exquisite," she admitted, unable to contain herself.

Her reaction pleased him. "My late father's sister, Gertrude, sent me the bulbs from Holland. I must confess I wondered if it would work, but my affection for Dutch flowers and the tranquility of a Japanese garden won out. Would that I could reconcile the West and East sides of myself so easily," he added with self-deprecating humor. "Come, let us sit down under the oak tree over there."

She followed. "I cannot believe how you've improved this place. Alice, I mean her Grace, the deceased owner, always treated me like an adult. Imagine an eight-year-old sitting out here, sipping tea, pretending to be a grand lady. I would rattle on about my vast knowledge of ships and cargo, while the dear lady would listen as if she thought me the most important person in the world. But my last visit, about four years ago, before . . . I became ill, I was saddened to see how the weeds and vines had overtaken the place. After Lady Alice's husband died, she lost interest in everything. They said she died of a cold that settled in the lungs; I think it was a broken heart." For a moment Amy thought about her mother. "I don't understand that type of love—so intense that it can destroy the other person."

The vision of his own parents flashed across Toshiro's mind. "Yet, if one is blessed by such a powerful love, isn't it a rare gift worth cherishing, even if it means facing adversity?"

Unable to answer at first, she pondered his question. "I don't think I'd ever want to face such a test." With a desire to move away from this serious topic, Amy managed a half-smile. "If I were a Buddhist, I would shrug and say my karma of reward or punishment will take care of itself."

Interested that she'd studied such philosophical theories, Toshiro ran his fingers across his smooth jaw. "Now," he mused playfully, "what possible misdeed could you have performed in another life? You who are as sweet and gentle as a lovely yellow flower."

Without comment, Amy allowed him to seat her in the garden chair with the comfortable cushion on it. Her host took the one opposite her. It was clear they'd been expected. She observed the embroidered tablecloth covering the round wooden table, the crystal stemware, the delft dishes that had been carefully arranged. When she looked up to compliment his excellent taste, their eyes met. Instead she blurted, "You do not know me, sir, my dark side."

Confused by her remark, Toshiro didn't get the opportunity to question her further because Sumi and Iwao came out with the wooden serving cart carrying their lunch. The dark-haired man reminded himself there would be time in the weeks ahead. Today was for her enjoyment only. "I hope you will partake of my humble food."

Amy brushed aside all thoughts of fate and cosmic theories. When she eyed the roast chicken with cinnamon apples she grinned. "Humble? Toshiro, this is a feast. Thank you, Sumi and Iwao," she said, when both Japanese bowed after serving her. "Please tell . . . Ethel, is that right, my Lord?" He nodded. "Please tell Ethel I appreciate all your work to arrange this picnic."

"Picnic?" Toshiro asked.

She giggled. "We English call eating outside—well, if we'd put everything in a basket, tossed a blanket on the lawn and sat down—it would be an official picnic."

When they were alone, Toshiro lifted his glass of cool lemonade to her. "To Amy Stockwell. Never did I realize doing business with the head of an English shipping company could be so pleasant."

Lifting her own glass, she touched his. "To our joint venture."

For the next hour they ate and talked. Toshiro noted she had second helpings of the chicken, fresh vegetables, fruit and cheese. A polite host, he asked if she cared for wine or sherry, but she declined both. She seemed most fond of Sumi's almond cookies, he noted. More comfortable in his presence now, he realized she did not feel the need to fill every space with conversation. He made certain food was available for her, yet he did not push. As he suspected, a little exercise, a tranquil setting away from her squabbling uncles, and Miss Stockwell showed a healthy appetite.

"Oh my, I'm going to burst," Amy said, then laughed at herself. She folded her napkin and placed it next to her plate. "I've eaten more than Grog this noon."

"Not at all. And do not forget I was the one who polished off the squash and cheese potatoes."

An imp peeked out from her expressive eyes. "I'm too well-mannered to comment on it. However, you must have to give Ethel Jenkins a sizeable food allowance to keep you fed."

"Quite so. I had to convert the East Wing into a pantry," came his dry reply. He looked over her shoulder to see Sumi return with Iwao. While Iwao cleared the crockery away, Sumi set two small cups down on the table. "I will serve us, Sumi. Thank you." With the customary Oriental bow, Sumi and Iwao went back toward the house.

"I prefer sake to brandy after my meals." He reached for the earthenware bottle, holding it with a linen towel. "Would you care to try our rice wine, Amy?"

"Ah . . . yes, I would," she decided, then held up her cup.

After pouring her some of the warm liquid, he served himself. "Like many things in life, it is best sipped slowly. Let it play along your tongue for a moment before swallowing it."

Amy followed Toshiro's actions in lifting the small cup in both hands. She took a tentative sip. It tasted warm and sweet. "I like it," she declared after the third sip.

"I almost forget, Amy-san, I have a small gift for you." Toshiro put down his cup and excused himself for a moment.

She watched his back as he walked quickly and gracefully across the grass. Opening the wooden gate, he headed toward a smaller wooden building next to the stables. Not as tall as David, she thought, but he was definitely an attractive man. There was an aura of mystery about him that fascinated her. When she heard his boots on the gravel path, she could not explain why her pulse quickened. Perhaps it was the sake or the unaccustomed amount of food she'd devoured. She smiled at her own foolishness. The count was merely showing his gratitude because she was willing to do business with him. Politeness was a way of life for him, nothing more. She stared at the slender object he carried in his right hand. It was wrapped in colorful yellow and blue paper. He handed it to her.

"My Lord, really, you are too generous. First the lovely bolt of aqua silk." She hesitated, not wishing to offend him, yet reluctant to accept another present from him after such a short acquaintance. "I am well compensated by our business venture, as you can attest from the profit margin I've wrangled from you."

"Please. It is a trifle. Besides, it will make my next suggestion that we walk about the garden more practical."

"Now I am curious." She accepted the gift, then began pulling away the colorful paper. "I should like a walk after that mountain of food I consumed, but . . . oh." She stopped speaking when she held up the mahogany walking stick. It was sturdy and functional, yet crafted with elegance in mind. The solid tip was inlaid with silver and gold in that sword-shape pattern she remembered seeing on the side of the count's carriage. It was superior workmanship, no detail overlooked, including the handle that contained the carved outline of a flower with large petals above that slender stem repeated from the base. Then she recognized it. "The iris," she said aloud.

"It is the crest of the Akashis, my mother's family."

She recalled his remarks about his Dutch father teaching him the joys of carpentry. "Toshiro, you made this?"

"Yes."

"But I know this took many hours of work. How

could you have made this for me? We have just met, and . . . ?"

"It belonged to my father. With age, the joints in his right leg stiffened, causing him discomfort when he walked. Since I have no immediate use for it, I thought perhaps it might assist you at those times when you feel up to leaving your wheelchair and taking short walks about your grounds and home."

She brushed her fingers across the smooth wood, then down to the carved leaves of the iris. "But I cannot allow you to part with such an expensive and precious family remembrance."

"Please, I wish you to have it, Amy." He placed his hand over her slender fingers. "The warm memories and affection I have for my honorable father are always with me in my mind and heart."

Moved by his gift and his words, she relented. "Thank you."

"You honor me by accepting it."

"Oh, Toshiro, I do adore your polite ways. I've never known a man like you."

Lost in the warmth and humor emanating from her sky-colored eyes, he couldn't speak for a moment. "Come, let me show you my lotus pond."

Getting up, Amy tried out her new gift. She held on to Toshiro's arm, while using the sturdy cane in her right hand. "This is much better. After all, I don't always want to roll somewhere. Try going to the privy with two huge wooden wheels bumping against the doorframe." She colored at her lack of reserve. "I beg your pardon." Then she came to a complete halt. "Listen, can I just apologize all to heck for any outspoken comments I'm bound to make in the future? It stems from my childhood preference for the company of salty mariners rather than cultured little girls my own age. Dare say Aunt Clarice is correct. I do lack the Townsend polish. I'm more like my father."

He could see this time she was jesting with him, and he delighted in her trust enough to joke this way. "Apology accepted for now until infinity, so you can say anything you wish in my company. Actually," he went on straight-faced, "how do you manipulate your wheelchair during those private times?"

"Never you mind." Despite her attempt at reserve, she giggled. "Guess I asked for that one." When he patted her hand, she went back to walking. They sat down on the wide ledge surrounding the man-made pond. Contentedly, she watched the lotuses and goldfish. It was mesmerizing the way the white flowers turned in the water when the fish brushed near them.

As the minutes passed, Amy realized Toshiro's company was like a calming breeze. He was a firm steady rock in her world of shadows and inner turmoil. A peaceful feeling she'd never experienced settled over her.

"Amy, you are safe here," came the voice next to her.

"I know," she answered. "It is a magical garden."

He did not touch her but his voice held her. "Amy, a Buddhist monk, Iwao's brother, was my teacher in Japan. Do you know there is a way to unlock hidden memories of the past by staring at the tranquil lotus on the water?"

Panic seized her at his innocent question. Amy jerked her upper body away from the pond. Toshiro caught her walking stick before it toppled into the water. He placed it on the side of the bench. She tried to cover her initial reaction. "How . . . how interesting."

He could smell the fear on her delicate skin. He took

her cold fingers in his. "Amy, I only meant that my wise teacher taught me a way to retrieve what lies hidden in our past. You should trust your own instincts. Truthful memories can never hurt us." He'd come this far, so he went the last mile. "It is only when we distort our memories with inaccuracies or shadows that we can be harmed."

She pulled her hands away. "I would not be so sure, my Lord." Shrugging, she peered over her purple-covered shoulder to pretend flippancy. "We English are a more practical people. I believe things should stay buried in the past where they belong. We do not worship the dead or the past."

His own features became a mask of restraint at her veiled insult. "Of course. I did not mean to offend you."

"None taken," she answered too quickly.

With self-consternation, Toshiro realized he'd played this card too soon. He sought to repair the damage. "May I show you the rest of the garden?"

She saw the uncertainty in his expression. "Of course, I should like a closer view of those hyacinths and yellow tulips." After he handed her the walking stick, they resumed their promenade. Neither of them mentioned the past or karma. They stayed within the realms of pleasantries, aware an unspoken agreement had been made: Amy Stockwell would not discuss even the possibility of remembering things that happened fifteen years ago.

When they entered the small structure next to the barn, Amy saw the rough wooden workbench, lathe, assorted saws, and planes. A well-used copy of Thomas Chippendale's book, *The Gentleman Cabinet Maker's Director* rested on a nearby table. Everything was orderly and clean, as if the place just waited for its owner to find the time to work here.

Almost reading her thoughts, Toshiro added, "This is probably the last time you will see my workroom without inches of sawdust on the floor. I have a tendency to get immersed in my work."

Amy smiled but did not comment. She had the impression this young man gave one hundred percent in whatever he undertook.

The rest of the late morning passed pleasantly. Amy found herself laughing more than she had in months. Toshiro listened with such attentiveness, she almost believed he really was interested in her banal activities. However, she couldn't refrain from asking more questions about Canton and Tunis. He enthralled her again with more exciting tales of his travels.

"Oh, Toshiro, how I envy you visiting such fascinating places." A wistful sigh escaped as they sat down on the chairs next to the table. She noticed with amusement the presence of more fruit, a lemon sponge cake, and a pot of steaming tea on the table. Ethel, Sumi, and Iwao were clearly working behind the scenes. At home the tea table was always set with noise and complaints from the young servants about how much work they had to do. While here, even understaffed, Valerius Hall ran like clockwork. She laughed at herself when she accepted a large piece of cake on a blue Wedgwood plate. Without hesitation, Toshiro went about pouring their tea.

"I've never been served tea by a gentleman before. In English homes, the lady of the house usually pours. You do that very well. In truth, my Lord, I'm more amazed that I'm really going to eat this piece of cake."

"Walking works up an appetite," the black-haired man

remarked, then took a hefty slice of cake from his own fork. "I like your English custom of high tea."

"But," she pointed out, enjoying their banter, "high tea takes place in the afternoon. What time is it?"

Toshiro made a production out of reaching into his embroidered vest pocket to pull out his watch on the gold chain. "It is only noon, but in Nagasaki it's tomorrow, so you see, we're already late."

She chuckled at his witty remark, then coughed when the lemon cake went down the wrong way. She reached for her teacup, then waved the Eurasian back when he appeared ready to spring to her aid. "I'm all right, *Hyo*. Guess I never expected you to be as outrageous as I am."

He relaxed. "So, you have heard of my nickname."

She took another swallow of the dark tea. Watching him from beneath lowered lashes, she studied his green eyes, dark hair, and muscular frame. "You did resemble a panther ready to pounce to my rescue just now. Of course, it was entirely my own fault for stuffing my gob with cake. You won't believe this, but I don't think I've eaten or laughed so much in one morning." She leaned over her side of the table and whispered, "Are you sure you can put up with me for two more hours? You did tell James Conroy I'd not be home until two this afternoon."

Equally amused, he copied her actions and placed his elbows on the small table. "I give you my word, *koneko*, I have never enjoyed a day more than these hours in your company."

She was lost in the warmth emanating from his eyes. Time stood still as they gazed at each other, words unnecessary now.

Toshiro reached out and took her hand in his. "Amy,

I want to—" His words halted when they heard loud voices from behind the wall that surrounded the garden.

"Wait, I tell ye the lass is all right," they heard Dover Jenkins shout.

"Out of my way, you country clot. Norbert, tell this oaf, I'll have the magistrate and ten of His Majesty's fiercest dragoons on this heathen place if he doesn't step aside."

"Love a duck," said Amy, horrified, "it's Aunt Clarice!"

Five

Amy Stockwell could never remember seeing Clarice so distraught. Dr. Norbert Wakefield, the white-wigged physician, struggled behind her, as he pushed Amy's empty wheelchair over the grass and gravel. The elderly man looked out of breath and as frazzled as her aunt.

Stifling a lurid curse, Toshiro rose from his chair. "Miss Townsend, what an unexpected surprise."

"Infidel," Clarice declared, her ample chest heaving with indignation. "How dare you kidnap my niece!"

"Madam, I assure you, I did not—"

"Don't try that Oriental kowtowing with me. I'm on to your weasel ways. I'll have you arrested, see if I don't. My brothers and I hold a very high position here in Bristol. We know how to deal with you foreign upstarts. I tried to be a Christian, allowed you into our home, let you sit at our table despite my brothers' misgivings. See where it got me?" she ranted. "David tried to warn Amy and me that you are more Jappo than Dutch, but one of us," she hoisted, eyeing her shorter niece, "is apparently too beguiled by your peculiar ways to act sensibly."

"All right, Aunt Clarice, please. If there is any fault, I am to blame for—"

Clarice dismissed the girl with a flutter of her hand. "Amy, you are too trusting and haven't a clue about the true ways of the world." The dark-haired woman zeroed her attention back on the grimly silent man in front of her. "The very idea," she continued, "getting innocent young girls into your pagan quarters for God only knows what illicit activities. And don't think I haven't heard of your East Wing. David and I saw all those Japanese ornaments going in there. My brothers still haven't figured out what goes on behind those wooden shutters, but I know. Well, you'll not lure our Amy into your den of debauchery."

Amy could not believe the vileness of her aunt's accusations. She caught her breath when Toshiro's military posture straightened even more. Right now she thought he resembled a threatened panther ready to spring on his unsuspecting prey. She saw the narrow line of his jaw harden. The dark green of his slanted eyes mirrored the colors of a stormy sea. She could believe he'd earned his nickname right now. "Please, Aunt Clarice." Overcoming her own discomfort, Amy grappled for the cane that Toshiro had placed next to the table. Struggling awkwardly, she got to her feet.

"Oh, my God, Amy, what are you doing? Norbert," Clarice ordered over her shoulder, "get that damn chair over here before Amy kills herself in a fall." Ignoring the count, Clarice marched over and clamped an arm about Amy's waist. Her demeanor lost some of the outrage as she clucked over her niece. "When will you learn not to be such a daredevil?"

With Clarice coming at her so swiftly, Amy lost her

balance. The walking stick slipped from her fingers. With a cry of alarm, she pitched backward. The Eurasian was at her side instantly.

"Don't you dare lay your uncivilized hands on my niece," Clarice ordered. She fussed over the younger girl. "There now, I've got you, poor lamb."

And she did. Feeling suddenly helpless in the wake of Clarice's outrage and fretting, Miss Stockwell allowed her aunt to lead her over to the wheelchair. She sank down on the cushioned seat. "Clari, you must listen." She gripped the leather-covered arms. "I asked the count to take me for this ride." Only a small lie, but Amy knew she had to do something to keep Toshiro from being arrested, let alone more insulted by her aunt's protective stance right now.

Apparently Clarice finally heard Amy's words. She looked down at her niece. "Amy, what has gotten into you? It isn't like you to be so brazen. To go to a strange, foreign man's house, alone—"

"Oh, no," Amy piped up, "I never went inside. We just had lunch in the garden."

Clarice folded her cloak-covered arms across her chest. "And I suppose without maid or proper chaperon, you believe it's all right?" She shook her head when Amy didn't answer. "Merciful heaven, child, what if any of our friends saw you? Think of the family. Your business. What of your reputation? I can tell you the fine families of Bristol will take their business elsewhere if they ever get wind of this."

Amy swallowed, for the first time getting a completely different picture of the day's events. It was to have been an adventure, nothing like Clarice was describing. Biting her lower lip, she made no protest when Dr. Wakefield reached down and took her wrist in his fingers. Earlier, her iris colored riding habit had felt warm enough; right now she shivered when a spring breeze ruffled her hair against her cheek. She looked up and gave Toshiro a silent apology, hoping he would forgive her for this disastrous end to his welcomed gesture. He probably wouldn't ever want to set eyes on her again, and she couldn't blame him. Even from their brief acquaintance, she could tell how much it cost him to remain mute in the face of such unfounded allegations against his honorable behavior.

While Amy wished she had the courage to say something more supportive to the count, the Englishwoman couldn't speak. Tears of mortification glazed her eyes.

Toshiro warred with his outrage at the intrusion of Clarice Townsend and that mountebank who dared to call himself a doctor. Yet, he was not so far-gone that he didn't recall Rigby's warning about Amy's loyalty toward her kin. It galled him to have to stand here and allow Amy to take the blame for getting a short reprieve from that stifling atmosphere of Stockwell Hall. However, he knew from the pleading expression in her eyes that Amy wanted nothing but his compliance right now. So be it, he thought, forced to grind the backs of his teeth to steel his features into a mask of polite restraint. As Clarice walked over to him, he berated himself for underestimating the Townsends' long reach where Amy was concerned. This round definitely went to Clarice Townsend, and she knew it.

"Well, my Lord," said Clarice. She even smiled up at him. "It appears I might have been too hasty in my words. You must understand how much our fragile Amy means to us. I have raised her since she was a baby, and protectiveness is second nature to me." In a gesture of dismissal, Clarice pulled the skirt of her cloak away from his black riding boots. She hunched down next to the wheelchair. "Amy, I was so worried when James told me where you had gone. I know you miss having a normal life, and if it were in my power to change things, you know I would gladly give it to you."

"Clari, I never meant to worry anyone. It was just such a lovely day, and I. . . ." Amy couldn't help remembering all Clarice had done for her. She was certain she would never have made it past that long, terrible period four years ago without Clari and David. Looking briefly at the count, she knew she'd also been selfish today. Too romantic for her own good. And hadn't she proof she would never have a normal woman's life? Clarice and her uncles protected her. What if she had let something slip this morning? Toshiro was a man of high intelligence and sensitivity. Even not meaning to, he could destroy her. When she saw the concern on his aristocratic features, Amy came to a decision. But it cut to face reality.

Clarice watched the myriad of emotions brush across her niece's slender face. It seemed to calm her. Rising, she moved behind Amy's wheelchair. "Come, it is time we went home." Miss Townsend pushed the chair back out through the open gate.

Sizing things up, Toshiro walked behind the three English people. "Am . . . Miss Stockwell," he amended after Clarice glared at him. "May I offer the use of my carriage? With the chair and all, I should think if you and your aunt ride in my coach, it—"

"Thank you," Clarice cut in. "However, the Stockwell carriage will suffice. I assure you, Count Valerius, we are well used to accommodating Amy and her wheelchair."

He gave a cool nod of acceptance, then glanced down to see Amy's hands clamped against the arms of the wheelchair. In only a few moments, Amy's aunt and doctor had managed to undo all he'd accomplished this day. The blond-haired woman was again as tense as a coiled spring. Never, he vowed, would he allow anyone, not even Amy herself, to put him in such a hopeless situation where he was powerless to defend her, either in word or action. He knew he'd been defeated badly by the Townsends in this first unexpected skirmish. And what enraged him the most was that Amy had taken the brunt of the attack.

Iwao and Dover stood near the Stockwell carriage. Toshiro said something in Japanese to Iwao.

"Hai. Domo goshinsetsu ni." The older Japanese servant bowed and quickly went back through the gate to the garden.

Amy took a deep breath when she saw it was time for her to get into the carriage. She looked back at her host. "Count Valerius, thank you for your kind patience in taking me for a ride with Grog, the delicious luncheon, and. . . ." Her voice broke and she had to stop for a second. "And for showing me your lovely Japanese garden." She was learning his ways enough to know how much she must have offended his sense of hospitality by having her relative and doctor descend on his home like a pack of angry wolves. "I humbly apologize for the unfortunate misunderstanding just now." She was warmed by the change that came into his panther eyes, before he bowed to her.

"You have honored my house by your visit."

An iron weight lifted from her chest at the return of his calm acceptance. She did not want this man to despise her, though she couldn't fault him if he was promising himself this would be the last time Amy Stockwell or her ill-mannered kin ever set foot on Valerius property.

Amy pressed her lips together and turned back to the task at hand. At home there was always someone scurrying over to help her, but for some reason she did not want to ask Clarice or Wakefield for assistance right now. Gritting her teeth, Amy pushed her hands down hard on the leather-covered arms and hoisted her frame up. Having felt so wonderful earlier, she couldn't explain why her legs now wobbled like a newborn colt's. She calculated the strength needed to make it up the three steps to enter the coach. A glance up at the youth atop the conveyance told her he wouldn't do a thing without direct instructions from Clarice. Yes, unlike other times, today Clarice was going to make her ask for help. Damned if she would, Amy thought, irked at her right now.

Toshiro eyed Clarice, the doctor, then the coachman. He couldn't believe after all the aunt's carrying on, she wasn't even going to. . . . *"Unko,"* he muttered, then stalked past Dr. Wakefield and Clarice. Before anyone could say a word, he had Amy in his arms. With a gesture of distaste, the Eurasian nudged the wheelchair out of their way with the toe of his black boot.

Amy let him see her gratitude. She took in his raven hair and dark clothes. "I confess," she whispered, "I always did prefer the Black Knight in my storybooks even though he was supposed to be the villain. I found him much more intriguing than golden Sir Percival." The curve of his sensual mouth enthralled her when he smiled. "You have been chivalrous in your patience this day, my Lord. Please know that I do appreciate it more than I can say."

Patience? he thought. God, he wanted to run with her in his arms up the stone steps, past the English entryway to his East Wing, bolt the door and keep her with him, anything to get her away from. . . . He stopped, aware how much his compliance meant to her right now. With the care he usually showed her, Toshiro walked closer to the carriage. "Will you not open the carriage door for your lady?" he asked the sullen coachman.

The wigged lad looked down at Clarice, saw her nod, then did as the count asked.

Clarice bustled over. "Amy, my dear, I think it best if you do not see the count again. Today should show you that only unpleasant consequences result from this man's company. After all," she said, giving the count a cursory stare, "this is merely a business arrangement. Do you not agree?"

Devoid of energy, Amy's mouth went dry.

Still holding her securely in his arms, Toshiro looked down at her. "Amy, is this what you wish?"

Oh, God, she couldn't face anymore of this pulling back and forth. Drawn to one, yet loving her aunt and uncles. Duty and loyalty against . . . what could she call this feeling? Infatuation, the delight in hearing about his exciting life? She rubbed her aching temple, almost wishing for Dr. Wakefield's vile medicine that took away anxiety during those short blocks of oblivion. She felt the pressure of Clarice's and Toshiro's attention as they waited for her answer. *I can offer this man nothing. It isn't fair to him, for I can never be a normal woman; he doesn't know what I have done; he thinks I'm sweet and good; he can never learn the truth I hide,* shouted through her mind. Unable to look him in the eye, she focused on the silver buttons of his riding jacket. "Perhaps it would be best for a short time, my Lord. Joshua Rigby can better handle all future correspondence between us if the need arises."

Hurt by her decision, years of self-discipline rescued him. "As you wish," he said, the formal politeness back in place. He eased her onto the leather upholstery of the Stockwell carriage. Then he could only watch as the coachman went about strapping the wheelchair on the luggage rack with practiced ease, before coming over to assist Clarice into the other side. Toshiro noted Clarice gave the young man a flirtatious smile. Amy never noticed the exchange.

When Iwao rushed toward his master with the walking stick, Amy's heart lurched. Now she knew what Toshiro had instructed Iwao to do in Japanese.

The Eurasian took the carved cane from Iwao. Iwao wasn't totally correct in his earlier Japanese comment that Toshiro was being kind in giving the golden lady this cane. The count admitted it. He also wanted Amy to remember their time together. Perhaps the memory would reach something inside of her to keep her fighting against that unnamed evil he felt lurked within those gray stones of Stockwell Manor. Without hesitation, he placed the walking stick inside the coach, right next to Amy's velvet-covered legs. He ignored her aunt's huffing sound of disapproval. "I would not wish you to forget your gift. Even a few moments each day about your room will strengthen your legs with time, I am sure. I hope you will continue to use it. As the body heals, the inner place becomes more self-reliant, too." For a second he wished he wasn't so Japanese and committed to politeness or else he'd have added she should feel free to use the sturdy wood to clout a few of her obnoxious relatives.

Through her side of the open window, Amy gave her host a sad smile when he stepped back from her carriage and shut the door. "I shall treasure your gift always. Thank you, again. Goodbye, Count Valerius."

He would not admit defeat in front of her aunt and doctor by saying "Goodbye" to Amy—not in any language right now. *"Gokigen yo kudasai,* Amy-san." His words—part request, part prayer—he followed by a deep bow in her direction.

When he straightened, the Eurasian saw the question on her expressive features. He went close to the carriage window and whispered the translation for her ears alone, "Stay well, please."

Unable to find any words to respond, Amy glanced over Toshiro's shoulder to see that her physician was still outside. "Dr. Wakefield, aren't you returning with us?"

The wheezy doctor brushed some specks of snuff off the cuff of his tan coat. "In a moment, Miss Amy. I want to have a few words with the count."

Alarmed, Amy turned to her aunt. "Please, Clari, I have already said Mr. Rigby will handle all future correspondence required between the count and myself for this joint business venture." Her aunt sat stonily looking ahead. "I have read much on Japanese history and culture. Clari, I beg you, tell Norbert Wakefield to get in the coach." Enough unfounded insults have been hurled at the count this day to convince him Englishmen were totally lacking in manners. "Aunt Clarice." Amy's right hand tightened on the ledge of the open window. "Do not humiliate me this way."

"Tut-tut, child, don't fret yourself," said Dr. Wakefield.

"Not good for you. Your aunt only has your best interest at heart, always has." He walked slowly over and gave her fingers a fatherly pat. "Besides, I merely want to ask the count about getting me some special herbs on his next voyage to the Orient. Supply is getting low, and who better to get them than one of the natives."

Her protectiveness toward him and the distress in her voice nudged Toshiro into saying, "It is fine, Am . . . Miss Stockwell," he added for her sake in front of these English snobs. "The doctor and I will go inside for a moment. I will take down the items he requires. In a few weeks I will be traveling to London anyway to bring you back that cargo from China." He did not add that he hoped to have word from his uncle in reply to his letter about his father's murder. "I am sure there will be some roots and herbs I can set aside for your doctor," he said, nearly choking on the words of hospitality. However, he was rewarded when Amy nodded in relief and sat back against the upholstered cushions.

"Norbert, dear," gushed Clarice as she peered across Amy's shoulder to address the elderly man. "Pray, do not keep us waiting over long. I own, Amy has been out in this unhealthy air too long as it is."

Adoration in his rheumy eyes, the doctor doffed his hat and presented a courtier's leg to the lady. "Your humble servant, Miss Townsend. I shall be back posthaste."

As Toshiro expected, when he closed the door of his paneled study, the white-wigged Englishman came to the point.

"If the earl weren't in London right now, I'm sure he'd call you out for this despicable behavior," grated Wakefield. His full-bottomed wig slid forward in his agitation. "And to put Clarice Townsend into such a state of worry is only the work of a brutish cad. I do not know the custom in Amsterdam or Nagasaki, but I can tell you, sir, in Bristol we expect more gentlemanly behavior toward our womenfolk. Bad enough Mrs. Cranshaw, the vicar's wife, spotted you riding near the wharf with Amy Stockwell, who I'll remind you is a paragon of virtue in this community, and head of one of the most prestigious companies in England. How dare you drape Miss Stockwell across your saddle! Why, you paraded her through town like a warrior with his battle prize. Mrs. Cranshaw even said Amy shouted a greeting to Captain Murphy, acting like a common . . . peasant lass." Clearly overwrought, Wakefield took out a dingy pocket handkerchief and mopped his perspiring brow. "Gad, sir, I cannot fathom what you were thinking. Miss Amy's tender years and sheltered upbringing excuse her. But you," he accused, peering up into the taller man's face. "Woodcroft said *you* had gone to Eton!"

As if going to Eton was the sole criteria for making a man fit to live, Toshiro knew he had to curb the angry outburst that had been hovering near his lips since Clarice Townsend and this old goat charged into his garden and ended his idyllic day with Amy. He thrust his hands behind his back to gain more control of his emotions. Aware this man would relate everything back to Amy's aunt and uncles, he chose his words carefully. "Yes, the earl and I were classmates. It would appear I am still learning about your customs."

The younger man's calm reply took some of the rancor out of Wakefield's bluster. "Well, that is more like it. I could see little Amy was all in a dither about it. Guess Clarice does have a tendency to overreact when it comes to the girl. Suppose no real harm done, now that you understand everything. Rigby will handle all the business nonsense. You just let him guide you. Man has sense."

"The ladies, sir?" Toshiro interrupted, goading the doctor into leaving so he could pursue some physical activity, like practicing his kendo skills with Iwao in a hidden part of his property where the trees thickened into a dense forest. He wanted the feel of that bamboo stave in his hands right now to work off these strong emotions before they strangled him.

"Yes, of course." The elderly Englishman turned toward the door. "Oh, meant to tell you. I like what you've done to the place. Good solid English architecture. You've done wonders to the hall and this old study. Hope to see the rest someday."

"Of course," Toshiro answered, equally smooth now that this ordeal was coming to a close. "I shall probably give a ball here next spring. By then, perhaps Miss Townsend and her brothers will see I am not the ogre they believe. I should very much like to line up with the other Bristol gentlemen to share a minuet with Amy Stockwell."

Toshiro's pleasant statement did not have the effect he anticipated.

His veined hand on the brass door handle, Dr. Wakefield turned his horrified gaze back on the dark-haired man. "Why . . . I . . . never realized. . . . Didn't Clarice tell you?"

Alert to danger, the panther moved back from the smaller man. "Tell me what?"

For the first time Norbert Wakefield stared at Toshiro with sympathy. "Why, my dear count, Amy Stockwell will never see another spring. She is dying."

* * *

Three days later when Joshua Rigby came to call with copies of the signed trade agreement, the rotund solicitor saw the change in his new friend. For a gentleman who usually projected an aura of inner calm, Toshiro Valerius appeared distracted this afternoon.

The count related what had occurred with Amy and her doctor.

"I can hardly believe it" Joshua said. He placed his half-filled brandy glass back on the side table and stared out the window. "Lord love me, a tragic business."

Today the count ate nothing. He placed the untouched cup of tea back on the saucer next to Rigby's brandy. "Wakefield said only he and Clarice know the truth. Joshua, I can tell she is too thin and often gets short of breath, but I never dreamed. . . ." He leaned forward on his chair to rest his elbows on his thighs. "Wakefield says she has the wasting sickness, and her heart is very weak."

Rigby read the torment in the younger man's eyes.

Aware he'd shown more of his feelings than intended, Toshiro got up and walked over to the unlit fireplace. He pressed his fingers against the pink marble while he grappled with his emotions. He'd jumped at the chance when he learned the owner of Stockwell Enterprises was none other than his childhood friend, Amy. All during the long voyages of the last four years, he'd kept that Gainsborough portrait in his cabin that reminded him of the sweet ten-year-old who once befriended him. Something had broken through his usual wariness when he realized that enchanting child had grown into a beautiful woman. Even after she first tumbled into his arms when he rescued her, he felt there was hope. Her legs were not damaged. The spine he'd felt when he held her was straight and unharmed. But now to learn she only had a few months to live. And he couldn't even give her a few months' happiness, for Clarice had gotten Amy to agree not to see him again.

Coming to a decision, Joshua Rigby grabbed his glass in his meaty hand and downed the rest of the liquor. He pushed his large frame out of the comfortable chair and came over to his client. "Here is my professional opinion," he said in his brisk manner. "As your lawyer, Valerius, I should advise you of the poor prospect if you form any attachment to a dying heiress, but blast it all, I can see you already have . . . a regard for the young lady. Myself, I've little use for all that hearts and flowers nonsense. I'm fond of my Doris, the children and all, but Doris and I understand each other. We merged our assets, and passion never entered into it. And if you take my advice, which I'm sure you won't, you'll stay away from Stockwell Hall."

Irritation at the Englishman's blunt words replaced his earlier reaction to the truth about Amy's health. "Joshua, I cannot leave her to face this alone. Even if I have only a few months or weeks with her I won't. . . . She has touched me in a way I've never known before. It isn't pity. There is a life force inside her. I know it," he added with conviction.

"Um. Well, then, I can't let you stay here pining over her. Just listen, Toshiro. Think of me as your older saffron-garbed tutor from your youth—all right, plus a few stone in weight," quipped the solicitor.

Toshiro nodded. "Go on. I am listening."

"Tell you one thing, my boy, I'm breaking one of my cardinal rules. Never usually get personally involved with my clients, that's my motto. Lord love me, it must be the large fee you're paying me."

The count's shoulders relaxed. "Perhaps, Mr. Rigby, you like me as a friend."

"A lawyer in my position can't let friendship interfere with his business. No, I just feel sorry for you." However, Rigby's smile proved the lie to his words, then he blustered, "I'd not put all my faith in what doctors tell you. Besides, you said yourself Wakefield is a mountebank. Gad, you must be besotted to swallow Norbert's pronouncement like pap to a two-year-old."

"Besotted?" echoed the count. "I'm fond of Amy, but I don't believe I'm besot—"

"Oh, don't get into a twist about it. Thing we have to do is think of a plan of action."

Hope sprang in Toshiro's chest. "I have a friend, Dr. Keith Stewart. He studied in Edinburgh. We met as boys in Eton. He was one of my few friends in those days. If a way could be found to have Keith check Amy. . . . You know I always thought consumption included spitting up blood. I never noticed Amy coughing and such. Joshua," he added, then grabbed the man's shoulders. He couldn't help grinning. "You are the crust of the earth. No," he said, then laughed at his mistake with the English. "Sorry. I mean, you are the salt of the earth. Is that not right?"

"Well," said the amused Englishman, "there are a few up at Stockwell Hall, I'll wager, think crust is a better description for me. Good to see you relax some of those courtly mannerisms once in awhile, lad. Shouldn't keep yourself all bottled up. Can't be healthy no matter what your customs in Japan say. Self-control has its place, but you should let your Dutch side pop out occasionally, just for a little air, if nothing else."

"Thank you, Joshua. You are a true friend."

Rigby's voice bounced off the four plastered walls. "Don't think this means I'm going to start sending you flowers, you understand."

It took the Eurasian a moment to comprehend the man's gruff joke, then he grinned. "Yet, how do I go about seeing Amy? I cannot visit the house now that she has asked me not to." He started pacing across the polished wooden floors, deep in thought. Rigby joined him.

After fifteen minutes, Rigby puffed back to his chair. "Lord bless me, Valerius, I can't keep up with you." He rubbed his leg. "Blasted gout's been actin' up again." He straightened in his chair, ignoring Toshiro's look of sympathy. "Gout? That's it. Romance through gout!" he shouted, then pressed his big hands together, like a philosopher who'd just explained the meaning of the universe.

Confused, the count came back and sat opposite the Englishman. "Joshua, I know I'm still learning about English ways, but how do you see your gout as a means to court my Amy?"

"Clifton Hotwells?"

"The spa? Yes, I've heard of it, but how . . . ?"

Joshua leaned over the arm of his chair, but his whisper could have carried across Scotland. "I met Amy's Uncle Henry at our club yesterday. After five brandies he became rather talkative. I'm not such a rotter to repeat his bragging stories about his mistresses. However, he let slip that his sister, Clarice, is taking Amy two miles up to Clifton again, while David is away in London on business. Seems Amy has been more despondent the last few days, not eating, and . . ." He saw this bit of news caused a worried frown to etch across the count's features. "Ah, well, Bath's Beau Nash may be dead, but the Master of Ceremonies at Clifton Hotwells still runs his place by Nash's rules. Mind you, it's no lark—dissipated roues, mamas in search for wealthy husbands for their daughters, dress codes, no swords allowed in the Assembly Room, up early—Gad, I'm fatigued just talkin' about the regime. It means there will be an Assembly Ball at night, gathering at the Pump Room to guzzle the waters in the early morning, dips in the hot spring. Who could blame me if Bristol's prominent solicitor and his new friend, Count Valerius, accidentally bump into Miss Stockwell? Though you'll have to be wary of the aunt, it would give you five days to . . . conduct any scientific studies you like," the older man finished with a roguish wink.

Could it work? Toshiro asked himself, then smiled at the prospect of seeing Amy again. He knew he had to try.

As she stared ahead at the arrivals parading up the path to the Pump Room, Amy unconsciously ran her fingers along the sword-shaped leaves carved on the side of the cane she held across her lap. Her second day at Clifton Hotwells was turning out like so many other visits. With Clarice abed in the mornings, Amy was left on her own until late afternoon. While she didn't mind the solitude, at least at home she had her logbook and business to take care of. Here she spent most of the time alone just watching the crowd. Of course, she always enjoyed the view from the gorge. Perhaps Clarice would take her there this afternoon.

The spa was one of the few places where class distinctions temporarily blurred. A duke might be soaking in the hot springs next to a tradesman's wife—tall, short, lean, fat, some healthy, others not. They all came to take the waters.

Though Amy tried not to think about him, Toshiro came to mind again. She missed their talks, the way he walked into her study and lit up the room. One moment his voice could soothe her with its low timbre, then excite her with entertaining stories about colorful ports. Bursting into her humdrum life, Toshiro made her realize she'd never really lived. Just once before the chance was gone, she had suddenly wanted to have an adventure; something to hold close that would bring a smile to her lips and color to her cheeks in remembrance. It might have sustained her during those empty years she could see stretching ahead at Stockwell Hall.

But it was over. Of course, it was impossible; she'd always known it. Amy placed her cane on the footrest of her wheelchair. Such maudlin thoughts weren't like her. The count was out of her life, and that was that. Nothing to do but keep going, just like she'd always done.

However, for the first time in years, Amy didn't feel very brave at the moment. The nightmares of the dragon had returned—one reason she fought sleep lately. Compressing her lips, she put her hands on the wooden wheels and pushed herself up the ramp. The staff was handing out glasses of the mineral water. She wheeled herself up to the wooden bar.

"Oh, Miss Stockwell, good to have ya back, dearie,"

said a plump, red-cheeked woman from behind one of the spigots.

Amy managed a half-smile. "Nice to see you again, Liz. Bigger crowd than last year."

"Oh, aye. More from London I'd say," answered the servant. "All that high living brings them down here eventually. Bath gets too crowded, so we get the overflow."

"Here, Toshiro, grab a glass," came the loud baritone to her right. With a start, Amy turned her head. Something fluttered inside when she saw the tall features of the count. He was standing with his back to her, sipping a glass of the waters with Joshua Rigby. The Eurasian was dressed impeccably in dark blue coat and breeches, white hose above leather shoes with unadorned silver buckles. His black hair was clubbed back in a simple queue. When he turned sideways, she studied his straight nose, lean jaw, and high cheekbones. He laughed at something Rigby said to him, then turned to see her.

Both gentlemen appeared surprised, then smiled as they headed in her direction. Happiness was the first reaction Amy had upon seeing Toshiro Valerius; she couldn't deny it. For once, she was glad her aunt always slept late. Joshua gave her a warm greeting. Toshiro took her hand in his, leaned over, and kissed the sensitive skin across her knuckles. His piercing gaze devoured her. "I never expected to see you again . . . here," she corrected.

Rigby frowned into his glass. "Devil take it, gout flared up again. Doris says the spa should help me. Asked Toshiro to go with me. Help me down the stairs into the water. Besides, if he's going to live in England and eat our food, he'll need to know where our cooking and drinking leads. Another glass, Valerius?"

One sip had all the appeal of swallowing warm irons. "No, thank you, Joshua," he replied, hiding his revulsion to this mawkish liquid. "I believe I've had enough curative for today."

Joshua shrugged, then looked about the crowded room. "Your aunt isn't about, I see."

Amy put her empty glass back on the wooden counter. "No, Clarice usually joins me in the late afternoon for supper at the Assembly Room."

A spark of irritation nudged the Eurasian. While the Townsends fussed over her at Stockwell Hall, in his mind they showed a lack of care for their niece by leaving her alone to fend for herself in the mornings at this spa. They probably assumed one of the attendants bustling about would help her. Yet, he knew Amy wasn't the type to bother people by asking for assistance.

"Lovely weather, isn't it?" Amy tried, then called herself a goose for asking such an inane question.

Idiot, say something. "Yes," Toshiro remarked. "Spring is my favorite season." Now that he was with her again, he wasn't sure how to ask her to spend time with him.

Joshua took in Amy's nervous features and Toshiro's uneasy countenance. He cleared his throat. "Miss Stockwell, would you do an old man a great favor?"

"Why, yes, Joshua, if I can," Amy answered, giving the Englishman a shy smile.

The solicitor bent over to rub his bandaged right foot. "Ungrateful thing is starting to ache again like the bloody devil—beg your pardon," he apologized for his phraseology in front of her. "After all the work I've done to give that foot the good life, see how it repays me? Lord love me, I'm going back to my room to rest. Toshiro said earlier he wanted to take the waters in the communal room downstairs. Know I should have let him swim in the pool first, but would you mind? That is, if you're planning to go down yourself—hate to impose, but I don't feel well—"

"Of course, Joshua. I should be delighted to act as guide and protector for our guest." A spark of mischief entered her eyes when she looked up at the count. She read amusement in his panther eyes at her light teasing. "I understand from my studies of Japan, shared bathing is very commonplace in your country. This will remind you of home."

"Fine," said Rigby, his voice carrying throughout the large room. He watched as Toshiro went behind Amy's wheelchair. "Thanks for minding the lad."

Amy turned her head and gave Toshiro a saucy look. She called back to their hulking friend. "Not at all, Mr. Rigby. I'm very good with precocious tots."

Six

Amy stood in the shallow part of the enclosed pool. "Now, pray do not be afraid, Toshiro. I am with you." She gave him an encouraging smile.

Toshiro managed to hide his true reaction to this English phenomenon of "taking the waters." Attired as most of the other ladies in here, Amy wore a shapeless linen gown with wide sleeves stained yellow by the waters. Her gold ringlets were encased in a ruffled cap. A ribbon about her slender neck held a small wooden tray that held handkerchief, perfume, and what looked like a bit of food. Though how anyone could eat a biscuit in this murky water was beyond him. He could hardly believe some of the ladies and a few of the gentlemen even wore their powdered wigs in here. Most of the men had on their hats. A woman in her sixties struggled to keep upright, clearly so the powder and paint on her face would not be "ruined" from immersion. Forced to don canvas drawers and jacket, he had been informed by the male attendant in the men's dressing area that this was the proper wading attire for a gentleman at the spa. However, the count drew the line on wearing his three-cornered hat in here. He felt ridiculous enough already. When the Eurasian placed his foot on the first step, he realized Amy had misinterpreted his initial revulsion of unwashed men and women sharing the same brackish water in the guise of good health. She obviously thought he was hesitant because he was a foreigner in unfamiliar surroundings. He felt a few stares in his direction as some of the English bathers moved out of his path. Little did Miss Stockwell realize he'd grown up with such reactions since childhood. However, unlike his usual response, today with Amy near him, he found humor in the situation. Indeed, a hearty laugh almost escaped at the discovery that these clothed English people probably feared the "foreign devil" might contaminate their Hotwells. He only hoped he didn't get a raging case of the trots from cavorting in this slimy water.

"Careful, my Lord, the water is hot."

Hot? Used to a long soak in his Japanese tub at home, Toshiro found this water barely tepid. "I will have a care," he reassured her, then followed when she walked to the back of the rectangular pool. The water came to her chest but only managed to reach his abdomen. Apparently many of the others felt his presence deserved solitude, but for once he was glad to be different. It gave him more privacy with Amy.

"I have attar of roses in one of the bottles on my tray. It's to help if you feel faint from the heat."

More likely overcome by the stench of body odors, but he said, "Thank you, I am fine. Amy . . . it is good to see you again."

The intimacy of his voice and manner touched her. She looked down at her tray, then back up into his eyes. "I have thought about our last meeting," she began in a nervous rush, wanting to get the words out before her courage faltered. "Toshiro, I never expected to see you again after what happened. I mean, after you behaved like a perfect gentleman and all."

"Amy-san." He came closer, then stifled a curse when he bumped into the blasted tray that hung in front of her breasts. With a deft motion, he slipped the ribbon-held tray over her head and placed it on the stone platform behind her.

An older attendant came over and gave him an unfriendly look. "Here, miss, are you all right?" she asked Amy, with a pointed stare at the tall Eurasian.

Aware the spa employee wrongly thought she might be in need of assistance, Amy smiled and shook her head. "Oh, yes. The count," she emphasized his title for this woman's benefit, "was kind enough to take away the tray when I complained of its weight. I still do not know how to swim, and he gallantly offered his assistance when I appeared ready to topple. I am finished with the tray, thank you."

For once Amy had obviously sounded dismissive and not apologetic with a servant, for the woman grunted and picked up the tray. After putting it on a nearby table, she went back to her post on the other side of the room. One of the heavier gentlemen had just leapt feetfirst into the center of the pool, splashing everyone in his path. Horrified squeals and male swearing by those sprayed from the tidal wave gave the attendant and her partner more pressing matters to handle.

Amy couldn't help giggling at the raucous goings-on at the other end of the enclosure. "I fear we are not making a good impression on you, my Lord. You are always so polite, in control."

A sardonic expression cut across his strong face. He waded closer to her. "The Japanese believe we should present a pleasant or reserved appearance so as not to upset the harmony of those around us. Our word *'men'* means both 'face' and 'mask.' " He took her hand in his and gazed intently into her vivid blue eyes. "Amy-san, do not be deceived into thinking that what you see only with your eyes is all there is to our emotions."

Amy's skin fired where his fingers stroked her arm's slippery flesh where her sleeve ended at the elbow. Even clothed, her wet flesh felt branded where he touched her. Telling herself she should pull away, Amy knew she didn't want to. "Toshiro, I don't know what is happening to me. I was so unhappy at the thought of never seeing you again."

This time he did smile. "Oh, *koneko,* you will never know what it cost me to stand mutely while your aunt and doctor took you away from me. I read your silent request that I 'not make a scene,' as you English call it."

"Yes," she admitted sadly. "You see, reserve is not the sole prerogative of the Japanese."

"But what is it you want now, Amy?"

Toshiro's warm breath fanned her cheek. His masculine frame shut everything else out of her mind. Time stood still. She no longer heard the chattering about them, for she was captured in the depths of the panther's gaze. "I would like to know you better. Of course, my intentions are honorable. Learning more about shipping is not my only reason."

Touched by her openness, he said, "And my intentions are equally honorable, Miss Stockwell. But I must confess coming with Joshua purposely to see you. Will you be vexed with me if I admit I've brought Grog and my own horse with me? If you like, we could take a short ride."

He did have a wonderful smile, she thought. "Oh, yes, I should like that very much. How thoughtful of you to bring Grog for me."

When he saw how her warm expression lit up her sweet face, suddenly he wished they were alone, not in this scummy water, surrounded by these noisy, splashing people. No, he could not believe this vibrant woman was going to die soon. It caused him too much torment even to contemplate losing her. "How long is it expected we must remain in the water?"

His impatience delighted her, for she'd been thinking the same thing. "If we get out now and dry off, I shall take you to my favorite spot overlooking the grotto. It has a lovely view high above the cliffs."

"Do many spa visitors go there?"

She understood his meaning. Amazing, but she was learning to read beyond his politeness. "No, not this early in the day. We should be quite alone."

"Good," he added, equally learning to show more of his emotions to this captivating Englishwoman. He held out his hand to assist her. A thrill of pleasure engulfed him when she placed her small hand in his.

About an hour later as she and Toshiro rode slowly across the grassy knoll, past a flock of sheep that led toward the cliff, Amy studied Toshiro's black mount. She had never seen a Japanese horse. He was muscular and hardy with a heavy head. This animal looked like he could easily carry the weight of two samurai in full armor. "My Lord, you called him Kori. While I've guessed it is Japanese, what does the name mean?"

Toshiro looked at her atop the gray gelding. *"Kori* means 'ice.' He is related to the Mongolian pony." The count patted the black stallion's sturdy neck. "We have been together since his birth. He was a present from my uncle."

Ice? Amy thought it an odd name for a horse. However, as she watched the way Kori responded to his master's subtle directives using only faint pressure from his legs and hands, Amy realized the name suited this animal. "Kori acts as if nothing would ruffle him. A bit like his master," she commented aloud. "Not to be jealous, Grog," she told her comfortable old mount. "You and I are well-matched, too."

Grog blew air out his nostrils and lumbered alongside the trimmer stallion, who appeared impatient with their slow pace. Yet, to Kori's credit, he obeyed his owner's unspoken directions and stayed back with her and Grog. She inhaled the sweet spring air and turned her face up toward the welcoming sunlight. "I like coming up here to watch the water. Isn't the view magnificent?"

Toshiro continued watching Amy. "Breathtaking."

She flushed but was grateful when he did turn to take in the rocky gorge.

After a few silent moments, the count spoke. "I hired twenty-five Bristol servants this week. Ethel, my cook, has a warm way with people. The young girl, Becky, who now helps her in the kitchen, let slip that a certain Englishwoman visited the hiring office in Bristol to speak personally with the job seekers. It appears this well-thought-of shipping owner vouched for my character." Toshiro looked deep into her blue eyes. "I am most grateful for your kindness, Amy-san."

"Bosh. I should have known Becky would spill the beans after I asked them all to stay mum about it. Appears the lot had some misinformation about you, that's all. I just had a few words in some select ears. Papa always taught me if you want results, you have to go to the source. Besides, haven't you thought that as your business partner it's in my best interest to see that you settle comfortably in Bristol? I don't want a competitor in London stealing away my source of Oriental goods."

He knew she was trying to save his face. "Amy, will you accompany me to the Assembly Room one evening?"

Pleased that he accepted her efforts to help him, she nodded. "I should be honored." As they turned their horses back toward the spa, Amy could not help admitting, "I like being in your company. You have a most agreeable effect on—"

Suddenly, Amy heard a woman call her name. She saw Toshiro frown.

"Amy! Wait!" came the feminine voice again.

"Please, my Lord, we must stop."

"As you wish," he said, unable to hide his disappointment.

Clarice Townsend was a vision in a mint green riding outfit. An expert horsewoman, she rode next to a young man dressed similarly to the count in buff riding coat and jacket. "Amy, you remember Alice's brother, Lord Anthony Fairfax?"

"Yes," Amy answered and finished the introductions. Riding sidesaddle across Grog's wide back, Amy was grateful Clarice wasn't alone. At least that saved a scene in front of others. If she was astonished to see her niece out riding with the count, Clarice didn't show it. Perhaps her aunt finally realized Amy was old enough to arrange her own personal life.

Clarice stared at her flush-faced niece. "Amy, I do not think it is healthy for you to be up here so soon after your immersion in the waters."

"Bilge." Amy waved her hand. "I like the morning air. I do feel much better today. You did get my note?"

"Yes," Clarice answered. The area near her mouth appeared pinched. "My maid gave it to me just a little while ago. Kind of you to let me know where you were so I would not worry myself to death upon not finding you in the card room. Come, let us go back. Rachel Throckmorten and her mother are expecting us." As if all was settled, Clarice and her auburn-haired companion turned their horses about.

Toshiro waited with difficulty, but he forced himself to remain silent. If Amy did want to spend time with him as she said earlier, she would have to prove she meant it. For an instant, he thought he'd lost when she turned to smile at Clarice and her younger admirer.

"Thank you, Clari, but I believe I would rather stay up here and watch the sky and water for awhile." She did not flinch when her aunt scowled. "This gorge is my favorite spot at the Hotwells. Pray give my best to the Throckmortens, but tell them I am unable to join them at cards this afternoon. I am sure the four of you will have no difficulty finding another player, a far better player than I am anyway. Cards are not my specialty. As David and you can attest, I always lose more than I win."

But not this time, lovely Amy, Toshiro thought, wanting to hug her for her polite but firm reply to her aunt.

He knew Clarice was livid but determined not to show it, especially in front of Lord Anthony Fairfax. And she didn't dare remind Amy of her agreement never to see Toshiro again. Everyone here but the affable Anthony realized Clarice had coerced Amy into that promise.

Clarice nodded. "As you wish. However, do not be late for supper and the ball this evening. I am sure Lord Anthony will wish to spend time with you."

Verbally nudged, Anthony spoke up. "Yes, Miss Stockwell, I should look forward to dan . . . I mean, sitting with you for a cozy chat," he stammered, clearly remembering this young woman was a cripple confined to a wheelchair.

"Thank you, my Lord," Amy managed politely.

Outmaneuvered a second time by Amy's cheerful rejoinder, Clarice stated, "Well, then, we shall see you at dinner."

Amy watched as her aunt and Lord Anthony rode back down the hill. They had met him last year at the spa. Strange, Clarice trying to push her off on Fairfax this way. Usually Clari wanted her niece to spend time thinking only of David. Amy took a quick glance at Toshiro. Could the Eurasian's presence have caused this change in her aunt?

This second round belonged to him, Toshiro told himself with wicked satisfaction.

Before going down to dinner on their fourth and last evening at Clifton Hotwells, Amy knocked on the adjoining door to her aunt's room.

"Enter."

Using Toshiro's gift, Amy leaned on the mahogany

cane as she walked slowly into Clarice's large suite of rooms. "Aunt Clarice," she said in the tone of a peace offering, "you're ravishing in that deep rose." She looked down at her own pale gown and wished the lutestring cream were a more vibrant color. She noted the perfume bottles and expensive Chinese jewelry strewn carelessly across the top of the dressing table. "I do want you to know how much I've appreciated your understanding these last few days." Though there had been no harsh words between them, Amy had been aware of a new restraint since their conversation at the gorge when Clarice first spotted the count at the spa.

The older woman readjusted one of the ivory combs that held her lustrous dark curls away from her smooth features. "As Joshua Rigby is so fond of telling me, you have passed your majority, and I have little to say in how you conduct your affairs."

Amy gnawed her lower lip. "Oh, Clari, I know you always have my best interest at heart. But, well, I believe you, David, and my uncles have misjudged Toshiro Valerius. He is patient and kind. He doesn't seem to mind that I am—"

"A cripple," Clarice finished.

"I was about to say 'shy,'" the younger woman corrected, briefly stung by her aunt's word. She took a deep breath. "I just wanted to thank you for not.... Clari, this is our last night here. Can't we be friends again? I've missed our closeness. I feel more sister to you than niece. I have always tried to do as you wished, but, please, you must trust me on this. The count and I are merely friends. He is a stranger in a foreign country, and I truly believe he enjoys my companionship. It's also in my company's interest to see that he fits in here. I want those Japanese goods each year, and, if I can smooth his way in Bristol society, he'll be less apt to take an offer from one of my competitors in London. This business venture is important to me." Amy walked slowly over and sat down on the sofa.

Clarice's posture lost some of its earlier stiffness. "But what of David? You know he adores you. How will he feel to learn his intended is going out every morning on rides with another man?" Not giving her niece a chance to answer, she got up and stood over her. "Our friends here are starting to talk. They have seen you in the Pump Room, Assembly Room, even out of your wheelchair actually walking with your hand on that man's arm."

Amy shook her head and smiled. "The count was merely assisting me by offering his strong arm for support." She looked down at the tips of her embroidered slippers. "I own my legs are feeling stronger with the use of this cane. I think Dr. Wakefield is wrong to insist I always stay in my wheelchair. Admittedly, I can't walk any long distances alone yet, but I'm feeling much stronger than a few weeks ago."

"Before Count Valerius entered your life," added Clarice.

Amy thought for a few moments. "I don't understand everything myself, but I suppose you are correct. I am changing. Won't you be just a little happy for me?"

"Well, I suppose I should be grateful for anything that improves your health." She gave Amy a speculative look. "But please be careful, my dear. I don't want to see you hurt. You only know David's generous ways. A man like the count arrives like a whirlwind into your life and captivates you with his fanciful stories and attentions. We know so little about him."

"I will be cautious. We are just friends, after all," she assured her aunt again.

"Just as well. Word about Bristol is that the count must marry soon. Probably came here to check the prospects for a wife to grace Valerius Hall."

Amy couldn't think of anything to say at this bit of news. It made sense, of course, but until now she hadn't thought about his need for a wife.

Miss Stockwell stole another glance at the man standing next to her as they watched the dancers and listened to the orchestra play one of Handel's slow tunes. Though she tried to be discreet, Amy could not deny Toshiro was good-looking in his dark blue suit, ruffles at his throat and cuffs. The diamond stickpin across his cravat gleamed in the candlelight. And he had clearly gone out of his way to greet Clarice tonight, before she danced away on the arm of Anthony Fairfax.

Amy's conscience bothered her. "My Lord," she whispered to Toshiro, "I believe I will go over to sit with my friends. I have not paid my respects to them. Rest assured, I shall continue to help you, though."

Toshiro followed her gaze and frowned. "You usually spend the evenings here sitting among the dowagers?"

Amy couldn't keep from giggling at his expression. "My Lord, I am quite used to fending for myself. I assure you those ladies are very pleasant company. Besides, you should be dancing with the eligible young ladies here. It would please me to see you enjoy yourself. Oh, there is Alice Fairfax," she whispered, then waved to the auburn-haired young woman across the press of people. "No," she whispered, "Alice is pretty, and you would acquire a good dowry there, but the Fairfaxes are a bit too high in the instep if you get my meaning. They might not appreciate your special qualities."

The Eurasian could not believe Amy was actually matchmaking for him. "You mean her family would not stand for their lovely Alice marrying a man not of their race."

She did not miss the biting edge of his words. "You must trust me to introduce you to people who will treat you with respect and consideration." She motioned a brown-haired beauty over.

"Rachel Throckmorten, I should like you to meet my new neighbor. Count Toshiro Valerius."

Rachel bobbed a curtsy. She blushed when the count bowed politely over her hand. "We have heard fascinating tales about your new business partner, Amy."

Amy smiled, then turned to Toshiro. "Perhaps you can tell Rachel more about your travels as you dance the next set."

Unable to do anything but request Miss Throckmorten's company for the next minuet, Toshiro felt a stab of irritation at Amy for manipulating him this way. As he led the agreeable Rachel out into the middle of the floor, he watched as Amy walked haltingly over to the other side of the room to join the elderly ladies. Their warm greeting showed him they were used to the entertaining company of their youngest member.

Amy watched as Toshiro lined up with the men, and Rachel took her place among the ladies across from him. While enjoying his company, she reminded herself it wasn't fair to monopolize his time.

When the dance ended and Rachel took the count over to acquaint him with some of her friends, Toshiro had the impression Amy had also planned this part of the evening. While he appreciated her efforts to introduce him into Bristol society, something began nettling him about her methods. When asked, he went after large glasses of fruit punch and plates of cold ham and turkey for two of the young ladies. An older gentleman talked with him about investing in Stockwell Enterprises. Apparently the investor, who turned out to be Rachel's father, said he'd heard good things about Toshiro from Miss Stockwell.

Pleased with herself for helping the count, Amy watched like a doting parent when he went back for more ratafia.

Two hours later, Toshiro managed to extract himself cordially and head over to where Amy sat talking with her own court of older ladies. She looked like a ray of sunshine as she sat there in her cream-colored gown, her golden curls arranged in a more becoming manner than her severe style of the past. "Miss Stockwell, may I have the honor of this dance?"

Was he mocking her? Everyone knew she never danced. Amy looked up into his green eyes. It surprised her to find a challenge in his gaze. "Thank you, my Lord, but I must decline."

"Why?"

This was intolerable, Amy thought, embarrassed. "Sir, this is the first time in four years I've even attended this assembly without my wheelchair. You see I can barely walk with a cane, let alone go dashing over the floorboards."

Her reproach didn't faze him. "I am sure you can manage a minuet, as expertly as you have managed to introduce me to Bristol's finest young ladies."

His barb wasn't lost on her. Expecting his gratitude, she wasn't prepared for his ire.

"Oh, do dance with him," one of her friends encouraged. Then another added, "Do you good to dance for once, my dear. I am sure the count will have a care for you."

Toshiro gave the older woman a grateful smile. "How kind you are to assist me, ma'am. Amy is so shy, is she not?"

Shy? Hell, right now she was furious. However, the Englishwoman managed to bite back a nautical retort that would have surely amazed the ladies about her. "I must decline, but I am sure Miss Throckmorten would love to stomp out a jig with you."

"I do not wish to dance with the lovely Miss Throckmorten. Come, I did not take you for a coward."

Amy winced. "That is unfair, sir. Just because I do not wish to humiliate myself by capsizing at your feet like a poorly made skiff in a gale, I will not be called a coward. And you . . . you're a bounder to suggest it. I am not afraid of anything or anyone. So there." It wasn't totally true, she conceded, thinking of the dragon and the nightmares that haunted her, but she'd make certain this man never found out.

All fire and outrage, spots of color bloomed on her smooth cheeks. "Your pardon, feisty one," he murmured for her ears alone. However, something nudged him when he added loudly, "Then it must be that you do not trust me to insure you will not fall. I am crushed."

She saw amusement hover near his mouth, but she knew he appeared only attentive to those about them. Equally determined to keep her features placid, she added, "My Lord, you are a roguish sea captain, and I am not deceived into thinking I have wounded you. However, it will serve you right if I trip all over your feet. If you get bunions from this, remember I warned you."

"Full of sauce," said the dowager, then tapped Amy playfully on the arm with her folded fan.

"Yes," agreed Toshiro. "She is quite full of impudence at times."

"And, you, sir, are full of shi—" Her coarse rejoinder halted when Toshiro reached down and hauled her up by her white-gloved arms.

"Yes, I'm glad you have reconsidered," he said smoothly, then bowed gallantly to the women who tittered behind their fans.

"My walking stick," Amy protested.

"You will not need it to dance."

"I want it to clout you over the head."

Toshiro just kept moving. As they walked onto the dance floor, Amy couldn't refrain from pointing out, "I resent being manipulated in this manner."

"Then you understand my feelings when you sought to pick out my dancing partners for the evening. I appreciate your efforts to help me in business matters; however, I insist on running my personal life myself."

Her chin lifted as they stood across from each other waiting for the minuet to begin. "I was only helping you meet suitable young women."

Keeping his left hand behind his back in the proper stance, his dark brows slanted at her. "Suitable for what purpose?"

"Why, for your wife, of course. For what other purpose do you suppose I'd be introducing you to young women tonight?" His leer in her direction scorched her. "That is beneath you, sir."

Their gloved fingers touched as they moved close to each other to execute the intricate steps of the dance. "Young lady, I do not require or desire a matchmaker, let alone a procuress," he bit out. "When the time comes and I wish to marry, I shall choose my own wife. Stockwell Enterprises does not need to provide that particular service for me."

Stung by his words, Amy missed a step and briefly lost her balance. However, Toshiro's strong hands over hers kept her from falling over. "Thank you."

"Tell me," he said as they finished the dance. "Do you often resort to that barnyard derivative for manure?"

She didn't flinch. "I use the word that fits the occasion. If I offend your delicate sensibilities, you have my permission to return me to my friends. I assure you Rachel Throckmorten never uses such language."

"Though Rachel is a pleasant young lady, I would much rather spend the rest of the evening with you, salty language or not."

As Amy allowed Toshiro to lead her away from the dance floor, she managed a polite greeting to her aunt and Tony Fairfax as they passed them. Toshiro's words just now took the fight out of her. "My Lord, I believe I've irritated you unintentionally. I should warn you my relatives inform me I've inherited my father's bluntness."

"That is old news," said her companion. "I knew you were used to winning the minute I signed that trade agreement and conceded so much to you."

Amy shot him a combative look but then spotted the humor in his eyes. "All right, perhaps I was wrong to start this, but I only had your best interest in mind."

"Then we will let the matter rest, now that we understand each other. No more maneuvers along that line, all right?"

"I agree," she answered. "Would you like another glass of ratafia?"

"Yes, dancing and being the brunt of your verbal arrows always makes me thirsty," he admitted. "I still have not managed to learn how to deal with you when you send such cannon fire across my bow."

She laughed outright this time. "Yes, I've noticed you usually remain silent when I start up. It is really charming, but sometimes I find it irritating. You can look so wooden, I'm tempted to check you for termites. Please, I don't want you to be afraid of me."

God, he thought, both amused and frustrated that they had so far to go toward understanding each other. He wasn't scared of this direct Englishwoman, but he'd been raised believing it was impolite to disagree openly in public. He sighed. "Let us have some more of that delicious fruit punch."

After they finished another glass of ratafia, Toshiro suggested they go out in the garden for some air. Amy agreed. He went back to get her walking stick, and they went out the glass-paned doors.

Aware of the female giggles and male voices in the dark garden, Amy smiled before she spoke to her companion. "Toshiro, perhaps I should have warned you, young people often use this hedged garden for romantic trysts."

"You are with me, so I will not be afraid," he teased. Indeed, he'd thought often during the last few days of locating a private spot where he could take Amy into his arms for their first kiss. When she stopped walking, his breath caught in his throat. He leaned against a wooden post along the flower-strewn arbor. There was just enough light from the many candles in the Assembly Room to make out her lovely face. "I like the way you have your hair tonight, Amy. It suits your slender neck and small-boned features. You are beautiful," he whispered.

"Thank you," she said, then felt the warmth in her cheeks. "Not getting out much, I don't receive such compliments often."

Oh, yes, he ached to kiss her, to caress her soft, pink lips. In this quiet place alone with her, they would have their first kiss. Gently, he changed places with her to hide her from everyone's gaze but his own.

She knew he was going to kiss her, and she welcomed it. Leaning against the firm wooden beam, she gave him a look of encouragement.

He bent his dark head, his lips inches from hers, and. . . .

Suddenly, there was a whooshing sound. Something hit the wood near Amy's head. Startled, she looked down and tried to pull the shiny object out. But she couldn't budge the embedded thing. "What ever?" She moved aside when Toshiro shoved his white gloves into his coat pocket and wrenched the object from the beam. Amy took it out of his hands before he could stop her.

"It looks like something from a horse's harness. One of the grooms in the whiskey, no doubt."

"May I see it?"

Amused now, Amy handed it to him.

Toshiro moved away from her and held it up to the light. It took effort to hide his reaction. He slipped the pointed silver star into the deep pocket of his coat. Never had he expected this—his father's killer now stalked him. Horrified, the Eurasian realized he'd endangered Amy.

Turning her at the last minute away from the light, he'd put her in the deadly path meant for him.

His expression confused her. "My Lord, are you unwell?"

"Yes . . . no. Please, I would like to go back into the parlor . . . no, it is the wrong word. I mean, the Assembly Room."

"Of course." Perhaps, she told herself, the public display embarrassed him. Beginning to know him, Amy realized he only struggled with the English words when upset. She should have remembered from her studies about his culture, kissing and other public displays of emotion were not thought proper by the Japanese. Had he just realized she wanted him to kiss her and felt uncomfortable at the discovery? Good thing one of the inebriated stable lads had tossed that piece of harnessing. Toshiro looked in a hurry to be gone from this romantic spot. Amy gripped her cane and began walking next to the count with her halting gait. "I'm getting better at this," she remarked, clearly trying to ease things back to normal. She was puzzled that Toshiro kept looking behind them, almost as if he searched for someone or something. "He's probably gone to sleep it off in the barn. Clarice had to fire one of our stable hands for getting foxed all the time."

Her companion took little notice of her words. Worried over Amy's safety, he cursed himself for being so careless. Toshiro was certain the Japanese assassin still lurked on these grounds. He knew he had to get Amy inside—now. "Forgive my forwardness," he apologized first, then leaned over and placed his left arm under her gown-covered knees. He lifted her high against his chest and began running with her along the grass that led out from the high boxwood hedge.

Amy held her cane out of his way. "My Lord, I assure you I can walk." Not alarmed, yet she was baffled by his odd behavior.

Toshiro saw her confusion. Not even out of breath, for she was light in his arms, he continued racing out of the maze. "I . . . have an urgent need to be back in the Assembly Hall," he said, trying to explain his outlandish behavior.

Amy thought a second, then the reason hit her. After he bounded with her up the stairs, taking two at a time, Toshiro put her down just outside the glass doors. Like a wary panther, he darted glances left and right before opening the door. He hustled her inside. "My Lord, I do understand," she whispered, then patted his arm reassuringly. "What you are looking for is through the door to your right, under the stairs."

It was the Eurasian's turn to look perplexed.

Dear me, she didn't want to embarrass him, but her sensible nature won out. "My Lord, I just assumed after the three tumblers of fruit punch you consumed, you are in need of the . . . ah . . . necessary."

He discovered he wasn't too old to blush. However, he decided this explanation would have to do. He wouldn't alarm her with the truth. "Yes," he managed, not having to pretend his sheepish expression. "Thank you. I shall be right back."

Amy watched him leave, finding him quite endearing just now.

After he returned, they settled on one of the upholstered benches along the periphery of the ballroom. Amy spotted Clarice coming over with a servant carrying a glass on a tray. "Bother, it's time for my medicine again. Clari never forgets. Oh well, nothing for it," she said with resignation.

Clarice handed her niece the goblet. "I am a bit fatigued, and the carriage will arrive early to take us home. Forgive me, Amy, but I believe I am going to retire early."

Amy's reaction changed to gratitude. It was evident she was trying to show Amy she accepted her new friendship with Toshiro. "Please do not give it a second thought, Clari. The count will escort me to our rooms in just a little while. I promise to drink every drop of my tonic," she added, as a conciliatory gesture.

Clarice patted Amy's arm. "Good night, my dear. I'll see to the rest of the packing. You enjoy yourself."

Toshiro stood up and bowed to Clarice. "Good night, Miss Townsend. I wish you and Amy a pleasant journey home tomorrow."

Clarice smiled at him. "Thank you, my Lord."

After Toshiro sat back down next to Amy, he noted she stared at the rim of the glass in her hand. "What are you thinking about?"

"I was thinking how sorry I am to be leaving tomorrow. For the first time, I actually enjoyed my stay here at Clifton Hotwells." Turning to face him, she said in a rush, "Oh, Toshiro, I regret those words last week in your garden. I do want to see you again. I know I sound brazen, and I'm sure you're too polite to show how shocked you are, but—oh, bilge—will you come to dinner next week at Stockwell Hall?"

The count let her see how much he wanted this invitation. "I shall be most honored," he said. "You have made me very happy."

Joy engulfed her. "You should smile more often, my

Lord. It makes you even more handsome. Thought I might as well get it all in while I've got my brass up."

His rich laughter escaped. "Oh, Amy-san," he said, as they sat on the bench in the corner of the large room. "You are adorable."

Despite her earlier behavior, she blushed. To steady herself, she looked down at the full glass in her hands and made a face. "Oh, well, I might as well heave to it."

Toshiro looked at the glass in her gloved fingers. "When I was a little boy, Sumi had a way to get me to eat my seaweed soup. She always took a taste first. May I?"

"Oh, I don't think you'll like it," said Amy, amused by his efforts.

After taking the goblet from her fingers, Toshiro took a generous mouthful. He held it on his tongue.

"God's night rail, you look ready to spit it on the floor," she commented, then giggled.

He swallowed after a few seconds. "Lord, you are right, *koneko*. It is vile stuff."

Laughter bubbled up inside of her. "Love a duck, Toshiro, I tried to warn you." With a shrug she took her medicine. "It has to grow on you. I'm getting used to it. Down the hatch."

As they talked, Toshiro became aware of the slight changes in Amy. Less animated, her words drifted off. That luster in her blue eyes dulled. "Come, golden lotus, I shall walk you up to your rooms." He reached across her gown-covered legs to retrieve her cane. Like a limp doll, she allowed him to put a supportive arm about her shoulders and lead her out of the ballroom.

Amy smiled sleepily. "Must be the warmth from the

crowd in here," she murmured. "Sorry to be such a bore."

Silently walking next to her, Toshiro was buffeted by the two discoveries. First, the horrible realization that his father's killer now stalked him. He was still shaken by the danger Amy had been in because of him tonight. Then he thought about that "tonic" her doctor had been prescribing for her. Despite the bitter herbs that were added, obviously to cover the taste, Toshiro recognized the sweet flavor.

Why, he wondered, was Dr. Norbert Wakefield giving Amy Stockwell opium?

Seven

"Come on, my Lord. I'll race you up to the edge of my property." Amy patted Grog's wide neck, then looked across at Toshiro, who was dressed in snug riding breeches and forest green coat. "Kori may be bred as a samurai destrier, but Grog and I have been practicing every day."

Toshiro was too lost in her mischievous smile to deny her. "All right, Miss Stockwell." Leaning over his black stallion's saddle, he tweaked Amy's upturned nose. "However, you are to have a care of that stone wall. Yesterday you took five years off my life by jumping over it."

She smirked. "Told you Grog has potential."

"Amy," he said in warning.

"Oh, all right. No stone hurdles," she conceded, but the deviltry never left her eyes. "I'll win the race anyway."

He chuckled at her audacity. "Aren't you concerned that Kori and I might win?"

"Not a chance," she tossed over her shoulder. "I never lose in wagers or business deals." Off in a flurry, she pressed her knees to Grog's thick flanks, and horse and rider charged across the meadow.

Toshiro knew he wanted her to win. Laughing, he rode after the enchanting Englishwoman, making sure Kori kept back just far enough to add spice to the race. "I'm right behind you, *koneko.*"

"And the back of us is all you'll see, my Lord Panther." She bent her head over Grog's neck to increase their speed. Today she felt healthy and reveled in the changes within her. Having given her word to the count, Amy took Grog past the stone wall, not over it. She raced to the right, the shortest way to the edge of Stockwell lands.

However, when Amy looked up, she realized they were heading toward the cedar tree near the edge of the cliff. Suddenly, Grog reared up on his hind legs. He whinnied in protest and wrenched his neck back. Shoved forward, she nearly fell off with their abrupt halt.

"Amy!" Toshiro yelled, his cultured voice filled with alarm. He bounded off Kori and raced toward her. Without hesitation, he reached up and pulled her off Grog's back.

"I'm all right," she protested. "Put me down . . . please," she added, trying to sound less frantic.

Concerned, nevertheless, Toshiro did as she asked. He set her boots on the dew-covered grass.

She gave a nervous laugh. "Grog must have lost his footing. There are a lot of stones up here. Maybe it was a hole."

Her companion watched the way she rubbed the upper part of her hands. He studied the low spreading branches of the cedar tree to the left, then peered ahead toward the edge of the cliff. He walked over to Grog. The horse's mouth was bleeding where the bit had cut him.

Amy joined them. She looked at Grog, while Toshiro tended to him. She knew that the count now realized it hadn't been Grog's fault. Amy had pulled up on the reins, forcing Grog to stop. Yet, he said nothing. When Toshiro stepped away, Amy came closer and hugged Grog around the neck. "Oh, Grog," she whispered against his soft gray nose, "I'm so sorry I hurt you." What was wrong with her? She wasn't a child anymore. There was nothing to fear up here.

Amy turned to find Toshiro studying her intently. "My Lord, I . . . I am feeling tired. I should like to go home now."

The Eurasian nodded and helped her mount.

Silently, they made their way back down the hill. Amy knew the count must be perplexed, probably even repelled by her behavior. If only he knew she didn't understand her actions just now either.

"How's David doing?" Henry Townsend asked, then took another nostril-full of powdered tobacco from the back of his right hand.

"Fine, I believe," answered Amy. She walked slowly over to the green sofa and sat down. "I've written him often, but as usual, he is occupied with business matters. I only received a short note from him two weeks ago."

Simon was busy wiping off a wayward glob of cherry tart that had cascaded down the front of his canary yellow waistcoat.

Henry looked eagerly at his niece. "Wait until you see the catch I bagged this morning. Always was an excellent marksman. Told that new cook of yours to fetch it in later so you can admire them, Amy."

"Hah," mumbled Simon, his jaws bulging with another fruit tart, "wager you had your gun carrier do the stalking. You couldn't hit an elephant if it sat in your living room sippin' tea."

Henry sneezed, then folded his limp handkerchief back into the deep side pocket of his brown coat. "Well, mutton face, if you'd get your jowls out of the trough once in awhile, you might appreciate the great outdoors. It infuses a man with vigor." He gave his rotund sibling a critical look. "Poor Mabel must have given up on having any more children. Her parts rusting away from disuse, are they?"

Simon's features mottled to crimson as he waddled over to his brother. "You . . . snuff-snorting, gutter-mouthed. . . . Ain't enough you're overrunning Bristol with your bastards. Don't let me catch you dancing about my wife, else I'll mount your balls in one of your own trophy rooms, right next to that boar's head you *said* you shot last Christmas. Gray beast probably keeled over from old age or did you offer it more of that stinking tobacco you're always blowing about the place?"

Amy fought the familiar tensing in her stomach. "Please, let's not have any more quarrels tonight." The count and Mr. Rigby would be here soon. Surely Toshiro would not keep coming to see her if he was forced to listen to her family bickering each time. She hadn't missed the way he recoiled that first night when he'd sat down at her dinner table.

Clarice went over to her niece. "Now, you mustn't upset yourself." She shot her brothers a warning. "You know Dr. Wakefield said it isn't good to excite Amy."

Her features softened when she turned back to Amy. "And she has made such progress. My dear, you are not as peaked as you were weeks ago. And a new gown," she exclaimed, her dark gaze taking in the unfamiliar dress. "Clever girl, how ever did you shop for it?"

Amy touched the watered silk material of her skirt. "Well, I do own the store," she said with humor. "I saw it in the window that day I went for a ride with the count." She took in her aunt's amber-colored gown and matching slippers. "You look lovely tonight, too, Aunt Clarice," she said, confident to add herself in this praise.

"My, my," Clarice mused aloud. "I own, the spa did wonders for you this time, my dear."

Much of the tenseness left Amy's body. "Oh, yes, Clari, I agree." Deciding to keep the count's major role in her improvement to herself, she smiled at her relatives. "See, Uncles, I'm able to walk with just my cane. I hardly use the wheelchair anymore."

Giles came over and stood in front of her. "But Amy," he said in his unsteady voice. "Do you think it wise to invite Count Valerius again to dinner, let alone accept his gifts?"

Amy hadn't expected this. Of all her uncles it was light-haired Giles who usually sided with her. "In Japan gift giving is seen merely as politeness. Besides, it was just hanging about his house, now that his late father has no use for it." Like those times before her servants, Amy was provoked by the way her usually protective relatives were making her feel so defensive. "The count and I are business partners. Why shouldn't I have him to dinner in the proper setting with my family? For heaven's sake, it isn't as if I'm sneaking out to have my way with him along the docks. I hardly think I'm a scarlet woman because I go for horseback rides, see a male acquaintance at a spa, or invite him to dinner."

Giles appeared uncomfortable and stepped to the side of the sofa. An oppressive silence fell over the sitting room.

"Thunderation," Simon bellowed as he raided the nut dish on the table next to him. "Enough of all this stepping about on eggshells. All right, Amy, I'll come right out with it: my brothers and I think this Jappo upstart has designs on you. And I ain't talkin' about architecture or calligraphy."

"Shush," pleaded Giles, his voice high-pitched. "Will you lower that bellow, Simon, before the servants hear you."

"Oh," said Amy, "I am sure the count only sees me as a friend, as I view him." Then a stronger emotion at Simon's remark took hold of her. "Not that I would be anything but flattered if he did find me worth courting in a proper manner."

"Did you hear that?" Simon exploded to his siblings, nearly choking on the glob of nutmeats in his mouth. He ignored Giles's nervous waving of hands for him to decrease the volume. "We should all be bloody thankful Amy is barren. Can't you imagine having to explain to our neighbors that our niece has lapses, where she can't even remember what she's done? If she were a normal woman, we'd likely have one of those slant-eyed little bastards turn up on the Stockwell doorstep. And what would you tell your sacred neighbors, Giles, when Amy there twisted the little bugger's neck one evening during one of her blank spells? Damn me, her husband would have to count the whelps each night to be sure she hadn't strangled one of them inadvertently."

"Simon!" Clarice shouted in horror.

Giles mirrored his sister's reaction. "Really, Simon, you go too far."

"Well, Henry, don't tell me you've forgotten four years ago?"

Henry shrugged. "Hasn't happened in four years, Simon. No reason to suspect it will. David would make a better husband anyway. He says it doesn't matter that Amy's a bit off. He'd still care for her. Besides, a man ought to be running the business. David understands these things."

Amy's knuckles whitened with the pressure she exerted to keep from saying something she knew they would all regret. Right now her relatives spoke about her as if she weren't even in the room. None of them had brought up this disturbing subject in years. It unnerved her. When she spotted the cane against the side of the brocade-covered sofa, she reached for it. For some unexplained reason, it made her remember Toshiro's encouraging words. The coiling inside her abdomen receded. She ran her fingers along the carved iris leaves. No, she would not comment on those remarks. Better to talk about the present. "I do not love David, and I have told him so," she admitted. "He is a dear friend, nothing more." Something lurched inside her chest, but she forced herself to continue. She looked at her aunt, then glanced at her three uncles who hovered over her as if they thought any second she would collapse or begin shrieking like a bedlamite. "You need not fear on that account. Rest assured, I'm aware of the legacy I carry from my mother." She'd been abruptly reminded of it this morning when she got near the cedar tree on her way to the cliff.

"Well," blustered Simon, "glad that's settled. Come

on. I'm starving. Scent of coriander over that crown roast of lamb is killing me. Let's go into dinner. That cheeky young cook told me it wasn't my business when I asked what was in the porcelain bottle she had in a pan of water over the fire. And the delft custard cups? Is it for that Chinaman?"

Amy retained her composure with difficulty. "Toshiro is Japanese, not Chinese."

"Whatever," countered Simon. "They all look alike to me."

"Not to the Chinese or Japanese." Amy got up and began walking awkwardly toward the door. Clarice and her uncles followed.

"Now you've got me curious," admitted Henry. "What is in the bottle?"

Amy gave her uncle an enigmatic smile. "We shall see later," was all she would divulge.

"What kind of a queer answer is that?" Simon demanded. He scowled at his youngest brother, who looked ready to remind him again about his English whisper. "Curse you, Giles, and all the servants. I don't give a bishop's fart if the whole house hears. What in bloody hell has gotten into Amy? She's even beginning to sound like that bloody Jappo."

"Oh, come, Uncles, won't you try the sake?" Amy poured some for Toshiro, Joshua, Clarice, and herself.

The Townsend brothers all declined. Giles peered at the clear liquid in the tiny cups and shuddered. "Sorry, but I'll pass. I've a delicate stomach for such outlandish concoctions."

Pleased with the way the cordiality of the predinner

conversation had progressed so far, Amy told herself everything was going to be fine. Prudently, she'd not included the rest of the family in this dinner. Less chance of upheaval. "I think it is good to stay open to new adventures," she said, then looked up at the count. Dressed in black evening clothes, Dutch lace at throat and cuffs of his fine tailored shirt, his hair gathered back with a black ribbon, Valerius looked every inch the well-dressed aristocrat. She touched the skirt of her rose gown. When she saw the warm appreciation in his gaze, she was glad she'd requested one of the clerks from the store to bring this new dress up to Stockwell Hall.

"It is most kind of you to go to so much trouble," the Eurasian commented. "May I ask, how ever did you acquire this rice wine?"

Merriment transformed her features. "Captain Murphy is a great source of information for me. He told me your ship, *Nightingale,* was back in port after you'd sent her up the coast for a few minor repairs. I had one of my clerks from the store offer to purchase some sake from your second in command. Of course, dear Mr. Roonhuysen would not take any money for the bottle I desired."

"Jan did not mention it to me."

"No, my Lord, I asked him not to. I wanted it to be a surprise."

"And a thoughtful one it is." Toshiro took another sip of the warm wine.

"Don't drink too much of the stuff," cautioned Giles, "else you'll become foxed."

His niece chuckled. "This sake isn't any stronger than sherry. I like it," she added. Amazing, but around Toshiro, she became more outspoken with her uncles. It wasn't an unpleasant experience.

"Of course," said Joshua, as he held the tiny cup in one of his heavy hands, "I admit being partial to your brandy, Toshiro, but this rice stuff isn't bad."

"My Lord, I wanted to ask you about . . . ?" The words stuck in her throat when a young man dressed in green livery entered the room. Amy stared transfixed at what he carried in his right hand.

Toshiro saw Amy blanch when she spotted the three dead rabbits strung with leather on a wooden pole. Blood matted their brown fur.

Henry beamed. "That's right, James. . . ." He took a closer look at the red-haired lad. "You're not James Conroy. Who in blazes are you?"

The young man of about eighteen smirked. "He don't work here no more. Went back to bein' a journeyman in London. I'm Brian. Miss Clarice hired me yesterday. I left the birds out in the slop sink. Cook said I wasn't to make a mess on the floors."

"Lord," admonished Clarice to her brother, "you never said they were rabbits. Oh, Henry, how could you?"

When Simon saw his niece's ashen face, he gulped another swallow of liquor and gave his younger brother an incriminating look. "Henry, you've got all the sensitivity of a pregnant sow in a milliner's shop." Then he noticed there weren't any more filberts in the dish. "Damn me, isn't it time for supper yet?"

No one answered.

Toshiro put his cup down. He caught Amy's before it landed on the Oriental carpet at her feet. He noticed the way she kept pressing the upper part of her hands together.

Chagrined, Henry blustered, "Now, Amy, you're all right. Your trouble is, you don't breathe in enough."

"Damn me, what she needs," offered Simon, "is more red meat and port. Makes more blood. I'm going to waste away if we don't get victuals soon."

"Look, mutton face, I tell you the girl doesn't breathe enough."

"Oh," wailed Clarice, "look at her; she can't even hear us."

"What the deuce is she doing with her arms?" Henry asked.

"She's rubbing her hands again," Clarice pointed out.

Joshua eyed the count, as if asking him if he was going to let this tomfoolery continue.

Toshiro could not believe Amy's relatives let her stand there. Years of conditioning warred and lost within Count Valerius. With a muttered curse in Japanese, he rushed to her side. "Amy?" Her eyes were transfixed on something none of them could see. Toshiro glanced quickly at the Townsends.

Recoiling, Clarice held a hand to her throat. "It's starting all over again."

"Just like Jane," said Giles.

Henry looked chagrined. "Lord, I forgot. Brian, take the cursed things back to the kitchen."

Aware the Townsends knew what Amy was reliving in her mind, Toshiro surmised they weren't about to enlighten him. He turned back to her. "Amy, please tell me what you see."

Nothing.

"Amy," he called again, both concerned and confused by her reaction. It was evident there was something more here than the tasteless exhibition of Henry Townsend's hunting prize. Her gaze focused straight ahead, as if she watched some horrid scene played out for her eyes alone.

"The dragon," she whimpered. "I can see his blood-red eyes. No, please."

Her anguished cry tore at him. "Amy, what frightens you?"

In her mind, Amy saw herself in the garden again. She was awakening after a pleasant nap. She looked down. "Fluffy," she greeted, happy to see her brown rabbit had joined her as usual. Then she realized her playful little pet wasn't moving. His mouth gaped open. Blood dripped from his ears. His eyes bulged. She raised her hands and saw the blood, glanced down and found it soaked the cream-colored skirt of her summer gown. "God, no!" she screamed. The dragon had come back. She recognized that dark haze from her nightmares and knew he meant to harm her. She'd told herself four years ago if she closed that door and pretended the dragon didn't exist, she would be safe. Clarice and her uncles would keep her secret, and the dragon would never find her again. But now, alone in this heavy mist, he was stalking her once more. She felt his putrid breath on her skin. What did he want? "Who are you?" she asked aloud. "Please, leave me alone. I don't remember. I won't tell."

"Amy!" The hairs on the back of his neck bristled in alarm at her outcry. In a movement that now felt the most natural in the world, Toshiro reached out and encircled her slender waist with his left hand. Gently, he tipped her face up to his. "Amy, you are safe," he whispered, his mouth a hair's breath from hers. "I am here, *koneko*."

"Oh," said Clarice Townsend, clearly alarmed at the young man's boldness. "Simon, Henry, do something."

Simon took a step forward. "Sir, unhand my niece at once. Damn me, if you persist in these liberties, my brother Henry will call you out. You've already seen how he pulverizes rabbits. He'll shoot you right through those slanty eyes of yours, see if he don't. Tell him, Henry."

"Me?" Henry echoed. "You weigh more than I do, mutton face. Why don't you teach the foreign devil a lesson?"

"Perhaps," Giles pointed out in a nervous squeak, "if the three of us circle the blackguard we can—"

"Stay back, all of you!" snarled Toshiro. Distress over Amy and anger at her relatives collided within him.

Clearly affected by the unexpected growl from the dangerous panther before them, all three brothers stepped back.

"I never," huffed Clarice. "Men. Weak as water, the herd of you."

Rigby took hold of Clarice's satin-covered arm when she made a motion to charge over to her niece. "Now, Miss Townsend, I'd go along with the count if I were you. Haven't you heard of these Oriental ways of curing? All hush-hush."

Clarice looked skeptical but allowed the solicitor to ease her over to her brothers a few feet from her niece. "But . . . but that man is holding her."

"Dear me, what if the servants hear about this?" Giles's face crumbled when he saw the Eurasian bend his head closer to Amy's. "Good God, what's he going to do now?"

Toshiro said her name, this time with a new fierceness. When she did not respond, he pulled her body closer. "I'd never anticipated our first kiss would be in front of all your astonished relatives," he said against her mouth, "but by God I can think of nothing else to bring you back to me."

Count Toshiro Valerius pressed his warm lips firmly against her cool, parted mouth. All the passion and longing he'd kept under tight control raged to the surface, and this time he made no effort to quell it. He stroked her, teased her with his lips, then demanded her response as he prolonged this first kiss between them far beyond the boundaries of propriety in either England, Holland, or Japan.

The waking nightmare suddenly changed within Amy's mind. The Black Knight, a gleaming sword in his armored hand, sat astride a midnight destrier as he began charging after the dragon. Her rescuer shouted something in a language she did not understand, but the red-eyed dragon must have, for he turned suddenly and moved his green talons away from her. The ice began melting from her veins. A glimmer of light guided her away from the vaporous fog. Her hands reached up and felt sinews through the velvet-covered arms that held her now. Unconsciously, she pressed herself into the strength of this offered shelter. Through the rose silk of her gown she felt the warmth of his hard body. Confusing images spun about her, and she had to cling to this steady rock as the Black Knight battled the dragon for her. He had not killed the beast, but he frightened him away. She would be safe for a time. Her lips moved against the sensual mouth that continued claiming hers and spoke to her in a way no words could ever convey. A new forcefulness entered their kiss and she accepted his unspoken promise that he would protect her from the dragon, but there was a price: She now belonged to the Black Knight.

"Yes," she murmured, automatically accepting the bargain. "I need . . . please, I want. . . ." The awakening fires caused her to protest when her champion pulled back. Her lashes fluttered against her alabaster skin. Breathing hard, she looked up into the familiar eyes with their golden flecks. "Panther eyes," she whispered, then colored at his smoldering gaze. Amy didn't want reality to push its way into her mind just yet. She wished to return with the Black Knight to their secret place where nothing would harm them, where culture and race didn't matter, and her own past couldn't destroy them.

"Welcome back, *koneko*."

His smile was almost boyish and it warmed her, along with that mesmerizing voice that suddenly made her want to yield everything to him. It stirred something deep inside her. A memory? But then it departed when Amy realized they weren't alone. She looked over the count's shoulder to see her aunt and uncles, then Joshua Rigby. They came at her at once. She flushed, aware she still clung to Toshiro's upper arms. Shaken, Amy managed to step back.

"Such liberties," Aunt Clarice complained. "Positively indecent, seducing her right before our eyes."

Amy tried to fight her lethargy. "No, you must not blame the count," she defended. Though she strove to hide it, never had she experienced anything like this searing kiss. "I am grateful for the count's intervention. Silly of me, really. I've seen prizes from Henry's hunts before. I'm usually not the vapor sort."

"Then," Giles asked, "you were not aware that he just kissed you?"

His niece touched her sensitive lips. She realized it all right. "Yes, of course." She saw the unfriendly expressions on her uncles' features. They looked ready to call the magistrate. The count didn't seem to notice, for he kept watching her, as if he needed to be certain she was truly going to be all right.

"I am fine, my Lord. Thank you for your quick, if somewhat unconventional, intervention," Amy added, trying to put them all at ease.

"But," Clarice protested, seeming at a loss. "Such forwardness."

"Bilge," countered Amy. "The count merely performed an effective clinical maneuver. We must understand he is not cognizant of our English prudery about such things. Now, please let us speak no more about it."

Toshiro understood she meant to defend him. However, he knew there was nothing in the least medicinal about that kiss. And he'd felt her torrid response. She'd opened to him like a delicate lotus reaching for sunlight. The thought warmed him. However, it was muted at the realization that Amy and her relatives were hiding something from him.

"My dear, you gave us such a fright." Clarice patted her niece's shoulder. "Leave it to Henry to act the buffoon."

"I said I was sorry," Henry pointed out. "What do you want me to do? Grovel and bow like the count's two Jappo servants? I ain't the toadying type," sniffed Mr. Townsend. "Jane did enough of that in her day, may she rest in peace."

"Love a duck . . . I mean, let us all proceed into dinner," Amy corrected, only wishing to put the incident behind her.

* * *

After the dishes had been cleared away and the men, except Toshiro, were having brandy and port, the evening was interrupted again. A servant came in and whispered a message to Clarice. She rushed out into the hall but did not return alone.

"Amy," Clarice gushed, then beamed at the Englishman dressed fashionably in brown brocade. "Our David is home!"

For the first time in her life Amy realized she wasn't overjoyed to see David Saunders. The timing was all wrong. However, with the help of her cane, she managed to get up from the overstuffed chair and make a hesitant promenade over to him.

"Why, Amy, you are walking!" Instantly, he bent down and gave her such an exuberant hug, her slippers almost fell to the carpeted floor.

She returned his smile but was relieved when he unhanded her. With a need to steady herself, she clutched the head of the walking stick with more force than necessary. "You are back a week early."

He gave her a lopsided grin. "I missed you so much, Amy, I had to return early." He placed a possessive arm about her shoulders, frowned at Toshiro, then kissed Amy on the cheek. "Had to see my girl."

As David greeted Amy's uncles, Toshiro watched her. A spark of something he'd not experienced before nipped him when he saw Amy allow David to lead her over to the sofa, where he sat down, closer to her than necessary. Not for an instant did the Eurasian believe that only missing Amy had caused David to cut short his London trip. He scanned the room unobserved. But which one had written the Earl of Woodcroft, clearly advising him to return posthaste to protect his interests at Stockwell Hall?

When the count saw her smile at a whispered comment from David, the unwelcome thought came to him that Amy herself might have written the brown-haired Englishman. Had she wanted rescuing from her foreign neighbor? It wouldn't be the first time an Englishwoman had changed her mind about him. He remembered her complaint that David had to travel to London on business so often. Had Amy Stockwell been using his attentions to nudge David into a more active role as suitor for her hand? This last question unsettled him.

As the minutes went by and everyone fussed over her and David, Amy felt errant as the count sat quietly alone on the overstuffed chair across the room. As hostess, she did have certain responsibilities. Excusing herself, Amy stood up, this time congratulating herself on not even needing the cane. She picked up the tray with the cups and empty porcelain bottle. Going to the kitchen, she heated the rest of the rice wine herself. It was a small gesture, but she hoped the count would appreciate it.

When she came back into the parlor, she found everyone but Joshua Rigby still ignoring Count Valerius. Her aunt and uncles spoke to David in hushed tones. Without hesitation, she went over to Toshiro. "My Lord, would you like another cup of sake?"

Touched by her gesture, Toshiro felt some of the strain leave his shoulders. "Thank you." He took one of the cups from the tray she'd placed on the round table next to him, then watched as she filled his cup two-thirds full from the cloth-covered jar in her hands.

"I'm sorry," she whispered, "I did not know David would be visiting tonight."

Her admission lightened his mood instantly. "It is of little importance," he assured her.

She smiled, then turned away. As she neared Joshua Rigby, the older man said out of the side of his mouth, "Port side. Storm warnings."

Amy turned, then saw David scowling at her. "Would you like some sake, David? Only Joshua and Clari would try it, but I'm certain you'll—"

"God, Amy, look at yourself!" he demanded. "I leave for a few weeks and come back to find you shuffling about like a bleeding geisha tart."

Singed by David's accusation, at first Amy couldn't reply. Never had he spoken to her in this manner. "David, I am only acting as hostess. It is a courtesy, similar to when I offer you a glass of cognac, as I often do."

David's tone became vicious. "Heard about your ride through Bristol and your assignation in the count's private garden. What the hell has come over you?"

Toshiro gave nothing away as he placed his delft cup back on the table. One of these people had definitely been busy writing to the earl. He would give David only a few more minutes to back down, then despite protocol or Amy's wishes, he was going to take matters into his own hands. He'd had a bellyful of Woodcroft's insults. And had she been his niece, Toshiro would have tossed David out on his expensive breeches by now. Not for the first time was the Eurasian appalled at the dichotomy between her relatives' cosseting on one hand and their callous neglect on the other.

"Really, David," Amy admonished. "I hardly think this is the proper place to air our differences."

David looked disgusted. "Why not? It seems all of Bristol is buzzing with your cavorting about the town, arranging a rendezvous at Clifton Hotwells, only a stone's throw from my very home," he added, his voice rising an octave.

"There isn't any need to blow your boiler over it," countered Amy. "All this slop from my serving the count sake?"

"Aspire to more than geisha, do you?" demanded David. "I wonder just what other little courtesies you've performed for your Jappo neighbor behind my back."

Tempted to grab the bottle of sake off the table and heave it at David, Amy stifled the urge when the count's calm voice intervened.

"Woodcroft, I must protest the misapprehension you are under." In a gesture that belied his true feelings, Toshiro stretched his legs out in front of him and folded his hands across his chest. "The ladies of the Yoshiwara in Edo would be highly insulted at your mistake. The word 'geisha' means 'accomplished person,' nothing more. The geisha houses in our pleasure districts are licensed and clearly not what you have implied. Geishas are professional entertainers with years of training in dancing, playing the samisen, flower arranging, and singing. A geisha may, if she chooses, bestow her favors on a wealthy patron. However, geishas are not whores, as you imply." His panther eyes confronted the Englishman from across the room. "And a geisha always has the right to refuse entertaining any client she feels is . . . unsuitable."

Not even her uncles were squalling now. Tonight Amy had fretted they would instigate a rumpus. Never had she dreamed it would be jovial David who would cause an unpleasant scene tonight. "Well," she said, intent on taking charge of this volatile situation. "Isn't that interesting? Other cultures are fascinating, are they not?" she offered the silent assembly.

"Damn me," Simon muttered, "I need another brandy."

As Joshua passed the count to amble over to the decanter of brandy, Toshiro stopped him and whispered something in his solicitor's ear when he bent over the count's chair.

Amy saw Joshua look up sharply, then catch a warning in Toshiro's expression. He nodded grimly but said nothing.

What was going on here?

David and her relatives went back to conversing. However, her relief was short-lived when she spotted David's usual congeniality depart once more.

"He did *whaaat?*" David bellowed. The Englishman bounded to his feet, face crimson with strong emotion. He charged over to Toshiro. "By hell, Valerius, you go beyond the bounds of decent society. You're not in Japan now. How dare you paw and kiss Amy. Isn't it enough you practically kidnapped her and took her over to that house of yours, along with pestering her at Clifton Hotwells?" he dredged up again. "We've ways of dealing with your sort in England."

With a sigh of exasperation, Toshiro stood up. "I assure you, I would never do anything to harm Miss Stock—"

"I know why you've been sniffing about Amy," David cut off, "but it won't do you any good because—"

"Woodcroft, I advise you to cease speaking of Miss Stockwell using that phraseology." Toshiro's voice was more menacing in its quietness. "If you care to discuss this in private later, I—"

Without warning, David reached out and backhanded Toshiro across the face. "Name your second."

Toshiro's green eyes darkened, but he did not flinch or touch the red welt that now colored his left cheek. The words pushed through his teeth. "I would prefer not to."

"Told you he was a coward," Simon pointed out with derision. "Knew it the minute he said he didn't ride to the hounds."

"Uncle Simon, please." Alarmed, Amy reached for her cane and moved unsteadily between the two combatants. She confronted her longtime friend first. "David, you have been misinformed about the count and me." She glared briefly at her relatives, peeved to realize they'd spoken this way to the Earl of Woodcroft. "David, his Lordship's behavior since we first met has been nothing but gentlemanly and above reproach. Your bullying tactics at the moment are giving him a terrible impression of English hospitality." When David looked unconvinced, her irritation increased. "Hell, the count merely assisted me earlier when I was overcome by a weakness at seeing the dead animals Uncle Henry shot today. Really, David, I cannot understand how you could so misconstrue my relationship with the count. He is my business partner and my friend. You know," she finished, her voice faltering, "that is all I could be to any man."

When Amy turned to him, Toshiro saw the humiliation in her blue eyes. He thrust his hands behind his back to keep from responding in a more physical way right now to David's insulting remarks. He wanted to take Amy in his arms and comfort her, instead he had to stand here and grimly read in her expression what she wanted from him. Damn it to hell, she asked a great deal of a man.

If he didn't believe she was in some sort of danger in this house, he'd have stormed out of this moldy mansion, never to set eyes on these cursed Townsends or Woodcroft again.

"My Lord," she addressed Toshiro. "I am sorry that you have been so rudely treated in my home. However, let us put this misstep behind us, shall we?"

"It is David, not you, who needs to apologize," said the Eurasian. "There is nothing of which you need concern yourself, Miss Stockwell."

The formality of his reply had the opposite effect on her nerves. "Thank you, but I would prefer a more direct answer to my question."

"Fighting is always the last choice," Toshiro stated.

"Bah," grumbled Simon. "A Jappo pansy. Didn't I tell you, Henry?"

Even David smirked. "Well, don't expect me to apologize to Amy, Valerius. She knows I never apologize. Against my religion, you might say."

Ignoring the others, Amy pressed for the reassurance she wanted from the count. "Valerius, let me make my position clear. There will be no duel. I will not allow any one's blood to be spilled on my account." She had enough blood on her hands already, she thought, then rubbed her forehead as the area behind her eyes began to ache. Right now she found dealing with the complexities of the Oriental mind a tedious endeavor. When Toshiro stood silently in front of her, she turned back to the earl for help.

"David," she entreated, then batted her blues eyes in his direction. "Of course, I'm not asking for any apology. Come, just something that will end this idiocy." She felt better when she saw David smile in his familiar way. "I know you regret slapping the count. It was too bad of you, but no one has died."

Obviously sensing his advantage, David took Amy's slender hand in his. "I can never refuse anything when you look at me that way, Amy. It was never my intent to insult or hurt you. Protecting you and your good name has become a habit with me. Such an innocent in the ways of men like Toshiro," he said, then kissed her fingers. "You know how much I've admired you since we were children. I only wish to show you more of my devotion in the future."

His gallant speech was more than she expected. "Thank you, David. Then you will not cross swords with the count?"

"No, I will not, since that is your wish, Amy."

Pleased with her success in ensuring there would be no duel, Amy was taken aback but didn't protest when David quickly pulled her into his embrace and kissed her briefly on the lips. While irked he was taking advantage of the moment, Amy reminded herself she had David to thank for extracting them out of this potentially dangerous situation with her foreign guest. It was the first time David had kissed her this way in public. Though she tried to hide it, she was acutely aware of the difference between this kiss and her earthshaking reaction to Toshiro's passionate embrace earlier. When she pulled away, Amy glanced over David's shoulder to find Toshiro watching her. Her aunt and uncles looked amused. Well, she thought, challenging the count with a look of her own, she wouldn't even be in this position if Toshiro had not been so vague about not fighting that foolish duel.

When David went over to Giles to get another glass

of brandy, Amy addressed the count once more. "My Lord," she began, "since the earl has graciously backed down and clearly regrets striking you, it only leaves you to reassure me the matter has ended. No more hedging, no more obtuse phrases. I demand your promise."

Both his Dutch and Japanese blood fired at Amy Stockwell's arrogant demeanor. He cursed David and all the Townsends for placing him again in this mortifying position. As a guest in this house, he knew he was in an absolutely untenable situation. He bowed stiffly. "As you say, the matter has ended."

Again, they were not the words she sought. "My Lord, I would have a more direct answer in front of my family and friends."

"We shall see," replied the count.

Amy bit her lower lip and fumed. He obviously meant there wouldn't be a duel, but he was just being stubbornly Eastern in his response. Tempted to press further, something in the chilly tone of his cultured voice warned her just now to proceed with caution. Yet, George Stockwell's daughter did not heed it. Her chin tilted up. "David is an excellent swordsman, my Lord. He killed a man last year in London who had the misfortune of cheating at cards. Now, let us have an end to this nonsense. Do you understand my meaning?"

He sucked in his breath at her tone. "Yes, as clearly as I understood precisely what Woodcroft meant by his words tonight. Now, if you will excuse me, I must leave. There is just so much English hospitality I can take in one evening."

She nodded, equally cold in her adieu. Still irritated with him for his evasive reply when they both knew there wasn't going to be a duel, Amy let David see the count and Rigby to the door.

"Amy!" Clarice cried, then shook her niece again.

"What the . . . ?" Groggy, Amy rubbed her eyes and sat up in bed. She tried to focus on the brass clock over the fireplace. "God, Clari, it's hardly first light."

Clarice shoved a crystal goblet under her niece's nose. "Here, you'd best drink this before we leave. I've sent word over to Dr. Wakefield to meet us in the wooded grove past that man's property."

"Aunt Clarice, what in blue hell are you blathering about?"

Clarice looked incensed. "Count Valerius didn't keep his word last night."

Amy gulped her tonic, then coughed when it sloshed against her windpipe. This was the first time she'd ever had another glass in the morning, but now she felt she was going to need it.

Clarice wrung her hands. "David is going to be vexed with me for telling you, but I can't help it," she whined. "After you went to bed and your uncles left, David confided to me that Toshiro would not relent."

"Barnacle balls!" Amy swore, almost choking on the murky liquid halfway down her throat. And Toshiro knew they all believed the duel had been called off.

Clarice spoke again as her niece finished her medicine. "David is definitely the superior swordsman. I am certain he'll be unharmed, but our family could be injured if this scandal leaks out."

"Come on," said Amy. She swung her legs over the side of the bed. "Please help me dress. We've got to keep David from killing that damn, stubborn. . . . Bilge water," she snapped when her toes bumped against the heavy wooden bed frame. "Damn the man," she said, thinking of Toshiro.

Eight

All during their ride in the carriage, Amy could not understand how Clarice could sit next to her, calmly peering out the window.

Clarice arranged a dark curl back in place. "David will teach that heathen a lesson. Not to worry," she added, then patted her niece's arm. "Joshua Rigby will help us hush things up. We'll keep the scandal out of the papers."

But it wasn't the threat of gossip that plagued Amy. A more horrifying picture buffeted her. Toshiro never wore a sword when he went out, unlike David and her uncles. He showed he was against violence, his calm politeness in the face of adversity. God, Clarice was correct: David would make mincemeat of Count Valerius!

The blond-haired girl pressed her lips together. Though at the time it seemed a good idea to ward off her agitation at this shocking news, right now Amy had to fight the effects of her medicine. The early morning air whipping through the carriage window chilled her. However, Amy shoved back the hood of her traveling cloak, hoping to keep her wits about her. No, she would not give in to that familiar sluggishness that threatened. She had to face what was taking place beyond this thick grove of oak trees.

Amy's agitation increased when they reached the clearing. Listening, she could hear no clanking of steel against steel. "Oh," she said with hope, "they haven't started yet, thank heaven." She saw the two carriages in the distance. But when she spotted a man in his late twenties head toward the Valerius carriage, she clutched her hands tightly in her lap. It was the square wooden medical case with the leather strap over his shoulder that unnerved her. She was too late; the duel was over.

God, Amy thought, it was Toshiro who was killed or mortally wounded, just as she'd feared when Clarice first told her the news. She gripped her cane and bolted out of the carriage before it scarcely came to a halt. She recognized the gold circle with the iris leaf carved on the door. Using her cane, she rushed toward the Valerius coach.

The man with the reddish-brown hair stopped her. "Easy, lass. I've already checked him. Let me see to his wound first. Miss Stockwell, is it not?"

"Yes, now if you will move aside, I must see—"

"Oh aye." However, the man did not step out of her way. "I'm Dr. Keith Stewart. I set up my practice here in Bristol last year."

Why was this doctor studying her so intently, almost making pleasant conversation at such a time? "Excuse me," she blurted, then darted past him in an attempt to see Toshiro. This time the man did not try to stop her. "Oh, Toshi. . . ." Amy's jaw dropped when she saw who was sprawled across the Moroccan leather seat of the Valerius coach. "My God, David!" She knelt on the wooden floorboards.

It took David a few moments to open his eyes. "Amy. Sorry I couldn't get out of it. God, I'm dying."

Her eyes widened when she took in the blood that soaked his shirt. Was the wound close to his heart? "Doctor Stewart," she called in alarm.

"Oh, David," she sobbed, then pressed her hand to his cheek. "I'll never forgive myself for this. Please, David, you must be all right."

David groaned. "I . . . don't think I'm going to make it."

"Miss Stockwell," said the physician as he peered inside the coach. "You'd best wait outside so I can do my work. You'll only crowd us in here. Ye look ready to faint yerself. Best get some air. There's a good lass."

Though she did not wish to leave, Amy realized this Scot was being practical. Reluctantly, she allowed the doctor to help her out of the coach. "Please, Dr. Stewart, please save David."

Before he could answer, Clarice arrived. She took one look at David and screamed. "David, my poor boy." Despite the physician's advice against it, Clarice Townsend pushed her way into the coach and placed David's head on her lap. She cooed over him, fluttering her hand against his forehead.

"Oh," David whimpered, "I'm dying, Clari."

"Doctor," Clarice said, "our own physician will be arriving here any moment. Your services are not required. Perhaps you should see to the count."

At the mention of Valerius, Amy clutched the handle of the coach. "Dr. Stewart, where is the count?" Fear gripped her insides. If David was wounded, that meant Toshiro had to be. . . . "Is . . . he dead?"

The ruddy features of the physician softened into a

smile. "Nay. Even in our boyhood days at Eton, Toshiro could withstand any fracas and come out on top. He's way over by that tall oak with Mr. Rigby." Clearly, feeling the matter of David was more pressing, Stewart leaned into the opened carriage. "When Wakefield gets here, I promise to leave," he told both women. "In the meantime that gouge needs stitching, so, madam," he addressed Clarice, "if you're prone to the vapors at the sight of a needle mending flesh, I'd suggest ye close yer wee eyes."

At such directness, Clarice said nothing when Keith started about his business. He set his wooden box on the floorboards of the coach, shrugged out of his gray coat, rolled up the sleeves of his shirt, and proceeded to tend to his patient.

"He . . . really will be all right?" Amy asked in a small voice.

Intent on threading his needle with the catgut string, Dr. Stewart looked briefly at Amy. "Aye, Miss Stockwell, his Lordship will have a sore shoulder for a few weeks, but he'll be just fine. Off with you now and find a place to sit down. Ye look ready to collapse."

Relieved David was going to survive, Amy left him in Clarice's tender care. Even if Keith Stewart was more blunt than Dr. Wakefield, the Scot appeared to know his business.

While relieved Toshiro was unharmed, Amy grappled with her strong emotions against the count. It was almost consoling when Dr. Wakefield's rickety carriage arrived. The coachman held the door open for the elderly doctor.

Wearing his full gray wig and dusty coat and breeches, Norbert would have gone automatically to the Woodcroft coach if Amy hadn't steered him over to the count's carriage.

Clarice welcomed the doctor.

David moaned, "The rack would torture me less."

Amy saw that Dr. Stewart was finishing the last stitch on David's torn flesh.

"Get your Scottish paws off my patient," Norbert commanded.

It was then Amy realized these two men knew each other.

When Keith kept his attention on David, Norbert demanded, "And how in blazes do you happen to be up from your little office on the other side of Bristol? Running out of paying clients, are you?"

After tying a knot and snipping the thread, Keith turned to the elderly gentleman who stood glowering outside the open carriage door. "Good morning, Dr. Wakefield."

Amy's physician spat on the ground then turned back to the younger man. "Never mind your Highland jabber. Answer my question."

Dr. Stewart began putting his medical supplies back in the drawers of the wooden chest. "Count Valerius sent word last night he wished me to accompany him in his coach this morning to a . . . certain meeting on his property. It was his wish that the earl be placed in his coach, for it is larger and more comfortable than the Woodcroft carriage."

"Bah," grumbled Wakefield. "I want him out of there and in his own coach right now."

"Do you believe it wise to move him?" Amy asked, peering at the earl's chalky features. David's groaning increased.

"Of course," said her aunt. "I think it would be best to get David home." She placed an arm about his shoulders. "David dear, we are going to help you back to your own carriage. I shall come home with you. Would you like that?"

"Yes, Clari, please. Oh, I'm dying. That Scot wouldn't even get my brandy flask from my coach."

Miss Townsend brushed strands of his brown hair away from his face as she clucked over him. "There, there, my brave boy. I'll take you home."

It took some doing, but they all managed to get the whiny Englishman into his own carriage. Clarice joined David.

Leaning her head out of the Woodcroft conveyance, Clarice spoke to her niece. "Amy, are you sure you will be all right going back in our carriage alone?"

"Certainly, Clari. Brian knows the way," she said in an attempt to ease her aunt's burdens. "Please look after David for me. As you take such good care of me, I can see you'll be a comfort to poor David. Thank you for being so good to us."

The woman in her early forties continued to cradle David's upper body in her lap. "I suppose I enjoy mothering you both."

A crusader on a mission, Norbert pushed his spindly legs over to Keith Stewart before the Scot could mount his horse. Though loyal to her family physician, Amy did not believe Keith should be blamed for honoring his friend's request to come here. When a wave of dizziness assailed her, she had to stop walking for a second to catch her breath. Lord, she thought, first the duel, David injured, now sparring physicians. "What a morning," she muttered.

As the elderly doctor vented his spleen on the taller Scot, Amy began feeling sorry for the younger man who stood silently taking it. "Please," she called to her wigged physician. "Dr. Wakefield," she shouted.

The Englishman stopped, looked across at the slender girl wearing the oversized gray cloak. "Amy, you should be home in bed. It's not healthy for you to be up and about in this morning air. Good God, woman, where is your wheelchair?"

She really wasn't up to more of this right now. Her smile was strained. "I . . . the spa helped as you advised," she said, trying a stab at diplomacy. "I'll tell you more about it later, sir. I am worried about David. Won't you hasten to Woodcroft Hall?"

"Well, but—"

"Dr. Stewart was merely being kind to answer the count's request that he be in attendance." Out of the corner of her eye Amy saw Joshua Rigby and Toshiro heading their way. She turned her attention back to Wakefield. "Count Valerius," she added in a voice that carried to the two men approaching, "apparently recognized his inferior abilities with our English swords and sought to have a physician handy to see to his anticipated injuries."

Wakefield appeared to back down. "I could have seen to that foreigner's wounds myself."

"Aye," said Keith Stewart with spirit, "and before you got your leech box out, you could have just dumped Valerius at the church graveyard to save time."

His eyes shooting venom, Norbert lunged for the younger man, only to have Keith step back with a jeering laugh. "How dare you imply my patients die . . . you, Scottish Highlander. You're just jealous because my practice is larger, and I have the cream of Bristol society."

"Weel," said the Scot, "from what I hear, more of the cream is now under the sod than on top of it."

"Sir, that will do." Amy gave the Scot a censuring look. "Thank you for seeing to David, but I believe it best if you leave. Send your bill to me, and I'll see you are paid. Dr. Wakefield has diligently looked after my family for years and will continue to do so. Good day, sir."

With her icy dismissal, Keith Stewart's expression sobered. "The count has already seen to my payment. Your servant, Miss Stockwell." He mounted his horse. However, he gave Toshiro and Rigby a jaunty wave before he rode off.

Amy finally got Norbert to leave.

With only Brian atop the Stockwell carriage waiting for her, Amy looked down at the tips of her shoes. While Toshiro talked with Joshua, his back to her, Amy braved her first look at him.

Dressed in simple black shirt, breeches, and leather boots, his raven-colored hair was clubbed back against the collar of his shirt. A leather belt about his lean waist held the scabbard and rapier against his left hip. It was the presence of that silver-handled sword that shoved her against the heated wall she'd been trying to escape for the last half hour. She reproached herself because her first fears had been for Toshiro's safety, not her childhood friend's. When she heard Toshiro laugh at some remark from Joshua, her eyes narrowed. Ignoring the urge to sit down until the vertigo passed, she leaned on her cane and walked over to him.

She glared at the count's back. Rigby saw her expression, and the smile left his bulldog features.

"Why did you lie to me, Valerius?" she demanded without preliminaries.

Sizing up the situation, Rigby excused himself and said he'd wait for his Lordship in his carriage.

Slowly, Toshiro turned around. Determined to remain calm, the Eurasian knew her anger also stemmed from fear. But was it only for David that she came here today? he couldn't help wondering. He saw the pinched look about her mouth. "You should sit down. We can talk later, golden lotus." He reached out to help her. However, his hands dropped to his sides when she vaulted back from him.

"I demand a direct answer," she hissed, "not Japanese evasions." She gripped her cane to steady herself. "You knew I believed you would not fight this duel."

"Yes."

"But all along you intended to cross swords with David this morning. You even arranged for Joshua to act as your second last evening," she accused, remembering when the count whispered something to his friend.

"Yes."

Though she'd expected it, his calmly spoken answer slashed her. "I thought you were my friend. Why did you lie to me?"

"I did not lie. My exact words were, 'We shall see.'"

"Son of a sea . . . you are the most irritating man I have ever met," she shouted. "Why in bloody hell didn't you just tell me then?"

"It would have been impolite to tell you no," he said, as if explaining the obvious. "Also, it would have been ill-mannered to upset the harmony of your house. I deeply regret Woodcroft went to your aunt about our duel. It was a matter I intended to handle quietly."

"Disrupt the harmony of my . . . ? Rat farts!" She gasped as outrage threatened to strangle her. "You almost murdered my dearest friend, and you have the audacity to spout remorse about a bloody breach of etiquette?" She swiped at a strand of blond hair when a breeze ruffled it across her face. "You insufferable. . . . David is right. You are an uncivilized heathen."

His posture became more rigid, but he remained silent.

"David could have died."

Toshiro's equanimity came with more effort. "Then he would have been the first man to expire from a scratch on the shoulder. You were correct. Woodcroft is a skilled swordsman."

"But you are better," she hoisted with sarcasm.

"Perhaps it is because I never glance away from my enemy's eyes. That is how I knew what he would do next."

"You told us you could not use a sword," she added, refusing to give an inch. "Liar."

The panther's eyes darkened. He forced a chilly breath of morning air into his heated lungs. "That is not the first time you have tossed that word at me. Be warned, fiery one, I like it not."

"Too bleeding bad. When my family or friends are threatened, I don't roll over and play dead."

He frowned at her but managed to ignore the barb. "I merely stated I am uncomfortable wearing a sword as Englishmen do; I never said I was ignorant of its use. While growing up in Japan, I became accustomed to different sorts of weaponry, however, my father arranged lessons with a fencing master at our home in Amsterdam when I was older."

Some of the starch went out of her, but George Stockwell's daughter wouldn't back down. "You have a ready answer for everything, don't you? I was a fool to come over here to try and sort this out. I won't make that mistake again." A haughty expression on her face, Amy turned to leave with what little dignity she could muster. "After I went to the trouble of begging David on your behalf, I should have known you wouldn't even—"

A squeak of surprise escaped when Toshiro swooped down on her without warning. Flustered, she dropped her cane.

The count took her firmly by the shoulders and whirled her around to face him.

"Let go of me at once." She struggled, astonished at his uncharacteristic behavior. Despite her exhaustion from the morning's trying events and the tonic, her Stockwell temper blasted to the surface. "I'm warning you, Valerius."

"You are going to listen to me if I have to glue . . . *Unko*," he swore, emotion causing him to trip over the English words. "Even if I have to tie you to that tree."

"Just try to keelhaul me," Amy challenged. "I'll scuttle your gizzard. I won't listen to any more of your bilge." She pushed against his chest but couldn't get free. "I can't believe you dare . . . let go of my arms." She aimed a kick at his booted foot, but the villain easily avoided it. "Damn you, I have had enough of your dockside antics for one day."

"And I have had enough of your bossy, rude behavior," he countered. Fully prepared to let her go, something in her manner scalded him. "You will hear what I have to say, like it or not." With an easy strategy he'd learned as a boy in Japan, he held her arms in a way that would not harm her, just keep her still before him. "Last night when you went simpering over to Woodcroft, pleading with your English peacock, I wanted to charge over and haul you out of his arms."

Amy saw him close his eyes as he took another ragged breath. His touch on her arms relaxed. She realized he was using some mental technique to dissipate his fury. It affected her, and she stopped brawling. "I know David should not have struck you," she conceded.

He shook his head and looked down at her. Disappointment tinged his reply. "Do you know me so little that you believe my ego would demand satisfaction from such a trivial thing? Amy, search your inner place for the answer."

Confusion buffeted her. "I don't understand any of this. Why . . . ? You explained that a geisha is an entertainer, not a . . . well, not a prostitute." Her face heated, but she got the word out. "David said he wouldn't fight you because I asked him not to. You must understand David is a very proud man. All right, if it was just a slip in semantics, why did you cross swords with him?"

"Because David meant his words to be an insult. Japan does have courtesans who sell their sexual favors in the pleasure districts, just as there are whores along the Bristol docks. You and everyone else in that room last night knew David implied I had bedded you. Woodcroft disparaged not only your good name but mine. And when he refused to formally apologize to you, he sealed that duel in my mind. I have been forced to overlook much in my dealings with you English, as I did that first night at your table," he added, reminding her he knew full well he'd been the butt of her relatives' jokes. "But with my honor and those I lo . . . those who are my friends," he amended, "I bend not an inch."

At first Amy could not meet his gaze as the truth of

his words washed over her. She focused on his open shirt where the three buttons were undone. Strange at such a moment, but it occurred to her that this man's chest was hairless unlike David's. She blushed at the brazenness of her thoughts.

Toshiro did not miss her observation. He stepped back and touched the beginning dark stubble on his jaw. His rich voice was now laced with amusement. "Even though my uncle in Nagasaki has a mustache, I once complained to my father that I inherited from him the necessary task of shaving my face daily. But as you can see, Amy-san, we Japanese have bare chests." His smile became roguish. "Of course, I will not be so indiscreet as to ask how you know mine is different from an Englishman's hairy upper torso. I'll not deny it pleases me to realize Woodcroft keeps you on a pedestal. It is clear you are unsuited for each other. I knew it last night when he kissed you without passion, more in the manner of a dog marking territory."

"Oh . . ." Amy blustered. "How dare you say such a carnal remark to me."

"But you said earlier you wanted me to be more direct in my speech," the count pointed out with relish.

"Yes, but I . . ." She stopped, amazed when she couldn't come up with a counterattack. "You surprise me this morning. I am unused to your coming back with rejoinders." Despite herself, amusement entered her voice. "My Lord, my friendship may be having a disastrous influence on you."

He did not join in her humor this time. "You know there is something stronger than simple friendship between us, Amy. I have tried to fight it, as you have. Don't you think I know the problems we will face? You are an inconvenience at this time," he admitted, aware of the danger until he found his father's murderer, who now stalked him. "As I know I am an unwelcome burden in your life. But there it is, Amy Stockwell. So do not think you can fire your broadsides at me, and I will let you walk away. I know you lash out hardest when you sense danger. You are afraid of something, and I give you fair warning, I am going to find out what haunts you, with or without your help."

The determination on his face took her breath away. Her mind warned her to run. The danger right now was from this man, not her past. And she was certain he'd feel different about her if he learned the truth.

When he saw the terror in her eyes, Toshiro took her gently into his arms. He held her close and stroked her cloak-covered back. "You are not alone, Amy-san," he whispered close to her ear. "I will not rush you. We will have plenty of time to get to know one another."

His arms were too comforting to pull away from on her own. "It is impossible. You don't know what you are asking." She inhaled the musky scent of him, felt the strength of his healthy body. "Didn't you hear what I told David last night? I can never be anything but a friend to any man. I . . . I am not like other women," was all she could divulge, as misery assailed her.

Toshiro lifted her face to his. "Shall I prove you are wrong, golden lotus, just as I did when we shared our first kiss yesterday?"

Desire and regret warred within her. "Please don't."

He sighed before stepping away. "Then I better take you back to your carriage, else I will kiss you with or without your permission."

She watched the play of emotions across his face. The

combination of hectic events, no breakfast, and her medicine made her light-headed again. She tried to reach for her cane on the ground but had to give up when the horizon began spinning before her. "I'm sorry, I feel so. . . ."

Toshiro noticed that her pupils were now dilated. "Amy," he demanded, "did you take more of that . . . ? I thought you only took it at night. Answer me."

Why was he so cross? She tried to answer, but her tongue felt like cotton wool. "I need it. Keeps away the nightmares, calms me." Amy staggered to the right, as if to flee to her coach in the distance. "Brian," she called in a raspy voice, but even she realized the Stockwell coachman couldn't hear her. "My Lord, I must leave now before I. . . ."

The panther sprang in front of her, just catching her before she would have landed on the dew-covered grass at his feet.

Joshua Rigby saw her collapse and came bustling out of the count's carriage.

Toshiro held the blond-haired woman against his chest. "Damn those jackals," he swore, "they've drugged her again." He stalked over to his own carriage. Rigby opened the door for him. Toshiro placed her carefully on the cushioned seat across from him.

The count was not surprised when the Stockwell coachman appeared unconcerned that his employer wasn't going home with him. The gold coins Toshiro tossed him were of more interest to Brian than his Lordship's instructions for Clarice Townsend.

The Eurasian climbed back in the coach next to Joshua. He tucked the lap rug more securely about Amy's legs then ordered his driver to take them home.

"You know, Joshua, I have come to the conclusion there is not one loyal servant at Stockwell Hall."

When a deep rut in the road rattled the coach, Joshua watched as Toshiro got up and placed a protective hand against the unconscious girl to keep her from falling forward. The count sat down, this time opposite Rigby, with Amy across his lap, her upper body cradled in his arms. A few details became clearer to the Englishman, but he did not verbalize them.

When they arrived at Toshiro's home, the count sent his coach immediately for Dr. Stewart. In only a short time his friend arrived. Toshiro showed Keith into the East Wing, where he'd placed Amy.

Both Toshiro and Joshua stood up when Sumi showed the Scot back to the English sitting room.

"Keith, how is she?"

Keith took in his friend's anxious features. "She will be all right after the effects of the drug wear off. There is no congestion in the lungs. You say Wakefield has been giving her opium?"

"Apparently Wakefield adds bitter herbs to counteract the sweetness, but I could swear that's what he's giving her."

Keith shook his head. "Miss Stockwell is clearly undernourished, pulse is weak. I was able to get a few medical facts out of her, though she probably won't remember telling me when she awakens."

"Her heart, Keith, what about her heart?" Toshiro pressed.

"Weel, 'tis hard to say. The aftereffects of taking opium slows the rhythm, but I'd say it's a sound heart. Though there's no mistaking the lass needs better care than she's been getting."

Toshiro couldn't hide his exuberance. "Sound heart." He felt foolishly giddy. "God, a sound heart," he repeated. "Did you hear, Joshua?" He went over and pumped Keith's hand. The Scot looked as if his usually reserved friend had taken leave of his senses.

Rigby enjoyed Toshiro's unusual display. While Toshiro went over to the other side of the room, clearly to compose himself, Joshua explained to the doctor what Wakefield had told the count. For once Joshua managed to keep his voice to a whisper. "Until now I hadn't realized just how distraught that young man has been over Norbert's pronouncement that Amy Stockwell would be dead within the year."

Toshiro came back to them in time to hear Keith say, "The lass is nae in any immediate danger of dying from natural causes. However, if she keeps taking that much opium, I cannot vouch for her future."

Neither Joshua nor Dr. Stewart commented on the dark look that crossed their friend's features.

After Keith left, Toshiro and Joshua sat down to wait for Amy to awaken.

Joshua took another slice of Stilton, placed it between the fresh pieces of crusty bread and began munching on it. He noted his companion ate little. "I'm sure she'll be all right," he managed between mouthfuls. "Amy's got her father's pluck."

"Pluck?" Toshiro repeated the word, his brow furrowing. "You mean to grasp? No, Amy is not greedy," he defended. "Look at the donations she gives to St. Mary's Foundling Home, the stipends she pays the seamen's widows, much to her uncles' irritation? No, you are quite wrong, Joshua."

"No, no, my Lord," Rigby protested. "Lord love me,

I keep forgetting you weren't raised here. By pluck, I mean Amy has her father's gumption . . . ah . . . she's a real fighter." Mr. Rigby did not comment on his surprise that the count had made it his business to find out such details about Amy Stockwell.

"Ah, I understand. I hope you are correct. She looked so pallid just now." Toshiro shoved back strands of black hair that had escaped during his sword fight with Woodcroft. So worried over Amy, he'd not taken the time to wash or change. When he touched his jaw, he remembered he also needed to shave.

"She'll pull through," Joshua tried again. "Saw out the carriage window the way she lit into you." His wide face split into a grin. "Fists flying, shouting at you. A real spitfire."

Toshiro couldn't join in the older man's high spirits. All he could envision was her tumbling into his arms and the way her small fists had felt like butterfly wings when she tried to pummel his chest. "God, Joshua, sometimes I do not understand her. I tired to retain my composure with her, even after she started punching me. I walked away when she disagreed with me last night. I keep trying to act correctly, but it only seems to make her more agitated."

"Agitated?" Joshua snorted with mirth. "My Lord, she was mad as a hornet this morning. And I wouldn't wonder if you say you always act that way around her."

The Eurasian's face mirrored his puzzlement. "Maintaining harmony in one's relationship is paramount, is it not?"

Joshua ran a meaty fist across his chin. "Well, of course, everyone likes tranquility once in awhile, but are you so certain that is the only thing Amy needs for the rest of her life?"

Listening intently, the count mulled over Joshua's question. "I would say Amy requires more peace in her life away from those squabbling relatives. She does not eat well when they quarrel. I have seen the way her body coils like an over-wound clock when she sits among them."

The gray-haired man leaned forward on his chair. "All right, I give you that, but think, my Lord. If Amy disagrees, even slightly with any of them, they usually back down. Clarice fusses over her; the uncles treat her like fragile glass. Even Woodcroft never says no to her. Why, I've never heard David raise his voice to her. Last night didn't count because it was clear he was picking a fight with you, not Amy.

"And there is Amy," Joshua continued, "intelligent, used to winning in her business dealings, but for the last four years confined to a wheelchair with only David and her relatives hanging over her. I've witnessed them constantly telling her whatever she wants is fine with them, always urging her to eat more, get more rest, and not excite herself. Well, Count Valerius, I'm hanged if that mustn't get downright tedious for a spirited girl like Amy Stockwell. She's like a gale coming up against meringue—she can't fight them, and there is no way to blow off steam. In the fours years I've known the young woman, I've only gotten a glimpse of that Stockwell rancor, but it's enough to convince me that any man who hopes to court George Stockwell's daughter had better be able to handle himself in a fracas, else she'll make a milksop out of him."

"Go on," encouraged Toshiro.

Like a barrister presenting a vital case, Joshua pressed

on. "You enter her life. She likes talking with you, enjoys your company. I can see for myself you care what happens to the girl. However, when she disagrees with you, what do you do? You leave. Either physically, similar to last night when you left abruptly, or emotionally, when you don that inscrutable mask of reserve and clam up. Amy's left huffing, ready to burst. I saw it happen last night and this morning."

"But I am not sure I know how to rectify—"

"Tell you what you need to do," Joshua interjected. "Go out in that garden of yours once in awhile and shout a few colorful phrases to the sky in Japanese, Dutch, or whatever. Put you in better form the next time you and Amy disagree. I often do it in my study at home. Makes me feel wonderful, gets rid of a lot of inner turmoil. Contemplating lotuses on a pond has its place, but just once in awhile you ought to let loose a good bellow." He gave the Eurasian a pointed look. "You've got promise, I can tell. It's all in the expansion of the chest, and your voice is a good baritone if you ever choose to project the sound. Lord love me, I bet you could get out a loud roar if you set your mind to it."

Toshiro chuckled at Joshua's last remark. "I will think over what you have said. These are views I had not considered before." He sighed. "It is clear I still have much to learn about living among you English." He was also thinking of the scene with the dead rabbits yesterday. Amy did not trust him enough yet to tell him what tormented her.

"Then you plan to court Miss Stockwell?"

Toshiro turned back to his guest. "Yes," he answered, a new resolve showing on his features. "I do intend to fight for her."

Nine

The scent of ginger tickled her nostrils. Amy heard a tinkling sound of light metal bars brushing against each other. She opened her lids slowly and spotted the circular piece of wood with wire that held the thin chimes near the window frame. Someone had opened the window a crack. She was reclining on a futon, thick brocade-covered mattress stuffed with cotton.

With a start the Englishwoman realized she was on the floor in a room that was clearly not English. Tatami, woven reed mats of rice straw, covered the wooden floor under the mattress. There was a comforter over her. She noticed the unusual cloud pattern against a bright blue background. Though she'd read about Japanese furnishings, she noted someone had placed a comfortable pillow beneath her head, rather than a firm block that she knew the Japanese used. Across the room there was a six-paneled wooden screen with purple irises painted on a gold background. This room could have been out of the illustrated book Captain Murphy had found for her at her request. Intrigued, she tossed off the coverlet and stood up carefully. She was in her stocking feet. Her traveling cloak had been removed. It was folded neatly over a low lacquered table. A charcoal fire in an iron brazier warmed the room. Slender sticks of ginger incense burned in a ceramic stand on one of the low tables, a lighted candle beside it. She took the brass candlestick in her hands and began walking on the thick tatami toward the next room.

This room was large with a low ceiling. A huge mattress was on the floor with a wide wooden wardrobe in the corner. A table held mirror, basin, razor, and shaving brush. Against the wall there was a black lacquered stand with the gold Akashi crest painted on the base. Two thread-wrapped scabbards, one long, the other short, rested on each wooden rung of the stand. Fascinated, she walked over and opened one of the wardrobe drawers. The white paper rustled as she carefully moved it to get a glimpse of black silk, a wide sash. The garments were clearly Japanese. Quickly, she slid the drawer back, suddenly realizing this had to be Toshiro's bedroom, at least his Japanese bedroom. Really, she shouldn't be creeping about the count's Eastern Wing. Her uncles had been speculating for months about the strange renovations in this part of the late owner's home. At least she might be able to tell them this wasn't any den of iniquity or sacrificial rooms to pagan gods. Giggling, she stole a peek in the room that her uncles had been so vexed about because they couldn't inspect it. There was a large, square wooden box with a cover over it. Small stool, with a few wooden buckets on the tile floor. She couldn't imagine what this room was for, nor why the present owner had wooden shutters on the three windows inside here. The room was pitch-black. Surely, the count's servants didn't cook anything in that deep box, did they?

But it did have a lid on it and was raised above the floor. Would they light a fire under it? Amy reproved herself. They weren't cannibals. However, she decided not to mention this room to her uncles. On second thought, she'd best not say she'd been in the East Wing at all, given their strong opinions against the count already.

She heard voices. Racing back to the room she'd awakened in, Amy returned the candlestick to the table and darted for her bed. Without a usual door, she noted that resinous timber with paper-covered screens looked to be the way one entered this part of his home. She forced herself back against the pillow and pulled the coverlet up to her chin.

She heard Sumi and Toshiro speaking in Japanese so she couldn't tell what they were saying. One of the wooden panels slid to the right. Toshiro left his shoes outside. Amy watched as he bent his dark head and entered the dimly lighted room. In his stocking feet he walked over to her and sat down on the floor, cross-legged. The Englishwoman felt his shrewd gaze as he studied her.

"Amy-san, you are better?"

"Yes, thank you."

"Would you like some tea?"

"Oh, yes, my Lord, that would be delightful."

He got up with the grace and ease of one accustomed to these non-Western furnishings. After clapping his hands once, apparently in a prearranged signal, Sumi opened the partition. Toshiro bent down, thanked his servant, then took the full tray from her.

He came back and hunkered down to place the tray on the low table. Then he sat next to her and went about pouring hot water into an earthenware bowl. With a small spoon he measured out a bit of green powdered tea from a wooden box and sprinkled it into the bowl of scalding water. Amy noticed he tapped the edge of the wooden spoon twice against the rim of the shallow bowl. Never could she imagine David making tea for her. Yet, there was nothing effeminate about Toshiro's precise, unhurried actions. He reached for a bamboo whisk and began blending the tea and hot water.

When he offered her the shallow bowl, Amy took it in her hands. His blunt-edged fingers touched hers. Something surged through her, and when their eyes met, she knew he felt it, too. She raised the bowl to her lips and took a slow sip. Unlike the tea at home that was always served with lemon, sugar, and heavy cream, this plain green tea had a slight bitter taste, but it was just what she needed at the moment. She took another swallow. The dryness left her mouth. "Umm, I like this tea." When he smiled, she could not help giggling at the picture he presented.

"What are you thinking, *koneko?* I can see the mischief in your eyes."

"My Lord, I really should not tell you. I fear you might be offended." After another sip of the steaming tea, she put the bowl back down on the wooden tray. Her features become more serious. "And I would not insult the dear friend who has been so kind to me."

So, she still thought of him as her friend only, he mused but would not press the matter now. "I have come to learn your nature, Amy. I realize your humor does not contain the thorn of cruelty. Come, tell me what made you laugh just now."

After she remained silent, he reached out and took the

half-empty cup from the tray. Instead of turning it, he drank fully from the spot where her lips had touched.

His patience seemed boundless as he sat watching her. It would be so easy to trust this man, she thought. Time stood still in his company. There were no problems of the past, just the moment to enjoy. She sat back against her heels, then decided she'd be more comfortable tucking her legs to the side of her. "I dare say, I'm a bit clumsy in gown and stays. You are most gallant not to mention my awkwardness."

"Your demeanor is charming, Amy-san. Now," he pressed good-naturedly, "what is it about my smiling just now that made you laugh? Have I grown floppy ears," he added, outrageously checking his head. "No, that is not it."

She laughed again at his antics. "All right but if you suddenly decide to catapult me out of your home for good, it will be on your head." When he chuckled at her impudence, she felt more at ease. "Well, first let me point out that I have fared no better this day." She looked down at her wrinkled gray gown, then tossed back strands of her uncombed hair that hung about her shoulders in disarray. "I look right now like a sack of rumpled laundry," she said, amused at the picture she must present. "However, when you grinned at me just now, I thought you looked like a rakish pirate in your black breeches and shirt, and the . . . um . . . dark stubble on your face." She took a hesitant look up, hoping she'd been right to let him coax her into such an intimate remark. Her heart sank.

Toshiro's features had returned to that reserved mask. He moved the tray to the side, leaving the path clear between them.

She might have known, she berated herself. "Oh, my Lord, I am truly sorry," she said in a hurry. "I said I looked just as unkempt." She was making things worse. "Oh, bilge, I tried to tell you, you wouldn't understand. I even like you this way . . . less stiff-rumped, not as fastidious. I've always been partial to the Black Knight." Rising to her knees, she moved closer to him as he sat straight and silent. "Please don't look so wooden. You remind me of that Buddha I saw on the altar next to the futon in your bedroom." His brows arched, and she saw something flicker within the green depths of his eyes. Drat, she hadn't meant to give away she'd been prowling about his rooms like a Bow street pickpocket. "Look, my Lord, I said I was sorry I called you a rakish pirate. Love a duck, if you're shocked and offended by that, you should hear me when I really lose my temper. Captain Murphy says I can turn the air blue for twenty minutes without repeating a word." She saw Toshiro's shoulders jerk, but he kept that impenetrable expression on his aristocratic features. "What in blue balls do you want me to do, grovel on my knees?" She looked down at herself. "Come to think of it, I'm already on the floor." Regretting she'd unintentionally hurt his feelings, she said, "All right, I'm lower than dirt. My shadow isn't worthy to cross your path. Is that groveling enough?"

Silence.

"And if it isn't," she hoisted, a gust of fury in her voice, "you can just take that damn tea pot in front of us and shove it up your Japanese arse!"

The back shook again, then Amy saw him shatter from his confined restraint. Boisterous laughter exploded from him as he threw back his head, clearly overcome by her outrageous remarks. "I . . . wondered, feisty one . . ."

he gasped for breath . . . "just how long you could continue your apology." Another fit of ribald merriment overcame him, and he doubled over.

"You . . . blackguard! You were never affronted; only teasing me. Scoundrel. Jackanapes. Blighter." Sputtering, she grabbed the nearest missile, the earthenware bowl.

Still chuckling, Toshiro straightened to look across at her flushed face and heaving bosom. "I should very much appreciate it if you do not clout me with that heavy crockery."

He said it so politely, without moving, her own mouth twitched, then a gurgle of laughter popped out. "Well, I suppose I did walk right into that one. Guess I'll spare your life." She placed the cup back on the table. "Should have remembered the Black Knight from my storybooks always had the hide of a rhinoceros."

Toshiro reached out and pulled her closer to him.

Lost in the mixture of humor and something else in his gaze, Amy found herself in his embrace. He sat down with her upper body supported in his arms.

"Oh, Amy-san, you are adorable, like a golden butterfly and mischievous kitten. So sweet," he breathed against her lips, just before he lowered his mouth to hers. He tasted the soft, pliant warmth of her lips, delighted in the feel of her slender neck, curve of her firm breasts through the tight lacing of her corset and wool gown.

She moaned and arched her body closer to his. He felt her hand on the back of his neck as she pulled him closer. His healthy body responded to this woman in a way no other female had ever affected him. He forced himself to pull back, for his sake as well as hers. Then he saw the faint redness on her cheek. He caressed the scorched skin with his fingers. "I must shave, Amy-san. My face is like a bramble against silk."

A lethargic smile on her lips, Amy opened her eyes. She rested her cheek next to the soft material of his black shirt. "I didn't mind. In fact, I enjoyed it. You kiss very well, you know."

He smiled at her directness. "Thank you."

"Is it very late?"

"No, only about two in the afternoon. Joshua went home. I will see you back to Stockwell Hall."

"I'm surprised Aunt Clarice or my uncles aren't storming the Black Knight's battlements. Knowing you, I'm sure you told our driver that I would be home shortly. Maybe my relatives are finally getting used to my choosing your company." She yawned. "Oh, beg your pardon."

Toshiro was relieved it was a natural tiredness this time, not drug induced. "Come, I shall take you home. You need to go to bed."

She made a mewl of protest. "I like it here. The chimes, the incense. It's so peaceful."

Peace was the last thing her companion experienced at the moment. The erotic image of her in his bed, the scent of roses on her soft skin as she nestled against his body . . .

"Ah . . . Amy-san, I will tell my servants you are to have access to my home at any hour. You must feel free to come back again."

After Toshiro helped her up, Amy stood in the middle of the floor while he draped her traveling cloak about her shoulders. "Toshiro, do you sleep here? I mean, you do not have an English bedroom?"

He finished the last button near her throat. "Usually I sleep upstairs. Other than these three rooms, the rest of the house is in the English style. Sometimes," he said wistfully, "I miss Japan or have trouble falling asleep. Then, I come down here to my other bedroom. It acts as my bridge between East and West."

She understood. "We all have need of bridges from time to time."

Despite her attempt at lightness, Toshiro did not miss the shadow that crossed her face.

She tried to cover it. "Oh, when we reach my home, I'll just get out quickly. No need to have you come in. My aunt will probably start fussing over me anyway."

"Of course," he said, trying not to reveal the thoughts that plagued him. "You must at least let me see you to the door." He bent down and slid the paper screen open.

"No, Toshiro." She took his hand in hers. For the first time she noticed the strain at the corners of his eyes. "It has been a hard day for you, my Lord, and I would not have you confronted by my well-meaning but sometimes difficult relatives right now. You should rest also. In fact, you don't even have to stop the coach when we reach Stockwell Hall," she quipped, as she walked down the two steps that led out into the hallway. "Just push the door open and toss me on the stoop."

"Rascal," the count called her, but he was touched by her concern. "I shall see you properly to the door."

She imitated a martyred expression. "No doubt, I'd better go along with you." She let him lead her down the hall, each step closer to the Western part of his home. Dutch paintings on the walls, delft ware bowls on a sideboard, red and gold Oriental carpets on polished floors. "You do have exquisite tastes, my Lord. The renovations inside are as beautiful as those you've done on the garden."

Amy continued admiring the rich furnishings. "Yes, I'd best humor the Black Knight, else you're liable to challenge me to a duel. Wouldn't want to break anything in here as I trounce you." She made a playful swish with her right arm, hoisting an imaginary sword. "I warn you, I'm a better fighter than David, just in case I ruffle you again, which I'll probably do with my unruly tongue. I'll be ready if you challenge me to a duel, so you'd best be on your guard."

He gave her an arched look. "Perhaps it is the English kitten who should be wary."

Not the least intimidated, Amy gave him an impudent grin. "Doubtful, my Lord Panther. I've read your philosophy. You're too full of Zen stoicism for loutish behavior, especially to a fragile woman. Think it has something to do with all that Oriental reserve you've stored up, kind of stuffs all the senses. You might say it froze your emotions."

"Think so, do you?" he asked, sharing her audacious mood.

"Oh, I'm certain of it. In fact, I take comfort in knowing how completely safe I am with you. Sort of like being around a bonsai tree."

"Ha, Amy, a bonsai tree is miniature."

She looked up at the taller male. "I'll soon cut you down to size, my Lord."

"Impudent brat," he countered. "What can one expect from a race that rides to the hounds, dresses in such confining garments, and seems to have a terror of daily bathing?"

"Blackguard."

"Yes," admitted Toshiro, "I suppose you bring out the Black Knight in me after all."

"It suits you well," she admitted. "I enjoyed this afternoon, and not just because you kissed me."

At the open look in her expressive eyes, Toshiro stifled a groan. No, the next few days were not going to be easy, he thought, aware she trusted him to continue behaving like a gentleman. He switched his traveling cloak over his arm to hide the proof that he was affected by her nearness. How wrong she was, he thought, then smiled self-effacingly. He wasn't a block of wood at all.

The next morning Amy decided she must go over to check on David. Arriving home yesterday, she'd been surprised to find that Clarice was still tending to the Earl of Woodcroft. No one but the servants were about, so she had a large bowl of beef stew before going to bed. Her sleep had been refreshing. Forgetting to take her tonic hadn't made a difference. She ate a hearty breakfast of eggs and ham, then put on her printed day dress and ordered the coach.

A few hours later when she arrived at Woodcroft Hall in Clifton, one of the servants ushered her into David's rooms upstairs. "David. I just wanted to come and check. . . ." She stopped speaking when she saw her aunt move hastily off David's bed, where she'd been spooning hot broth into the earl.

"How are you this morning, my Lord?"

David wiped his lips on the damask napkin across his chest. He gave her a pleasant smile. "I am much better, thanks to your aunt's diligent care."

Amy wondered why Clarice appeared so nervous. Well, Amy thought, her aunt wasn't usually up this early. Perhaps Clarice felt embarrassed over Amy's lack of concern for the man who challenged a foreigner to defend her honor. "David, I am sorry about this whole thing." Clarice busied herself with putting away the tray items.

"Come, let me look at you." David patted the area next to him where Clarice had been sitting earlier.

Using her cane, Amy walked over to the earl's bed. She sat down on the edge.

David took in her shining eyes, healthy color, red ribbon holding her curls lightly away from her face, and flower-printed dress with large ruffles at the elbow-length sleeves. "Why, Amy, you're positively radiant this morning. If my fighting Toshiro for you has brought about this change, I'd take more gashes in my shoulder."

"Oh, David, please don't joke about it. I still blame myself for being the cause of your injury."

"Why, little Amy, you have been worried about me?"

"Of course. You have been special to me since our childhood days. I never want to see you hurt . . . by anyone."

David put his arm about her shoulders. "Does this mean you have changed your mind and consent to be my bride?"

His unexpected question made her feel trapped. "My Lord, I am honored again by your proposal, but my answer has not changed. I do not believe I love you. In truth," she added in a rush, "I don't think I'm capable of loving anyone."

"Oh, innocent Amy, don't you know few English couples in our class marry for love? Anyway, my love will be enough for us."

"No," she said with more feeling, then moved off the bed. "My Lord," she added, trying to soften her words, "please do not speak of it."

David's wounded look was only temporary. "Amy, you needn't feel sorry for me. I take comfort that I've enough memories of having bested that Jappo devil many times in the past to make this mortal wound on my shoulder endurable."

Confused, she turned back to him.

Clarice came back and fluffed the pillows behind her patient's back. "You have no fever," Clarice said, then smiled down at him.

A look Amy recalled seeing before passed between Clarice and David, but she was more intent on finding out what David meant concerning the count. "Have you crossed swords with his Lordship before?"

David's conviviality returned. "Even better, Amy." Then he told her about the time he'd put glue on their headmaster's chair at Eton, then locked Toshiro out of the dormitory. There were other incidents: having Toshiro's clothes stolen out of his rooms, Toshiro's name signed to derogatory sketches of their teachers. As David went on relating all the tasteless, often cruel pranks he played on the Eurasian when they were at Eton, Amy could only listen grimly. Clarice laughed at David's antics; Amy could not. Her heart lurched for the proud, quiet lad. For the first time in her life, she glimpsed a cruel side of David she'd never seen before.

"How clever you are," said Clarice.

Clearly, the young man basked in her praise. "And didn't I make certain everyone in Bristol knew what a dangerous foreigner had moved into our cozy English community? Valerius still wouldn't have a servant in the place if it was up to me. The count probably had to offer them a king's ransom to get those townsfolk to work for him."

Merriment danced in Clarice's brown eyes. "I always thought it was one of my brothers who spread those wicked tales across Bristol."

With the excuse that she did not wish to tire the invalid, Amy left, not even commenting when her aunt said she would not be home for supper.

On the ride back, Amy could not get David's gleeful admissions out of her mind. On top of everything, David had insulted the count in her own home. No wonder Toshiro hadn't backed down when David challenged him. It only amazed her Toshiro hadn't fought with David before this. And Toshiro had shown remarkable consideration in having David placed in his coach, asking his own doctor to see to his scratched shoulder. In the same situation, Amy thought she just might have left the mean-spirited David on the ground to fend for himself.

All the horrible things she said to the count yesterday came back to taunt her. Instantly, she knew what she had to do. Using her cane, Amy pounded on the roof of the coach. She poked her head out the open window.

"Take me to Valerius Manor . . . at once."

The young coachman pulled on the horses' reins, then jerked the carriage to a complete stop. He frowned down at her. "Sorry, miss, yer aunt gave me strict orders I was to take you back home."

"Roast your liver," Amy shouted. She rapped her cane on the edge of the open window. A piece of wood splintered from the fragile frame. "I pay your salary, not my aunt, and this is my bloody coach. Take me to Valerius Hall at once, else I'll sack you on the spot."

The astonished young man gulped. It was clear he'd heard from the other servants how passive Miss Stockwell was. But when he took another look at her set features, he turned the carriage around. In an instant they were off.

Amy sat back against the lush interior of her coach. Agitated, she rubbed the carvings along the wooden cane she held across her lap.

The coachman drove the horses hard, but Amy felt it had taken forever to reach the Valerius estate. When they stopped, Dover Jenkins came over.

"Well now, Miss Amy, good to see you again." Without hesitation he helped her down the coach steps.

Already untying her cloak, Amy rushed up the stairs. She met Sumi in the hall. The Japanese woman bowed and smiled. "My master will be happy to see you. He is in the East Wing. Do you wish me to announce you?"

Amy shook her head. "No, thank you, Sumi. I can find my way." The urgency of her feelings came to the surface once more. The reality of how David had treated him, her own despicable words yesterday when she'd first confronted him—she rushed down the hall, turned right where the corridor narrowed. Quickly, she slipped off her leather slippers. Now that the moment was here, she hesitated for a second near the sliding wood panel. She heard his resonant voice. It was a faint chanting sound. She left her cane outside with her shoes and slid the partition open. Silently, she walked up the two steps and placed her feet on the tatami.

Toshiro was kneeling in front of the altar she'd seen yesterday. Incense sticks wafted the scent of ginger throughout the room. Never had she seen him dressed in his Japanese clothes before. His straight hair was tied back as usual, but he wore an ankle-length black kimono, belted at the waist and tied in back. His eyes were closed, his hands rested on his thighs. Suddenly, the chanting in Japanese stopped.

He'd been praying for guidance. Toshiro had tried to take things slowly, yet he had to leave for London in the morning. It was ironic that he'd been impatient waiting for word of his ship from China with his uncle's message. Now that it was here, he did not wish to leave Amy with things so unsettled between them.

He felt Amy's presence, like the soft breeze of spring. He opened his eyes and turned to see her. She was dressed in a charming gown patterned with bright wildflowers. It was the first time he'd ever seen her in something so suited to her light coloring. Her hair was tied with a red ribbon that left the soft golden curls free against her shoulders. He stood up.

Amy held her breath. His clean-shaven features, the welcoming look in his panther eyes undid her. "Oh, Toshiro, I had to come today. I visited David, and he told me . . . I mean, I. . . ."

Seeing her face so full of anguish, he opened his arms to her, an invitation if she wanted it.

Like a storm-tossed craft spotting a safe harbor, Amy rushed into the circle of his arms. "Toshiro, I'm so very sorry for everything." She clung to him as if her heart would break. "David told me—actually sounded proud of all those cruel things he did to you at Eton. And I couldn't believe he'd been the one to spread those horrid rumors about you throughout Bristol. I almost challenged him to a duel myself," she added with feeling. "I said such terrible things to you, shouting at you, and you stayed so calm yesterday." She stepped back from the haven of his embrace. "I'll never know how you remained placid while I ranted at you for crossing swords with David."

A half-smile softened his features. *"Koneko,* I could never translate all I was thinking at the time. I have the same feelings as any other man. However, my Japanese reaction only means I've been taught to hold the mask in place at such times. I am sorry David upset you by telling you such things."

"Telling me?" she repeated. "He was bragging about it. I am ashamed of him and myself. I could think of nothing but getting out of his house, leaving him with Aunt Clarice so I could race over to you. I'm appalled at the wrongs we've done you, my Lord."

Moved by her words and the suffering on her face, Toshiro pressed her upper body against his chest as he sought to comfort her. "Amy-san, even growing up in Japan I learned at a young age people of one race do not always tolerate another. The group is more important in Japan than the individual, and I was often reminded of my mixed blood, subtly and in more direct ways."

For an instant, Amy got another view of his childhood in Japan. His green eyes, height, Eurasian features would have been strikingly evident against a sea of pure Japanese children. "Oh, my darling." She reached up to touch the angular planes of his face. "I wish I could take all the hurt away from you."

"As I would take yours away, golden lotus."

Certain he did not know the nature of her past demons, her smile was rueful. "Unlike you, my Lord, it appears my face gives too much of my emotions away."

"I would have you as you are, Amy Stockwell."

She looked up into his eyes with their golden flecks and realized he would not kiss her this time until she asked. "As I would have you as you are, Toshiro Valerius." Straining on tiptoe, she pulled his dark head down to hers and kissed him full on the lips. It was a brief declaration, a promise. She would try not to think of the past or the future. There was only right now. When Toshiro's arms came about to support her back and their kiss deepened, she welcomed his tongue when it sought hers. She clung to him, needing the assurance of his solid strength. Her remorse from yesterday melted away, allowing her to show him just what he was beginning to mean to her. Out of breath, she pulled back a little but had to hold on to his shoulders for support. She smiled up at him. There was nothing aloof about him now.

"Amy," he whispered to the top of her head. "You remember I told you I would be going to London soon?"

"Yes. I was the one who got you to agree to bring the Chinese cargo back to Bristol instead of selling it in London." She smiled into his coat. "Rigby couldn't believe I wrangled that concession from you, but I wanted that entire shipment for Stockwell Enterprises. Told you I'm used to winning . . . in my business deals," she added, aware of her vulnerability in other areas.

"I must leave tomorrow." The disappointment in her eyes when she looked up pleased him, for he realized he might eventually become as important in her life as she already was in his. "I shall be gone for a few weeks, but I cannot wait to settle things between us." He took her hands in his. "Amy Stockwell, will you marry me?"

As the silent moments ticked by, Toshiro was not prepared for Amy's reaction. He would have understood surprise or reluctance to his marriage proposal. However, panic was the one emotion he'd never envisioned.

Ten

Amy knew she had to say something. She moved farther away from Toshiro. "I never meant. . . Oh, no, my Lord, I could never marry you."

He blanched at the unexpected bluntness of her refusal, but he forced a calmness he didn't feel into his voice. "Is it because we have only known each other for a few weeks?"

"No," she answered. "From the moment we first met I. . . ." She pressed her lips together. It was her own fault, for she'd known the danger if she kept seeing this man. But she couldn't help herself; he was like a breath of sea air, swirling into her sheltered life. Never had she known such happiness as when they were together. "I tried to warn you, my Lord. I told you a normal woman's life could never be mine."

"Is there someone else, David perhaps?" The Englishman's name was acid on his tongue.

"No, I have already declined David's proposal."

Her answer helped, but not enough. He'd felt her response to his kisses, saw the flicker of desire in her blue eyes when he'd held her. But then why would she not consent to . . . ? He frowned as an unpleasant thought shoved against his strained emotions. "Is it because I am of another race?"

Silence.

"Yes, I see," he bit out when she did not answer, a warrior's self-discipline forcing him to look at the truth. "You are willing to enter into a business agreement with me, pity me for past ill-treatment by your countrymen, but to marry me . . . ah, yes, that is something entirely different, is it not? Forgive my obtuseness. Because you seemed to enjoy my company, I assumed . . . now I do understand. I had forgotten how you English can cloak hypocrisy in a mantle of polite behavior." He turned toward the open panel. "As you found your way in here, I trust you will find your way out." His back rigid, he stepped down the two stairs and slipped his sock-covered feet into the leather sandals. He had been a romantic idiot to harbor such impossible hopes, buying that painting of her, trying to court her, and. . . . He glanced back to see her still standing in the center of the room. God help him, he still wanted her. He was a fool not to turn his back on her.

Amy stood watching him. How could he believe her capable of such cruelty? "Your race, my Lord, has nothing to do with my refusal."

Like ice on the Avon, she challenged him with her expression. "Then why, damn it?" He charged back into the room, not even bothering to take off his sandals. "Why?" he repeated. "Amy, can't you see what you are doing to me, to us?"

The torment in his voice cut deeply into her. She reached out and clasped his shoulders. "Oh, Toshiro, don't you know how difficult it is to refuse the one thing I want most in the world right now?"

He thrust aside his own wounded feelings when he glimpsed the pain on her face. She looked ready to burst into tears, but that Stockwell reserve would not allow it. He held her close, rocking her back and forth, without saying anything. He didn't understand. Nothing was solved, but he only knew he couldn't bear to see her so lost and frightened. It was evident she felt unable to tell him all that stood between them. "I see the dragon is back, Amy-san. You spoke of him the afternoon Henry had your servant display his hunting prize." He massaged her tense shoulders and the muscles at the back of her neck beneath her thick golden hair. He nuzzled the rose-scented locks, welcoming the softness of her. "All right, we will call a temporary truce with the dragon, shall we?"

Stepping back, Amy noted his almond-shaped eyes watched her with sadness now. She owed him part of the truth. "Toshiro, I hope soon I can tell you everything, but for now, I must tell you this: I am barr. . . ." She found the word difficult to say. "I can never have children, my Lord. I am barren." She saw the disappointment etch across his features before he could hide it. Yes, she thought, Count Valerius was the last of his house. She knew he desired an heir. What man in his position would not?

It was an unexpected blow; he could not deny it. By the certainty in her voice, the count knew Amy believed it to be true. His practical side intervened, however. "Amy, you have never been with a man; you cannot be certain of such things."

She noted he wasn't saying it did not matter. Uncomfortable divulging more personal details, she chose her words carefully. "I have seen a doctor in London on this matter." She looked down at the tatami-covered floor. "I do not always have . . . that is, my woman's times are not . . . ah, during the last year sometimes I go three months without . . . my flux."

Suspicions plagued him: until recently she'd not been eating well, the tensions at Stockwell Hall, the lack of proper exercise. The murky liquid she took each night flashed across his mind. He bit back a lurid curse. If he found other motives at work here besides getting Miss Stockwell a quiet night's sleep, someone would wish they'd not been born, he vowed.

Amy thought he was angry with her again, for his expression had changed. She supposed it truly was over between them now. Well, at least it saved her having to tell him the truth that she'd inherited her mother's illness. Taking a deep breath, she thrust out her hand to him. "I wish you a safe journey to London, my Lord. I have only felt honored by your marriage proposal. However, as you can see, it is completely out of the question."

So English with the inflection of finality in her speech. Toshiro looked down at her slim hand. He took it in his. "This is not farewell, Amy. It is a temporary separation. Let us leave the matter open between us. I still wish to marry you. No, you will not pull away. I won't allow that," he said, though his voice had now returned to its earlier tenderness. "My need to leave tomorrow, when now I do not wish it, caused me perhaps to rush you before you are ready. I only ask that you think about the possibility of accepting my proposal." He knew he was close to getting this concession and added something more to entice her. "Sumi is very fond of you, and I have observed you like to speak with her. May I have her stay with you for the weeks I am away? My Aunt Gertrude in Holland taught her the skills needed to be a European lady's maid. I am certain you would find her helpful. Besides, she can tell you all about Japan and our ways, no doubt fill your head with embarrassing stories about what a horrible little boy I was growing up. All right, Amy-san?"

His smile was disarming. It would do no harm to think about what they had discussed. And the prospect of having Sumi to talk with in the mornings triumphed over Amy's initial trepidation. "All right, my Lord, I should enjoy having Sumi stay with me. I believe you knew I would be too tempted by the prospect of learning more about Japan to turn down your offer."

"Perhaps," he said, pleased at least she'd made this concession. Though she only thought it was for her entertainment, the Eurasian knew he'd rest easier with Sumi watching over Amy while he was away.

She laughed up at him. "Yes, panthers are known for their cunning. Be on guard that I do not turn you into a common house cat," she added, giving him a saucy look.

"You are always welcome to try, *koneko*." He kissed the tip of her nose. "I would enjoy such tousling before we pillow."

"Pillow?"

He chuckled, aware she did not know what he meant. "Pillowing is how we describe making love."

"Pillowing," she tried the word on her tongue. Amazing, but she wasn't shocked. "I like the term; it sounds cozy." A way out of her dilemma occurred to her. And this time she was not uncomfortable talking with him about such an intimate matter. "Toshiro?" She ran her hands along his arms.

"Yes, golden lotus." He kissed the slender nape of her white neck.

"I am twenty-five and well aware of such worldly matters," she began. "I just thought of a way we might solve both our problems without the complication of a marriage that could never give you an heir and would be impossible for me. I know pillowing is done even in England without the formality of a marriage contract. Just think," she added, fascinated by the wonder of it. "It could solve our dilemma without hurting anyone. I would be your concubine, and—"

"No, absolutely not."

"Mistress, then."

"It is the same. No."

The finality of his tone and the new roughness in his embrace didn't startle her. "Well, it was only a suggestion."

He gave her a gentle shake. "Not a very flattering one. I do not wish a submissive wife. That is why your fire and impudence captured me the first time. . . ." He couldn't mention it for she had no memory of that time when she was ten. "From the moment you landed in my arms," he corrected. "However, head of Stockwell Enterprises, I will have you honorably as my wife or not at all."

"Umm, thought you might be stiff-rumped about it. I'm the one who's never been anywhere, and you're supposed to be a well-traveled man of the world, yet I think I'm being more sporting about the matter."

"The correct phrase is 'impudent brat,' Amy." He

chuckled when she made a face at him before pulling away.

"We shall see, noble Valerius, we shall see. A lot can happen in a few weeks," she teased. "When you return you may just take me up on my offer." Inside, she was pleased he felt this way about her, but she could not resist speaking with him this way. No one had ever matched her verbal sparring so adroitly before.

He placed his arm around her as they headed for the door. "Amy-san, I shall write you such persuasive words every day while I am away that you will have the Anglican minister waiting for me when the *Nightingale* puts into port at the end of May," he countered.

She laughed up at him.

"Yes," he mused aloud, as they walked down the corridor toward the West Wing. "Joshua was correct."

"About what?" Today she kept up with his longer legs without needing the cane.

"He advised me to stop being so Japanese in my habit of walking away when you spouted . . . bilge," he said, using her familiar word. "I like this form of verbal chess playing. It is most stimulating."

Amy giggled. "You see, my Lord, serenity does have its place, but so does knowing when to stay and tousle." She stopped when she saw Iwao coming toward them. Two English servants were busy polishing the silver in one of the open rooms to their right. Iwao's prideful stare of reserve touched something inside her today. She stopped and crooked her index finger at Toshiro. "I need to whisper something in your ear. It's a private matter."

Toshiro bent his head toward her. "Yes, darling?"

He'd never called her that before. Happy at this new freedom between them, she moved the shoulder-length queue aside and placed a tender kiss on his earlobe—just before she nipped the soft flesh with her teeth. "And let that be a lesson to you," she said, then followed it with an exaggerated Oriental bow.

The Eurasian knew Amy expected Iwao's presence and his years of training would keep him from any public display. As he rubbed away the light sting from her small teeth, the count read her smug look of triumph. They resumed walking sedately out toward the entryway.

But with a ninja's reflexes, Toshiro's kimono-covered arm snaked back, and he landed a playful swat across the center of Amy's gown-covered derriere.

A squeak of surprise, not discomfort, tumbled out of her. She stopped dead in her tracks, astonished at Toshiro's counter maneuver.

Casually continuing to walk a few paces ahead, Toshiro turned back to see Iwao's startled look that the older samurai quickly struggled to conceal. But it was Amy's slack-jawed amazement that had his attention. "Yes," the Eurasian said slowly, "I . . . am . . . learning. How I am learning."

Toshiro Valerius, dressed for travel with gray cape over his wool coat and breeches, a three-cornered hat under his arm, arrived with Sumi at the prearranged time the next morning.

Amy was sorry to see him go, even though it was only for a few weeks. His carriage waited outside, so she knew their parting must be brief. She was determined to help him on his way. "I thank you for allowing Sumi to keep me company." She turned to the servant who carried a small leather satchel.

Dressed in blue linen kimono, leather sandals under her white socks, Sumi bowed to Amy. "I shall be honored to serve the Amy-san."

"And please teach me some words in Japanese," Amy added, with a humorous look at Toshiro. "I have a feeling they will come in handy, Sumi."

Toshiro didn't want to make this trip, however, he knew there was no choice. It wasn't just that he'd signed an agreement to deliver the cargo to her in Bristol. More importantly, he had to straighten out this business of his father's murder before he could plan his own future. Hope sprang within him, for he could feel Amy was opening to his idea of marriage. Yes, there was something she kept from him, but perhaps when he returned from London she would finally tell him, let him face her dragon so they could be happy together. "I will miss you, *koneko*."

She hid behind flippancy. "No doubt, the gaiety of London will help you pass the time. I've heard about the Drury Lane district," she snorted.

He took her hands in his. "I *will* miss you."

This time she couldn't deny her feelings. "I wish you a pleasant journey and a safe return. I'm glad you came this morning before everyone else was downstairs." The tenderness in his eyes made her secure enough to ask, "Will you kiss me goodbye?"

"Did you think I would not?"

"I wasn't sure . . . I mean, public displays and all." When he moved closer to her and held out his arms, she came to him. She inhaled the scent of white ginger and ran her hands across the nubby wool of his coat under his open traveling cloak. When she moved her face up to his and his lips claimed hers, she was buffeted by the mixture of pleasure from his skillful kiss and heartache that he was leaving. Yet she felt his promise as he held her close.

"I will be back as soon as I can."

Amy heard a mew of protest, looked down, and saw a dark head pop out from the deep right pocket of his coat.

Toshiro followed her gaze. "I almost forgot. I have a present for you." He reached into the pocket and pulled out the black kitten. He went to hand the pet to her but was surprised when she stepped back. She put her hands behind her back. "Amy?"

"Thank you, my Lord, but I really couldn't."

The fear in her eyes was the last thing he expected. "You like animals. I have seen it. My love, it is only a harmless kitten. He won't hurt you."

She struggled with her reaction, trying to stifle her panic. "Yes, well, I do like animals, but they . . . they do not seem to take to me." She saw the olive green eyes, noticed a smudge of white across the kitten's nose. Wasn't she being ridiculous? It had been over four years. Right now, as she read the affection in Toshiro's eyes, she felt more sure of herself. She walked now without assistance. It was in the past, just as Toshiro said. She was not just her mother's daughter. George Stockwell was strong, some said even ruthless, and his blood ran in her veins. She reached out to take Toshiro's present. "Thank you, my Lord. He is adorable." When Toshiro smiled, her world brightened. "What is the Japanese word for cat?"

"Neko," he answered. He was certain now she was pleased by his gift. It still annoyed him that none of her relatives saw she needed company, that she was starving to give affection to others, including a needy kitten.

She held up the purring ball of fluff. "Neko," she called the sleepy animal. His eyes opened and he meowed again.

Amy laughed. "I'd best get Neko some milk from the kitchen." She knew he had to leave, understood about obligations—both personal and business. "Safe journey, my Lord. And thank you again for letting Sumi come to stay and for Neko."

Aware the time to leave was upon him, Toshiro looked deep into her blue eyes. "Amy-san, have the greatest care of your health for me." He turned quickly and walked back down the steps. "Oh, and Iwao will bring my other present around to your stables."

Amy saw Iwao, dressed in brown livery, untie a horse from the back of his master's coach. She recognized the gray head, wide neck, and lumbering gait. "Grog!" she shouted, unable to hide her delight at the prospect of riding out across Stockwell lands each morning. "My Lord, I should not, but I am too delighted with having Grog to spout proper words."

He laughed at her directness. "I am pleased, Amy. Besides," he added from the bottom of the steps, "I must admit he prefers you to my heavier weight. As you have said, Kori and I are better suited to each other."

She returned his smile. "Thank you, Toshiro. I will think of you every time I ride him."

Of course, he knew the gentle way she meant the words, but he could not help arching his dark brows at her.

Suddenly, the double meaning of her words hit, and her cheeks heated. "My Lord, I did not mean to imply. . . ." She read the amusement in his eyes. "You, sir, are learning

English ribaldry far too well," she replied in mock indignation.

"I was only thinking how much I envy Grog," protested her admirer.

"Go, my Lord, before Neko and I chase you down to the wharf."

Sumi opened the carriage door for her master. Toshiro's humor departed. He leaned out the open window to speak with the woman who'd taken care of him since he was an infant. "Your kindness in staying with Amy means a great deal to me, Sumi. There is nothing we can do about the tonic they give her each night. That will be my responsibility when I return. I would not have you confront those relatives of hers. Just be company for her. This journey is important, but I am heartsick at leaving her."

Sumi could never recall seeing Toshiro so worried. "My Lord, you must not distress yourself." She touched the area between her breasts where the wooden tube held the sheathed dagger under her kimono. "I will watch over your lady."

"I will not have you endangered. You are not to confront these English. Just observe, for I will want a full report when I return." His features relaxed. "I can never express my gratitude properly."

When Toshiro Valerius bent down and kissed Sumi on her lined cheek, she was astonished by this public display of affection. Could her husband be correct? Iwao told her their master was now beginning to act like these hairy barbarians with their outward display of emotions. She placed a hand nervously against her mouth, then bowed to cover her embarrassment.

Toshiro looked up to see Amy waving from the window of her sitting room downstairs. She held the kitten in her hands and kissed his silky head. The Eurasian waved back.

As the carriage began moving, Count Valerius sat back against the leather seat. Something began to ache inside his chest at the thought of parting from her for even a day, let alone the weeks ahead.

Clarice Townsend wrinkled her nose when the black kitten jumped across the inkstand on her niece's desk to land with a thud on the papers. Her expression proved Clarice couldn't believe Amy just giggled and scooped up her pet to place him on her lap while she went about writing in her account book. "Really, Amy, I cannot understand why you accepted such a scruffy creature." Her dark gaze shifted to the gray-haired woman sitting on a chair near the raised window as she embroidered flowers onto a large swatch of red silk. "And what would our friends say if they knew that creature—Gloomy, isn't that her name—was encamped here? Does she really understand English?"

Amy put down her quill pen. "Her name is Sumi, Aunt Clarice, and yes, she speaks perfect English, as Jan Roonhuysen told us the first day we met Sumi and her husband. Therefore, I would appreciate it if you treat my friend with the same courtesy I always have shown your English friends, not to mention the servants you hire."

Clarice did not say a word. Amy sighed at her aunt's hurt expression. For the last week and a half, Clarice had found excuses to enter Amy's study in the afternoon. Never did the older woman leave without some complaint to Amy about Grog, Neko, or Sumi. She never brought up the count, most likely storing up ammunition for when he returned. For her aunt's sake, Amy softened her features. "Clari, I thought you would relish the chance to visit your friends, go shopping. With Sumi to tuck me into bed each night," she quipped, "I hoped you'd enjoy this brief respite from the chores of tending to me. Soon enough, I'll be a burden to you again, for his Lordship will need his servant back at Valerius Hall."

Her reassurance that Sumi was not a permanent fixture seemed to placate the dark-haired woman. "Yes, and perhaps his Lordship will bring back a bride from London. I understand he is in the market for a woman to bear him sons to fill that huge house next door."

Amy's hand slipped, knocking over the pot of black ink. Instantly, she grabbed Neko and stood up, nearly toppling the chair over with her haste.

Clarice gave her niece an indulgent smile. "I'll have Brian send one of the maids in to mop that up. Oh, and Amy," she added over her shoulder, "I really wouldn't sleep with that feline across the bottom of your bed cover. You never know what these sneaky creatures have been eating. Lizzy found a half-chewed mouse in the scullery yesterday."

It shocked Amy that her aunt's allusion about Toshiro could unsettle her. Doubts assaulted her. Of course, she would never blame Toshiro if he changed his mind. He had every right to seek a wife who could give him children. They'd left things open between them, as she'd wished. She bit her lower lip, then petted the black kitten in her arms. "Neko wouldn't touch mice. He's too little, and he prefers fish anyway," Amy defended him to her aunt's back.

After the mess of black ink was cleaned up and another pot brought in, Amy looked down at the ruined sheet of notes and tossed them into the wicker basket with the empty ink bottle. For some reason she didn't want to go right back to work. Reaching behind her head, she readjusted the ribbon that held her hair loosely away from her face. She walked over to the half-opened window. As usual, Sumi had a plate of Amy's favorite almond cookies on the tea table. Absently, Amy took three from the plate and began munching on one. "Sumi, I hope you know how much I enjoy having you here, despite what my aunt says."

Sumi looked up from her work. "I understand your aunt does worry over you, Amy-san. I am not offended."

"Well," said Amy, after devouring a second cookie. "Today I find her downright annoying." She looked at the other woman's noncommittal expression. Something told Amy it wasn't going to hold today.

Sumi started to giggle, then quickly put a hand over her mouth. "I, too, have enjoyed our rides in the morning and our talks. You learn quickly, Amy-san."

"Only because you are an expert teacher." She peered down at the kitten, now swiping his paws at a piece of embroidery near her feet. "I would like to learn as much as I can about Toshiro, his homeland, and—"

Her words ended with the arrival of Iwao. It was evident Brian disliked letting this foreigner into his employer's office, but he said nothing when he opened the door and announced the daily visitor.

All letters from Toshiro came directly through Valerius Hall. "Though it makes more work for your husband, I suppose the count feels it's easier to toss his letter to me in the same dispatches with the work he sends Iwao."

Sumi looked down at the silk in her hands. She could not tell the young woman Toshiro did not trust Amy's

211

relatives or servants to deliver his missives to her. She gave a proper greeting to Iwao, who acknowledged it with a cool nod.

Keeping her features set, Amy went over and said, "Iwao-san, *Tegami ga kite imasuka?*"

"*Hai.*" He handed the sealed envelope to Amy, accepted her letter to his master, but then it registered she'd asked if there was any mail for her in perfect Japanese. "Mmm," was all he said in the way of approval. He reached into the leather pouch over his shoulder and pulled out a brightly wrapped box. He bowed, then left without another word.

"Sumi, I fear Iwao does not approve of me."

Sumi could not tell Amy-san her husband called her "another of those straw-haired barbarians who stink of sour pork." She looked down at the floor, then back up. "My honorable husband believes our master would be happier with a Japanese bride."

Amy did not take offense. She thought of her own relatives. "I can understand Iwao would rather his lord make an alliance for the Akashis in Japan."

Sumi said nothing.

"And do you also believe it would be best for Toshiro?"

"It is not for me to say, Amy-san."

"But if you had an opinion, Sumi, what would it be?" she pressed, both amused and frustrated by the woman's answer.

Sumi studied Amy for a few moments. "I have never heard my lord laugh so much as when he is in your company. He prefers less docile ladies, one reason my husband does not understand."

Amy chuckled. "Less docile. Love a duck, that's putting it mildly." Eagerly, Amy went over and sat down on the Oriental carpet at Sumi's feet. "Of course, I should read his letter first." She looked at the unopened box. "No, I can't wait." She began tearing off the bright paper.

A smile began forming at the edges of Sumi's mouth as she watched Amy. "My master was just the same when his honorable father would come to visit us and refill his ship. Lord Pieter Valerius always brought a barrelful of gifts for his young son and his lady wife."

At the mention of Toshiro's mother, Amy stopped unwrapping the layers of paper. She looked up at the older woman. "You have told me Haru Akashi is in her forties and lives with her brother's family. Rice is grown; they raise horses, but, I notice you say little else about them. The count only hints about his people, too. Sumi, I want you to understand I do not hold the Akashis in a lesser light just because they are. . . ." She didn't want to use the word "rustics," or worse, as David said. "As people with little means. Farming is a noble profession. Indeed, my father had no aristocratic bloodlines. He began as a common sailor." She went back to the square object in her hands.

Sumi veiled her reaction to Amy's clear assumption that the Akashis were peasants. Toshiro had warned both his Japanese servants that, for the time being, these English were to learn as little as possible about the Akashis. It had to do with his late father's manner of death.

Amy peeled away the red silk cloth covering her gift. It was a carved wooden box. The crane standing beneath a cheery blossom tree had been inlaid with gold and mother-of-pearl. The smooth background was painted in dark lacquer. "Oh, Sumi, it is beautiful." She opened the lid and gasped with surprise. A double strand of pearls lay inside the red interior. She pulled them out. "See

213

how they capture the light. I have never seen such pearls with that pinkish hue. It gives them a warm appearance." She quickly tried adjusting them around her neck but was grateful when Sumi put down her sewing and helped with the clasp. Amy touched the beautiful gift, then turned the box over. "His crest," she whispered, running her hands affectionately over the carved iris with its sword-shaped leaves, surrounded by a gold circle. "He realized I would know he'd carved this box himself. He is so wonderful and generous. What a dear friend he is, Sumi."

A slight smile transformed Sumi's features. Certain the English girl did not realize it, Sumi saw more than friendship in those blue eyes.

Amy got up and took the carved box over to her desk. With great care, she placed it on the corner of the oak top. When Neko scampered over and began purring for attention, she took him up on her lap again. "All right, Neko, but you must be quiet while I read his Lordship's letter." Cutting the seal that held the four pages together, Amy began reading:

Dearest Amy,

I am most pleased to hear that Sumi, Grog, and Neko are keeping you well-occupied, along with running Stockwell Enterprises. Not a day or night goes by that you are out of my thoughts. I miss your golden laugh, your sweet smile, your mischievous ways. I long to walk along the water's edge as we did at Clifton; the memory of you nestled in my arms as we rode gentle Grog's back across the green meadows of Bristol plays about my senses like a nightingale's song.

When I reached London, I could not appreciate the city's sights, for when I saw Ranelagh Gardens, I longed to share it with the lady I hold above all others. Even meeting King George and his wife was not as remarkable as an afternoon sparring verbally with my koneko.

He wrote that the cargo from China was taking longer than he'd expected to load properly onto the *Nightingale*. He went on in the next few pages to explain he'd spoken with the king and his ministers. They seemed interested in doing business with Stockwell Enterprises. Apparently, now that Amy had secured the trade agreement with him, and Japanese goods were a certainty, King George warmed to the idea of making a profit on their venture. Toshiro wrote he requested His Majesty's financial advisers to write to her directly so that Miss Stockwell and her solicitor could draw up a formal proposal.

Pleased by his gesture, Amy knew he felt the final decision should be hers as head of Stockwell Enterprises. He was the secondary partner, according to their signed agreement, and he would not usurp her position by making deals on his own. She knew many English merchants who would have ventured right ahead and negotiated a contract without consulting her, even going so far as to attempt to cut her out of her share of the profits. The count was again showing her he was a man of honor.

She giggled when she came to the end. Apparently, her outrageous remarks, written in moments of merriment to get the usually serious young man to laugh, had not gone unnoticed. His long letter finished with:

Please keep writing to me, beloved. Your letters have become as necessary to me as sunlight. However, do not think I have overlooked your occasional saucy remarks. It appears distance gives the golden kitten a warrior's courage. The panther is keeping careful accounts of all your impudent salvos hoisted through the post. And you will account for them when next we meet—if I am not too busy smothering your adorable face with kisses or caressing all your lovely curves. The days will not go fast enough until I see you again.

Enclosed are two small gifts. The crane is a symbol of long life and constancy. Know that I hold your mind, heart, soul—all of you close to me.

He signed his first name boldly across the bottom of the page. So like the Eurasian himself: correct, strong, yet tender. Distance, she realized, affected him also. The passionate nature of that intimate part of his missive warmed her. Was he trying to seduce her with words, too? she wondered, then discovered she did not mind.

As she stroked Neko's head, the Englishwoman began thinking about the day Toshiro would return in a few weeks. How would she greet him? She always babbled so when she was nervous, while he usually appeared calm and in control. What would she wear? The question made her smile, for it was so unlike her to fuss about clothes. Yet, she wanted to please him. No, she corrected, his absence made her wish right now to do more than please him. What he accomplished with his written words, she wanted to do the same in another medium. Surely she didn't mean to seduce him? she thought, taken aback by such a blatant thought. Well, perhaps just a little. A way occurred to her. "Sumi?"

"Yes, Amy-san?" The small Japanese woman turned her head toward the blond-haired girl.

"The count gave me a present of a large bolt of aqua silk to seal our business venture," she mentioned offhandedly. "Do you think, if I helped you, we could design something that might resemble a lady's kimono for me to wear when your master returns?"

Sumi brightened at the prospect. She was certain of it now. There was definitely more here than friendship between her master and this English lady. "Yes, I believe we could manage it. But we should begin as soon as you can find the time."

"I'm ready now," said Amy. She got up and placed Neko back in his wicker bed that she'd bought for him. "I'll show you the sewing room we have upstairs. If you need anything, you must tell me, and I'll have one of the servants get it for you." As the shorter woman walked beside her, Amy verbalized her uncertainties. "Hope I won't look foolish. I know I'm not remotely doll-like, but maybe we could stretch the silk to cover me."

Forgetting her place, Sumi patted the younger girl's arm. "You are trim, and there will be plenty of material, I am sure. Do not worry, Amy-san. You will dazzle my master with your beauty."

"Well," quipped her companion, "I'll settle for just blinding him for a few hours until he forgets some of the totally irreverent remarks I wrote him."

Sumi was too polite to display her shock that Amy would be anything but courteous to Count Valerius. Never would she consider such behavior with Iwao. However, it was clear her master delighted in this outspoken, complex Englishwoman. He had known beautiful women in both Japan and Amsterdam; however, none of them, Sumi was certain, had ever touched him this way.

"Maybe I shouldn't have called him stiff-rumped again in writing," murmured Amy, then shrugged, as if she really wasn't concerned about the matter.

Sumi could only look down at her sock-covered toes as she struggled again to conceal her amazement.

Eleven

It was during the next week that Amy Stockwell came to a decision. She was standing on a stool, while Sumi draped the aqua material about her and showed her how to tie the *obi,* the wide sash, behind her. The arrival of Toshiro's latest letter that afternoon had helped make up her mind. As the days passed, influenced by his loving words and the way Sumi answered most of her questions about Japanese culture, Amy realized she wanted these days to continue. And she wanted to share them with the man who'd instigated these wonderful changes in her life. Yes, she missed the way Toshiro's calm voice soothed her, the feel of his strong arms around her, the taste of his warm lips on hers. He continued writing her words that gave her hope.

Lately after taking her tonic at night, unlike other nights before she'd met Count Valerius, there were no nightmares from the past. She now had dreams she'd never experienced before. There were visions of a Black Knight springing like a panther as he rescued her from the dragon. His kiss was gentle at first, then deepened into a blazing fire that left her throbbing and wanting more of him when she awakened.

As she peered at herself in the full-length mirror while Sumi pinned the cloth and took more measurements, Amy saw herself in a different way. She was no longer pale and fragile-looking, no longer afraid of the past, nor apprehensive about the future. Her life was in her own hands now, as Toshiro had been trying to tell her all along.

When they finished, Amy went down to the second floor to see her aunt.

Clarice was trying on a new gown. It had been a long time since Amy had been in her aunt's suite upstairs. When Clarice bade her enter, Amy walked into the glimmering room. She saw the French rococo style with gilt-edged white furniture, the elaborate bed hangings of lace and ruffles—all too elaborate for Amy's simpler tastes. She sat down on a gold brocade-covered chair.

"Oh, I don't know," Clarice mused aloud, "do you think the yellow or green goes better with my complexion? You don't think the yellow makes me look too full about the bosom, do you? I wanted to wear my gold and jade pin with it."

Amy looked across at her preening aunt. "Either gown will be beautiful, Clari."

Though pleased by the expected praise, Clarice put down the dresses and went over to sit across from her niece on the upholstered stool of her dressing table. "Good to see you looking so fit," she remarked, then turned to check herself in the gilt-framed mirror above the lacquered dressing case of inlaid woods that rested on the marble tabletop. She pulled out a circular gold and jade pin with Chinese lettering across the edges. She tried it near her shoulder. "Yes, I suppose that brooch will go best." Still in her nightgown and wrapper, it was evident Clarice had just arisen. "Giles sent word that he and your other uncles will be joining us for supper tomorrow. I had Brian pop around with an invitation for the earl. I thought poor David could use an afternoon out now that he is recovering."

David's disclosures about his despicable behavior toward the count still rankled Amy. However, she realized Toshiro had put it aside. She attempted his example. "That will be nice, Clari."

Amy had decided to tell Clarice first. Tomorrow she'd talk with her uncles and David. "Clari," she began, trying to keep up her courage. "I have thought deeply about this during the last few weeks." She saw her aunt shove the Chinese pin back into the jewelry case and lock it with the small key. Clarice looked as if she expected a blow. "I haven't even told the count yet," Amy went on. "I felt it would be better in person, not a letter." Strengthened by the thought of Toshiro, she stated, "I have decided to accept the count's proposal of marriage."

Leery that her aunt would shout, rant, perhaps even faint, Amy quickly realized Clarice must have been expecting this announcement. Of course, even the servants saw how happy and healthy Amy was, all because of this special man's presence in her life.

"I see," Clarice Townsend stated after a few silent moments. "Well, you are of age, of course. You do not owe me or your uncles any allegiance. Valerius does not mind about . . . ?"

Amy flushed, then interjected, "No, he wrote me again that he accepts the possibility there will be no heir for the House of Valerius."

"Possibility?" echoed Clarice. "Certainty, you mean."

Clarice was taking this better than Amy had hoped, so she let the remark go. Certainty was a more accurate term anyway, she thought, trying not to be sad on such a momentous day.

The following afternoon when David and her uncles arrived, Amy could tell by their grim expressions Clarice had already told them. They were polite but distant. By the time the dessert of baked apples ended, Amy was ready to follow them into the sitting room.

David spoke first. "So, your mind's made up, is it?"

Amy nodded and tried to press home the advantages she knew concerned her relatives. "Yes, David. I know there will be difficulties, but Count Valerius is from a noble Dutch family, educated in our English schools."

"Bah," grumbled Simon, "Eton and Oxford can't turn a Jappo into a gentleman. Mabel and the whelps don't like it, I can tell you that."

"Well, I'm sure in time you will come to see his Lordship's fine qualities. Of course, we will have a long, proper engagement with parties, time for all of us to become better acquainted."

Henry searched his vest pocket for his enameled snuffbox. "Suppose you don't mind the rake is probably only after your money and Stockwell Enterprises."

"What will our friends say?" Clarice interjected.

Giles nodded. His eyes showed his distress. "I do wish you would reconsider . . . at least for the family's sake."

All through their misgivings, Toshiro's written words kept coming back to Amy. No, she was not alone this time, and she would stand firm. "I appreciate your concerns," she told Clarice and the four men watching her. "However, I have made my decision. You must know," she added softy, "none of you will suffer financially from this marriage. I am certain Toshiro would want you all to retain your holdings in the business."

"I'll just bet," grumbled Simon. He looked over his stomach to the sparkling buckles on his shoes. "We'll all be wearing last year's waistcoats, our wives forced to patch old gowns, the little ones not even getting their Grand Tours. Mark you, I'm not one to complain, but you might have a care for your father's business. George built this place up with his bare hands, poor bugger."

"You look tired, my dear," Clarice remarked abruptly. "I'll get your medicine. We can talk more about this another day." She turned to the men. "I believe we should close the topic on Count Valerius. If it is Amy's decision to marry that man, I think there is nothing we can do but accept it." Without another word, Clarice left the room.

She returned with the glass containing Dr. Wakefield's prescription.

Indebted for Clarice's assistance in ending the unsettling topic of her intention to marry, Amy accepted the glass and drank it quickly. "Sumi is upstairs still working in the sewing room," she remarked. "I think I'll sit in the garden for a while before going to bed." She stood up. "Thank you all for coming tonight," she managed in a polite voice. "Toshiro and I would be so grateful for your support, but if you cannot give it, I will understand."

On such a balmy May evening, Amy only took a light shawl with her to the garden. The scent of hyacinths engulfed her. It reminded her of Toshiro's Japanese garden where spring flowers bloomed ahead of hers. Boxwood hedges, precise, straight plantings—her English garden did not have Toshiro's tranquility, but it was enticing just the same. She sat down on the wrought iron bench and leaned her head against the base of the oak tree she'd sat under since her childhood days. Pleasant thoughts of Toshiro washed over her. All would be well now. For the first time in her life, she had found a safe harbor.

An hour later, Clarice Townsend stepped back into the sitting room. Her dark eyes softened to a maternal glow. "Poor lamb, Amy is fast asleep on the bench outside. David, we may need you to take our Sleeping Beauty back to her room before you leave."

David nodded. He held out his glass while Simon poured him another brandy. "God, I still can't believe she is really going to marry Valerius. He is totally unsuitable."

"Here, here," said Henry. Even Giles nodded in agreement.

Clarice's peach-colored gown swished when she walked across the room to join the others. She sat next to David on the sofa. He gave her a searching look, but she turned back toward Henry. "I know. But I can see little we can do about it."

"Another thing," Simon grumbled, clearly intent on chewing more of this topic. He plunked his half-empty glass down on the table next to him. "I don't like that sneaky Jappo crone hovering about the place. She doesn't say anything, just squats in Amy's rooms, even while our niece works at her desk. Downright repulsive. The hag sleeps on some cushion on the bloody floor at night right in Amy's bedroom. Amy says the Jappo is more comfortable on the mat than in a proper English bed. Primitive, that's what it is. That queer foreigner, along with

Now you can get Heartfire Romances right at home and save!

Heartfire Romance

GET 4 FREE HEARTFIRE NOVELS
A $17.00 VALUE!

Home Subscription Members can enjoy Heartfire Romances and Save $$$$$ each month.

ENJOY ALL THE PASSION AND ROMANCE OF...

Heartfire

ROMANCES from ZEBRA

After you have read HEARTFIRE ROMANCES, we're sure you'll agree that HEARTFIRE sets new standards of excellence for historical romantic fiction. Each Zebra HEARTFIRE novel is the ultimate blend of intimate romance and grand adventure and each takes place in the kinds of historical settings you want most...the American Revolution, the Old West, Civil War and more.

SUBSCRIBERS $AVE, $AVE, $AVE!!!

As a HEARTFIRE Home Subscriber, you'll save with your HEARTFIRE Subscription. You'll receive 4 brand new Heartfire Romances to preview Free for 10 days each month. If you decide to keep them you'll pay only $3.50 each; a total of $14.00 and you'll save $3.00 each month off the cover price.

Plus, we'll send you these novels as soon as they are published each month. There is never any shipping, handling or other hidden charges; home delivery is always FREE! And there is no obligation to buy even a single book. You may return any of the books within 10 days for full credit and you can cancel your subscription at any time. No questions asked.

Zebra's HEARTFIRE ROMANCES Are The Ultimate
In Historical Romantic Fiction.
Start Enjoying Romance As You Have Never Enjoyed It Before...
With 4 FREE Books From HEARTFIRE

TO GET YOUR 4 FREE BOOKS MAIL THE COUPON BELOW.

FREE BOOK CERTIFICATE

Heartfire Romance

GET 4 FREE BOOKS

Yes! I want to subscribe to Zebra's HEARTFIRE HOME SUBSCRIPTION SERVICE. Please send me my 4 FREE books. Then each month I'll receive the four newest Heartfire Romances as soon as they are published to preview Free for ten days. If I decide to keep them I'll pay the special discounted price of just $3.50 each; a total of $14.00. This is a savings of $3.00 off the regular publishers price. There are no shipping, handling or other hidden charges. There is no minimum number of books to buy and I may cancel this subscription at any time. In any case the 4 FREE Books are mine to keep regardless.

NAME _____

ADDRESS _____

CITY _____ STATE _____ ZIP _____

TELEPHONE _____

SIGNATURE _____

(If under 18 parent or guardian must sign)
Terms and prices subject to change.
Orders subject to acceptance.

ZH1293

Heartfire Romance

GET 4 FREE BOOKS

HEARTFIRE HOME SUBSCRIPTION SERVICE
120 BRIGHTON ROAD
P.O. BOX 5214
CLIFTON, NEW JERSEY 07015

AFFIX STAMP HERE

that scurvy cat, will probably give Amy some tropical disease. I'll warrant Norbert Wakefield would agree with me. I hate cats," Simon muttered. "Thing's black, with eyes like Valerius, curse them both. Speaking of which, Clarice, you said those letters have been arriving like clockwork. Why is he writing her so much? Ain't just business and romantic slop. Bet that foreign devil is trying to turn her away from us. His power over her increases everyday, and—"

A shrill scream tore through the room, cutting off Simon's diatribe. Another followed.

"Amy!" Clarice sprang from the sofa and ran toward the doors that led to the garden outside. David and the uncles followed.

Clarice and the four men stood on the gray flagstones, at first unable to move closer toward the grisly sight before them.

The screams continued tearing from Amy's raw throat. "Neko," she sobbed as she looked wild-eyed at her hands then back down on her lap. "No, please God, noooo!" The small black kitten lay in her lap, his jaw rigid, pink tongue coated with blood. A slimy ooze trickled from his nose and ears. A fetid stain seeped across the skirt of Amy's gown where the cat had clearly lost control of its bowels from the force of being strangled.

"My God, like that rabbit four years ago," Henry whispered next to his brother Simon.

Giles thrust a hand over his mouth, obviously fighting the urge to vomit. David appeared ready to bolt from the place at the first opportunity.

"Simon," ordered Clarice, "take that wretched cat away—bury it, put it in the dustbin. I don't care; just get the damn thing off Amy's lap."

Aghast, Simon stared back at his younger sister as if she'd just asked him to slaughter King George and toss him in a cooking pot. "You know I can't bear the sight of blood, let alone the stench of droppings, neither can Giles. Cor, I can't even get near my own whelps until they're housebroken. Why ask me to do it?"

"Because you're the oldest, mutton face," said Henry.

Simon glowered at his brother. "Henry, I'm not touching that beastly mess, and that's an end to it. Get your burly wife, Penelope, to haul it away. Hear she's fond of dead creatures. Have to be to stay married to you while you prowl about the stews at night."

"Mutton face, you just watch your—"

"Dash it all," muttered David, clearly out of patience with the Townsend brothers. The earl reached into the side pocket of his hunter-green coat and pulled out his pocket handkerchief.

David went over to the Englishwoman who now sat staring into space. Deftly, he scooped up the remains of Neko and walked straight ahead into the denser part of the garden. "I'll get a spade from the garden keeper's shed. It will take me a little while, for I mean to bury it at the edge of the rose garden. Last thing we need is for Amy to find it."

Clarice walked over to Amy and got a firm hold on her arms. "Come, Amy, I will take you back into the house." She increased the pressure from her fingers to pull the blond-haired woman up. "Amy, stand up."

Automatically, Amy did as bidden, however, her legs wouldn't support her, and she fell back on the hard iron bench. "I'm sorry, I can't—"

"Henry," Clarice commanded, "send for Dr. Wakefield at once."

"I can't stand," Amy cried, panic again on her face.

Clarice turned to her remaining two brothers. "Simon, you and Giles get Amy's wheelchair from her bedroom."

Amy looked down at her hands again. "Oh, Clari, I . . . I'm so frightened," she cried, then covered her face with her hands as wracking sobs engulfed her.

Clarice went to her knees before her distraught niece. She hugged the girl close, rocking her back and forth. "Shush, little Amy, I am here. I'll keep you safe. I'll protect you, just like I always have."

Toshiro Valerius stood on the deck of the *Nightingale* as the ship pitched through the choppy water. He translated the hastily brushed characters of his uncle's letter once more:

My Honorable Nephew,

Your letter arrived with the sad news of Pieter's death. Through her grief, your lady mother has made me promise to find those responsible for his murder. I have sent spies out into the countryside. Their news is not what I'd hoped. Your suspicions have proven correct. I believed this matter ended years ago; it has not. Apparently, Lord Masao will not let the matter rest. I have asked the Shogun to order Lord Masao Nishikawa to meet with my council. Our families, as you know, are not on speaking terms. However, it is vital that you be present at that meeting.

A final word of warning, Toshiro. I have had the Port of Dejima watched constantly since I received your letter. To my shame, my spies tell me that

Pieter's assassin is not dead, nor has he returned to Japan. Masao's ninja was seen boarding a Chinese ship. He is in England. You must be more samurai now, Toshiro—move with caution, trust no one. I have not told my sister this, for she is grief-stricken enough with the death of your father. However, I firmly believe the panther will be in the gravest danger until he returns to Nagasaki to end Masao's revenge against our house. Come home quickly, with the greatest care for your safety.

Toshiro shoved the paper back into the folds of his plain dark coat. However, something more urgent pressed against his strained emotions than this danger from a Japanese assassin out to end the House of Valerius. It was his growing worry that something was wrong at Stockwell Hall. For weeks he'd heard nothing from Amy. At first he'd tried writing her coaxing letters. Then when he received no response, he reprimanded her playfully for being a naughty tease by proving her power over him with her silence. Later, he became irritated, then angry when there was no reply. Even the command in his final curt note that she write him at once had met with failure. During the last few days fear twisted his belly, keeping him awake at night and unable to eat. Had Masao's instrument of revenge been stalking him all along and found the one chink in his armor, where he was most vulnerable? "Amy," he whispered, concern for her safety slashing against him like the cold wind on his face. Or had David and her relatives succeeded in turning her against him in his absence? Their arguments had probably worn her down, convinced her of the folly of wedding someone not of her own kind. "Amy-san," he whispered against the hard-driving wind. "Be strong for me. Hide from the dragon until I can come for you."

They had to go faster. "Roonhuysen," he barked over his shoulder. A few feet ahead, three of his crewmen backed away and silently went about their duties.

"Jan Roonhuysen!" bellowed the enraged captain.

The man in his fifties came up the narrow wooden stairs from below deck. Taking the long-stemmed clay pipe out of his mouth, Jan smiled at Toshiro, then noticed the reception wasn't as usual. The Dutchman's cheeks became more ruddy. "Sorry, my Lord, I was checking the hold. The speed is rattling the barrels and crates something fierce."

"Damn it to hell, Jan, I pay common sailors to check on the hold. Next you'll be hanging from the bloody halyards stitching sailcloth. Your job is above deck. No wonder we're moving at a snail's pace. At this rate we'll be lucky to make Bristol before we're all in our dotage." Thrusting his hands behind his flapping coattails, Toshiro stalked back across the rolling ship. Used to the feel of a pitching deck beneath him, he had no trouble keeping his body ramrod straight.

"Blimey," murmured one of the older sailors, as he worked to retie a thick piece of rope on the rigging. "Never seen the captain in such a foul temper." When he saw Jan tap the tobacco from the stem and place the fragile pipe back in the pocket of his coarse shirt, the English sailor shook his head. "Watch your starboard, Mr. Roonhuysen. The panther looks right ready to tear the throat out of the first man who opens his yap."

Jan walked slowly over to the younger man, who stood gripping the curved wooden railing of his ship as if he wanted to break the heavy planks between his bare hands.

Concern for his longtime friend warred with his obligations to his ship and her crew. He cleared his throat. "Tosh . . . my Lord," he changed, "you are pushing the men too hard. Brigs over there," he said, nodding to the gray-haired sailor, "hasn't been in his hammock in thirty-six hours. She's a fast ship, but you'll tear her masts apart with this speed. We'll get there, lad." He dared more by placing a brotherly arm on his captain's rigid shoulder.

For a second Jan saw the raw anguish on the Eurasian's features before he concealed it with a stoic mask.

Toshiro stepped away, turning back to gaze at the foamy green water. "God, Jan, I fear it might already be too late."

Not even stopping to wash or change, Toshiro bounded off the gangway the minute the *Nightingale* reached Bristol. With an instinct he did not want to analyze, he knew it was imperative to speak immediately with Iwao. He winced when he saw both Japanese servants standing in the hallway. Iwao looked grim. It was Sumi's distraught features that gripped him.

In a gesture of complete subservience, Sumi dropped to her kimono-covered knees and pressed her forehead against the toe of Toshiro's boot. "My Lord, I have dishonored you. My shame is too great to bear."

Sumi was weeping so intensely, the count couldn't get her to tell him what had happened. Finally, he had to bend down and pull the groveling woman away from his boots. Never had he seen her so upset.

"Gomen nasai," Sumi kept crying, striking her fist to her breast.

As she continued repeating she was sorry, Toshiro realized Iwao was embarrassed by Sumi's lamentations. Yet, Iwao did nothing to comfort his wife, years of training making him aware his first duty was to his master. Automatically, Toshiro put his arms about the elderly woman's shoulders and steered her to the edge of the room. He eased her down on the upholstered bench against the wall. *"Daijobu desu.* Sumi, *daijobu desu,"* he repeated, hoping with all his heart everything really was all right. It was clear he'd get nothing more out of her right now than disjointed phrases about "Lost face and complete failure."

Toshiro rubbed his throbbing temples as he walked back to Iwao. "For God's sake, Iwao, tell me what the hell has happened."

Impassively, Iwao related what little he knew. "My dishonorable wife returned a few weeks ago during the middle of the night. Her arms were badly bruised by the force with which she was evicted from Stockwell Hall."

"Who dared harm my servant?" demanded the Eurasian. "Was it the Earl of Woodcroft or one of those brazen-faced servants?"

Iwao shook his gray head. "No, my Lord, it was the raven woman."

"What?" Then the count remembered the dark hair and sultry gaze. "You mean Clarice Townsend tossed Sumi out of the house in the middle of the night?"

"Hai." Iwao's brown eyes never wavered from his master. "That is all we know. Sumi was not allowed to see Amy-san. English servants bar the entry. Only the earl, her uncles, and Dr. Wakefield are allowed inside. My Lord, I, too, am sorry. My wife has failed in her duty to protect your future consort."

Toshiro was no longer listening. He charged upstairs to get his pistol. "Have Kori saddled immediately," he ordered.

When he reached Stockwell Hall, Toshiro jumped off the black stallion's back and took the stone steps three at a time. He almost shoved the brass knocker through the carved wooden door as he announced the manor had a visitor.

Brian appeared at the door, with a new footman behind him. "Sorry," said the red-haired lad with disinterest, "Miss Stockwell is unwell and has ordered that you never be admitted here again." He went to close the door but found the Eurasian's muscular frame hampered the task.

The loaded pistol the count pointed at both servants got their attention.

"Step out of my way or else Clarice Townsend will be needing two new footmen."

It was clear the young men found the calmly stated words more lethal than if he'd shouted them. They stepped back.

Familiar with the downstairs, Toshiro went immediately to Amy's suite of rooms. He could hear nothing from the slightly opened door. Prepared for a fight with David or those uncles of hers, he kicked the door open with his booted foot. Like a springing panther, he vaulted into the room, his green eyes darting quickly, searching for the danger he was ready to confront.

However, the scene that greeted him almost shattered him. Amy was sitting in that cursed wheelchair, her face colorless and drawn. The rosy glow of returned health that brightened her face before he left had disappeared completely. She stared ahead, watching him but not registering any emotion. Toshiro ground the backs of his teeth in frustration, then fury. Practically pawing the ground in his readiness to do battle with their enemy, he'd arrived to find there was no dragon left to fight. It had done its worst, leaving nothing concrete he could crush with his hands or kill with his pistol. The Black Knight was too late. He lowered the gun in his hands and placed it on the corner of Amy's oak desk. A stack of papers strewn across it gave evidence she had not worked here in days. There was an empty glass on the tray. He picked it up, sniffed, then peered at the dregs left in the bottom. Wakefield had been called to bring more of his filthy opium.

"Hello, my Lord," Amy said in a monotone. "I . . . I've been expecting you."

The emptiness in her voice made him want to reach down and shake her, for his rage was against this evil house, her stifling relatives, and against Amy for not having the strength to fight them, but mostly against himself for having left her. "Amy," he said, his throat constricting with emotion. "I am too weary to argue with you now. I want to take you out of this house immediately. You cannot stay one more night here in this gilt-edged tomb."

A spark ignited her blue eyes. She braced her hands on the leather-covered arms of her wheelchair. "No, my Lord, I can never leave." She looked about her room and focused on the closed green drapes that kept the summer sun away from her. "I belong here. I'm safe here. Glad you came, though," she said offhandedly. "You know I cannot marry you."

"Noo!" he shouted, a mixture of anguish and fury in his voice. In an instant his tortured features were inches from her face. He gripped her hands against the arms of her chair. "Damn it, I won't let it end this way. Amy, look at me. What has happened? Tell me," he demanded.

"Count Valerius." Clarice Townsend rushed into the room with Brian and the new footman behind her. "Don't you dare harm my niece."

Toshiro whirled about to confront Amy's aunt. "Harm her? By God, I've come here to get her out of this coffin you and those brothers of yours have buried her in."

Miss Townsend's tortoise pin of sapphires and diamonds shimmered against the material of her gown where her ample bosom moved up and down with her indignation. *"You* are the black devil who is trying to destroy this poor child." She dabbed at the corner of her eyes with a lacy handkerchief. "I beg you, sir, please leave."

Amy blinked and saw her aunt standing a few feet away with their two servants hovering nearby. "Please don't cry," Amy said in a bland voice. She turned back to the count. "Yes, my Lord, I pray you leave. I do not wish to see you again. I tried to tell you I could marry no one. I warned you. You wouldn't listen."

"Amy," he snapped, near the end of his patience. "I won't leave until you tell me why you say such things. Answer me, damn you! Why?" He gripped her upper arms.

"Let me go." She couldn't get free. "I can't marry you," she shouted.

"Why?" he pressed, afraid he'd lost her for good.

Without warning, Amy burst into tears.

Clarice nodded and the two male servants came at his back.

The Eurasian saw something in Amy's eyes when she looked over his shoulder. He moved swiftly. His booted foot landed in the center of Brian's stomach, while his fist slammed into the other man's face. He glared at Clarice, warning silently he was ready to use more of his Eastern skills if she pushed him.

For the first time genuine fear showed in Clarice's eyes. She walked past her prostrate servants and sat down on a chair. "I will not leave Amy," she said firmly but made no move to oust the unwelcome guest. "You shall answer to David and my brothers for this rowdy behavior."

Ignoring her, Toshiro turned back to Amy. "Now, by hell," he commanded, his voice carrying to the next room, "answer me."

Appalled by his violent actions and the promise of a more physical response if she did not obey him, Amy felt something surge within her veins. "All right, have the truth then. I killed my mother. Yes," she said, watching the shock in his eyes. "She strangled my spaniel, Timi, and I pushed her over the cliff. My father jumped in to save her, but they both drowned. What an irony." Her laugh was harsh. "I now realize my blood is as tainted as hers. Four years ago when I killed that rabbit, I wanted to believe it wasn't true. I thought I could hide it, master it. Neko is dead, Toshiro. I strangled him with my bare hands." She held up her hands to him. "God, you are a fool," she shouted. "You thought it was only because I'm barren that I couldn't marry you?"

"Amy," he whispered, his mind and emotions a jumble at this totally unexpected declaration. "I don't believe it. You were only ten years old and—"

"Are you blind?" she jeered, angry and bleeding inside because he was forcing her to experience this horror again. "Aunt Clarice and I are the only ones who know the whole truth. Even my uncles think Jane killed herself. Still want a murderess for your wife or concubine, Valerius? Better let Sumi scout a proper Japanese bride for you."

At the mention of Sumi, Toshiro shook his head, trying to take all this in. "Sumi is distraught over having left you. She blames herself for. . . ." A new terror seized him as he recalled Sumi's words, remembered Iwao's grim look. "Loss of face, shame," he murmured aloud. So distracted with his fears over Amy's safety, he'd not been thinking clearly, let alone recalling all he'd learned growing up in Japan.

He grabbed his pistol off her desk. "I must leave. Amy, I will be back tomorrow, and we will talk again." He gave Clarice a hostile look. "It is not over yet."

When he arrived back home, Dover came over to greet him. "Got Kori in a right lather, my Lord."

"Dover, where is Sumi?" Toshiro demanded, devoid of his usual politeness with this easygoing Londoner.

The Englishman scratched his gray head. "Don't rightly know, my Lord. Place has been real quiet since you charged out of here."

Rushing past a puzzled Dover, Toshiro forced himself to think rationally for a minute. Sumi would not risk defacing her master's home. She would want some private place outside. He began running toward the back of the large stone structure, through the opened wooden gate to his Japanese garden. The whole world was going mad, he thought. His nerves hovered near the breaking point as the insanity caught hold of him, too. He charged across the carefully raked gravel, stomped on the new beds of iris he'd planted himself. "Sumi? Iwao?" he shouted in alarm. Then he saw them.

Sumi, dressed in white, her legs tied with a wide piece of cloth to keep her body still when she plunged the point of the sharp knife into her throat. Her hair hung straight down her back, gathered simply with a piece of purple yarn. No longer in his Western clothes, Iwao had on his gray kimono, insignia of the Akashis on his sleeves, front and back. The older samurai stood behind his wife. Sunlight glittered off the water droplets on the lethal blade as he raised it, ready to assist Sumi by cutting off her head at the proper time in this ritualistic suicide.

"Stop!" Toshiro bellowed. *"Yamero-yo!"* he thundered, feeling the power of the dragon's breath crush him.

Twelve

"My dear, can't you eat a little more? You've hardly touched your plate," said Clarice.

More in control today, Amy gave her aunt a wan smile. "Perhaps later I'll have something."

Simon moved away from his two brothers to eye her plate. "If you aren't going to eat that custard, can I have it?"

"Simon, really," his sister admonished.

"No sense of it goin' to waste."

Amy looked indulgently up at her uncle. "You are welcome to it."

"Better keep your sword arm ready instead of shoving food into your snout," Henry advised. "He'll be here any minute."

Giles wiped perspiration from his forehead. "Dear me, what will the servants say? And did you see the black eye the footman has from that infidel's massive fist? Brian said the count soared like a falcon and attacked them in midair."

"Oh, just that Oriental stuff. Comes from eating raw fish and all that bowing they do . . . limbers up the spine," remarked Henry, sounding like someone in the know.

Pushing with her hands, Amy moved her wheelchair away from the small table. She winced and shielded her eyes at the sun coming through the glass panes. "Please, Clari, will you close the drapes. One of the maids must have opened them."

Her aunt went over and pulled the heavy green velvet across the thick panes of glass.

"This must be the last time I see the count," Amy informed her aunt. "I hurt him deeply yesterday. I saw it in his eyes."

Clarice came back and pulled a bulky overstuffed chair across the rug to sit next to her niece. "Amy, do not torture yourself. If Valerius hadn't forced his way into your life, filling your innocent head with promises of marriage, exciting schemes, you would never have been through the last agonizing weeks. We would have gone on as always, the family taking care of you, keeping you safe. That foreign devil pushed you over the edge. He made you relive all that suffering, the way your parents died. If his unnatural power over you hadn't caused you to think about those buried memories, you never would have insisted I tell you the truth. It was monstrous of him. I shall never forgive him."

Amy glanced at her four relatives. "Please, I do not want a scene. I'm so tired of fighting. It is over."

The sudden loud knock echoed through the silent room. "Let him in, Uncle Simon. Allow me to handle this. Just stay quietly on the side of the room."

Something fluttered against her heart when Amy took in Toshiro's appearance in dark coat and breeches. But she stifled it when he strode into the room as if he owned it, showing them all he was ready to fight anyone again who stood in his way, even Amy herself. Yet, she could not help spotting the lines of strain at the corners of his eyes and mouth. He appeared more haggard than she'd ever seen him. However, she knew she had to steel herself against these soft feelings. For his sake as well as hers, she had to ensure this was the last time he called at Stockwell Hall. She watched his cold greeting to her aunt and uncles.

When Amy spotted the quick shuffling steps of the woman who walked behind Toshiro, her whole demeanor changed. "Sumi," she cried, overjoyed to see the Japanese woman.

Sumi looked up at Amy and made a motion to come forward, then stopped and peered hesitantly up at her master.

"Look," sneered Henry, "he's got the old crone so terrified, she daren't say boo without his permission."

Amy shared her uncle's umbrage at the regal, almost arrogant stance Valerius held as he stood in the center of the room. "My Lord," she addressed with formality, "I should like a few moments alone with Sumi first. Kindly go into the next room and wait for me in my library. What I have to say to you will not take long."

Her dismissal rankled. Yet, he realized he could not deny his beloved servant a chance to check on her English friend. "As you wish."

Amy watched as the count said something in Japanese to Sumi. The woman bowed low, then gave an appreciative look up at her master. When Toshiro nodded, Sumi bowed to him again before he walked imperiously to the right to enter Amy's office.

Having expected him to go over and sit down on a

chair, Amy was disconcerted when he remained standing. She must have shown her discomfort, for he arched a dark brow and merely turned his back on her, seeming content to look at the various leather-bound volumes that lined the bookshelves along the wall.

Grateful her relatives were keeping their word to let her handle this, she pushed her chair over to Sumi. "How pleased I am to see you. Sorry I frightened you into leaving." She rubbed her forehead absently. "I . . . I can't remember all that happened after. . . . It is better that you returned to the comfort of his Lordship's home. I would not have you unhappy, dear friend."

Sumi could not hide her puzzlement. She bent down on her knees to speak face-to-face with the Englishwoman. "Amy-san, I do not understand."

"It doesn't matter." Amy's eyes misted. Despite her obvious terror of Amy's bizarre conduct, Sumi had bravely come back here to see her. Automatically, Amy leaned over to hug the smaller woman.

Sumi was not able to stifle her outcry when Amy's arms encircled her back.

Amy pulled away, as shocked as Sumi by her reaction. "Sumi, what is wrong? Are you ill?"

"No, Amy-san. I am fine."

Not to be fooled, Amy realized this woman was hurt. With a surprising show of determination, Amy pushed aside one shoulder of Sumi's patterned kimono.

"No, hold still," Amy ordered in a voice she'd never used with this woman before.

Used to commands, Sumi did not move.

Carefully, Amy ruffled away the white under-kimono from her shoulder. She gasped when she saw the thin red marks across Sumi's upper back. Someone had beaten this small woman. "Son of a . . . Sumi, who did this to you?" She heard her aunt gasp at the stripes on the woman's smooth skin.

Sumi rose with haste and readjusted both parts of her kimono. She tightened the *obi* at her back. "It is of no importance, Amy-san."

"The hell it isn't." Amy thought of the red-haired Brian. "By hell, if one of my servants has done this to you, I'll have him in front of the magistrate before noon." She turned her wheelchair to face her relatives. "Clarice, Uncle Simon, did you have a hand in this? I know you did not approve of Sumi being here, but I'll never forgive you if—"

"Amy," came Clarice's indignant voice. "The Townsends never beat their servants; we just fire them. My brothers and I don't know anything about this."

She watched her relatives, and decided Clarice spoke the truth. "What was used? The marks are thin. Giles, you went to Eton. Is it something like a schoolmaster's cane?"

"Hardly. Too thin," answered Giles nervously.

"Let it go," said Henry. "She's only a servant."

"Sumi," Amy addressed again, sparks flying before her eyes. She winced when the servant stepped back from her in obvious distress. "Please, you do not have to fear me or anyone in this room. I will have this person arrested. I have connections in Bristol. Tell me the Englishman's name. Was it Dover or Ethel at your estate? God, was it one of the Bristol servants I sent over to hire on at Valerius Hall?" Remorse assailed her.

Sumi shook her gray head. "No."

"I know those marks didn't just appear on your skin, woman. You didn't fall into a patch of nettles. Stow the evasions. I won't rest until the culprit is punished for such savagery. Practically using a pillar to—"

"No, Amy-san, it was thin bamboo," Sumi corrected in a soft voice.

The younger woman swallowed, trying to control her outrage. "Someone beat you with a strip of bamboo?"

"Hai . . . I mean, yes."

The words came out in a dead calm. "Who? Do you mean to tell me that your own husband dared such brut . . . ?"

"No, Amy-san. Let this matter rest, I beg you. Do not distress yourself. The matter is settled."

Something Amy could hardly take in pushed its ugly way into her mind, even though she tried to run from it. She glanced across at Sumi's placid expression, then darted a look at the black-haired man who stood with his back to her as he perused her bookshelf. The terrible question pushed through her lips. "Count Valerius beat you?" When Sumi did not speak, Amy read the affirmative answer in the woman's almond-shaped eyes. A rage she'd never experienced took hold of her. Before anyone could stop her, she pushed down on the wheels of her chair and charged toward the unsuspecting count at ramming speed.

Unprepared, Toshiro whirled about, nearly losing his balance when he was forced to jump out of the way. His legs just missed being crushed by the heavy wooden wheels. *"Unko!* What in blazes are—"

"Wharf rat! You yellow swine!" she hoisted, using one of David's derogatory expressions. She reached for a large volume of English ship designs and heaved it at him with both hands.

Toshiro ducked. The heavy book landed with a loud

243

crash against the wall. His own control began sailing to the irritated side. "Amy, will you tell me what the devil is the matter now?"

Despite her weakened condition, Amy hauled her body out of the chair to do battle. "How could I have ever considered marrying you? I . . . I don't even love you," she tossed. "Here I'd been apologizing all over the place, eaten by remorse today because I thought I'd hurt you. You don't have a heart. You're just a . . . cold machine with polite manners! I wouldn't marry you if you were the last man on earth."

Her behavior right now almost convinced him she had actually taken leave of her senses.

"Konketsuji!" she called him, deliberately using the one word Sumi had warned her against saying to her master.

His head snapped back as if he'd just received a physical blow. The snows on Fujiyama could not have been colder than his reply. "That is a word I have not heard for a long time. The last man who made that scurrilous reference to my mixed lineage soon learned it could be detrimental to his health."

She sensed the sudden danger from this man, but she would not back down.

"Amy, I am warning you. The last two days have pushed me closer to violence than I've ever experienced in my life." Toshiro took her firmly by the arms and pushed her none too gently back down on the cushioned seat of her wheelchair. "Now, you will explain yourself," he ordered, every inch the captain of his ship.

With a mutinous scowl in his direction, Amy demanded, "Did you or did you not beat Sumi?"

Hell, just what he needed. Nothing settled between

them, now this. "Amy," he tried, "you do not understand our ways. There is more here than you see, but I do not have the time, nor the patience to explain it to you now. Another day I will be glad to—"

"Bastard," she called him. "I'll not tolerate any Japanese hedging right now, or noncommittal smirk. Answer me yes or no, damn you."

His jaw tightened as he fought his own demons. "It is always black or white to you, isn't it? Just like all you English, you do not try to understand us. All right. Have the answer then. Yes!" he shouted, his voice carrying to the next room. "I beat Sumi yesterday. Does that satisfy your English sense of justice?"

Her first reaction was betrayal. She'd never considered this man capable of such an action. She looked at him as though he'd turned into something Dover would muck from the stables. "David was right. You are an uncivilized coward who picks on defenseless women. Get out of my house before I have the servants throw you out." She turned her chair about and headed away from him.

"Sumi," Amy called, "you do not have to go with that cruel monster. You can stay with me under my protection. No one," she added, glaring at Toshiro as he walked past her, his features set in marble. "No one will ever beat you here."

Sumi's normally placid face mirrored distress. "Oh, Amy-san, I could never leave my master. I am happy there. Iwao and I have always served the Akashis. Forgive me, but you do not understand."

"Like a whipped cur," muttered Simon. "The hag still follows him."

Amy knew from the way the muscle in his jaw worked, Count Valerius was furious. However, she was too far gone with outrage that he could be such a bully. This could not be the same man who'd written her poetry, carved cherry blossoms in a wooden box for her, laughed with her, been gentle and patient. . . . "I do not know you, Valerius."

His tightly held countenance broke for an instant. With a low growl, he lunged for her, clearly intent on a direct response to the vile words she'd hurled at him. Only at the last moment did he catch himself and pull back. Breathing hard, he clenched his hands into fists at his sides. "No, Miss Stockwell, it is clear you do not know me. Perhaps you are right. You do belong in this stifling tomb of Stockwell Hall. You have become like the other jackals here," he said, looking disdainfully at her relatives. "I thought you a woman worth fighting for, a woman of honor and courage. It seems we have both made a grave error."

She grabbed her anger to use as a shield against the softer emotions that would soon make it impossible to hold back tears. "You ever beat Sumi again and I . . . I'll cut off your cock and nail it like a barnacle to the bow of your damn ship!" she vowed.

This time Toshiro did not flinch from her filthy words. He saw Clarice's smirk, took in the triumphant looks of Amy's uncles as they reveled in his defeat. He noticed Sumi's expression of horror, then sympathy when she looked up at him, reminding him of the countless times she'd sought to comfort him when the Japanese children taunted him because he was not of pure blood. Her look almost undid him right now. He cleared his throat. "Miss Stockwell, I will not come to your house again. Soon, I will sail back to Japan, for I must see my uncle. When I return I will sell my Bristol estate. The business contract between us I will honor. But Joshua Rigby can handle all the details, as your aunt correctly pointed out that afternoon in my garden when she came to . . . rescue you." He bowed stiffly, without warmth, without respect. It was a gesture of Oriental disdain and finality. Turning his back on them all, he appeared every inch an aristocrat among English peasants as he walked slowly out toward the hallway that led outside.

Forgetting even to bow, Sumi raced after her master, intent on following him home.

Drained, Amy's anger changed to a sorrow so deep she doubled over with the stabbing ache of it.

Her aunt came to her. "My poor lamb," she fussed.

Amy straightened. "Please, I'd like to be alone now."

When everyone had gone, Amy rolled her chair over to her desk. She sat looking down at the carved wooden box Toshiro had made for her. The crane and cherry tree blurred as tears filled her eyes. She brushed at them impatiently but could not stop them. Sobs tore from her as she held her face in her hands. Everything was lost, there was nothing in the future except long empty days and even longer nights. Norbert's tonic could never take away this pain. She thought of her own culpability in her parents' deaths that she had discovered four years ago. How could she have been such a fool to think she could marry Toshiro? Ignoring her usual good sense, she had deluded herself into believing she could marry this man and have a normal life. "Fool," she called herself.

When the tears finally stopped, Amy continued staring at the top of her desk. Peace, how she longed for it. However, she knew right now it would never be hers. There was no quiet place where her mind and heart would stop tormenting her. There was only one way to bring the release she so desperately craved.

"Tonight," she whispered, holding the word like a balm against her tortured soul. Then it would be over. She couldn't tell Toshiro what Clarice had divulged last night. His pity was the last thing she wanted. No one could help her now. But she would not keep that vigil throughout the next months, feel her heartbeats slip away into oblivion. George Stockwell's daughter would choose the time and hour. No more would she wait for the dragon, for she knew his identity now. Clarice had revealed it to her last evening. Now Amy knew the dragon's name—it was Death.

After tying Kori to a nearby branch, Toshiro tossed his outer coat over the horse's saddle, then walked slowly along the deserted shore of Stockwell property. It was late, and his muscles ached from the heavy work of unloading the cargo off the *Nightingale*. If Jan Roonhuysen was surprised to see the captain with his sleeves rolled up, working like a dock hand, he'd said nothing. Toshiro needed the backbreaking labor this afternoon, anything to blot out the ache that Amy was lost to him. Bereft, he had no more weapons left to fight for her. When she told him she did not love him, hinted she never had, he realized it was over. As he walked along the empty shore, the count no longer cared what happened. He almost wished the assassin stalking him would visit tonight. Nothing mattered now.

Weary in body and heart, Toshiro stopped and leaned against the large boulder. The Eurasian called himself a fool for haunting this place like a specter returning for something he could never possess. But the memory of their first meeting here caught him. The way Amy's eyes reminded him of sunshine on the Adriatic. Out of breath and frightened, yet she'd delighted him with her spirit when he'd checked her for injuries. An unexpected smile tugged at the corners of his mouth. Early on he had guessed she longed for adventure, an opportunity to travel on one of the many boats she owned but could never use herself.

The count's gaze shifted from the shore of the Avon to the area near his outstretched legs. The strewn pieces of wood scattered about the ground reminded him that Amy Stockwell could have lost her life in that accident. Typical of her lax servants, he mused with irritation. When sent back to retrieve her chair, they left the broken pieces from the left wheel behind. With a carpenter's eye for salvage, he bent down and pawed through the rubble. Axle, box, hub, spokes of the wheel. At least some of the parts could have been reused. Distractedly, he sat down on the ground and began putting wooden pieces together while he listened to the water lapping against the shore. The full moon gave him enough light to see by. A spring moon, he mused, thinking of Japan. A time of cherry blossoms, warm nights, lovers' trysts.

However, something in the way the slender pieces of wood fit together nudged him. He picked up another, then arranged it on the ground. When he ran his thumb over the edges of the broken pieces, he felt the gummy paste inside the smooth cut. He peered closely at the pieces. The impact of the wheel hitting that huge boulder with such force would have shattered it. All these pieces were cut clean. They fit together perfectly, their edges too neat. It was like putting back the pieces of a puzzle.

His blood chilled when he realized the spokes in this wheel had been precisely and expertly cut halfway, then filled with a mixture of weak glue and sawdust, the kind a carpenter used only when a hasty, temporary repair was desired. But who had tampered with her chair? Who would try to kill her? A rival shipping owner? A disgruntled servant? Had to be enough of those around at Stockwell Hall with their surly manner. Any of those grasping relatives of hers could have secretly paid someone to do it. It must have galled her uncles when George Stockwell left everything to Amy. How about David, the Earl of Woodcroft, the spurned lover? Toshiro's trip to London had convinced him the earl had other interests in that city besides business.

He picked up the pieces of wood, stood up, and carried them back to Kori. Toshiro put them in the leather bag that hung across the horse's saddle, not really certain what he would do with them. He only knew he could not turn his back on this. God help him, he still wanted to protect her, even though it was clear she loathed him.

Ready to put his booted foot against the leather stirrup, the Eurasian stopped when he saw something white head along the empty shoreline. It looked like a woman. He shook his head. These Englishwomen were certainly eccentric to go about in their nightgowns for midnight swims, or perhaps she was meeting her sweetheart and. . . . He pulled back from Kori and strained to make out the familiar figure heading toward the water.

Moonlight danced off golden hair that streamed about slender shoulders. Alarmed, Toshiro began running toward the shore ahead. "Amy?" he called.

Not looking left or right, Amy continued toward the river.

Fear knotted his gut, and he shouted to her again. He pumped his legs as fast as he could. She told him at the spa she couldn't swim. "No, Amy. Come back!" The water was up to her waist, then her shoulders. When he saw her head disappear, he rushed into the cold water, not even taking the time to remove his boots, breeches, or shirt. He swam with hard, frantic strokes to the spot where she'd disappeared. He dove, searching, praying, then cursing when he couldn't find her. His lungs burning, he had to kick upward to gulp deep breaths of night air. Then he made a second dive, this time plunging deeper than before.

Finally his fingers latched around strands of silky hair. He grabbed her and began pushing upward.

Holding her head out of the water, he grasped Amy under the chin as he continued swimming for shore. When he reached the shallow area of the river, he stood up with Amy in his arms. Exhausted, he staggered as he carried her out of the water and placed her limp body down on the hard ground. Her lips were blue. Putting his ear close to them, he could feel no breath. His finger at her throat detected no pulse. "No, Amy, I won't let you die," he cried, a man at the end of endurance. He cradled her upper body in his arms. He pressed his mouth against her cold lips, begging and commanding her to respond. His fingers tangled in the mass of her wet hair. He ran a hand along the sodden remains of her nightgown that covered her soft body. "Fight it, Amy. Fight the dragon with me," he pleaded.

As a last resort, he turned her over on her side and pressed her stomach and back several times. A rivulet of water trickled out of her mouth. He increased his efforts. She made a strangling sound, then he felt the upsurge within her stomach, just before she released the portion of the Avon she'd swallowed in her attempt at suicide.

Toshiro held Amy's head until the heaving stopped. He undid the three buttons of his shirt and pulled it over his head. After using it to wipe her face, he propped her against the smooth edge of a rock. "I'll be back," he said, not sure if Amy could even hear him, for her eyes were still closed. He ran back to Kori, grabbed the coat off the saddle, and mounted him in one fluid motion. When he returned, Toshiro went to his saddlebags and pulled out the bottle of brandy his second in command had thrust at him tonight, apparently deciding the younger man looked in need of libation. Uncorking the bottle, he went back to Amy. "Here, take a swallow of this."

She sniffed the strong liquor then moved her head back. "I don't like bran—"

"Damn it, neither do I but drink it!" her rescuer ordered, in no mood to be crossed. He knew her attempt to kill herself had changed something permanently within him.

Amy took two mouthfuls. The liquor made a heated splash through her empty stomach. She slumped back against the rock and closed her eyes.

Toshiro put the bottle to his own cold lips and, despite his usual distaste for brandy, he drained half of it in one uninterrupted swallow. His pulse racing, he shivered, and knew it was reaction from the terror of almost losing her. He raked his shaky fingers through his thick black hair, then realized the leather tie had come off in the water during his rescue. When he looked back at Amy, he saw that she'd bent her knees to rest her head on her arms. Her shoulders shook. Without hesitation, Toshiro moved over to her. He began chafing her arms and legs to restore the circulation.

"You should have let me drown."

He stopped, dropped his hands to his sides and sat back on his heels, Japanese fashion. He'd never seen her this way, so like a beaten animal. Yesterday he'd read sadness in her eyes, then fury when she'd discovered he'd whipped Sumi. But right now there was nothing of Amy Stockwell, the spitfire or successful businesswoman. As if a spark of light had gone out of her forever, a new self-destructiveness had taken its place. She had judged herself guilty, then sentenced herself to death. "Amy," he said, keeping his voice low, "I still do not believe you are capable of harming anyone, let alone committing murder."

Her lashes opened slowly. "The evidence proves otherwise."

He wanted to hold her but sensed from her wary expression, comfort was the last thing she'd accept right now. "You were only a child, and clouded memories make those shadows you view from the past unreliable. No one saw you, so how can you be sure?"

"My aunt saw me push her sister over the cliff," Amy said, as if explaining truths to a child that the adults already knew.

"I'll never believe you hurt anyone in the past or will in the future."

His stubbornness unnerved her. "You still don't understand, do you? Valerius, I have no future." She bolted upright, angry that he was harassing her this way. "Two days ago my aunt and Dr. Wakefield told me the truth. I only have a few months to live." When he stood up, she found his unyielding expression irksome. "Don't you see? I'm dying!"

Toshiro wasn't sure if he was more angry at Clarice for telling her niece this news or at Amy for believing it. "We are all in that process, Miss Stockwell, however you are the only person I've ever met who makes a hobby out of dying, the way some people collect coins."

"Oh, you insensitive. . . ." She choked, unable to believe he could resort to sarcasm at such a moment. Her heart was breaking because she would never have a future with this man before her. She was a murderess and insane like her mother. "No one is safe with me."

"Rubbish," he countered. "You suspect the worst in yourself because your uncles and aunt have been spouting those false notions to you since you were a child. Like a hothouse plant, they've raised you to become an invalid."

"I'm dangerous," she pointed out, "both to animals and humans."

"I'll risk it."

"How can you be so cruel? I trusted you with the truth. I thought you were my friend."

His green eyes turned to stone. Tonight had changed him, and he knew he'd never be the same. "Forgive me, Miss Stockwell. I tried courting the dying virgin, but found I desired more than just worshiping at the altar no man is ever allowed to touch."

"You wouldn't be so smug if you woke up one night and found my hands around your throat."

"If I awakened to find those adorable little hands lower, I am certain I would not mind."

How could he behave this way? "You are horrible to

make such a lewd remark. I'm only trying to do the right thing, to take responsibility for my actions."

Toshiro snorted. "Well, young lady, from a clinical observation I'd say you will fare better under my protection than you've done so far in the bosom of the Townsends and the Earl of Woodcroft. Your relatives hover about you like vultures waiting for a plump turkey to expire so they can have lunch. They cosset you, spoil you, yet neglect even to watch out for your safety," he added, thinking about the neatly carved pieces of wood across Kori's saddle. "As for David," he bit out with distaste, "you can bid farewell to that dishonorable Englishman without a tear." He saw her shock and outrage but continued just the same. "Business trips to London you thought? I did some checking while I was in London."

"Spying, don't you mean?" But the man before her only shrugged. Never had she seen him this way. What had happened to Count Valerius?

Almost reading her thoughts, he stated, "I am learning to fight you English on your own terms. Imagine my surprise to find your sainted Earl of Woodcroft spends most of his time in the brothels and gaming houses along the seamier streets of London and not toiling away at business, as his parents and a certain naive English chit believe? No doubt your death would clear his way to live openly with his mistress. I think his common tastes lean more toward brunettes like your Aunt Clarice."

With a shriek of outrage, Amy pulled back her arm and slapped Toshiro across the face.

His dark head snapped back with the force of her hand. For such a fragile-appearing woman, she packed an amazing wallop. Holding his back rigid, he just managed to clamp a long-practiced stranglehold on his temper.

Inwardly aghast to realize she'd actually struck someone, Amy took the offensive. "I'll not have you say such odious things about David and my family. After you left yesterday, David came to visit me. He said you would try to discredit him. You want to hurt me just because I rejected you."

Toshiro cursed himself for not anticipating David's attempt to cover his tracks. He should have remembered their Eton days when Woodcroft made certain he never took the blame for his misdeeds.

"Leave me alone," Amy yelled. "My life was peaceful until you charged into it."

As he rubbed his smarting left cheek, his smile mocked her. "Yes, working diligently to die in that moldy house must have been a tedious pastime."

He was laughing at her? "I cannot believe how unfeeling you are." Moisture smarted the corners of her eyes. "I've always read the Japanese view suicide as a happy ending. You are showing a decided lack of understanding. If I want to end my life, it's my business."

All humor departed in a rush. Blood pounded against his temples, heating him like a volcano, especially when he saw the blond-haired woman head back toward the water. "Amy Stockwell, get back here. Now!" he thundered. For the first time in his life he found he couldn't summon the control his Bushido master had spent years teaching him. Nor did he even try to reach within his inner place for a meditation to calm the raging fire that sent flames before his eyes. "I . . . have . . . had . . . enough of your morbid theatrics!" he shouted at her back, then charged after her, his ruined boots sliding on the slippery stones.

"Stay away from me," she yelled, whirling on him, her own ire up.

A few feet from her he stopped and made a last attempt to move back from the precipice that threatened to consume him. "I'm willing to . . ." he tried to catch his breath, ". . . overlook your first attempt to drown yourself, for I believe it stemmed from despair. However," he grated, "this second time you're acting from spite, nothing more. And that I will not excuse." His voice became more dangerous in its calm. "Come here."

A lethal panther ready to lunge—that's what he appeared to Amy. She stepped forward, then caught herself. "I'm not Sumi. Do not think you can browbeat me with your tyrannical ways." When he planted his fists against the waist of his ruined breeches, she turned and rushed back to the water. Discarding thoughts of drowning, now she only wanted to learn to swim posthaste to escape this side of Valerius she'd never glimpsed before. In a desperate move, she bent down and picked up a rock. "Stay back. I'm warning you, Valerius. Full to the scuppers, you must be."

His green eyes never left hers. "No, I am not intoxicated, just more enlightened," he stated without losing a step.

When he continued stalking her, she held his gaze, changed the aim at the last minute, then hurled the stone.

It caught Toshiro on the left cheek in the same spot where the fading imprint of her hand had landed earlier. It was then he realized she had remembered his remark about watching his enemy's eyes to anticipate his next move. The edge of the jagged stone had swiped across his skin, but he did not feel the cut. He was too far-gone in his fury. "Hellcat," he growled at her.

Horrified, Amy saw blood trickle down his face. Was she turning into a virago? What was happening to her? But she knew there were more pressing matters at hand than analyzing her complete departure from dying rose. She ran for the safety of the water, but only managed to plunge knee deep before she felt the panther's hot breath on her neck. He turned her roughly about. The wind was forcefully pushed from her diaphragm as she landed across his left shoulder. Water and rocks spun around her as he hauled her roughly back up the embankment. When she struggled, he clamped a hand about her ankles and pressed her hard against his body. She pounded her fists against his muscular back. "Put me down. This behavior proves I was right to run from you. I . . . I'll talk with you when your usual reserve comes back." When that didn't work, she grew incensed. "Stop acting like a dockside bully, do you hear me?"

Ignoring the moss on a large boulder, Toshiro sat down and easily transferred Amy's form facedown across his wet breeches.

"You have no right to treat me . . . I'll not stand for your savagery."

"Nor will you sit comfortably for it either," snapped the enraged panther, just before his right hand landed with a loud thwack across the wet seat of her ruined nightgown.

Amy screeched in outrage, then began hurling nautical terms at him, some she'd never used in her life. However, as his punishing hand continued to land across her fiery hindquarters, her swearing ceased along with her futile efforts to get free. "Stop . . . you've made your point. I'm sorry I hit you with a rock."

After six well-placed swats on the curve of her pert

bottom, Toshiro felt more in control. He bent his head closer to hers when she craned her neck to look up at him. "You know that's not why I'm paddling you, Miss Stockwell. Let me know when you've decided suicide isn't the answer to your problems." He pulled back his arm.

"No, wait! All right." She sighed, then rested her head on the backs of her arms. "I wasn't trying to kill myself the second time," she admitted. "I was just trying to get away from you."

Slowly, he lifted her up to cradle her on his lap. "How relieved I am to hear it," he bit out, but his touch was now comforting.

Dizzy, Amy had to rest her head against his bare chest. "I've never seen you this way before. It frightened me."

He cupped her chin in his fingers. "Truly, *koneko*, I've never felt this way before. No woman I have ever known has been able to get under my skin the way you do. One minute I want to spank you, the next I want to smother your face with kisses."

She swallowed, then reached up to trace the familiar line of his jaw. When she viewed the cut on his face, she couldn't help wincing. "I'm sorry about that." She reached down to tear away a square of the thin nightgown and used it to blot his face. "I do not understand myself tonight. I'm usually quite deferential. Ask anyone in Bristol."

He took her ministering hand and kissed her fingers. "Everyone doesn't know you as I do, fiery lotus."

Lost in the look from his green eyes, the blond-haired woman could only stare transfixed as he continued holding her in his arms.

"Marry me," Toshiro whispered against her lips. He

kissed her eyes, her nose, the planes of her cheeks. All the while his hands stroked her body. His lips and tongue savored the salty taste of her skin.

"I . . . I can't, my darling," she whimpered. "It is impossible."

"Marry me," pressed the panther, just before he captured her lips, this time setting them both on fire with his passion. His hands slipped the sodden nightgown from her shoulders, and he began caressing her small, firm breasts. He teased the pink nipples until they became hard pebbles against his fingers.

He was sucking the very breath out of her, and all Amy could think of was her desire to yield everything to this man who was so thoroughly seducing her. She belonged to Toshiro, her mind and heart shouted. A moan of earthy pleasure tore from her when he gently nudged her legs apart and began stroking the inside of her naked thighs.

Overcome, Amy had to pull away. "Oh . . . I've never felt. . . ." She couldn't breathe. Perhaps it was the trauma of trying to drown herself; more likely it was this man's skillful lovemaking, but Amy Stockwell felt the world spin about her. "Please, I think I'm going to. . . ."

Alarmed, Toshiro scrutinized her face. "Amy, did you take any more of that damn tonic?" he demanded.

She tried to clear her head, but it was a losing battle. "I . . . I thought it would help give me courage. I . . . I've always been afraid of the wa . . . ter. Had to take two . . . glasses."

"Unko. Bloody hell." He caught her just in time when she pitched forward from his lap. With self-consternation, the count told himself he should have thought to ask if she'd ingested more of that damn—with her lovely

curves distracting him, he'd had little room in his fevered mind for other considerations just now.

He shoved all his attention on getting her safely out of here. First, she needed to get out of that wet nightgown. He felt for the steady beating of her heart, reassured she'd just swooned. God, what had this seductive creature done to him? He was a totally private person when it came to the physical intimacies between a man and a maiden. But in the space of an hour, Amy Stockwell had just incited him into turning her across his knee, followed by his making love to her—right outside in the open!

Gently, he placed her next to the rock and raced to Kori to get his heavy wool coat. In an instant he had the white gown off her. He tossed it on the rocks, then bundled her carefully into his dry coat. He lifted her in front of him. Automatically, he headed left toward her home.

Then he pulled back on the leather straps in his hands. He looked down below to see the white lacy nightgown, shining like a beacon among the rocks. He thought of Amy nestled in his arms, the evidence in Kori's saddlebags that proved someone close to her wanted her dead. Yet, what of the danger from that ninja who stalked him? He knew what he risked, what his actions now would mean to this proud beauty. With a warrior's resolve, Toshiro pressed Kori's flanks and turned the horse about to head in the opposite direction. He would take her where she belonged.

"Despite what you say, this is your karma," he told the unconscious girl he held protectively in his arms. "We will do it my way now," he vowed, losing all patience with his failed efforts to woo her in the proper English manner.

Thirteen

"Did she rid herself of the Avon?"

"Yes," Toshiro answered Keith Stewart. "But double amounts of that vile opium was already in her bloodstream by that time."

"No bones broken, pulse slow but steady." The Scot went about checking his patient. "She's going to sleep for a good while until that drug wears off. I think she'll be all right in a few days. But, damn it, man, no more opium. She's got to get off that stuff before it kills her."

"She will never take that cursed muck again," said Toshiro, his jaw set.

Keith glanced at the bloody line across his friend's cheek. "My Lord, I should tend to that, too."

Absently, Toshiro touched his face. "Please see to Amy first."

"How did you come by such a gash?" the doctor asked as he and Toshiro removed the count's wool coat from the unconscious girl.

"The lady took exception when I rescued her from drowning."

Upstairs in Toshiro's master bedroom, both men had

placed Amy on the huge four-poster bed. The Scot made a clinical examination of the front of her. Satisfied, he turned the girl over. His reddish-brown eyebrows moved to his hairline when he saw the unmistakable pink marks of a man's hand print on each round cheek of Amy's backside. Keith shot a glance at the man standing on the other side of the bed.

With his usual reserve, the count remarked, "Whereupon I showed Miss Stockwell the error of trying to drown herself a second time in the Avon."

"Well," said the Scot, "your engagement is certainly getting off to a verra unconventional beginning. A simple announcement in the social section would have sufficed."

"You don't know my future in-laws," quipped Toshiro.

After he finished with Amy and tended to the cut on his friend's cheek, Keith went about putting his items back into his wooden medical chest.

Toshiro dressed Amy in one of his lawn shirts that went down below her knees. Keith watched as the black-haired man gently lifted her onto the lavender-scented sheets, then tucked the blanket and coverlet over her. "My Lord, you realize what will happen if she stays here alone in your bed?"

"I am not a man of rash actions, as you should know from our school days, Keith." His expression was tender as he looked down at the girl sleeping in his English bed. "She is my responsibility now."

The Scot shook his head. "I hope you know what you're doing. I'll stop by the day after tomorrow to see how she is faring."

The count's face relaxed into a grateful smile. "Thank you for coming over so quickly."

"If you have need of me . . . well, you can count on my support," said the Scot.

"I have a feeling I will need all my friends in a few days. I'm not sure whether I dread Amy's wrath when she awakens more than the Townsends' when they find out my plan. In any event, I had better get to those letters I need to write."

After he wrote his missives, Toshiro washed hastily and put on clean clothes. Sitting down on a straight chair near the bed, he watched Amy. The single candle on the table next to the bed threw flickers of light across her fine-boned features. She looked like an angel, with her alabaster skin and golden hair billowing like a halo across the lacy pillow. When she whimpered, he leaned closer to her and stroked her forehead. "You are safe, my love. I'm here. No one will harm you. Sleep. Think only of the white lotuses on the pond as they turn with the slow ripples in the quiet water. Rest, *koneko*."

She smiled, then turned on her side, facing him with her eyes still closed. Cuddling the pillow closer to her, she murmured, "Mmm, yes, I'm safe with the panther."

A tender look in his green eyes, Toshiro leaned back against the chair. Amy had placed her trust in him, and her giving, passionate response earlier had pleased him. Yet, as the night wore on and he kept his self-imposed vigil at her bedside, Toshiro could not help wondering if his English rose would understand why he had to do this. Jarred by the thought of Masao's assassin, he got up and walked across the carpet in his stocking feet to recheck the latches on each multi-paned window. He looked out onto his moonlit garden, then pressed his forehead against the cool glass. God help him, he'd never forgive himself if any harm came to Amy through this blood feud between the Akashis and Masao Nishikawa's family. Understanding the stealth and skill of the ninja, he knew he'd have to leave for Nagasaki as soon as possible. He had to settle this matter of his father's murder immediately. Amy and he were both in danger until he did.

Feeling suddenly older than his late twenties, Count Valerius walked back and slumped down on the chair. He watched the sleeping young woman in his bed. But would this proud, determined Englishwoman ever forgive him for this night's work that now sealed her future forever with his?

"Lord love me, Toshiro, I feel like a lecherous old coot standing here." Joshua Rigby managed to keep his voice down to a whisper. He fingered his cravat as though it strangled him. "Keith here is a physician and used to such things, but I'll have you know I'm not accustomed to prowling about a lady's boudoir."

Under the covers, his naked back pressed against a pillow, Toshiro Valerius gave his solicitor a look of sympathy. "Amy will be awake soon. Keith has checked her. This won't take long."

Amy snuggled closer to the warm smooth chest. She felt a hand caress her right breast. "Mmm, I like that. Again," she purred, then stuck out her pink tongue and licked Toshiro's hairless skin.

"Amy," Toshiro whispered. He followed it with a soft kiss on the sensitive flesh of her earlobe. "Darling, we have visitors." He hoped she would wake soon, for his body was responding to her closeness, as it always did around this fascinating woman.

Amy smiled. "Ohh, I don't want to get up. Please kiss me again."

He chuckled and uncurled her arms from about his neck. "Later, ravenous one. When we do not have guests."

The last word made its way into Amy's foggy brain. She was instantly aware of a faint scent of spicy soap. She felt a man's muscular chest against her cheek, heard the familiar voice near her ear. Her eyes flashed open, but they took a moment to focus before she saw Count Valerius next to her. He was smiling at her, his straight black hair about his shoulders—God, he was naked! She sprang away from him and scurried to her side of the wide bed. She looked down at herself, shocked to discover she wasn't wearing anything but a man's white shirt. Pushing back her curly hair from her face, she looked quickly about the room. "Wh . . . where am I?"

"This is my English bedroom upstairs," Toshiro answered matter-of-factly.

Her mouth opened when she saw the pink cut on the count's cheek. Memories crashed against her. "My Lord, I . . . do regret all . . . especially hurling that rock at you last night."

He saw her shade her eyes from the sunny glare coming through the window. "Apology accepted, but I must correct you, my Amy. This is the morning after your second day here," he pointed out with emphasis.

It was then Amy turned and spotted Dr. Keith Stewart and Joshua Rigby standing on the other side of the room. "Love a duke, what are they doing here?"

Uncomfortable but with a solicitor's efficiency, Joshua spoke first. "We . . . ah . . . are witnesses."

"Witnesses?" Amy looked back at the man in bed next to her but could tell nothing from his expression. "My

Lord," she said, still grappling with the situation, "just where did you sleep last night . . . and the night before that?"

One dark eyebrow arched meaningfully. "Why, my dear, where do you suppose?"

She tried but failed to keep the crimson stain from surging across her face. "I can't remember anything after you. . . ." Her blush deepened as she recalled the pleasure that tore from her when Toshiro began touching her between her. . . . She darted an accusing glance at the Eurasian but was mortified to realize he'd mentally completed the lewd sentence for her, too, though Amy knew she was the only one who could see that slight change in his well-disciplined features.

Then a more pressing problem jarred her. "Oh," she cried, totally flustered. "Aunt Clarice, my uncles—my family will be frantic worrying about me. I must go to them at once." She made a motion to jump off the high mattress, only to feel two hands pull her back to the center of the bed.

"You will stay put, young lady," said Toshiro. "Dr. Stewart says you require at least one more day's rest." When he read the threat of mutiny on that pink mouth he'd kissed so thoroughly the other evening, the Eurasian held up his hand in a gesture for peace. "Rest assured I sent notes two nights ago to Stockwell Hall, as well as to each of your uncles. Knowing your friendship for the Earl of Woodcroft, I wrote him also, assuring him you were safely under my protection. Alas, I have been informed David is back in London again. However, he'll get the note upon his return."

"Thought of everything, haven't you?"

He noticed the hurricane warnings and decided a temporary retreat was more prudent at the moment. "Keith, will you please hand me my robe on the hook behind you? I'd better shave and dress before the Townsends arrive."

Keith brought his friend the black Japanese robe with the Akashi crest on the back and sleeves.

With a squawk of alarm, Amy clamped her eyes shut when she felt the bed jostle as Toshiro got up. The last thing she expected was having the count prance about stark naked in front of her.

"You can open your eyes, shy one," said the count. "I will never understand your English aversion to nudity. We Japanese are more practical about such natural things as covering."

Her eyes flew open. "But nothing will cover that black devil's soul of yours."

This time he looked amused. "Reminds me of something Simon wrote and left downstairs yesterday when I would not let him see you. I believe his exact words were, 'I am unfit to live.' "

"My uncle came to see me yesterday and you refused . . . ? You had no right to treat a member of my family so callously. I'll not stand for it."

Toshiro's equanimity came with more effort this time. She'd never listen to his suspicions concerning her broken wheelchair right now. "You were still sleeping away the effects of that opium."

"Opium? What are you talking about? I took only two glasses of my tonic. Dr. Wakefield assures me it is only herbs and extracts from plants to soothe and help me rest at night."

Both Keith and Toshiro gave her a grim look. "Madam," said the count, biting out each word at her gullibility. "For the last four years Wakefield, with your relatives' compliance and your blind acceptance, has been pouring laudanum into you, of which opium is the main ingredient."

Horrified, Amy looked first to Rigby, Dr. Stewart, then back to Toshiro. "I never . . . I didn't realize. . . ." Something in their expressions told her Toshiro spoke the truth. "But it did help me sleep," she managed in a small voice. "Surely a little of it each night could never—"

Toshiro swore in Japanese.

Keith cleared his throat. "Miss Stockwell, I have every reason to believe from what the count has told me, you have been getting quite a lot more than is . . . medically prudent. Your body may crave that drug for a short time, and it will not be easy for you to give it up."

"But," interjected Toshiro as he walked over to the bed, "give it up you will. Never, do you hear, will I allow that vile stuff near you again. Do you understand my meaning?"

Count Valerius stood over her like a dark, avenging angel. She swallowed, reminding herself of her vulnerable position at the moment. Attired only in his shirt, sequestered in the panther's lair, she made a critical inventory of her position. Only a temporary state, but there it was. Shrewdly, she decided to bide her time. David would come for her and so would her relatives. She met his unrelenting gaze. "I comprehend better than you know, my Lord."

Believing the matter settled, Toshiro excused himself and went toward the next room.

"A moment, my Lord."

Hope sprang within him, for her voice had that usual sweetness. "Yes, Amy?"

Having dealt with rough sea captains for years and not totally unaware of the seamier side of life, Amy sized up the situation with her late father's critical methods. And, she noted, the conniving scoundrel before her had provided his own witnesses. The owner of Stockwell Enterprises stared up at her adversary. "I'm on to your game. David tried to warn me but more fool I, because I thought your Way of the Warrior code, your outward appearance as a man of honor would make this occurrence impossible. I was wrong. Well, Valerius, spit it out. Joshua can send for my money this day and have the coins in your hands by nightfall. How much do you want to keep this matter quiet?"

Toshiro recoiled from her question. "You believe I did this to extract money from you?"

With a bitter laugh, Amy ignored the shock on all three male faces. "I'm no green girl just out of the schoolroom. My father told me about your kind," she added with disdain. "I'm certain you won't be the last blackmailer I'm forced to deal with." She gave his robe-draped physique a critical once-over. "Only I never realized they came in such attractive packages."

This time it was Toshiro who colored in humiliation. She stared at him as if he were a prize stud horse she contemplated purchasing. Her vile accusation cut, then enraged him. With all the self-control he could muster, he thrust his hands behind his back. "Money has nothing to do with this. Now, if you will excuse me." Nodding curtly to Keith and Joshua, he walked out of the room, his rigid posture belying his calmly spoken words.

Sumi brought up tea and muffins for the men, then returned with breakfast for Amy on a tray.

Amy pulled the coverlet up to her chin. When she looked down at the slab of ham next to fried potatoes and eggs, she realized she was hungry. Practicality won over her first inclination to toss the tray on the floor in defiance. If she hoped to penetrate the count's unflappable reserve, she would need all her strength. Without speaking, she went about cleaning her plate. She heard Toshiro laugh at something Iwao said in the next room as he helped his master wash and dress for his English guests. Well, she thought, gulping down the hot tea, the panther had a surprise coming if he thought he could get the better of Amy Stockwell. Frowning, she realized she had no memory of the last two nights. But if Toshiro wasn't after her money, what the devil did he want? She looked down at herself. Or had the Black Knight already taken what he wanted? The thought unsettled her.

Toshiro came back into the room.

Amy could not deny he looked the well-dressed Englishman in black coat and breeches, an embroidered waistcoat over a pristine shirt, his hair tied neatly back against his coat collar. Save for his Eurasian features, he could have been any aristocrat just coming from a private audience with King George.

Then Amy heard the voices of her uncles downstairs. Keith Stewart quickly excused himself. She couldn't blame him for wanting to leave. How she wished to go, too.

Toshiro watched the way Amy clutched the bedcovers in her hands. Why couldn't she realize she did not have to be anxious over the Townsends' reaction anymore? She looked so small and alone in his bed, for an instant he wanted to bar the door and spare her what was about to take place. But he knew they could not go back. He took a deep breath, then nodded for Sumi to open the door.

After Iwao directed the four Townsends into the room, both Japanese servants bowed and left.

Amy was moved by her relatives' worried expressions.

"Gad, it's worse than I imagined," declared Simon. "If that manservant hadn't forced us to leave our dress swords downstairs, I'd run you through," he told the count. Then he eyed Toshiro's cheek. "Looks as if someone already skewered you. David been here?"

"I believe," Toshiro answered, "the earl is in London."

Clarice Townsend sobbed into her limp handkerchief. "My poor lamb," she cried and would have fallen if Giles hadn't placed an arm about his sister's shoulders. She leaned on him heavily as he led her over to Amy.

Amy almost burst into tears herself to see her aunt suffering so. Clarice was hysterical. "Please, Clari, you will make yourself ill. I'm unharmed," she said, trying to calm her aunt.

"Unharmed?" repeated Clarice, her dark eyes aghast. "Oh, it is not to be borne. My poor brave lamb." This was followed by more sobbing into the rumpled piece of cloth. "If only David hadn't been called away again to London, his shoulder hardly healed. This will probably kill that sweet boy." Clarice glowered up at the count who stood on the other side of Amy's bed. "When David returns, I hope he runs you through. Castration would be too good for you."

"Dear me," squeaked Giles. "Most distressing." He looked at his niece. "Your father would turn over in his grave if he knew what had happened."

Henry gave Toshiro a combative stare. "You bounder.

Ruining the girl, then having the audacity to send notes all around."

Simon almost popped the buttons on his yellow waistcoat as he confronted the count. "Henry's two mistresses knew about it even before we did. Amy's nightgown was seen blatantly hung across the main sail of the *Nightingale*. It flapped all day in the breeze right in the center of Bristol harbor until one of your crew finally took it down this morning. You've made Amy and all the Townsends a laughingstock."

Amy's blond head snapped up at this unexpected news. She glared at Toshiro, but he was back listening to Simon.

"All Bristol is abuzz with the scandal," Simon continued. "Damn me, Valerius, why didn't you just fly a banner from the eaves of this house proclaiming, 'Amy Stockwell is being ruined within'?"

Toshiro cleared his throat. "I think Amy and I should discuss the rest of this in private later."

"Don't let a crowd stop you," countered Amy. "Let's have it all out in the open, Valerius, since you've clearly sought to discredit me in such a public way. Continue, Uncle Simon."

Simon folded his beefy arms across his chest. "Well, my brothers and I are here to see you do right by the girl."

Toshiro nodded. "I am prepared to marry her immediately. From the beginning I wished to wed your niece. However, you have all succeeded in convincing Amy she is an invalid, both physically and emotionally." His expression condemned them. "You have made her believe she is incapable of having a normal life. I intend to prove otherwise."

"Hold on," said Amy, suddenly alarmed at this turn of events. "Stow that talk. I'm not marrying anyone," she declared, but no one paid any attention.

She tried again. "Uncle Simon, we must remember the count is still not accustomed to our ways. I fainted. He merely wished to see me cared for. I am sure he did not stop to consider our English views on such matters when he brought me here."

Aware it would go better for him if he remained silent, nevertheless, Toshiro spoke up. "No, Amy, I will not start our married life with a lie. I knew exactly what I was doing when I turned Kori away from your home toward mine. I gave the order to have your nightdress run up the halyards of my ship. Compromising a lady is the same in any language."

Horrified, Amy couldn't get any words out.

But Clarice did. "You, sir, are certainly no gentleman."

"Yes," agreed Henry, "he's lower than pig dung, you tell him, Clarice. Only a knave would ruin a girl after she fainted."

Amy winced at that word again.

Clarice straightened. "It is common knowledge, my Lord, that poor Amy will never bear children. Sons are all important to you Japanese, especially since you are the last of your house."

Toshiro never flinched. "Miss Townsend, Amy should soon begin her monthly flow regularly again. There is no reason she cannot—"

"Stop!" Amy shouted, her face scarlet. "Cease discussing me as if I weren't even in the bloody room. And you," she accused the count. "No well-bred man would ever mention such details about a lady in public."

"Your pardon, Amy, but I did try to persuade you to

allow me to finish this conversation in the privacy of our rooms later."

The reminder did nothing but rankle. Her chin came up. "Answer my question. Who told you about the return of . . . ? Don't lie to me and blame Clarice. My aunt is too much a lady for such vulgarity with a complete stranger."

That pricking at the back of his neck started again. "Of course, I realize nothing can be certain until . . . later. However, it was Keith Stewart who spoke with me. That afternoon after David and I crossed swords and I brought you here, he examined you and asked you questions about—"

"All right," she cut off, cursing herself for not remembering she had answered Dr. Stewart's pointed inquiries. Amy hunted for another weapon.

He did regret making her uncomfortable. "It was my concern for your health that prompted me to speak to Keith that way. I would never seek to harm or embarrass you.

"How touching," Amy replied scornfully. "So sensitive to my good name that you wouldn't back down when David made a verbal misstep and challenged you to a duel. Yet, I notice no compunction when you brought me here, even though Stockwell Hall was an equal distance away." She saw his expression change and knew her barb had struck a nerve. "Why are you doing this?"

He knew she would never believe the truth now. Instead he stated, "I thought it best since you said you would not marry me on more than one occasion. When you lost consciousness, I decided to take matters into my own hands."

Something snapped within her at his calm proclamation. "Well, since the count needs an heir and my breeding prospects are shaky at best, Valerius, just shove the damn bed aside and you can mount me right here on the floor. We'll just wait nine months to see if you're correct. Sounds like a logical plan to me."

"Amy," he warned, "you are sailing on dangerous waters."

"Barnacle balls. I want to know what dirty little games you are playing here."

Silence.

"You bastard, answer me!"

The muscle against his jaw clenched. "I shall be truly angry with you in a minute if you do not curb that profanity. Two nights ago when you tried drowning yourself a second time, you learned my patience is not an ocean."

She squirmed automatically across the mattress but managed to give him an unfriendly look. "Don't expect thanks for taking advantage of me when I was unconscious."

He looked appalled. "Taking advantage?"

Her chin lifted. "Don't give me that inscrutable look. What did you do to me while I slept?"

A ruddy hue stained his features. "Your maidenhead is still intact . . . is that blatant enough for you?"

"Then why in hell are you doing this?"

He saw the strain on her face and knew she was close to exhaustion. "Because you refused my offer of marriage too many times. While this is not the way I'd prefer to have you become my wife, your stubbornness has forced me into seizing this opportunity when you fainted two evenings ago."

"Fiend," Clarice called him.

"I won't marry you," Amy said again, this time with more force. "So all your plotting has been for nothing."

As Toshiro expected, her three uncles did not agree.

"Now," Simon began, "don't be hasty, Amy. Think of the family. Your cousins wouldn't be able to show their faces in polite society if Valerius doesn't make an honest woman of you."

Amy couldn't believe her uncles, who were so against Toshiro from the beginning, were now pressuring her to marry him.

Clarice leaned over and patted Amy's shoulder. "Don't you let them bully you, my dear. You don't have to marry that man if you don't want to." She scowled at the count. "Amy and I know you just want her money."

Toshiro glared at the Englishwoman. "I will not touch Amy Stockwell's money or property. Mr. Rigby is also here as a witness that Amy's will stays as written."

Amy rubbed her throbbing temples. "If it isn't money, and you haven't had your way with me, there is no bloody reason for us to marry."

Simon didn't give Toshiro a chance to speak. "Of course you have to marry him. Even if the rakehell hasn't humped you, he might as well have, for your reputation is now in shreds. David could never overlook your peccadilloes."

Amy flushed. "I don't want David or anyone to overlook my peccadilloes, as you call them."

"Ah ha," Simon piped up. "Then you did let that Chinaman mount you?"

"No!" she shouted. Spots of color blossomed on each cheek. "And for the hundredth time, Uncle Simon, Toshiro is Dutch and Japanese; he is not Chinese."

"What will the neighbors say?" demanded Giles.

"Mutton face is right," spouted Henry. "Amy, you've got to marry—"

The door opened and Dr. Norbert Wakefield shuffled in.

"Damnation," Toshiro muttered. "This is all we need now."

Clarice went right over to the wigged physician. "Thank you for meeting us here, Norbert. You must see to our poor Amy at once."

When Amy saw Toshiro get ready to intercede, she blocked him. "My Lord, I beg a few moments alone with my family and our doctor. Will you and Joshua wait in the next room for half an hour? You must admit this is a momentous decision for me, and I need to discuss it with them."

Wary, yet not able to resist the sudden pleading in her blue eyes, Toshiro nodded his reluctant acceptance. He followed Joshua out the door into the next room. However, the look he gave Amy over his shoulder told her he wasn't going to change his mind.

Fourteen

Joshua Rigby sat in the count's sitting room with his hands folded across his chest. He watched the man next to him on the gold-covered sofa. "Surely, you're not going to sit here and allow that to continue. Listen to them."

The Eurasian frowned. "Amy asked me to stay away for one half hour." He glanced at the brass clock that hung against the light wallpaper. "She has fifteen more minutes."

Joshua shook his head but said nothing more.

Didn't Rigby realize it was taking all his self-control to stay put?

Henry and Simon were at it again. Now Giles added his nervous opinion. "Your mother was insane, but she was a good sort," Toshiro heard Giles point out. "She knew her duty and did it in marrying your father to provide for the Townsends. Just think about your innocent cousins. The girls will need dowries, the boys their Grand Tours. Even if you don't marry that yellow swine, the finest families all over England will cease doing business with Stockwell Enterprises. However, if you married the count, at least they'd see you were willing to pay for your mistakes. You'd be respectable again."

"Damn me," Simon intoned, "I don't know which I loathe more: A Jappo for an in-law or a niece whose become a fallen woman. Come, Amy, you have no choice. David can't offer for you now. The earl has his own family's position to think of. He's taken enough guff from his parents because you were in trade, not even titled. Now that you're ruined, that avenue is closed to us. Only one thing you can do: You have to marry Valerius to save the family. You won't want poor Clarice on the streets, tossed from the family home? You know that heathen doesn't like us."

"No, of course, I would never abandon you," Toshiro heard Amy say, her voice timorous. "You know I've always taken care of you. But . . . isn't there some way we could just say it was all a tasteless joke, that I was never ravished, and—"

"Bah," said Henry, "the news has already gone past Bristol. No one would believe the count hasn't mounted you."

Knowing the gossips, Amy could not deny it. And she suddenly felt selfish for not considering how this would affect her innocent Townsend cousins if her business collapsed and the family fortune dried up. Like her father before her, she was the breadwinner of this family. "Yes, I suppose you are right. I'm trapped, then."

Toshiro rubbed his hands across his knees in agitation. His plan to marry Amy was going awry. He wanted her to marry him because she cared for him, not because she saw herself as a sacrificial lamb. Those uncles were grooming her as the martyred offering to a foreign devil to save the family fortune. Henry demanded, "Amy, you don't mean to take the bread right out of our mouths?" When Simon started calling Henry "mutton face" and the arguments began, Toshiro bounded to his feet.

With a lopsided grin Joshua moved his large frame off the couch to follow. "Thought that last part would do it," he muttered, glad Toshiro wasn't going to let Amy endure any more of this.

Without knocking, Toshiro pushed the door open and stalked into his English bedroom. The sight that greeted him ignited his frayed emotions. Amy was reclining against the pillows, the sleeves of his shirt that she wore were rolled up, the top three buttons open. There were brown slimy creatures on her arms and one at the base of her neck. With a growl of pure rage, he charged over to her and began pulling off the loathsome leeches. He gripped the slippery creatures in his hands, shouting to Joshua, "Open the bloody window before I use my foot."

Joshua pushed up on the window frame.

Toshiro tossed the offending leeches down the three stories to the gray flagstones outside. He whirled on Dr. Wakefield. "You, sir, are a . . . a duck!"

Rigby translated to the befuddled physician. "I believe his Lordship is calling you a 'quack.' "

Without another word, Toshiro went over to his dresser and opened a drawer. He searched impatiently until he came up with a leather bag. Returning, he thrust the bag of gold coins into Wakefield's veined hands. "This should more than compensate for the loss of your patient."

Wakefield peered into the bag, clearly amazed at the generous amount. "I don't know what to say. Amy has always been one of my fondest patients, and—"

"Take the money and go," Toshiro advised. "Never do

I want you near my future wife again. Do you understand?"

Norbert turned his watery gaze back to Amy. "Is this your wish, Miss Stockwell?"

Amy thought of Toshiro's disclosure about the opium. Though she would not admit it to the count, she did like Keith Stewart's practical nature. "Yes, I think it would be best. I thank you for all your years of service to my mother and me, but I am quite recovered now," she lied. "It would not be fair to your other, more needy patients to take up your valuable time." Amy could tell from Toshiro's stance, he was just seconds away from hoisting this old man out the same window where he'd tossed the leeches.

Obviously more interested in his money, Norbert shrugged, picked up his tattered box of medical supplies, and prepared to leave.

"You cannot mean this, Amy," cried Clarice. When Amy didn't answer, she looked more alarmed when Norbert left. "And you mean to marry this horrid man?"

No reply.

"Well," said Simon, "I'll grant you, Clarice, his Jappo blood does nothing for him, but at least he is a count. With that Dutch title to fall back on, we can emphasize the Holland guff to our friends and play down his peasant Jappo blood, and—"

"Shut up!" snarled the count, completely out of patience.

Everyone in the room quieted. Even Amy sensed the peril.

Toshiro condemned Amy's relatives with his frosty expression. "Since the moment I sailed into Bristol, I have heard nothing except your disparaging comments about the Akashis. Know that I am proud of both my Dutch and Japanese heritage. I make no apology for either. How dare you criticize the Akashis, whose noble ancestors go back thousands of years, descending from the first emperors of Japan. My honorable uncle is the daimyo, the feudal lord of the province."

Simon looked irritated. "Well, why the hell didn't you say so, letting us all think you were spawned from some peasant hag in a rice field and—"

"Unlike you English," Toshiro cut off, "who are obsessed with aristocratic titles and pedigree, I was taught only boorish louts go about bragging to others of their family status."

The Townsend brothers scowled. Simon spoke first. "We at Stockwell Hall are—"

"Or Pisspot Hall as it is known along the docks," Toshiro interjected with satisfaction. "A rather apt description, given that George Stockwell made his first fortune from the manufacture and sale of chamber pots."

Amy, of course, knew this as did the rest of the family. However, her uncles appeared scandalized; Clarice near apoplexy.

"Oh," Clarice spurted, "how crude of you, how ignoble. Sir, we never mention such things."

Toshiro gave the dark-haired woman a reproachful look. "It is not George Stockwell's hard beginnings that I take exception to, Miss Townsend. It is the arrogance of those relatives who benefitted from his efforts, now his daughter's, that galls me. You spout affection for your niece and in the same breath badger her to marry me because you're afraid you'll lose your comfortable lifestyle."

Amy winced. Dr. Wakefield had seen her nervous state

earlier and said the leeches would help. She'd been ready to grab at anything to see this horrible day over. "Please stop," she whispered, more upset because she couldn't hide her distress. "Oh, what is the use . . . I can't fight all of you at the same time. Please, will you all just leave me alone."

Toshiro's anger fled in a rush of self-recrimination at her outcry. He cursed himself for having driven her to this. Her tears tore at him. Automatically, he came over to the bed, sat down, and took her in his arms. He held her the way one might comfort a forlorn child. "I'm sorry, Amy. I never meant it to be like this." It was true, he'd been fool enough to hope, once she got over her irritation, she'd see they belonged together. He hadn't counted on her deep pride. "I only wanted to protect you, be responsible for you," he whispered near her ear. "Isn't there some way you could find marrying me not a fate worse than death?"

Amy found herself responding to his tender ministrations and outrageous question. He really could be so supportive at these times. "My lord, I'm weary and confused right now. In this state I think I'd marry Grog just to get some peace."

"Darling," he called her, now determined to see that she got some needed rest. He let her move back against the pillows and settled the covers about her. Then he took her hand in his. "Will you trust me one more time to have a care for your welfare?"

She saw the pleading in his eyes and felt her resolve weaken, but she was still wary.

"Amy Stockwell," he continued, as he gently held her hands in his. "Will you do me the great honor of becoming my wife? I ask for nothing more, and you may set the terms of this marriage. You will continue running Stockwell Enterprises as before. I will not touch a cent of your money or your property. I only ask that you marry me and live here, not at Stockwell Hall."

"That is all you ask?" Amy repeated.

"It is," he stated truthfully, now aware her safety had become so important to him, he was willing to give up his hopes that she would love him, want him as a true husband.

She looked down at his hands, unable to meet his gaze. "Then you will not . . . force your attentions on me?"

Trapped by his own words, he winced at her direct question. Did she find him so loathsome even the idea of his touch filled her with horror? Old insecurities jeered at him. However, he forced himself to answer in a way even the Townsends would understand. "I promise if you marry me, Amy Stockwell, I will not make love to you unless you ask me. Ask me politely," he amended.

She couldn't believe her good fortune. "Then I am free of connubial chores."

Her pleased expression gnawed at him, but there was nothing he could do.

She thought this over. Knowing him as she did, she knew Toshiro would not break his word. "I will not change my mind, but I'm willing to leave the matter of sharing my bed open to discussion until after we are married."

"Wait just a minute here," said Henry. "No Englishman worth his salt could hold to such a vow."

For once Simon agreed with his younger brother. "My Lord, you'll have blue balls before the honeymoon is over," he scoffed.

Giles was busy supporting Clarice, who appeared

ready to swoon at the realization her niece was actually going to marry Count Valerius.

Toshiro looked every inch the samurai trained in Bushido as he peered down his nose at the Townsends. "As you have pointed out repeatedly, I *am not* English. I will keep that promise."

Convinced he would keep his word, Amy wasn't sure why she wasn't more pleased by the realization she'd now be a countess and a wife . . . a virgin wife, she corrected.

When her uncles told her that the wedding would take place at Stockwell Hall in one week, Amy could not hide her shock. After she mentioned the unseemly haste, her uncles pointed out that was even waiting too long to make an honest woman of her. She fumed in silence, aware this was an argument she couldn't win. Toshiro was no help, for he just nodded his agreement with her uncles.

Amy sat in a chair. Even for early summer, the evening was cool, and she was grateful for the fire. She watched the embers in the pink marble fireplace. Somehow she felt more secure here than in the room behind her. Though the four-post bed at Valerius Hall was comfortable, and she had Toshiro's word he would not make love to her, Amy felt anything but joyous on her wedding night.

She thought of the past week. Her uncles and aunt had bustled about, planning the private ceremony. Feeling David deserved to learn the news from her, Amy wrote him a letter. She only told David that after careful consideration, she'd decided to accept the count's proposal.

She didn't mention the circumstances that led to the reluctant decision. David would hear the gossip soon enough.

Determined to keep things as normal as possible, Amy had gone about her daily work of running her business. She saw the count each morning. He was attentive and patient. She congratulated herself on being able to manage an aura of English control. A few times she sensed Toshiro was frustrated by her lack of enthusiasm, but to her way of thinking, he only had himself to blame for manipulating her into this ill-advised marriage.

The gold band on her finger reminded her of the solemn ceremony this morning. It was more like a funeral than a wedding. Her Aunt Clarice wept from their exchange of vows right through the wedding breakfast. So morose, her uncles hardly fought with each other. Joshua Rigby acted as the count's supporter. Iwao and Sumi added the only festive color to the occasion. The elderly Anglican priest nearly fainted when Iwao came out dressed in his Japanese clothes. It was then Amy realized why his left shoulder drooped. Iwao carried the long and short swords of a samurai warrior in the sash of his purple kimono. Sumi wore an exquisite kimono of yellow and gold. Both garments contained the crest of the Akashis embroidered on the material.

Toshiro had been striking in formal English beige coat and breeches, gold waistcoat below a white neckband. It was clear he wanted to show Amy and her relatives he meant to honor her as his English bride. The groom gave his new wife a brief kiss on the cheek after the ceremony. Attentive, he'd turned to speak with her often during the wedding breakfast. Once, when he reached under the table to caress her cold fingers, she gave him a quick smile of gratitude. Of course, she reminded herself, he'd gotten what he wanted. One could almost say he looked triumphant as he led her out to his carriage to take her to his estate next door. Amy wished the ride to Valerius Hall had taken longer. When he looked like he might resurrect the English custom of carrying the bride over the threshold, something in her expression must have warned him against the intimation that she now "belonged to him." Instead, he'd bowed and allowed her to walk before him into Valerius Manor.

Yes, she cared for him, enjoyed his company. He was intelligent and charming. And never had she felt such a physical response to a man. Not even David's kisses had stirred her the way Valerius could. That was the problem. She was positive her feelings were not reciprocated. An English wife probably suited his purposes right now, and knowing some of the difficulties he faced because he was part Japanese, the count had shrewdly taken an English wife with money and position when the opportunity presented itself. As a successful businesswoman, she could not fault him there. He said this was for her own good; she doubted it. She'd tried to warn him of the dangers, of her tainted blood; he did not believe her capable of murder. While part of Amy welcomed his faith in her, she cringed when she pictured his expression when he finally learned the truth. It might take months or years, but somehow she was certain to fail him. Her illness would only get worse, and there would come a time when she could no longer hide it. Toshiro would see her for what she was: someone quite capable of violence. She shivered, despite the heat of the room. It was lucky she couldn't bear children, she thought, then bit her lower lip. Anyway, Toshiro had given his word not to make love to her. If she stayed calm and detached, perhaps they both might have a year or two of peace.

Remaining calm, that was the difficult part. She rubbed her wrists along the cloth-covered arms of the chair. So used to Clarice bringing her Dr. Wakefield's tonic each night, she now felt the growing need for it.

Startled when someone knocked on the door, Amy took a moment to answer. "Come in."

Instead of Toshiro, she was surprised to see Iwao enter the suite of rooms that had formerly belonged to his master. He bowed.

His close-cropped gray hair combed back, Iwao was now in his English livery of shirt and breeches. Aware he said little, Amy knew this man did not approve of his master's choice for a wife. She looked up at him. For once, his disdainful mask of reserve was not in place. It was evident he found beginning this conversation awkward. "Yes, Iwao?"

His guttural voice was softer tonight. "Countess, I wish to explain something. My wife asked me to see you while the count is downstairs seeing to other matters."

It was the first time anyone used that title. Rather than flatter her, it made Amy uneasily aware of her changed status. "Is there something you wish to say, Iwao?"

"Yes." Taking a breath, in the manner of readying for battle, Iwao plunged ahead. "My master forbade Sumi to explain that day to you. Though he would not like it if he knew I enlightened you now, I am under no order for silence. That day you learned Lord Valerius had...."

Amy frowned. "Beaten Sumi, you mean."

"I would not have used that word, but it is the matter I refer to. Sumi said she believes it hangs heavily against you, causing you unwarranted distress. I, too, can see by your reaction now, it still affects your feelings for my Lord Valerius. You see, my Lady, Sumi took the count's suggestion that she watch over you as a strict matter of family honor. There was much shame to her and for me, as her husband, that she failed in that duty."

At a loss, Amy said, "But my aunt forced her out of our home, and I was in no condition to see what was happening. Surely, you can see it wasn't Sumi's fault that she left."

Iwao shook his head. "The count said the same thing to Sumi when he raced back here to find Sumi preparing to commit seppuku." At Amy's puzzled expression, he translated. "Ritual suicide. It was the only way my wife could save face. I would assist her."

"Good God." Amy shuddered, positive she didn't want to know how this samurai meant to aid his wife. "But, Iwao, beating anyone is totally against all I believe. I still do not know how Toshiro could act so brutally."

"Brutal?" Iwao's expression changed to being affronted. "My master did not cut her skin, he used bamboo, not a studded strap. Even in his lady mother's house, punishments are three times as severe. Lady Akashi still berates her son for being too lenient with his servants. It is the same in Amsterdam. My Lord will not change his gentler ways."

Iwao saw Amy's face change as she mulled over his words. "I thought you should know how much it cost Toshiro to do what he did. It was the first time he'd ever beaten anyone, let alone the woman who'd taken care of him in childhood. He did it to save my wife's face, so that she would not kill herself. He did it because he knew I would be more severe, and it was Count Valerius's place as master of his house. But only Sumi and I know how much it wounded him. I will never forget the torment in his eyes. Sumi made him tea afterward, but he could not drink it. He stayed out in his Japanese garden all night, alone, at war within himself. My wife wished you to know this."

Amy could not speak. It did release her from one item that had made her reluctant to enter into this marriage. Since she'd seen Sumi's back, Amy had been wrestling with the contradictory images of Toshiro Valerius. It had unnerved her because all she'd known and experienced with Toshiro up to that moment had never prepared her for that morning. Even seeing him angry when she'd tried to drown herself a second time, he had never been cruel. Iwao and Sumi were correct. This had been bothering her. "Thank you," she told her husband's equerry. "I appreciate your sharing the truth with me. It has helped."

There was the faintest flicker of warmth in Iwao's dark eyes, but then he bowed and left.

As the minutes went by, Amy became more agitated. She stood up and began pacing back and forth about the sitting room. Hot then cold, she went over to the cherry wood table behind her and picked up one of her logbooks. She'd brought it over in a trunk full of her papers, accounts, and reports. Perhaps if she tried doing a little work, she could take her mind off this nervous strain that clawed at her insides. Yet, when she sat in the chair and attempted to read her entries, she couldn't concentrate. Toshiro should never have insisted she stop taking her tonic. Opium or not, she needed something to soothe her.

Her husband knocked, then entered their room.

Amy looked up to see that he'd changed from his wedding attire into more casual clothes of brown breeches, linen shirt, tan stockings above unadorned shoes. He carried a small ceramic bottle and two lacquered cups.

He smiled at her. "I thought we could have some sake."

Closing her book with more force than necessary, his bride clutched the volume tightly against her chest. "That was thoughtful of you," she managed. She could only watch as he put the tray down, lifted the tea table, and brought it over next to her. Her husband returned with another chair and placed it on the other side of the table. He poured the warm rice wine into each cup and handed her one.

She couldn't keep her hand from shaking when she took the cup from his fingers.

He studied her closely. He noted the stress on her face and knew the cause. "Amy, Dr. Stewart says this discomfort will pass in time. It is just your body's reaction to being denied the opium."

His soothing words had the opposite effect. She put the sake cup down so abruptly, some of the clear liquor sloshed over the side of the red rim. "Don't patronize me. I need that tonic to sleep. I always have."

"You will soon learn to sleep without it."

"Forgive me, but I'm not up to your warrior code that lets you face everything with a stoic reserve." Amy got up and returned to pacing back and forth, holding her arms against her chest. Regretting her harsh words, she knew her husband couldn't understand what she was going through. "I don't have your self-discipline, my Lord, so will you kindly leave me alone. There must be some other entertainment you can find tonight instead of watching me climb the walls."

Toshiro set his cup down and got up to join her.

Amy could not believe it when he started walking back and forth with her. His features were set, so she wasn't certain but demanded, "How can you mock me?"

He did not look at her or break his stride, but he reached down and took her hand in his. "I am with you in this, Amy."

He said it so sincerely, she could not do battle with him. It must have been over an hour that Amy pushed herself back and forth across the room. Despite her earlier irritation, Toshiro's warm hand against hers was comforting. Finally, her legs wobbled, and she knew she had to sit down. Toshiro led her back over to their chairs. She put her head in her hands. "You must be tired, my Lord. I shall not keep you from your bed. I will be all right now," she added, with more bravado than certainty.

"Amy, I spoke with Keith last week, and he thought my idea might help. Come, I have a present for you."

On guard, she looked across at him. "I'm not a child who requires toys to insure good behavior. Nor am I about to do myself or this room injury if that is what worries you.

"Point taken," he conceded. "But will you trust me? Come." He held out his hand to her.

She looked down at his hand. So strong and sure. She needed an anchor right now. Slowly, she placed her shaking right hand in his.

Fifteen

Toshiro led his bride downstairs to the Eastern Wing. Too distraught by her body's craving for the drug that would bring her sleep, Amy let him remove her bedroom slippers. He slipped off his shoes, then slid open the paper partition that led to his Japanese rooms. Past his sitting room with the Buddhist altar, past his bedroom, then into the dimly lighted room that she had briefly spotted after Toshiro had the duel with David.

Tonight steam rose from stones above a long, narrow brazier along one wall. She felt the tiles under her stocking feet. Her already clammy body protested this hot room. Silently, she watched Toshiro walk over and test the water with his hand in the six-by-six-foot wooden tub. "My Lord, I don't think—"

"You agreed to trust me." He followed with an engaging smile. "I wanted to be sure it was not too hot. I specifically warmed the water to a lower temperature than I prefer."

Amy couldn't hide her astonishment. Bathing preparations and heating her sake had been the tasks Toshiro performed on his wedding night? There were steps near the deep tub of water. Recalling David's words about the count's preference for bathing each night, Amy wasn't sure how this would work. At home, one of the maids usually assisted with the brass tub before the fire. The prospect of a bath did appeal to her right now. When he made no motion to leave but began rolling up the sleeves of his shirt, she grew alarmed. "I assure you, my Lord, I am quite capable of bathing myself."

"Ah," he answered smoothly, "but I want to show you the joys of the Japanese bath. And it is my pleasure to do this. I think it will help calm you."

Calm was the last thing Amy felt at the prospect of disrobing in front of her husband. True, he'd already seen her naked when he slipped her out of that wet nightgown a week ago and dressed her in his shirt. But that was different. She'd been unconscious then. Right now all her senses shouted caution. "Thank you, but I would prefer privacy."

"Come, English rose." Then he chuckled at her expression. "Maidenly shyness is one thing, but we are married now, my dear."

Perhaps it was his boyish smile or calling her dear, or the logic of his words, but she relented a little. Best test the emotional waters first, she told herself. "All right, my Lord, but I remind you of your promise."

For a brief second, sadness entered his green eyes, but he nodded his assent. "I will not forget my promise, Amy-san. Of all my faults, and I possess many, have I ever broken a promise to you?"

She thought about their times together and found he spoke the truth. Self-conscious, she looked down at her bare toes. After loosening the pink ribbon at her throat, she began undoing the buttons that went the length of the flowered robe. "I should like to thank you for all the beautiful clothes in my wardrobe," she said, both from gratitude and needing to cloak her nervousness. Her fingers still shook from the distress of not having her laudanum, and she was relieved when her husband took over unbuttoning her robe.

"You are welcome. I understand you have not had too many opportunities to shop in London or Paris during the last few years. All brides should have a trousseau." When he noticed his words reminded her of their haste in marrying, he regretted them. Yet, why couldn't Amy realize she wasn't the only one disquieted tonight? Did she hate him? The thought almost undid him, but he forced himself to face the possibility. The way Amy looked up at him now, trying to trust him despite her trepidations, made him more determined to cherish her. He slipped the nightgown over her head and placed it neatly on one of the low tables. "If you sit down on that wooden stool over there, I'll wash you."

"You mean we don't do it in the tub?"

"No, we clean ourselves outside first. In Japan many people often bathe in the same tub or bathhouse. We are a crowded country and cannot always afford the luxury of a private bath."

She went over to the stool where he waited for her. She recalled the expression on his face when they were at the spa in Clifton. Despite herself, she giggled. "Oh, Toshiro, no wonder you looked aghast when you saw the bathing pool at the spa. I thought you were going to bolt for the door."

He smiled but did not comment.

Amy watched him take a small wooden bucket and fill it with warm water from the tub. He picked up a bar of rose-scented soap and lathered it against a soft cloth. It touched her that he'd gone out of his way to provide her favorite soap. Then she felt the warm water trickle down her back and across the front of her breasts.

A sound of pleasure escaped her lips. "Oh, that feels marvelous." When he began rubbing her all over with deep yet gentle strokes, she almost purred with contentment. She closed her eyes. When he touched her breasts, then moved lower to the area between her legs, she stiffened. "Ah, my Lord, I'll get those areas."

He handed her the rinsed and freshly soaped washcloth. "As you wish." Giving her a little privacy, he busied himself with going over to check the stepstool that led into the deep tub.

Amy knew he was helping her again, and she appreciated it. His touch was warm, yet there hadn't seemed any eroticism about it. She was being absurd. In his culture, she reminded herself, both sexes bathed together all the time. She took a few moments to soap her long hair. Suds slithered into her eyes, and she tried wiping them away, then held out her hands to head for the tub. Her eyes stung, forcing her to shut them again. "Please be careful. I can't see and I don't want to trip over you. Ouch," she muttered, then rubbed her smarting eyes. "Guess I'm going to need more practice with this."

He walked over and turned her around. "No, not yet. First you rinse, then the tub. Here," he said, then laughed at her expression. "You look like a baby squirrel trying to get her eyes open." He led her back to the stool and hurriedly went for another bucket of warm water. Cupping the clear water in his hands, he rinsed her eyes and hair. "All right?"

"Yes, I think so." She looked across at him as he leaned over her.

"Poor *koneko,* your eyes are red. Here, bend over, shut your eyes, and I'll finish rinsing your hair and the rest of you."

"You know, my Lord, if you ever run short of funds, you could earn a fortune as a lady's maid."

"Impertinent one," he teased, "is that any respectful way to talk to your husband?"

"Not in the least, but I think you enjoy my tart tongue," she countered.

He ran his hands over her wet shoulders. "Yes, I do adore you just the way you are. You are beautiful, Amy Valerius."

The last name sounded strange to her, yet it did not displease her. "Countess to you, my good man."

Delighting in the knowledge she trusted him enough to be impudent with him, he asked, "Do all English wives deride their husbands so?"

"Only the smart ones." She helped with the rinsing, then blotted her long hair with a towel. "Have to train a husband early, sort of like housebreaking a puppy," she explained outrageously. "If you don't show them who's mistress early, they're liable to wreak havoc in the home or stray into the neighbor's flower bed."

When they stood up and walked over to the wooden ladder, the Eurasian could not help caressing her arm. "I shall never stray from home," he said.

She wanted to give him a saucy reply, but this intimacy between them was still too new. "I. . . ." She clamped her lips together when a spasm of pain shot through her body.

Toshiro saw it and knew the craving was back. He

wanted to lift her in his arms, hold her close, but felt she would be alarmed and believe he did not mean to keep his word. Instead, he supported her about the shoulders as she walked shakily up the three steps.

With her husband's assistance, Amy eased her throbbing body into the warm water. A contented sigh followed as she settled down on the smooth bench that had been carved along the periphery of the tub. "Oh, my, it feels almost decadent," she admitted, then closed her eyes and leaned her head against the back of the tub. "No wonder you like to do this every evening."

He went to the other side of the room and pulled back the long wooden shutters that covered the three windows. "Amy, if you open your eyes, you can see the rest of the present I have for you."

"Are you nude?" The bold query popped out, then she clamped a hand over her mouth. What had possessed her to say such a thing?

"Is that an invitation?" he asked, enjoying the way her face turned a deeper pink, this time not from the warm water.

"Truly, I really didn't mean . . . perhaps another time."

She sounded so polite and flustered, he could not keep from chuckling. He took consolation in noting her hasty words held some possibility for this pleasurable experience to be shared in the future. "Trust me, Amy-san. You may open your eyes for a far more satisfying view than just seeing your husband."

"My Lord, I have always found you most attractive, and—" She stopped when she saw the moonlight streaming across the Japanese Garden. "Ohh!" she breathed, enchanted by the view. "You planned this so beautifully. My uncles tried but could not find out what you kept hidden behind your boarded windows. They thought you might be performing human sacrifices or fertility rituals."

This time he made no effort to hold back his reaction. The levity escaped as he walked over to her.

The rich sound pleased her. "It is good for you to let it come out more often. Keeps you balanced."

Lost in her fathomless blue eyes, he felt that pressure in his chest again. "I shall keep your words in mind." Then he knew he needed to put some distance between them.

The Englishwoman watched her husband put away the soap, then he sat down on a wooden chair to look out the window. Relaxing, Amy closed her eyes again. He really could be so sweet, she thought.

"Amy," came a masculine voice near her head.

Her blond lashes fluttered open. "Just a few more minutes."

"It has been an hour, beloved. I don't want to cook you."

Startled, she couldn't believe it. "An hour? Love a duck, I mean, I'm sorry I kept you up so late. What tiring company I've been."

He shook his head. "Do not fluster so. I wanted you to have this quiet time. Come, I will put you to bed."

The sentence, said casually enough, caused the wariness to shove against her. Without comment, Amy let Toshiro help her out of the tub. He had a large fluffy towel ready but would not hear of her toweling herself. In truth, right now she felt as limp as a rag doll. However, his invigorating rubdown with the towel awakened her.

Finished, Amy was surprised to see he'd even thought to bring a fresh nightgown for her. As her husband put the silk material over her head, she marveled at the added chrysanthemum-printed robe that tied with a sash about her waist. "Oh, my Lord, you really are too generous. I have a wardrobe full of new gowns and riding outfits upstairs."

"It pleases me to give you a few small gifts."

"But I haven't given you anything. Even my money, you said you would not touch." Her own sense of fairness nudged her. "I do not feel right having such a one-sided relationship."

His expression became unreadable. "Perhaps one day you will find something for me. Let us leave it for the future, shall we?"

Puzzled by his words, she could tell he didn't want a big show of thanks for her new wardrobe. On their way out of his bathing room, she noticed the high table. "That's not Japanese with those long, sturdy legs. What do you use it for?" she asked to change the subject.

His gave her an enigmatic smile. "Another evening I will show you."

She let the matter go. Right now she was more concerned with how to handle the awkward moment when she went to bed.

Amy needn't have worried, for when they reached the master bedroom, Toshiro helped her out of her robe, placed it at the foot of the bed, then bade her get under the covers. The way he tucked her in, rechecked the window locks, she had to bite back a request for a bedtime story. He kissed her modestly on the forehead.

"I'll be in the next room if you need anything or become frightened in the night. May I keep the door ajar so I'll hear if you call me?"

He asked so hesitantly, she could not refuse. "Yes, my Lord. Thank you."

"You will be safe here, Amy."

After he turned and walked toward the adjoining room, Amy snuggled against the thick mattress. She was happy he was honoring his word, wasn't she?

Of course, she lectured herself, then turned over on her side. And she really did feel safe and more relaxed than she had all day. Yawning, the welcomed sleep overtook her. "A Japanese bath," she whispered aloud, then giggled to realize the staid head of Stockwell Enterprises had enjoyed herself. Amy repeated the words Toshiro had used about living among the English. "I am learning. How I am learning." She giggled into the fluffy pillow again.

Over breakfast the next morning, Toshiro asked his wife if she required anything.

Amy gave him a cheerful smile. "I am fine, my Lord. In fact, I believe I shall do some work today." She thought a moment. "Is there a small spot where I might have ink and paper to work at a desk?"

"Of course." He got up, walked over to her chair, and pulled it away from the table for her. "I shall show you the room that will be your office. Mine is next door."

They walked out into the hall, down a corridor. Toshiro opened a carved wooden door for her.

She entered, struck speechless when she saw the interior. Her globe, her desk, even her bookshelves. Amy scurried over to her carved oak desk. A shout of delight burst from her. "You brought all my office furniture over here!" She raced back to him, impetuously throwing her arms around his neck and kissed him on the mouth. Stepping back quickly, she couldn't keep the heat from her face. "Truly, I am overcome with your thoughtfulness."

It was his turn to color. He would never tell Amy the exorbitant amount Clarice Townsend demanded before she'd allow the count's English servants to cart Amy's office things over here. The woman knew he'd pay rather than drag Amy into another quarrel with her relatives. Besides, he told himself, Amy's pleased expression right now compensated him a hundredfold. "While we were getting married yesterday, my servants tiptoed over to Stockwell Manor and got your things. Since last week, the room has buzzed with activity. I took the liberty of picking a carpet with a nautical design for you."

She looked down. There was a ship in the center of the beige Oriental carpet, with blue waves over the bow of the frigate in full sail. A sextant was woven in one corner, a compass in another.

"I thought you could work more contentedly if you had your things about you."

Emotion filled her. "My Lord, I am most beholden to you. I've never known a kinder man than you." She noticed he looked embarrassed by her praise, so she sought to help him. "I shall set to work and write His Majesty today. You will be proud of the profits I'll make for us in this venture with King George."

His green eyes captured hers. "Amy, I am already proud of you just the way you are."

Words failed her. When he excused himself and went into his office next door, she almost regretted not asking him to stay. As she walked over to her desk, an idea came to her. Yes, she must come up with an appropriate wedding present for her husband. It would take time, but she was determined to find some way to repay him for his attentiveness.

That evening, Toshiro took his bride downstairs to the East Wing again. Like the night before, he was tender and giving, demanding nothing in return. She still felt the hunger for opium, but it was not as intense as the night before. Determined not to take her inner battles out on Toshiro, she said little.

However, on the fourth evening, after the Eurasian helped Amy towel herself, he stopped her from reaching for her robe.

"Tonight," he said, "I will show you what that English table is for."

He led her over to the oak table. A cushion had been placed across the flat surface. Unhurriedly, he brought the small wooden steps from the tub area and placed them in front of the table. "I would lift you up but something tells me you would rather use the steps. You are supposed to get on the table, on your stomach."

"Oh." Unconsciously she gripped the towel more securely about her body before putting her bare foot on the first step. On her knees, she managed awkwardly to roll on to her abdomen, while clutching the towel in front of her. "You're not going to do anything with fish heads, are you?"

"You really are a hoyden," he remarked affably. "Just stay put for a moment." When he walked to the other side of the room and closed the shutters, the light from the brazier cast elongated shadows across the room.

Still trusting him, yet without a clue of his intentions, Amy's humor bubbled to the surface. "If you come back here wearing a leather apron over your brown shirt and breeches, with a molding plane in your hand, I'll be off this table faster than you can say the lathe went to London for lumber." She heard him chuckle, but he didn't answer. "Has this got something to do with your carpentry hobby?"

He understood her outlandish question stemmed from an effort to quell her apprehension. "Well," he drawled, "you do look a bit *petrified.*"

Her guffaw echoed across the room. "I don't believe *you* said that. See, you can loosen your stays, in a manner of speaking. Not quite as stiff-rumped as you used to be, are you?"

He bent his head close to hers. "And you are blossoming into an even more impudent rascal than you ever were."

Not the least offended, Amy smirked. "I know. Now, don't be shy. No need to hold back. You can tell me how wonderful I am. I know you wouldn't change me if you could."

"True, though I would have you without the towel." Ignoring her squeak, he quickly divested her of this last impediment.

Amy squirmed on the cushion and sat up. Then she realized she didn't have enough hands to cover both breasts and the area between her legs.

"Can this shy rose be the same precocious imp who just advised me to loosen my stays?"

She didn't mean to, but she giggled. "Well, I had a towel around me then." When he continued patiently waiting for her to lie back down, she told herself not to be so prudish. There wasn't anything here he hadn't already seen every night when he'd bathed her. With a murmur of resignation, Amy went back on her stomach. " 'Would you at least tell me what you're going to do?' asked the piglet, before they tied her to the spit."

"Without a doubt, you have the most extraordinary way of expressing yourself." He showed her the vial in his hands, then uncorked the cap. "This is sandalwood oil."

She sniffed it. "Mmm. Smells very nice. All right, is that the basting?"

"I'm going to dump you back in that tub of water in a second," he threatened but spoiled the effect with a grin. "I put a few drops of the oil on my palms and then I massage it into your skin."

"Oh, just like bear grease on the pugilists at Gentleman Jack's in London." She went back to resting her head on her folded arms. However, her playful mood changed when she felt his warm hands begin kneading the tight muscles at her neck. An unexpected whoosh of air pushed from her chest as he expertly massaged her body. "You've done this before, Mr. Valerius."

"I have, Mrs. Valerius," he countered.

"To other women?" slipped out before she could stop herself.

"I have helped ease my father's rheumatism from his legs, and warriors in the bathhouses do this for each other. But, no, Amy, I have never done this to a woman."

His answer pleased her, but she was wise enough not to ask if a woman had ever done this to him. She knew he was not a monk, and she realized this part of his life before he married her was none of her business. "Ohhh," she purred when he went to the backs of her legs, even the soles of her feet. She hadn't realized she was so tense until he worked over her. His firm touch made her unclench. "Iwao and Sumi know how to do this?"

"Yes."

"So, Iwao could do this for me, too, when you're away?"

He stopped and placed a possessive hand on the jutting crest of her backside. "I wouldn't advise it if I were you. Sumi, yes, but that is all. I'm the only male who will perform this particular service for you. Do we understand each other?"

She could tell by his touch and the inflection in his voice, he was serious this time. "Yes, of course." She pressed her face into the pillow to muffle another gasp of pleasure when her husband resumed running his fingers over the fleshy curve of her bottom. She squirmed but didn't want to ask him to stop. Yet she knew she had to think of another topic, else she'd blurt something that proved she was finding this more than a medicinal rubdown.

"Be . . . sides," she managed, "I'm sure Iwao would have a conniption if I even suggested it. Were you . . . ah . . . ever that straightlaced? Iwao looks cast in granite sometimes."

Toshiro continued his pleasurable task. "Have I not mentioned you must not judge us by our outward reserve? We do remove the mask in the privacy of our homes."

When he went back to her legs, she felt more in control. "Well, the Japanese race has continued, so I suppose it means you must do more than bow to each other."

"English brat, turn over."

She complied, then held her breath as she studied his face in the soft light. His raven-colored hair was tied back against the collar of his linen shirt. With his sleeves rolled up, the muscles of his tanned arms rippled as he worked his slippery hands along her flesh. Dark brows, straight nose, high cheekbones—devastating, she mused. After he smiled down at her, she began experiencing that familiar weakness in her legs and was glad she had the cushion and sturdy table to support her.

While Toshiro went about massaging the front of her neck, shoulders, and arms, Amy became very aware that he avoided touching her breasts and the area between her legs. Involuntarily, she wriggled when his firm, graceful hands moved down her thighs to her ankles. He seemed to know instinctively just how much pressure to apply and where to use it. Yet, when his fingers brushed her right breast, she almost demanded to know why he didn't touch her there. Her pink nipples felt swollen, as if they anticipated what it would feel like to be fondled in Toshiro's hands. She searched frantically for something to distract her. "Do . . . Iwao and Sumi . . . do this?"

"I am certain they do. They also have the use of this room."

As she suspected, Iwao and Sumi were more like family to this man, not his servants. The thought made her recall Iwao's words about her husband and how he'd been crushed at having to beat Sumi.

Suddenly, Amy's heart went out to her husband. She wanted to take this mental agony from him but didn't know how to go about it. "My Lord, I am truly sorry I misjudged you. You were right. I do have much to learn about your Japanese culture. You have been more patient with me than I deserve."

He had not expected these words. They puzzled him, yet he continued touching her smooth, soft skin. "I told you I merely wished to massage you," he teased. "Did you think I had some ulterior motive?"

She stopped his hands with her own and sat up. Her legs dangled over the side of the table. "My Lord, I understand now why it was necessary to . . . find an honorable way to keep Sumi from killing herself."

Pain shot across his features. He pulled back and reached for a small towel behind him. Slowly, he wiped the oil from his fingers. "I am sorry you learned of this."

"Please do not be vexed with Iwao. I'm glad he told me."

His panther eyes looked haunted when he glanced across at hers. "Amy, I am not angry with Iwao. I am frustrated with the very heritage that runs through my veins. It was one of the hardest things I ever had to do in my life. God, I do not think I could face that situation again and not go mad."

"I know, Toshiro." Leaning over, she took his face between her hands and kissed him full on the mouth. Her heart lurched when she felt his shoulders shake as he released the painful memory that had been tearing at him since he'd taken that cursed bamboo in his hands.

He let her comfort him. She kissed his cheek, lean jaw, then pressed him closer. When her arms came around him, she reached under the queue that held his black mane and began stroking his neck. "My darling," she heard herself call him. "Let it out. I'm here with you." She sensed he needed her now the way she'd required him after that terrible vision with the dead rabbits.

The Eurasian could not speak; he just let her lead the way. She kissed him again, then continued whispering soft words of comfort. When his shuddering stopped, he felt released from the demon that had tormented him for the last few weeks. Grateful and humbled by her giving, he let her see his feelings.

When Amy caressed his cheek, she felt the moisture near his eyes. "We are in the privacy of our home, my husband. As you have said, you would have me as I am; I beg you to give me the same courtesy. Know that I would have you as you are, and that means showing me what you really feel. Pray leave the mask for out there," she said, pointing to the sliding partition. "Masks have no place at these times between a man and his wife in any culture."

"So wise and so beautiful," the count whispered, then pulled her into his arms. This time he was sure of his actions. He kissed her long and deeply, coaxing the response he desired from her tongue. His hands went to her breasts, and he caressed each turgid peak.

A primitive moan came from Amy as he placed feathery kisses against her cheeks, upturned nose, along the sensitive skin of her throat. She couldn't help squirming against the cushion under her. Closer to him now, she felt his strong arms as they encircled her. Delighting in the feel of his hard chest through his linen shirt, she kissed the skin where his shirt opened. When her husband pulled away, she couldn't stifle a whimper of protest, but then she saw he only wanted to pull the shirt over his head. When he came back, she reached out automatically to splay her fingers across his bare chest.

He kissed her lips, heady from her giving response. After taking some of the oil from across her stomach, Toshiro traced his fingers down to the apex of her thighs. He played with the soft golden curls, then gently separated her nether lips with his fingers. Back and forth in a teasing motion, he rubbed against her. He heard her stifled moan as she arched against his hand. "Would you have more, golden lotus?"

"Yes, oh, please don't stop. I've never felt . . . it is like a hundred fireflies fluttering against me. I'm on fire." Amy could not believe he could create this potent mixture of pleasure and torture within her woman's body.

Her sweet face showed desire and distress. He kissed her fevered lips, before tenderly spreading her legs to step between them. Holding her, he rubbed his index finger across her woman's core once more. "Do you like this?"

"Yesss."

"And this?" He touched her a different way and stretched the wet pink nether lips a little more.

"Oh . . . God, yes," she husked against his throat, then bit his skin, so lost in the throes of her erotic dance. "Do that again."

He did. "Come," he breathed against her ear. "Surrender your woman's nectar to me. I want to watch you as you take your pleasure."

The arousing tone of his voice, the increased pressure from his fingers were driving her to. . . . "No, I can't—"

"Yes, you can. I feel your honey on my hand." His voice became huskier as he described how the Japanese referred to this first release she sought but could not name. "You are so close to bursting fruit, golden lotus. Come, I am here to catch you."

"Oh, Toshiro, I. . . ." She could not finish her sentence as a shattering wave of exquisite pleasure engulfed her.

Her husband held her securely in his arms until her breathing returned to normal.

If she hadn't experienced it, Amy would never have believed such gratification existed. Nothing in her sheltered life had prepared her for this. "Oh, my . . . I never felt . . . I never knew marriage could be such fun."

He smiled and kissed her pink cheek. So open with her feelings, he found her adorable. Yes, he told himself, it was a good beginning. He was going to enjoy being married to this fascinating Englishwoman.

Amy looked down automatically, then averted her gaze.

When he stepped back from her, his smile became more chagrined. "There are some things I cannot totally control, Amy-san. One of them is my body's response to being close to you this way."

"Of course, I do understand; nothing for me to be embarrassed about," she added more for herself. "But I don't like to see you in such discomfort," she blurted, aware his breeches jutted to the starboard side. Yet, Mrs. Valerius wasn't sure how prepared she was to relieve him.

Her husband took pity on his wife. "Darling, I will recover. However, I think it prudent to take you back to your bed now."

She agreed, but before she could scramble for the steps, Toshiro placed his hands on either side of her waist and lifted her onto the tiled floor. Without hesitation, he handed her the clean nightgown and robe.

When they reached her bedroom and he began his usual routine, she tried to ease the tension between them. "Each night you investigate my quarters as if you expect to find someone in here with me. I assure you, my Lord, I am not such a ninnyhammer to even consider cuckolding you. Nor would I break the vow I said before the Anglican priest."

He tried to brush off his cautious behavior. He hadn't

forgotten that assassin's star outside the Assembly Room at Clifton. "I know, my love. Call it my eccentric precautions with such a precious jewel as my wife."

With his shirt still off, Amy could not help being affected by his manly physique in the candlelight. "I do like your chest without hair," popped out.

"As I enjoy yours," he teased. After he bundled her into bed, he kissed her cheek. Unlike the last three nights, Toshiro came back to the bed and took her into his arms. He nuzzled his face against her rose-scented neck. "Oh, Amy, do you really want me to leave?"

When she didn't answer, he released her. Right now she knew he wouldn't continue or join her unless she asked him. Something battled within her.

Toshiro felt her reluctance. Disappointed but determined to keep his word, he moved off the bed. "As you wish," he said softly. He walked toward his room and remembered to leave the door partially open. "In case you need me," he said mechanically.

Yes, her mind shouted. She did need him. Damn it, she wanted him, but could she risk it? If she was like her mother Jane, wouldn't it be kinder if Toshiro didn't learn to desire her the way she wanted him right now? Love could only destroy him, for he would have to learn the terrible truth that he still denied. It was inevitable that she would slip again and reveal her true nature.

Sixteen

Unlike the first three nights in this bed, Amy now found sleep impossible. Remorse and frustration consumed her, for she had wanted her husband to stay with her.

As the long hours ticked away, Amy felt stifled in the closed room. Getting out of bed, she padded over to the window and unlatched it. After shoving it open, she leaned against the wooden molding and breathed in the summer air. For such a health-conscious person, Toshiro amazed her by keeping all the windows shut at night.

She went back to bed and finally drifted into a troubled sleep. While her craving for the opium had lessened, something else bothered her. She came awake only two hours later.

Startled, Amy glanced to the right and saw the outlined figure. "Toshiro," she murmured, then smiled. He was going to make love to her after all.

But then the candlelight silhouetted a black-draped figure shorter than her husband. Amy saw the intruder dart glances about the room, as if he searched for someone else. When her eyes caught the glint of steel after he raised a sword over his head, she rolled quickly to the right. Terror constricted her throat, preventing her from crying out. Her stomach churned when she heard the muffled thud as the blade sliced through the pillow and mattress near her head. A snowstorm of feathers whirled about her. This time she did master her vocal cords. Her scream echoed off the four walls.

In an instant, Toshiro vaulted into the room. Later she would think herself mad for observing at such a time that, unlike most Englishmen who slept in knee-covering shirts, Toshiro was naked. Right now she was only aware that he growled something in Japanese. Then came the sound of steel hitting steel. In the dim light she noted the stranger was totally covered in black material. Only his eyes showed. He aimed a foot at her husband and kicked him in the chest. Toshiro somersaulted and sprang back up like a rubber ball. With a combination of awe and horror, she could not pull her gaze away. Toshiro seemed to hover in midair as his bare foot came out and kicked the man in the face. This was a form of combat she had never witnessed before. Then her husband blocked the other man's foot with his raised arm. There were more jerking movements and tumbling about. Sparks lighted the room as their swords clashed against each other.

"Amy, get under the bed," Toshiro ordered from across the room. "Now!" he bellowed when she didn't move right away.

She hopped off the high mattress and scrambled under the bedframe. On her stomach, all she could see were Toshiro's bare feet and the killer's wrapped in that same black cloth as his loose-fitting pants and shirt. A mahogany table crashed to the floor when the assassin's sword missed Toshiro, instead slicing the table in half. Amy knew she couldn't just stay here and not help. Her Stockwell verve came to the surface when she spied the empty chamber pot next to her. She mentally calculated the distance, then waited until the intruder came close again to the bed as he and her husband used that strange form of body fighting to block and leap in the air. She bit her lip in frustration when the assassin moved away too quickly before she could instigate her plan. Voices coming from the hall made her hope Iwao had been alerted downstairs to their unexpected visitor. Trying to concentrate the way she'd seen Toshiro focus, Amy took a deep breath and pushed the porcelain pot with all her might toward the black-swathed ankles. She heard it hit someone but the muffled grunt was indiscernible. God, she hoped she hadn't just crippled her husband! There was another whooshing sound, then a sickening crunch of steel hitting bone. A loud thud followed. Frantic, she peered along her vantage point but couldn't see anyone. Her heart hammered against her chest as the terrifying minutes went by. She heard footfalls, then saw blood puddling toward her. Someone was coming closer to the bed. She turned her head to the right when she heard him hunker down next to the wooden frame. A shrill cry tore from her when she felt a black draped arm reach under and begin tugging her from beneath the bed. This man had just killed her husband!

"Nooo. Let me go. You filthy bastard." Struggling harder at the determined black-clothed arms that hauled her out, Amy experienced an unleashed thirst for vengeance. She began using her fists and legs, oblivious that her nightgown now rode above her knees. "I'll kill you," she growled, tears blinding her. She clawed at the determined hands holding her arms.

"Damn it, Amy, stop fighting! It's me," came the irritated but dearest voice in the world to her. She blinked, at first not able to lower the right fist she held poised above her head, ready to strike the black-draped killer. Then her blue eyes focused on the handsome face of her husband. He'd apparently gone back into his adjoining room to shrug into the black kimono with the wide sleeves. "Oh, Toshiro!" Throwing herself into his arms, she began smothering his face with wet kisses. Her disheveled blond hair tangled about his chest as she held on to him as if her life depended on it. "I thought . . . I saw the black material. You are all right. Is he . . . ?"

He patted her gown-covered shoulder. "Yes, he is dead."

"I saw the blood." An involuntary shudder went through her. She heard Iwao's voice then Sumi's, but wasn't able to respond. As she clung to her husband on the floor, Amy heard Toshiro issue instructions in rapid-fire Japanese. "Why was that man trying to kill me? How did he get in here?"

"You opened the window, I see. Well," Toshiro went on, "it is partly my fault for not telling you everything. I had hoped to spare you." He helped her stand.

Amy glanced back at the bed. A mistake. She saw that Sumi had used the bedspread to cover the body. Blood soaked the carpet, but the Englishwoman was more unnerved when she saw Iwao return to the body with something held secretively at his side. There was a sword against the table leg. She recognized it as her husband's by the gold and silver inlaid sword-shaped leaf pattern across the side of the blade. But it was stained with blood.

Iwao said something to Toshiro. Almost roughly, her husband turned her away from the scene that held her with such grisly fascination.

"I . . . I don't understand. What is Iwao doing?" she asked. "What is he carrying?"

Strain made his voice harsh. "It is of no importance. Come, I will take you to my room." He placed a firm hand under her elbow and propelled her toward the next room.

Protesting this treatment without explanation, Amy jerked her arm away and glanced behind her. Another reckless error. She put her hand to her mouth when she saw the bloody object before Iwao lifted the bedspread and shoved it next to the body—it was the assassin's head. "My God."

"Must you always rush heedlessly into the storm when I point out a safe harbor?" But Toshiro's gruff scold was followed by the tender action of placing his arm around her waist. He turned her back to where he'd wanted to lead her in the first place. "I tried to warn you. Come."

She let the Eurasian direct her into his adjoining room. Even after he'd lost his temper when she defied him by charging back into the Avon, Amy had never considered just how lethal Toshiro Valerius could be when threatened. She recalled how fiercely he'd leapt into her room like a snarling panther. Usually polite and kind, he did not give the outward appearance of a man capable of . . . severing the head of an adversary. Yes, they still had so much to learn about each other.

When she entered her husband's room, she realized this was the count's former sitting room. There were bookcases and a desk along the wall. A small cot had been brought up. It couldn't have been very comfortable sleeping here, she mused. She sat down when he indicated the single leather-upholstered chair in the room.

"Would you like me to make you some tea?"

Her blond hair shadowed her face when she shook her head. "Perhaps later. Right now I should like to know why that man tried to kill me. If I hadn't rolled to the right . . . I'm sorry about the mattress. It's ruined beyond salvage, split down the center." Odd the things one blathered about at such a time, she thought distractedly.

Toshiro pulled the wooden chair from behind his desk and sat down next to her. "For God's sake, Amy, I don't give a damn about the bed. If anything had happened to you, I don't know. . . ."

Amy heard the anguish in his voice and reached across to pat his hand. "I am truly all right. It's amazing, but I felt a panther's courage and rage when I thought you'd been harmed. Docility was the last thing I experienced." She peered at him. "My Lord, are you unwell?"

He placed his hand over hers. "Emotionally, let us say, I have been better." He managed a lopsided smile.

"I know what you mean."

He did not miss the way her gaze went back to the closed door where Iwao and Sumi, along with two of the English servants, now worked to dispose of the body and clean up the mess. "Amy, you will be safe in this room."

"But where will you sleep, my Lord?"

"Do not fret. I will go downstairs to my Japanese rooms." He caressed her hand as it rested on his knee. "I am certain there will be no more Japanese assassins. My uncle has gained me a temporary reprieve from further attacks until I return to Nagasaki to straighten out this horrible quagmire. You will be safe here in my room."

At the earlier mention of his Japanese rooms, Amy thought of the positive feelings she experienced downstairs in the East Wing. "My Lord," she began before she could lose her courage. "May I stay there with you tonight? I don't want to be alone."

Something softened in his green eyes. "Of course. We'll go down right now if you like."

When they arrived in the outer room downstairs, Amy followed Toshiro into the bedroom she'd snuck a peek at that first time after his duel with David. It seemed so long ago. Toshiro went to his wardrobe and pulled out a beige-colored garment, then excused himself. When he returned, Amy saw the solid-colored under-kimono close to the nape of his neck under his black kimono. She noted the tray in one hand and pillow in the other. Quickly, he tossed the square pillow into a corner of the room. Amy was already seated on the tatami. She pulled the low lacquered table near the large mattress that served as the count's Japanese bed.

"I'll make the tea this time," Amy offered. "I'm not totally helpless," she quipped in an attempt to help them both over this traumatic encounter. After rolling up the billowy sleeves of her pink robe, she set about putting the green powdered tea into the round earthenware bowl, then added the hot water. She reached for the bamboo whisk.

"Far from helpless," Toshiro replied, admiration in his green eyes as he watched how she coped. "I know of few women—Japanese, Dutch, or English—who would have shown your courage tonight."

His praise warmed her. Surprised, she realized she was

proud of herself, too. Right now she did not feel like a fragile rose at all. "Of course, I did spend most of the interesting part under the bed," she said, as she poured each of them a measure of the steaming tea into two small bowls. "You know, I should be cross with you for having such an influence on me that I jump when you thunder the word 'Now' at me."

As her husband sipped the bitter, soothing tea, he watched her over the rim of his cup. "I have no illusion that such obedience will be a permanent fixture in our marriage," he replied dryly.

"Ruddy unlikely," she pointed out, then grinned. She set her cup down on the table and leaned back on her heels. "Toshiro, what will happen to the body?"

Aware their playful verbal sparring had ended, the count put his cup next to hers, then rested his palms on his thighs. "Iwao and I placed the corpse in a safe place in one of the barns. I shall ride into Bristol tomorrow with it and speak to the magistrate."

"What will you tell him?"

"The truth, as I will tell you now." He leaned back and brushed a strand of his shoulder-length hair away from the black collar of his kimono. "The assassin I killed was a secret warrior, a ninja we call them, in the employ of his master, Lord Masao Nishikawa. When he volunteered for this task, I am sure the assassin knew he could never return to Japan. A blood feud has existed between the Akashis and Lord Nishikawa's family for twenty-eight years. Masao Nishikawa was my mother's betrothed. Their marriage had been arranged when they were still children."

"Ah," said Amy, shifting her position to tuck her legs under her. "Then she met Pieter Valerius. From his son,

I can understand the instantaneous attraction. Dangerous men sailing into one's harbor can work havoc with a maiden's precarious plans." When she saw Toshiro's body relax, she knew she was correct to try and help him this way. "Please continue, my Lord."

"My father had been sailing into Dejima, the manmade port at Nagasaki harbor, for years. Of all the Dutch captains I saw firsthand, he was the most respected by the former daimyo, Lady Haru Akashi's father. The only daughter with six older brothers, not to mention a doting father to spoil her, I can say without disrespect my honorable mother was used to getting her own way. I have a feeling my father tried to fight his initial attraction to the unusually outspoken Japanese maid. However, someone who could use a bow as well as her brothers would find ways to meet the light-haired Dutch captain. Disguised as her maid, my mother met my father in secret. Their love blossomed. My father wished to go to her family openly and ask for her hand. Mother would not hear of it, for she knew they would never consent. Though my father was ever the gentleman when he related this to me, it is my own belief my mother instigated their first coming together. Only a maid of eighteen, she knew her own mind. Later, when she was certain she carried me, my father insisted they marry aboard his ship, then they would leave for Holland. Her maid was supposed to deliver a message to my mother's family the day after the ship departed, but I suppose the servant panicked at the thought of the Akashis' retribution. She gave the note to Lady Haru's father. Outraged, my grandfather and his sons, along with the jilted bridegroom, Lord Masao, charged to the *Nightingale* and boarded her. The wedding over, they found my father and mother in the captain's quarters in a compromising situation. Grandfather would have killed Pieter Valerius on the spot, save for his beloved daughter's intervention. The matter was turned over to the council of elders. Since Pieter had served the House of Akashi faithfully over the years until then, death was ruled out. When it became known Haru was pregnant, Masao Nishikawa had to be forcibly restrained from attacking my father. Insulted, Masao demanded the immediate death of 'the Dutch Barbarian.' The elders ruled otherwise. As punishment to my parents for their transgression, it was ordered they would always live apart. Pieter could still return each year to Nagasaki, but they could never live together as man and wife. My father managed to get the concession that I would live my first ten years exclusively with my mother's family, then I would be allowed periodic visits with my father in Amsterdam and later England. Father pointed out that I would inherit the title and position of the House of Valerius, and my grandfather in Japan agreed I should not suffer for my parents' poor judgment that brought shame to the Akashi household. Masao swore revenge. The council forbade it. Yet, from that day Lord Nishikawa refused any contact with the Akashis. Even the Shogun has not been successful in reconciling the former allies.

"But surely, now that your father is dead, Lord Masao Nishikawa will end this feud."

Toshiro shook his head. "I understand Lord Nishikawa's patience. That assassin I killed tonight was trained in stealth and cunning. I saw the silver star that slashed my father's throat that night in his study. It was the main reason I returned to England. In my previous letters I had arranged for my uncle to leave word for me on the first of my ships that reached London."

"The Chinese cargo," Amy added.

"Exactly."

"The silver star," Amy mused aloud. "You mean like the one in the wooden beam that night at Clifton Hotwells?"

"Yes, and I cursed myself a thousand times that my carelessness nearly harmed you. Tonight the assassin took advantage of the open window. He'd already found out where I slept. He hadn't counted on the bridegroom being anywhere else than with his English bride."

"So," she guessed, "that is why you must return to Nagasaki. Your uncle and the council will have this matter out once and for all with Lord Masao Nishikawa. When do you leave?"

"Soon. I should have left a week ago, but. . . ."

"Yes, I see." She thought of all that had happened between them. "You had not counted on me." She knew the trip would be long and arduous, and instantly she was filled with sadness at the thought of being separated from him. Yet, she understood family obligations. It could not be helped.

He saw something in her eyes before she tried to hide it. "I will stay another week until you are settled in your new home."

"Thank you." His consideration touched her.

With the return of her English politeness, Toshiro knew she was probably unsure of how to handle this moment. "Here, let me assist you." After untying the sash about her waist, he slipped the silky robe off her shoulders and placed it on a low table against the paper-covered wall. He reached around and pulled back the coverlet. "Come, Countess, your bed is ready."

She let him ease her onto the comfortable mattress. Like other nights upstairs, he tucked her in.

"Do you wish me to keep the candle lighted?" he asked.

"Yes, if you don't mind." The darkness still frightened her. When he went about taking off his kimono, she noted he kept on the other full-length garment and realized this concession was for her sake.

"Good night, Amy," her husband said. Under the covers, he went to his edge of the futon and turned on his side away from her. "Sleep peacefully, Amy-san," he whispered over his shoulder.

Not for the first time, Amy berated herself for having extracted that promise from Toshiro that he would not make love to her unless she asked him. Yet, she tried to tell herself it was for the best. He would be gone in a week, away for months. She rolled over on her side and clutched the cloud-patterned spread to her chin. What was the matter with her to even consider it? God, she thought, what if she had one of her spells while he was away? Her aunt always knew what to do if she lost consciousness.

Flopping over, she twisted to her edge of the mattress again. Well, she'd just have to work this out on her own.

If Toshiro was disturbed by her thrashing about, he seemed not to notice. Not once did he turn back to her or say another word. After tossing and turning for the first hour, Amy finally fell into a restless sleep.

When the count heard his wife's even breathing, his own body relaxed. He moved to watch her. Her blond hair tumbled about her face like spun gold. But he winced when she whimpered a few times. Her face contorted, and he knew she was experiencing one of those nightmares again. Better without the opium, he knew she still struggled with those hidden demons that her waking mind blocked out. He wanted to take her in his arms, felt his own body's ache, and knew where such contact would lead. What a brash fool he'd been to give that promise not to touch her unless she asked. Never had he known a woman like Amy. He should have realized how impossible a task it would be to keep his promise. He winced when he moved to the right. The throbbing ache between his legs continued. Simon Townsend's lewd prediction about the condition of the count's anatomy from such self-imposed restraint was proving true.

"No, I didn't mean it, Mama. Please. Nooo," Amy cried.

Damned if he could leave her this way. Toshiro grabbed her flaying arms and pulled her sweat-soaked body against his. Holding her sideways, he cradled her upper body close to his chest. "Shhh, Amy-san." While he was relieved she wasn't having a nightmare about their unwanted visitor this evening, he knew something from the past tortured her again. "You are safe, darling."

"No," she whimpered. "The dragon's green talons are reaching out for me."

He tried to let his hands convince her she was unharmed. He massaged her back, the sensitive area behind her ear. "It is only a dream," he whispered.

Amy became aware of soft linen and the faint scent of ginger. She nuzzled her face into the soft material. His warmth made her feel safe. "Oh, Toshiro," she said, her voice full of regret, "I'm sorry I woke you. Perhaps it would be better if I went back to the cot upstairs." She made an unsteady motion to pull away, then found she wasn't going anywhere.

"I would not have you alone tonight," he said truthfully. His panther eyes captured her wide-eyed gaze. "And I would not be alone tonight either."

The tenderness in his eyes took her breath away. She knew right now she wanted more than companionship. But how to ask for it? She was aware this proud man of honor would not touch her unless she instigated it. She had to look away, his gaze was so intense. It wasn't like asking for a logbook or more tea. "Ah, Toshiro," she began awkwardly.

"Yes, my love?" He rubbed her tense shoulders. When she did not speak for a few moments, he asked, "Do you wish me to leave?"

"Oh, no," she answered too quickly, then felt her face flush. "I mean . . . I . . . find it acceptable that you are here with me." There, was that Japanese enough for him?

He hid the beginnings of a smile in her blond hair. Yet, he reminded himself of his promise. He had to be certain of her wishes. He wanted no reproachful blue eyes staring at him over the breakfast table in the morning. However, he would help her now as much as he could. "You wish to ask me something, Amy-san?"

"Yes. I would like you to . . . that is, according to your promise, which I am sure you honorably intended to keep . . ." Floundering, she fiddled with one of the ruffles at her wrist. "Toshiro, I'm trying to ask you to . . . ah, give up your promise."

He kissed her forehead. "You mean, sweet wife, you are asking me to make love to you?"

Relief swept through her. She caught her breath when she read the smoldering passion in his green eyes.

"Yes . . . politely," she added, his reaction giving her the confidence to be mischievous at such a time. "And, I want the first time to be here in our Japanese rooms."

Nothing could have meant so much to him, and he let her see his pleasure. He kissed the smooth line of her jaw, then whispered near her ear, "You are certain, my love? There will be a point soon when I will not be able to stop if you change your mind." His mouth tasted the softness of her white throat.

"Yes, I want this," she admitted, breathless from the way he kissed her. Even when he eased her back against the mattress, they kept joined at the lips, clinging to each other as weeks of denied yearning surfaced. They were both panting when they pulled apart. Her gossamer nightgown felt too cumbersome. She sat up and pulled the frothy material over her head. Unashamedly, she delighted in the pleasure that ignited his panther eyes as he watched her.

"Beautiful," he whispered. "My golden lotus."

"Ahem. My Lord, may I see more of you also?" she asked. "I am not ashamed to admit I have dreamed of finally getting my Black Knight out of his armor."

He smiled and unwound the sash that rested against his hipbones. "I hope I will not disappoint you," he added, only half in jest.

"If you stand up, I'm more apt to get the full effect in the candlelight," she suggested, secretly amazed at her brazenness. "After all," she pointed out, "you have had more opportunities to view me."

"Point taken, Countess." With his usual grace and strength, he stood up as she requested. He admitted feeling influenced by her blatant perusal, but he couldn't refuse her anything right now. He folded the under-kimono and placed it on the woven mat.

Amy scrutinized him from his shoulder-length hair, dark brows, straight European nose, angular jaw, broad shoulders that tapered into a narrow waist, and well-formed legs. His tanned body was smooth except for the wisps of black hair at the junction of his thighs. "Oh, oh my," she breathed at the evidence of a healthy male in the state of full arousal. "Does . . . it hurt?"

Hands at his waist, Toshiro made a growling sound at the back of his throat, split between humor and exasperation. "Yes, impudent lotus. And I have felt this way almost from the first day you tumbled into my arms. I have come awake many mornings in this state which I can attest is most uncomfortable." He turned away, surprised how self-conscious he felt.

Intrigued, Amy added, "Ah, I see the back of you is equally well-formed, my Lord."

Abruptly, he turned to face her. His Amy could say the most outrageous things sometimes. "Thank you. I'd give you a formal bow, but I cannot possibly execute it in my present condition."

She looked up quickly and read the amusement in his eyes. "You really are learning to use your sense of humor. And you have the nicest smile of any man I've ever met." When he made no move to join her, she turned on her side to rest her head on the inside of her arm.

When she stretched her lithe body, he felt near to bursting from wanting her. "Amy-san," he said, his voice hoarse, "may I come back to our bed . . . *now?*"

Ready to give him a resounding yes, this new power turned her into a temptress. "Not yet. Perhaps later. I haven't seen the other side of you long enough."

Toshiro bit back a forceful answer. He spoke to her over his shoulder. "Enjoy your games while you can, saucy wife. But I shall remember this later." Her silver laugh sent shivers down his spine.

"Love a duck, I'm astonished how far you've let me take this. Show me your mizzen mast," she mimicked. "Let's get a gander of your topsail. You certainly are an accommodating frigate, my Lord."

Then he realized she'd been having a joke at his expense. "English hoyden," he snapped with mock sternness.

Her giggling turned to a squeal of surprise when the panther pounced on her. His strong arms kept his muscular weight from crushing her, but he trapped her easily beneath him.

"I did mean the part about finding you well-formed," she squeaked.

"Just as I mean it when I call you an impudent brat."

She colored at the lurid feel of his engorged shaft on the fleshy part of her thigh. "Perhaps this would be a good time to apologize for leading you on that way."

"No," he said, desire in his eyes. "This would be a good time for my adorable but naughty wife to allow her husband to make slow, passionate love to her." With that he claimed her lips in a long, searing kiss.

Her toes curled with the volatile images that flashed across her mind. "Ohhh," she breathed, then wrapped her arms about his neck. She ran her fingers through his thick hair and caressed the hardness of his smooth back. When her husband moved lower and began suckling the turgid pink nipple of her breast, she gasped. "Oh, that feels wonder . . . oh. Please, harder." He complied and she squirmed beneath him. He did the same to her other breast, all the while caressing her satiny flesh. When he lightly pressed his fingers against the blond curls between her legs, Amy thought she would swoon from this exquisite torture. Her hands tightened around his hips, and she pushed against him, wanting to feel more of his hard body against hers. They both moaned with pleasure when she managed to unbalance him so that his chest pressed into hers. Aware of his arousal, she was certain he had more self-control than she possessed at this moment. "Please," she cried, "I cannot wait. Touch me the way you did the other evening."

Knowing how much she wanted him added to his own pleasure. "Perhaps later," he said, giving back her earlier words. He regretted them instantly when he saw the hurt look enter her blue eyes. "No, fiery one, I only mean I would change the manner of that pleasure this time. I would never leave you unfilled. Will you trust me?"

She was lost in his tenderness. "Yes, with all of me, but I . . . I'm not as patient as you are."

Her honesty charmed him. He kissed her heated cheek. "Beloved, savoring is part of the delights of pillowing." Something lurched against his chest, his familiar response when faced with her vulnerability. He knew he'd die for this petite woman who'd bewitched him so thoroughly. Gently, Toshiro parted her legs and kissed the inside of her thighs. Unhurriedly, he bent his head to tickle the golden curls between her legs.

She gripped a handful of coverlet beneath her. "Barnacle balls," she swore. "I . . . need . . . now. You . . . you're killing me with this to . . . torment."

"But it is the sweetest of deaths, golden lotus," he whispered against her hot skin.

When she felt his tongue spread her nether lips so

carefully, before he began kissing the very core of her, she could not hold back the primeval sound of surrender that came from deep within her. Automatically, she tugged and pulled against his dark head, too far gone to know if she was trying to escape this exquisite torture or urge him on to complete what he so expertly began. Unlike before when Toshiro had used only his hand, this time his tongue was spearing her soft skin. "Oh, please, faster." Her body burned with needing him, and her hips moved off the futon in an effort to find the release she so desperately craved. When she tensed, Amy felt Toshiro plunge his tongue deep within her. He took a firmer hold on the swell of her hips. She called out his name as spasms of fire surged through her body.

Cradling her in his arms until she quieted, he kissed her damp forehead. "In Japan, we call your woman's bud, the praline," he whispered, then ran his tongue along her earlobe, before he used his teeth gently on her flesh. "They are right, *koneko,* for it does taste delightfully like a sugared almond."

"Oh, oh, God, Toshiro," she cried, aroused once more by his words and his touch. She pushed against his chest, not caring how boldly she behaved.

Beguiled, he complied when she shoved him down on his back. He huffed with arousal and amazement when she literally threw herself on top of him. She started smothering his face with moist kisses as she ran her determined hands along his hard body. The urgency of her reaction propelled him into the center of this whirlwind. He reached down to caress her back, the swell of her round bottom. When she encircled his lance with her small fingers and began moving up and down, he groaned, his plan for her slow initiation to love disintegrating. "Please, *koneko*—" He sucked in his breath at her continued onslaught. "There is no hurry. Sip this slowly," he repeated, trying to remember all that his Zen Master had taught him.

Amy rubbed her body against his. "No, I don't want to be patient," she growled, then nipped his shoulder harder than before. She flicked her tongue along the erotic bite. "Please. All my life I've had to wait, be patient, accept. I want to be your true wife . . . now. No more reading in books about it, no more dreaming about it. I want to experience this. Let me give you the same pleasure I've had from you."

"You do not know what you ask," he said, his voice husky. But he was lost to the pleading and sensuality of this woman hovering over him like a blond Viking ready to claim him as a captive prize. Indeed, his own body felt close to busting with the throbbing ache for her. Intuitively, he knew right now the way this beauty would respond best her first time. He only hoped he wasn't too over the edge to hold on. "All right, golden lotus." Gently, he moved her slender form so that she was sitting directly across his thighs.

She studied him. "What do the Japanese call this . . . it?"

So distracted with the need for her, he had to stifle his initial reaction to shout this was a bloody inconvenient time for a language lesson. Never did this woman cease to amaze him. "My countrymen often re . . . refer to it as . . . the stem of the tree."

She touched the smooth, hard head with the tip of her finger, then felt the two sticky beads of liquid escape from the opening fold at the top. She rubbed the moisture over the blunt tip of him. "Yes, it does resemble a hard tree limb right now."

"Kande. Motto fukaku!" he growled as beads of sweat formed across his forehead and moved down the straight bridge of his nose. His unsteady hands tightened on her hips.

Aware his usual control was slipping, Amy could not help smiling down at him. Heady with power, she asked innocently, "What does that mean?"

"It . . . is totally improper for a literal translation, fiery lotus. But it means you are going to have your way after all, for I could not wait if the house were surrounded by a hundred ninjas right now." He forced another deep breath into his overheated lungs. "Now, my seductive wife, you have a choice. You can either complete our pillowing by riding my stem above me, or I will finish this erotic dance with our positions reversed. Choose quickly," came out as both a command and an entreaty.

Amy knew immediately what she wanted and leaned forward. This first time, yes, she did want to be in control. And she was deeply grateful that Toshiro had sensed this about her. She kissed his cheek. "Thank you, my love, I would stay here. Please, will you tell me if I hurt you?"

The earnestness in her large eyes nearly strangled him. "It is you we must both have a care about during this first journey, sweet lotus." He experienced her hot wetness as she began easing his penis into her woman's sheath. They both felt the impediment of her maidenhead. "Easy, beloved." His own eyes stung when he saw her former rapture turn to discomfort as her narrow passage rebelled at being stretched this first time. He stilled her motions. "Wait, my love. You go too fast. Slowly."

She knew by the rapid pulse at his throat, the sheen of perspiration on his face, along with the shakiness of his hand when he reached up to stroke her breast that he, too, was suffering from this long wait. This wonderful man beneath her had given her a woman's pleasure on more than one occasion while denying himself. Toshiro had waited weeks for her to learn that she wanted this. His tenderness humbled her and suddenly made her determined to offer him this one gift only she could give him. When she felt his hands on the swell of her hips, almost as if he would move her away to safety, she clamped her lips together and plunged downward.

"No, Amy!" Toshiro shouted, but it was too late. Her muffled sob tore at him. *"Koneko,"* he said, half a scold, more in regret. He clasped her upper body close to his chest when she crumpled over him. Holding himself still within her, the Eurasian wasn't surprised when she moved her lower body away from the blunt lance that had just severed her maidenhead.

"I . . . I'm really all right," she said in a small voice, then sniffled into his bare chest. "I didn't realize it would . . . it was my own fault."

"Oh, Amy-san, sometimes you are so rash."

Clinging to him, the stinging began to recede. "I know. Guess I've always been too impetuous. We English are a determined race."

"So I am learning." He stroked her shoulders and back. "Beloved, I wanted only pleasurable memories for you tonight."

She pulled back to look down at his face. It shocked her to see the sadness in his eyes. "Toshiro, I am certain they will be. I . . . I believe it would be acceptable for you to finish this your way."

"Are you sure, Amy?"

"Yes."

Toshiro placed her beneath him. When he saw her maiden's blood mingled along the dark hairs surrounding his shaft, he looked down at his wife. She watched him, then held her arms out to him.

"I love you, Amy Valerius."

Her blue eyes sparkled as she held his words close to her heart. *"Aishiteru,* my Lord Husband."

In Japanese, she said she loved him, his mind shouted. Kneeling between her legs, he slipped his strong hands under her bottom and lifted her up to meet his lips.

Amy couldn't help squirming in mild protest. "But my Lord, you must not . . . the blood, I am not. . . ." The look in his panther eyes silenced her.

"I would have your bursting fruit once more before we join and take your pain as my own."

He licked against the soft folds of her pink flesh, soothing away the remembered hurt to leave a pulsating hunger in its wake.

This time she let him lead her. Her head thrashed from side to side. She clenched the coverlet beneath them as she told him openly what his skillful tongue was doing to her. "I . . . I don't know how you can wait so long for . . . this pleasure." Then coherent speech became impossible as she vaulted over the edge when Toshiro took the full nectar of her woman's release.

After he moved to hold her in his arms until she calmed, Amy would not have it. On her back, she opened her legs provocatively. "My Lord, I cannot believe it is natural for you to hold back this long. It cannot be good for you. Why, your whole body will explode if you do not—"

Aroused to the point of physical discomfort, Toshiro found his lips twitched in amusement at her sputtering. "I should die a happy man, audacious one."

Her look was pure seduction. "I would have you live even happier," she purred, reaching up to run her fingers through the panther's mane that fell about his shoulders.

Slowly, Toshiro eased into her. He watched her face for any sign of discomfort, but he saw only ecstasy and impatience on her flushed features. She was such a fascinating bundle of innocence and sensuality. Holding his weight by his arms above her, he moved back and forth. His pace did increase when his determined wife clamped her legs around his hips and pulled him deeper into her yielding flesh. No, he amended ruefully, even in this position, Amy was still calling the shots. However, he did not mind.

Delighting in these new sensations, she verbalized her pleasure when he thrust himself to the hilt inside of her after she raked her nails across his back. Deep within her woman's body, she felt him kissing her down there the way his tongue had done earlier. "Oh, yes, my love, I want this. Come to me. I would have the treasure from your jewel as you have had mine."

Her words sent him spiraling. Never had he felt so out of control. "I cannot . . . wait. . . ."

Amy tightened her legs around his waist, urging him to let go. "Yes, yield to me. Release the panther."

Toshiro's head snapped back. The corded muscles of his neck bulged with exertion, signaling the complete demise to his self-mastery. A deep growl tore from his throat as his hot seed gushed from his body.

This time it was Amy who did the calming. Their bodies were slick, but she managed to get the coverlet over them.

Toshiro kissed her damp face. Holding her tightly against him, he whispered, "My lovely wife. I never knew making love could be this earthshaking," he confided, still in awe of what they had just shared.

"You should have asked me," quipped the countess. "I'll teach you more things tomorrow." Then a yawn spoiled the effect of her audacious speech. With a contented sigh, she snuggled closer to him.

"You are definitely an English rogue," said her long-suffering husband.

She kissed his jaw. "Making love is most illuminating."

"As usual, the English understatement," countered her husband.

Even exhausted, her humor bubbled to the surface. "Oh, my Lord, aren't you going to soak in your tub tonight?"

"Madam," he said, only able to open one eye. "You so thoroughly ravished me, I barely have the strength to keep breathing."

Equally tired, she still smiled before sleep overtook her, too. The realization that he was so affected by their lovemaking pleased her to no end.

Seventeen

Waking first, Toshiro studied the woman cradled against his chest. Amy's golden hair spread about his bare skin. It was the light smile on her sensual mouth that pleased him most. It was clear she'd had no nightmares. He only wanted her to have sweet dreams from now on. This overwhelming protectiveness startled him, for he'd never felt so unguarded in his life.

Amy stirred as wakefulness languished over her.

"Good morning, golden lotus. You slept well?"

"Splendidly," she answered, then stretched her arms over her head. Leaning over her husband, she looked down at him. Even though he clearly needed a shave, she thought him the most attractive man in the world. "Thank you for being such a wonderful husband," she said, unable to state directly what she meant.

Attuned to her, he stroked the back of her head. "I, too, am most grateful for your consideration last evening," he added, echoing her Oriental style with words this morning. "My dear, would you like a warm bath first or breakfast?"

Her tummy growled almost on cue, making her blush.

She buried her face in the smooth skin of his upper torso. Finally, she looked up, and her embarrassment fled at the affection she read on his face. "Would you mind if I nibbled something first before we bathe?"

"Of course not." He enjoyed the return of her healthy appetite. "In truth, right now I could eat half a cow." After she turned her head, he should have been alerted when she sought to shield her eyes from him. However, he was too besotted to notice, he thought with happiness.

In the blink of an eye Amy darted between his legs. She slipped his male appendage into her soft mouth.

Startled by the unbridled lust that shot through him, he couldn't speak at first. "You," he managed between his teeth, "are definitely a scoundrel."

Her face a mask of innocence, Amy pulled back and sat up. "But my Lord, you did say I could nibble something before we have our bath."

Her small breasts with their pert nipples beckoned him, and he reached out to cup each one in his hands. "Can this bold little hussy be the same fragile rose I first met?"

She shook her blond head. "You make me feel so free and daring." Then her expression sobered. "My Lord, I cannot deny there are things in the past that I see only as a hidden mist," she admitted, alluding to her fears. "I pray each day that I will not cause you suffering or tarnish your honorable name. If the time comes and I cannot be with you—"

"My love, Keith says you are fit." Her sincere words alarmed him, and he placed his palm lightly against her heart. "It beats with strength, and I intend to keep you safe and well-satisfied in all areas," he added with a pat across her lush bottom.

Tempted to cry out that it was her mental health she fretted over, Amy squelched the urge because she could not spoil his happiness. For as long as it lasted, she would try to be a good wife to him. She knew the dragon was not vanquished, only sleeping. Amy had found a way to keep him distracted. But that dark corridor she feared to tread would one day beckon again, she had no doubt.

Toshiro realized a shadow from the past still tormented her. He also knew he would never press her to remember. He would not damage that fragile trust between them. Perhaps with time she would change her mind. He knew she did not wish to talk of it, so he went back to caressing her, trying to show he wished only to comfort her. "I love you, Amy," he whispered.

Her features relaxed. "And I love you so much," she cried, then hugged him with all her might.

He sat up with her still in his lap. "Come I'll help you on with your nightgown and robe. I told the servants we would probably want a late breakfast."

"Counting on my ability to seduce you?" she teased.

"I barely escaped with my life," he jested, then tickled her under the chin. "You'll like Ethel's breakfast this morning. It will be fresh and plentiful."

"Just like your lovemaking, my Lord."

He laughed. "Come along, hoyden, else I'll show you just how plentiful I feel, and you'll never get any food."

After a hearty breakfast, Lord and Lady Valerius returned to the East Wing to bathe. Amy soaped her body the way Toshiro had taught her. Occasionally she glanced up from her stool to watch him. He'd rolled up the wide sleeves of his black robe and was running the sharp edges of the razor over the planes of his soapy face. She marveled how such a simple act affected her. Yes, it pleased her to look at him. Though powerful, he moved with grace and agility. "Yes," she mused aloud, "I could have done a lot worse."

"I beg your pardon?" demanded her husband, pretending umbrage. "A brash statement, considering your unprotected state at the moment." His appreciative glance was almost a leer as he studied her soft curves. "I believe the correct phrase is, 'I could not have done better.'" After rinsing his face, he buried his face in a linen towel to hide his smile from her.

She liked fencing verbally, and Toshiro learned the game quickly. When his face came out from the towel, she gave him an arched look. "I'll have you know, sir, I've had dozens of suitors over the years."

Toshiro snorted. "Like the insipid Earl of Woodcroft, no doubt." The count tossed off his robe, went over to the stool opposite her, and began vigorously soaping then rinsing his body.

"David is not insipid." She poured a little water from the wooden bucket over her shoulders to rinse herself. "It's only that he's attentive to a lady's wishes."

"Spineless, like many of your powdered, bewigged, often unwashed Englishmen."

Her question this time was more serious. "My Lord, do you hold all Englishmen with such disdain?"

He stopped rinsing his body. "No, I have some English friends. Yet, it is the Davids of this world I dislike. They show up in Amsterdam, Nagasaki, and Bristol. It is an attitude that they are a superior breed above everyone else—that is what I abhor."

She couldn't fault his words. "For a man of only eight and twenty, you possess an elder statesman's wisdom. I wonder you have stayed a bachelor this long." When he did not respond with a quick rejoinder, she couldn't stop from asking, "Did you come close to an engagement before you met me?"

"There was talk between my parents of an engagement between Lady Akiko Yoshimitsu and myself, however, nothing came of it."

"How old is she?"

"Nineteen."

"Is she pretty?"

Toshiro knew this was not the time to tease her. He thought of Akiko's tiny features, dark eyes, and soft voice. "To others I am sure she is, but as I have told you, I did not want a timid wife. I would have a blond-haired termagant, with directness and a forceful right cross, who takes no guff. I like being married to a feminine English boxer."

She could not hide her satisfaction.

"Ahem," he said with exaggeration. "Now it is your turn to tell me you do not regret giving up all those English suitors."

She continued rinsing her long hair. Then she stood up and turned her back on him while she bent over to untangle the blond strands with her fingers. "Shrewd businesswoman that I am," she said over her shoulder, "I believe I'll wait to see how you work out before I make any more brash statements, as you call them."

"I'll give you a brash statement," growled the panther.

The next moment Amy shrieked when she felt her body sail through the air. She landed with a raucous splash in the large tub of warm water. As she sputtered awkwardly to the surface, she reached for the ledge, then realized she wasn't alone in this wooden tub. "How," she gulped, "do you move so fast without making a sound? I didn't even hear you come up behind me."

A smirk changed his features into a youthful prankster as he watched her tug her hair out of her eyes. He'd already tied his own hair back with a leather thong. "It takes years of practice. Of course," he added, snaking a hand about her waist in readiness for her response, "having a wife who galumphs about and shows everything on her face makes it easy."

"You miscreant of a Black Knight," she accused, then went for his ribs. "Oh," she said, ecstatic at the discovery when he burst out laughing. "So, you are ticklish. Another weapon for my arsenal."

The water sloshed over the side of the tub with their horseplay. His hands shot out and pulled her arms behind her back. He nudged his knee provocatively between her legs and began rubbing her. "My storehouse is not totally defenseless either, fiery lotus."

It certainly wasn't, and it unsettled her to realize just how quickly she responded to his lovemaking. He touched her, and she melted against him. "That is unfair," she charged. "You are bigger than I am. If I had an equal advantage, I'd take some of that bounce out of the panther." She squirmed, frustrated at not being able to touch him with her hands.

Wary, yet enchanted, Toshiro freed her arms. He sat down on the wooden seat and folded his arms across his chest. "All right. Is it to be chess, or . . ." His amusement vanished, replaced by an indrawn breath when Amy encircled his shaft with her fingers. He pressed against the wood at his back. Right now the look in his wife's eyes gave her every appearance of George Stockwell's daughter determined to win at all costs. "Amy, do not do this," he warned.

The anticipation of winning always empowered her. "Is the panther scared of losing?" Intent on giving exquisite torture, Amy began stroking him.

Not to be outdone, he placed his right hand along the soft tuft of gold between her thighs.

Unaccustomed to defeat in business matters, Amy told herself this would be no different. "Let us see who . . . blinks first," she challenged, adding a provocative tilt to her chin.

He realized full well what she meant. "I see the rose still retains some of her thorns. Perhaps a little pruning is called for." He eased his middle finger across her slippery cleft, saw her bite down on her lower lip, but she did not flinch.

Her delicate fingers moved easily up and down the pole of his flesh, and she felt him lengthen within her hand. "Perhaps it is the tree that needs cutting down to size."

His green eyes never left hers. "We shall see," was all the Eurasian would concede.

It was only a few more seconds before Amy discovered she was in trouble. Increasing her movements on him only made her own flesh burn. Damn the man! He knew her body too well, she thought, then had to close her eyes to fight her own arousal. She could feel his eyes devour her as his fingers demanded her response.

"That's right, *koneko*, I can feel you pulling my finger into you as the petals of your skin tighten about me." He increased the pressure and speed with which he played against her. "I adore the way your bud grows hard as I caress you. It is here for you. Take your pleasure.

Let it burst from you like the sweet juice from a pomegranate."

His words drove her in the direction she fought. "No, no, I won't." His wicked chuckle mocked her, yet she had to keep her eyes closed to battle the relentless Black Knight. Her fingers fell from their task. So overcome struggling against her need, she could only push against his shoulders with both hands. However, her determined conqueror gave no quarter. "No," she repeated, more for her own sake now, "you can't make me—"

"Can I not?" taunted the panther as he continued his thorough seduction.

If only she could say such lurid things to him, then she would make him lose control. She couldn't even think clearly right now, let alone turn phrases that heated a lover's body the way Toshiro expertly could. "Oh," she whimpered, knowing she should pull away, or call him that bad name in Japanese, but something told her from the ruthlessness of his arousing touch it would make no difference. She'd foolishly provoked him into this game. Looking up, she saw the male look of triumph in the depths of his eyes. Instead of pushing him away, she began clutching him, grinding her hips against his hand. In her fevered state, the countess was past the point where pride mattered to her. "Oh, yes, Toshiro, please don't stop. Please. I'm on fire."

"Your release is right here," he whispered near her ear as he gave her exactly what she craved.

Wanting to prolong this moment where her husband tenderly held her in the warm water and soothed her, Amy forced herself to look up at him. "You won, my Lord," she said, humiliated by her complete defeat.

When he lifted her, she draped her arms around his

neck, grateful he wasn't inclined to gloat right now. He thrilled her with his slow movement into her pliant flesh.

"Amy, look at me."

She raised her eyes, afraid she would find his mockery. But something she'd never anticipated showed on his face.

"Amy, we both win. Though I enjoy the games only a wife and husband in love can play, I'll never allow either of us to move into that dangerous realm where one seeks complete dominance over the other. I saw it in your eyes earlier. You thought to laud it over me, take away my face when you began this combat. Not a lover's game but combat, that's how you saw it, didn't you?" Holding himself still within her, Toshiro waited for her to admit the truth.

She looked at the water around them, both awed and ashamed at how much he really understood her. As George Stockwell's daughter she'd been used to dictating terms. Compromise never came easily to her. "You are right, my Lord. I'm sorry I insulted you."

He placed two fingers under her chin and raised her face to his. "Insulted us both. There is no I or you, winner or loser. It is us, sharing together. Do you understand, Amy-san?"

"Yes, I think I finally do."

The smile returned in his eyes. Amy ran her hands along his back as he began moving against her. When she felt the ridges along the smooth skin of his shoulders, she gasped. "My Lord, what happened to your back?"

He stopped for a second and gave her a rueful look. "I am a samurai, not a saint, my love. I practically shoved my back through the tub to keep from spending as your determined little hand went after me."

A sound of pure elation escaped before she strained up to kiss him. She moved her tongue with his, imitating the rhythm of their lovemaking as her husband skillfully finished what she had started.

"Oh, Amy-san, you have bewitched me."

"Yes, my love," she whispered, holding him. "We both win."

A few days later, while Amy was busy working in her study, Toshiro knocked on her door and came in. Her warm greeting muted when she spotted his frown.

"You have a visitor, my dear. The Earl of Woodcroft."

"Oh, I see. He's back early from London this summer." As a courtesy she'd written him about her marriage, yet was hurt when he didn't reply.

He watched the change of emotions across his wife's face. Dressed in a becoming yellow gown, with her hair tied loosely back with a matching ribbon, she looked like a lovely sunbeam this afternoon. "Would you like to see David alone?"

She knew what the offer cost him. "Yes, but would you please join us in about fifteen minutes?"

"I'll even bring in the cart."

"You are wonderful," she said, then kissed his cheek and patted his burgundy-coated shoulders. Amy was amazed to find she enjoyed giving him compliments. They came easily to her because they were true.

"Are you not afraid you will make me insufferably swell-headed with your flowery words?" he teased, then kissed the tip of her nose.

"No, for I know you are a man who has his feet firmly

on the ground. Besides, it isn't your head that usually swells when you are around me."

"Saucy rascal," he countered, then deliberately leered at the top of her bosom. Automatically, he reached down to tug up the frothy piece of tulle to cover more of her chest. "That gown did not look quite so low when I showed the seamstress the design from Paris," he mused.

She giggled. "I assure you, my Lord, this is quite a proper dress, almost dowdy by the Ton's standards."

"Hardly. Are you cold?" he asked, hope in his voice. "Would you like your traveling cloak over your shoulders?"

He really was quite endearing, she thought. "Thank you, but I'm fine."

"You certainly are," quipped her husband. "Oh, well, as long as the earl realizes you are married now and unavailable, I suppose I will survive the next hour."

Beginning to understand him, she knew there was something besides jesting here. Did David still bother him? Seeking to reassure her husband, Amy caressed his strong cheek. "I do so adore being married to you. It's not just the physical side that captivates me," she confessed, then colored at his knowing look. "I truly enjoy your company, our rides in the morning, cuddling next to you before I drift off to sleep. I am very lucky."

He felt that heaviness in his chest at her words, then remembered his responsibilities. His ship would sail at the end of the week. The thought of leaving her even for a day hurt right now. "How I wish we could just shut the world out and . . ." he caught himself. "Best not keep Woodcroft out there cooling his heels."

David brushed passed Toshiro when his host opened the door. The earl rushed over to Amy, took both her hands and raised them to his lips. "My poor Amy," he said with great drama. "You must tell me everything." It was clear he never heard Toshiro excuse himself and close the door.

As the minutes dragged on, David went on interrogating her, staring at her as though she'd been sacrificed to save her family from scandal. Amy began wondering when the count would arrive to rescue her. She tapped her fingers impatiently on the sofa arm. Really, now that she was married to a man like Toshiro, she wondered what she had ever seen in David. He really was a simpering twit.

"And when I got your note, I could not believe you married that brute."

There was a knock at the door, followed by the brute rolling in the tea service. Amy knew her husband had heard David's last comment but wasn't surprised to see the mask of polite reserve on his Eurasian features. Would that she could hide her emotions so expertly. Right now she knew her face showed her frazzled state. For his part, the count looked and acted the perfect host.

With a deep breath, Amy forced herself to concentrate on pouring the English tea and offering the cucumber sandwiches. Bless Ethel and Toshiro for being so efficient. She made a mental promise to take more interest in helping run her husband's home. Enjoying this honeymoon so much, she. . . . "Oh, I'm sorry," she apologized when she accidentally spilled tea on David's hand. Just thinking about her husband lately, and she started acting like a ninnyhammer. She chanced a glimpse at Toshiro, relieved to see he was feigning absorption in a bland question from David.

Unable to quell her nervous laugh, Amy saw both men

glance at her as if she'd slipped a cog. "My, isn't the summer weather lovely?"

David turned his back on the black-haired man and gave the countess his complete attention. "Hang the weather. Amy, your aunt is still distraught over the news. Inconsolable woman just rattles about that barn of a house."

"Really?" asked Toshiro. "I heard she was giving parties almost every night, all of Bristol society in attendance at Stockwell Hall."

David gave her husband an unfriendly look. "She tries to keep up a brave front."

The hostility thickened between the grim-faced gentlemen. "My, my, we haven't had much rain lately, have we?" Amy demanded, hoping to salvage the conversation. "Hard to know what we'll have next."

"Usually it is weather of some sort," offered Toshiro, his expression unchanged.

No doubt about it, Amy mused. She was definitely going to murder her husband. Her nervous laugh escaped again. "Ah, in a few days," Amy said, "the count and I hope to have my aunt and uncles over for dinner. We'd love to have you join us."

"Of course," Toshiro managed, struggling to hide that this family dinner was news to him.

"Dash it all, Amy," David blurted, then took her hand in his, "I have connections in London. I could get you an annulment."

"Really, my Lord," Amy said, floundering. She retrieved her hand. "I . . . this is so unexpected."

"You don't have to remain shackled to Valerius and his heathen ways."

The heathen in question popped another cucumber

sandwich into his mouth. He looked past Woodcroft's shoulder like a first-row opera patron waiting for the next scene.

"If you stay in this travesty of a marriage," David added, "I'll wager one day that savage will beat you."

"I already have," countered the lady's husband.

Amy blushed, reminded of the night she'd tried to drown herself a second time in the Avon.

"Good God," said David, appalled, "it's worse than I imagined. Amy, you have to leave this foreign devil at once. No Englishwoman could be expected to put up with such monstrous treatment."

"Please, my Lord," said Amy, then shot her amused husband a vitriolic stare. "Count Valerius is only having sport with you. He is a very attentive husband. My every wish is granted: I'm fed, exercised, and—"

"Dash it all, sounds like the care of livestock."

Toshiro folded his arms across his chest in a gesture that showed Amy he waited eagerly for her next remark.

"David, please, you must let me—"

"No, I can see he's bullied you. This is no life for you. Your uncles even told me of the vow that dolt took not to have his way with you. Amy, you are such an innocent in these matters. I'm a man of the world. You cannot live here the rest of your life like a cloistered nun."

The scarlet hue reached the roots of her blond curls. Certain there would be no help if she looked at Toshiro, she knew he was recalling their passionate lovemaking of the night before. She wheezed, then coughed. "Oh, that is, I'm content with my lot, David."

"Poor brave lamb," David said, then patted her shoulder once more. "All right, Amy, I can see saving your family and business are more important than your own happiness. But if you ever need me," he added, scowling at Toshiro, "you have only to send word to Clifton, and I'll come and rescue you."

"Thank you, my Lord," she said, touched by his offer. "You are most kind." When she got up to see her guest out, David stopped her.

"No, I can see myself out, little Amy. I'm a bit overcome," he said, rubbing his eyes theatrically. "I've lost you, but I console myself that you did it for a noble cause." After bending over to kiss her hand again, David gave Toshiro a curt nod and swept out of the room. He closed the door behind him.

"A Covent Garden performance," said Toshiro, before he popped another of the finger sandwiches into his mouth.

"Oh, how could you egg him on that way?"

"I hardly said three words."

"That's just it," Amy accused, then bounded off the sofa. She charged over to her seated husband. "You deliberately led him to believe that—"

"Amy, I sought to protect our privacy and save you further embarrassment. Would you have me tell him the truth that you've been pounding on me for days like a randy little monkey?"

"Oh . . . you Black Knight. That you can sit there smugly eating those blasted sandwiches, and—"

"Mind you, I'm not complaining, but I do have to keep up my strength to handle your demands." Prepared when she reached down to punch his shoulder, he hooted with mirth and caught her easily in his arms. He pulled her onto his lap before she could land a finger on him.

"I give up," she said in exasperation.

He caressed her gown-covered hips.

"It isn't fair. I can't ever get the better of you."

"Poor brave lamb," he said, imitating David's obnoxious phrase.

She wanted to be vexed but couldn't manage it. The thought of David's melodramatics made her upper body shake. Her giggle turned into a whoop of laughter. "I thought he was going to have kittens when you told him you'd already beaten me."

"And you looked demurely down at the carpet and said you were content with your lot. A sacrifice making love with me, is it?"

"I bear up bravely; David said so."

"I'll bare you in a minute," snapped the panther, before he swooped down and stole a heated kiss from his wife's saucy mouth. "Woodcroft will probably have your relatives march over here tonight with block and tackle, torches in their fists, ready to hang me."

Snuggling against the soft material of his jacket, Amy sighed with contentment. "I'd protect my panther." She wiggled on his lap.

"If the poor lamb does not intend to finish this, I would suggest she stop bouncing so provocatively across my thighs."

She caressed the back of his neck and breathed in the welcoming scent of his clean skin. "I wouldn't want to take advantage of your weakened condition," she chirped, then nipped his ear.

"As you have already noticed by the bulge in my breeches, I am more than ready to service my seductive wife."

"Sumi told me the new bed and carpet are in place

upstairs," Amy whispered, not certain she wanted to wait until they went upstairs.

"Tell me, Countess, have you ever made love on a sofa?"

Amy looked across at the gold brocade couch. "No, but is there enough room?"

Toshiro nuzzled her throat with his warm lips. "If one of us reclines on top of the other, I believe we could fit."

Amy licked the bottom of his lip, then began pulling at the three buttons of his breeches. "I can't get the cursed things undone," she complained.

Toshiro lifted her in his arms and stood up. After placing her across the sofa, he started for the door.

"My Lord?" she said, afraid he meant to leave her.

"I merely wish to assure privacy," he explained, then locked the door and quickly closed the drapes.

"Oh, I hadn't thought about it," she admitted, suddenly scandalized at herself. "You touch me, and I can only think how much I want you," she confessed.

Her words sent a surge of desire through his body. The area between his legs swelled. He tossed off his coat and shoes. "That is the entrancing thing about you, fiery lotus. I adore the way you lose control. But you are not the only one." He tore at the three buttons of his breeches. "Would it shock you too much if we did not remove all our clothes this time?"

"Come here," ordered his Viking princess. "Now!"

Amused and aroused, her husband obeyed her directive. This was playing not combat. He looked down at his desirable wife sprawled against the pillows of the couch.

"I feel like a French courtesan waiting for my lover,"

she admitted. When he came down to her, she was enraptured by his urgency when he sheathed himself forcefully into her. It wasn't often she experienced his complete loss of control, and she reveled in it.

"Goddess," he breathed against her mouth. "I want to taste every inch of your delectable body. You have conquered me."

She snaked her hand down and rubbed the base of him where they joined.

His fevered lips took hers roughly. "Seductress, you will not have me gently this way," he warned, then bit her soft neck. "I could crush you beneath me." The fierceness of his unleashed arousal proved his words. "You are driving me to madness."

"Just a little, but it won't do you any permanent harm," said the countess, just before coherent words deserted her.

"But I want to come with you," Amy said for the fifth time that morning. "I won't be any trouble."

The *Nightingale* was fully loaded and ready to sail the next day. Toshiro knew Amy understood why he had to go to Nagasaki; she just hadn't counted on staying here. "Darling, please, I have told you. It is a long, dangerous trip, certainly no journey for an Englishwoman. You will be safe here. Sumi, Iwao, and the English servants will look after you. Believe me, I only have your welfare in mind."

"But I've always wanted to see Japan. I've read about it for years. Sumi has taught me some Japanese and answered my questions about what would be expected of me. Besides, I really want to—"

"Enough!" he shouted. This time his tone showed he was master of his house. "You are not going, and that is final. Now, I would prefer my last day here to be a pleasant one before we have months of separation. However, I am fully prepared to show you I will never bend on this issue if you push me further."

She understood his warning. Devoted husband, playful friend, attentive lover he would be, but right now he reminded her he could also be a dangerous adversary when crossed. Her Stockwell blood came to her rescue. She recognized when negotiations had broken down. Walking the few paces over to the panther, who stood watching her somberly, Amy slipped her arms around his waist and buried her head against his shirt-covered chest. "All right, Toshiro, I promise not to ride down to the wharf to see you off, nor will I mention it again."

Toshiro felt the harshness leave his body. He stroked her gown-covered arms, then tipped her face up to his and kissed her tenderly on the mouth. "That's my lovely wife. I must know you are safe. Oh, darling, I am going to miss you more than I can say. That is one reason I do not want you to ride down to the wharf tomorrow. Jan would have to tie me to the crow's nest to keep me from jumping ship. You must know I would not go if there was any other choice."

Amy knew she couldn't let him see her eyes right now. She went back to holding him tightly around his waist. "Yes, of course," came out muffled as she buried her face against him.

"I must leave tonight to sail with the tide tomorrow. I always spend the last day on board. It is a precedent my men expect me to keep."

"I understand." Amy couldn't believe her good fortune. She needed that day alone tomorrow.

He would make it up to her. "When I return, I shall take you to Amsterdam, then we will have that trip to see the Adriatic. It is a promise. But right now let us have a quiet lunch, then . . ." his green eyes darkened with emotion. "I want to make love to you slowly, memorize every inch of you until I have to leave."

Amy clung to him like a limpet. Her samurai husband had taught her the importance of shadowing her eyes.

Eighteen

Amy pulled the wool cap down over her blond head. Over a week out to sea, as the *Nightingale* encountered rough weather, she had to take more care when the large barrel containing her few clothes moved back and forth across the wooden planks of the cargo hold.

With the pitching of the ship since yesterday, Amy had been occupied with the never ending task of restacking many of the lighter wooden crates that kept slipping off their perch. Well, she told herself with satisfaction, at least she was keeping things tidy down here. Perhaps she could use that argument when she sought out her husband tomorrow. With her fresh water and supplies dwindling, the countess knew it was about time to make her presence known. Perhaps she should get out of these boy's clothes and put on one of her gowns. It wouldn't hurt to try and make a good impression when she sprang this surprise on the count. She glanced behind her and saw the Valerius stamp on the barrel she'd enlisted into her service. Amy hoped Toshiro wouldn't be too upset when he found out she'd paid three of her most loyal dock workers to remove the bottles of Madeira to make room for her supplies. Bilge, she told herself, banking her courage. Hadn't Toshiro been the one to encourage her to grow, trust her instincts, back her own decisions? And this certainly qualified as an adventure!

When she heard voices, Amy crouched down to hide behind the wooden crates and barrels. It was early for the daily inspection down here. Peering to the side, she was amazed to see the ruddy complexion of Jan Roonhuysen, Toshiro's second in command. He was talking to the young sailor who usually came down to inspect the cargo hold.

"I can't help it, Mr. Roonhuysen," Amy heard the youth say, "there's something strange goin' on here." He pointed to the row of neatly stacked crates. "Thought it was just me imagination, but it's happened every day since we left port. With the swell and pitch of the ship, these crates are usually scattered all about the hold. Yet, every afternoon when I come on me rounds the stuff is sittin' there as neat as ya please. Downright eerie."

And here she thought she was doing everyone a favor by replacing what she could when something toppled over. Apparently, they just let the stuff tussle about down here.

"There's another thing," the Englishman went on, "I found these yesterday." He opened his palm. "And I could have sworn I heard humming."

Barnacle balls, Amy swore. That's where those two missing hair clips went. The other day the ship's motion caused them to slip off one of the crates she used as her dressing table. They'd dropped back under a barrel too heavy to move. The tortoiseshell hairpins had worked their way out with the increased motion of the ship. Then she castigated herself for her other slip. All right, so she hummed once or twice. It did get a little lonely down here.

Jan Roonhuysen reached for the pistol in the leather holster strapped across his chest. Waving it threateningly in front of him, he walked about the hold. "All right," he said in a loud voice, "show yourself, else it will go worse for you. The captain doesn't allow stowaways, men or," he held up the two hairpins, "one of the crew's doxies. Now, come out of there."

Indignant, Amy stood up and came out from her hiding place. "Mr. Roonhuysen, I am not anyone's doxy."

"Cor, it's a bloomin' girl!" said the astonished youth when he saw Amy take off her wool cap and shake out her long blond hair.

Jan's hazel eyes widened. He replaced his gun. "Not just any girl, lad. May I present Countess Amy Stockwell Valerius."

Amy smiled and made a proper curtsy, despite her attire. "I am pleased to make your acquaintance." The suppressed laughter in Jan's eyes was a good sign, wasn't it? "I suppose you would like to take me to see your captain."

Some of the humor left the Dutchman's lined features. "*Ja,* I'm sorry, my Lady, but the captain has strict rules aboard his ship."

As Jan helped her above deck, Amy reminded herself she was now in charge of her life, and seeing the Orient was high on her chart of unfulfilled dreams.

However, all her arguments for this venture fled when she saw the back of her husband. Dressed casually in high boots of supple leather, black shirt and breeches, his straight hair clubbed against his neck, Captain Valerius peered intently across his quarter deck as his crew went about their midmorning duties. She gulped. Originally she'd planned to find Toshiro early tomorrow morning in his cabin to inform him privately he had one more passenger.

Amy glanced about the crowded deck. "May . . . maybe I can just wait in the captain's cabin until dinnertime to . . . gladden him with the news," she suggested, then darted behind Jan's back. "He seems busy at the moment. No need to disturb him." With enough courage to plan and execute this venture, her verve suddenly abandoned her. Without opportunity to wash thoroughly, she felt at a complete disadvantage. She twisted her wool cap in her hands. Jan must have sensed she was about to bolt, for he reached behind his back and easily clamped a firm hand across her slender arm.

"Excuse the interruption, my Lord, but I found a stowaway in the cargo hold."

Frowning, Toshiro turned around absently. "A lad hoping for adventure at sea?" he grumbled. "Or is it another of those dockside whores hoping for . . . ?" He stopped when the unwelcome passenger was pushed gently forward. The count's green eyes widened as he took in a small pair of boots, tightly fitting brown breeches, a wide-sleeved shirt, and the smudged face of his wife. *"Li kagen-ni shiro-yo!"* he swore, then charged across the deck. Two feet from her, he yanked himself away from completing a more physical expression of his reaction. With his booted feet planted slightly apart, he rested his fists on either side of his waist. "I suppose you have some logical explanation for this?"

Amy looked down at her boots. Since Toshiro had left her little choice but to become his wife, he could damn well take her on her terms now. Looking up, she said,

"I'm glad Jan found me, for I was almost out of cinnamon rolls."

Some of the crewmen chortled at her feisty opener. Amy returned their grins. Now, if only her husband would smile.

He didn't. "I am waiting, madam. I should like to hear why you disobeyed my orders and came aboard this ship."

"We are too far out now to turn back, aren't we?"

Her question was a mistake, for his voice became dangerously low. "I am quite certain the head of Stockwell Enterprises already knows it is too late to turn back. Now, answer my question."

Amy could feel all the men's rapt attention as they watched their furious captain and his flustered wife. "Well," she tried, "as we are now also business partners, I thought I should inspect Nagasaki where you will be loading many of the goods I'll sell in my store. Also, I have always wanted to see Japan, and I wish to face any difficulties you may have with straightening certain personal matters out between the Akashis and Masao Nishikawa's family." There, she had managed to state her case as plainly as possible, even if the words had come out in a nervous rush. Waiting, she began twisting the gray wool cap in her hands again. And the other reason? Would he believe her if she confessed she did not want to be separated from him for months? He looked so formidable, she knew the next few moments weren't going to be pleasant. Anticipating he'd need time to blow off steam, she pressed her lips together, prepared for his verbal tirade.

Toshiro did not miss the way her slender shoulders squared. Despite his fury, he had to admire her resourcefulness. "You actually lived over a week below deck without being discovered until now?" He couldn't help asking.

She gave him a shy smile. "Yes. I brought food and fresh water aboard. My Lord, I should confess, I . . . ah . . . paid three of my dock workers to take out the Valerius barrel containing bottles of wine so I'd have room for my belongings."

"So you thought my private stock of Madeira would be the perfect thing to dump, did you?"

Affronted, she came to her full height. "I would never take anyone else's cargo. That would be stealing. The barrel did have our Valerius name on it. And I didn't dump it. I gave a bottle to each of my three Bristol workers; the rest we'll sell in the store."

"How economical," he grated. "Those bottles of Madeira were to be a present to my uncle."

"Oh. Well, I'm willing to reimburse you for the bottles out of my own funds," she offered. "I'll be certain to send Madeira on your next ship to Japan. Perhaps we can think of another gift for your uncle during the months it takes to reach him."

"I would not remind me of the long voyage ahead if I were you," warned Captain Valerius. "It is a hard trip; you will not like it. Women are expected to act differently in Japan than you are clearly used to behaving in England."

She brightened. "I have been reading about Japan for years, and Sumi has taught me a great deal about your customs. Besides, I shall stay out of the way."

"And obey my commands like any other crewman aboard this vessel?"

When he came closer, she nodded. "Yes, my Lord, I understand."

Toshiro took a deep breath. "Is it too much to hope that you saved Sumi and Iwao, along with your own relatives, worry by telling them where you were headed?"

Though resenting his tone, she managed to squelch the tart reply on her tongue. "Of course. I left notes for Sumi and Aunt Clarice. I am not stupid, my Lord."

"As this rash action of stowing aboard your husband's ship headed for Japan proves," he added, never attempting to disguise his scorn. "This is a working ship, madam, and I've no time to tend to a seasick wife or keep recalcitrant chits out of mischief."

"I won't be ill, and I've already promised to follow orders."

"We shall see," said her husband, an ominous gleam in his panther eyes. "Come, I shall show you to my . . . our cabin. Tom," he said and nodded to the young sailor with Jan, "will have your belongings brought up." Toshiro took a firm hold of her arm. "Jan, please see that another place at the captain's table is set tonight for my wife. And," he added in a voice that carried across the deck, "include a thick pillow for my Lady Wife's chair."

Jan blinked before the implication hit him.

Amy blushed. She saw the men around her try to curb their guffaws, but some didn't manage it.

"Very good, Captain," said Jan.

Toshiro's expression was unreadable as he hauled her toward his quarters. The crew's boisterous laughter rang in her ears.

Inside the small cabin, the count whirled on his embarrassed wife. "Damn it, Amy, for an intelligent woman, sometimes I don't think you use the brains God gave you. Rash is too mild a word for this stunt. You might have been killed if we'd had a major storm. One of those heavy crates could have landed on you. How the hell I ever thought you were meek is beyond me. You are stubborn, reckless, outspoken." He grabbed her roughly by the shoulders and gave her a forceful shake. "I wanted you safe back there in Bristol."

"Toshiro, please try to understand how much this means to me. I've never been anywhere outside of Bristol in my life. I've dreamed about this. Just once, before the chance is gone I want to sail to an exotic port. Besides, wouldn't your mother want to meet her son's wife? If I died before a year was out, wouldn't you be sorry that we'd had such little time together? I've just been married, and I don't want to be separated from you, not when the adventure is just beginning."

His hands on her arms relaxed. The thought of losing her made something hurt within his chest, but he couldn't dismiss the danger she'd rushed into. "I'll probably spend the next weeks either making passionate love to you or warming your unruly backside," he said, his voice husky. "Mrs. Valerius, you can be an exasperating woman."

She saw something soften on his features. "Then you aren't going to beat me?"

His wicked gaze never left hers. "Do you think I'd ever risk harming any delectable part of you?"

Amy was pleased at first, before the intent of his earlier words ignited her. She wrenched her arms free. "Then why did you humiliate me by letting the whole crew believe you were going to . . . ?"

The panther showed his even white teeth. "Consider that part of your punishment for disobeying my orders.

I've never truly beaten you, and you know it. Besides," he added, giving an ungallant sniff, "you need a bath first."

She tried but failed to hide a grin. "I brought my rose soap. The thought of not having a full bath for a week almost kept me home." Her look became flirtatious. "I don't suppose there is any chance I could borrow the use of the captain's brass tub?"

He tilted her gamine face up to his. "Checked to be sure I always travel with it, did you? Irksome wench." But the corners of his mouth twitched, spoiling his effort to be stern.

"I'll make it up to you," she promised.

"How?"

Amy held his gaze. "I could seduce you. After I've cleaned up and changed," she added.

If she only knew how much he did want her, Toshiro mused. He stepped back to take in her curves outlined most alluringly in those tight breeches. Her breasts strained against the front of the boy's shirt. "Never, do you understand, are you ever to wear this outfit in front of my men again."

She looked down at her grimy appearance. "I suppose I do look like a street urchin or a beached minnow at low tide. Sorry."

He was shocked to realize she had no idea of the arousing picture she presented. "Countess, it is because your alluring figure is too blatantly outlined in those boy's clothes. The voyage is long and my men, while the best crew in Europe, will be away from their wives and sweethearts. That is why I insist on more prudent attire, along with only going above deck when I tell you it is safe. Do you give me your word on these two issues?"

She accepted the wisdom of his directives. "Yes, I promise."

He nodded. "Then I will leave you to your bath."

That evening Amy dressed in a claret-colored gown, her recently washed locks tied in a becoming upsweep. Her husband and his officers rose when she entered the low-ceilinged dining room. She walked to the chair the count indicated, saw the large red pillow, took in Jan's worried expression, then moved the pillow off the seat and sat down. When she rested her back against the comfortable pillow, Amy saw Jan's expression relax immediately. It was clear the men now realized their captain had not carried out his threat.

Toshiro watched as his wife engaged in animated conversations with his men. She ate heartily and clearly enjoyed herself. However, he did worry about her ability to handle such a long voyage.

He needn't have. As the weeks passed, Toshiro was forced to admit his wife was blossoming. All the crew adored her. Not once did she complain or suffer from seasickness, as he'd feared. Indeed, her appetite for food, learning, and lovemaking delighted him.

Just three days before they reached Nagasaki, Toshiro as always allowed Amy above deck when he took his turn at the watch in the evenings.

As she stood in front of her husband, he guided her hands over the heavy wooden wheel that steered the *Nightingale*. Amy leaned back against him. She liked these quiet times at night when Toshiro let her come above deck when most of the men were asleep in their hammocks below. The summer air was almost sultry as they neared Nagasaki. She inhaled the smell of resin on the white pine decking and the odor of wet canvas sails.

"I like sailing, my Lord," she admitted. "I've never felt so alive in my life."

He kept his hands over hers as they both guided his ship. He lowered his lips and kissed her right ear. "I will admit I have never had such a captivating helmsman. And I am pleasantly astonished, golden lotus, how well you follow my orders. Is there any chance you will be so inclined when we return home to Bristol?"

She looked over her shoulder. "About as much chance as Grog sprouting wings," she tossed at him, then gave him an impudent grin. "While this is my first voyage, I have learned all I could about the life aboard ship from my captain. And I do enjoy the evenings, too. I never realized there were so many ways to make love in a bunk before."

"Saucy rascal," her husband whispered, then nuzzled her slender neck. "You are just taking advantage of me because my hands are otherwise occupied. Little hussy, stop rubbing your hips against me that way."

She giggled. "I thought you liked it when I instigate our lovemaking."

"You know I meant in the privacy of our cabin, brat, not right out here on deck."

"Oh, I beg your pardon," she said, not the least contrite. She made a motion to the right, then the left, exaggerating the gentle roll of the ship so that her plump derriere ground into his pelvis. "Must be we're picking up a southern breeze."

"I'll give you a southern breeze in a minute."

"I wouldn't," she advised. "Tom is coming toward us to take his watch." Plastering an angelic smile on her face, Amy greeted the young man. She watched as Toshiro stepped back, and Tom took over the wheel. For a minute the two men talked about the anticipated docking at Dejima.

Amy realized as they got closer to his home, Toshiro became more silent, less jovial. She knew it derived from this upcoming confrontation about his father's murder and the attempt on their lives from the ninja her husband had killed. Silently, she prayed she would be able to help him through these difficult days. It had been wonderful being away from Bristol for the first time in her life. The nightmares had almost stopped. Perhaps it would be all right now. If she kept the dragon asleep, he couldn't harm either of them, she told herself.

Amy stood breathlessly clutching the curved railing. She didn't want to miss anything as they sailed into the fjord-like inlet of Nagasaki. Flat ground with sudden hills—she marveled at how green Japan was. Using her spyglass, she recognized some of the tropical vegetation illustrated in the books she'd studied. She spotted palms and sugar cane. There were Japanese with their pants rolled up as they tugged their fishing nets out of the water. The air was warm and humid. Japanese workers dressed in gray loose-fitting pants and shirts boarded the ship to assist with the unloading. The man who obviously led the group came right over to Toshiro, knelt down, and touched his forehead to the floor. Amy noticed the Akashi crest on the sleeve of his shirt. He hid his shock quickly when Toshiro introduced his wife.

Tired from their long journey, Amy was grateful when Toshiro said she would be taken to their suite of rooms on the tiny fan-shaped island of Dejima, rather than go directly to his uncle's castle. Tomorrow they would be escorted to the mainland of Nagasaki.

Amy was even more appreciative the next day when Toshiro offered her the assistance of a young Japanese woman, who had learned English from the Dutch scholars that had been allowed to come to this settlement.

Dressed in a yellow silk kimono, the doll-like beauty entered their rooms after a servant slid open the paper and wood panel. The dark-haired girl had smooth pale skin, expressive almond eyes, and a childlike voice.

"I am happy to meet you," she said in excellent English. "My Lord Valerius has asked me to act as interpreter to make your stay more acceptable."

Amy returned the woman's bow. "I am most grateful."

"This is Lady Akiko Yoshimitsu. Her father is my uncle's chief adviser."

Amy remembered the name. This lovely girl was the lady the Akashis had wanted Toshiro to marry. Had these extensive Dutch and English lessons been allowed primarily to serve her future husband, Count Valerius?

As if reading Amy's thoughts, her husband added, "Lady Akiko is one of the few people who speaks both fluent Dutch and English. Her father has found her translation skills invaluable. We are honored that she accepts her father's request to act as your interpreter while you are a guest in Nagasaki."

Her husband's precisely spoken words reminded Amy of her manners. Toshiro had married her, not Akiko, but she could not help feeling drab in her brown cotton gown right now. "Thank you, Lady Akiko. I am grateful to have your assistance." She smiled.

Toshiro bowed to both ladies and went into the next room to change for dinner.

Amy turned to Akiko. "I would appreciate your help in putting on my kimono that I brought from Bristol. Do you know who Sumi is?"

"Yes, my Lady, she and her husband's family have served the Akashis for generations."

Though Amy heard politeness, something in the girl's demeanor made her uncomfortable. "Well, Sumi kindly made me a kimono and showed me how to wear it, but now that the time has come and I am to meet my mother-in-law for the first time tomorrow, I am not so certain I'll be able to get everything right. Tying the *obi* still confuses me."

The girl's porcelain features became more friendly. "I shall be happy to assist you."

Before Amy dressed the next day, Toshiro left to make their final preparations for traveling to his uncle's house.

While Akiko helped Amy dress, she explained how Amy would make the short journey to Akashi castle. When the time came to leave, Amy was led toward an enclosed sedan chair. Two Japanese servants on either side hoisted the long carrying poles over their shoulders. Peering out the one sliding window, Amy saw her husband. Toshiro looked more Japanese today in his wide-leg pants under a black silk kimono. Atop a white stallion, Count Valerius's wooden saddle of maple was painted in cinnabar and black lacquer. The gold sword-shaped leaves of the iris decorated the center rim of the pommel. He wore the long and short swords of a samurai thrust through his waistband.

When Amy had asked why she and her husband could not ride together without the large entourage, Akiko had not been able to disguise her shock at Amy's suggestion. "My Lord Valerius is *Hotamoto*," Akiko pointed out. A samurai knight of Lord Valerius's station apparently required more than Amy's preference for a quiet how-do with the kinfolk.

The Dutch port of Dejima was linked to the sheltered harbor of Nagasaki by a narrow causeway. As the retinue of archers, thirty foot soldiers in gray, and twenty mounted samurai went across the bridge, Amy realized how easy it was to guard and check who came and went. No wonder few Japanese ever left Japan.

The Akashi fortress was a five-storied wooden structure with each story smaller than the one below it. The black overhanging roofs contrasted with the white painted stories. On the highest point of the keep, elaborate decorations of gold dolphins gleamed in the sunlight. A thick forest surrounded the back of the compound. Following custom Toshiro went ahead to visit with his relatives first.

In her sandals, white socks, wearing the aqua silk kimono, Amy walked slowly into one of the rooms of the castle an hour later. The formal area was made of resinous timber with paper-covered screens. By English standards it was stark with little furniture, but there was a beautifully painted screen of a mountain and waterfall behind the dais where three people sat. Round cushions had been placed on the polished, dark-wood floor. Toshiro was already kneeling on one as he spoke to the two men wearing colorful kimonos over the same style of loose-fitting trousers as her husband.

Toshiro got up when he saw her enter. At first he looked pleasantly surprised to discover the use of his bolt of cloth that he'd presented to her that first morning in her office. Then he stared down at her sash. "Which of the servants assisted you with your kimono, Amy?"

His question was so unexpected and direct, the changed inflection in his voice alerted her. She looked at the gentleman sitting cross-legged on the raised platform. The full gray mustache Toshiro had once mentioned told her this distinguished gentleman had to be his uncle. The proud posture was similar to her husband's, yet the gray-haired man was shorter than Toshiro. There was an older man sitting lower and to his right, more than likely Akiko's father. Finally, Amy took in the red-and-gold-draped lady who sat so elegantly to the left of the men. Amy's face heated at their polite but obviously uncomfortable expressions. Instantly, she knew something was amiss with her attire. "I must have done something incorrectly," she gulped. "Please, my Lord," she addressed her husband. "What is wrong?"

Embarrassed in front of his relatives, Toshiro could hardly speak. "The way you have tied the bow in front. It is the sign of a courtesan. Respectable married ladies," he hissed, "tie the *obi* in back. Now, I realize you are still learning our ways, but I want to know the servant's name who helped you dress. It is clear there is something unpleasant going on here."

Amy looked at Akiko. Though the young Japanese tried to retain her placid countenance, Amy spotted a brief look of panic in her dark eyes. And she recognized the signs of jealousy; she'd felt the same when she first learned about this lovely girl Toshiro's Japanese relatives had hoped he would wed. Upset at not making a first good impression, Amy, nevertheless, tried to remind herself how swift and harsh Japanese justice could be. She shook her head. "I am sorry, my Lord. I thought I could dress myself. It appears I should not have let my stubborn independence stand in the way of asking for assistance. May I be excused for a moment to rectify my attire?"

Toshiro gave her a curt nod, then made her apologies to his relatives. "Perhaps Lady Akiko will accompany you this time," he advised. "She knows all about proper protocol and attire."

Akiko bowed and followed Amy out of the large meeting room. Once in a smaller private room, Akiko went about retying the sash behind Amy's back. For her part, Amy said nothing.

Finished, Akiko looked up at her. "You look most presentable." She peered down at her sandaled feet. "It was thoughtful of you not to tell my honorable father about my behavior."

"He is the man with my husband's uncle?"

"Yes," Akiko answered. "My father is Lord Akashi's minister."

"Well," Amy admitted, "I'd rather stay on your good side, as I may have need of your translating skills in the future. We English are pragmatic. I'm sure the count's mother was taken aback to see her son's foreign wife sashaying into the parlor proclaiming herself a tart by attire."

"Tart?" Akiko repeated the word. *"Wakarimasen."*

"No, I don't suppose you do understand. Well, no matter. Let's try again, shall we?"

This time Akiko seemed to realize the Englishwoman also offered a new start for them, too. "Yes, I will try."

Amy and Lady Akiko came back into the room.

Toshiro appeared relieved. For the first time he noticed the amethyst and gold clip in her blond hair. It was in the shape of an iris. "Please know that you are beautiful, in case I forgot to mention it."

"Thank you," she said, taking his arm. She walked over with her husband to the raised platform.

"I would like to present my untrained wife, Amy Stockwell Valerius," he said. "My uncle, the feudal lord of this province, Lord Kojiro Akashi."

Amy went down on her knees on the round cushion as Sumi had taught her, gracefully placed her hands on the floor in front of her, and bowed to her husband's uncle. "I am pleased to meet my Lord Husband's illustrious uncle," she said in perfect Japanese.

Obviously surprised at her grasp of his language, Lord Akashi's expression softened as he looked down at the blond-haired woman. "Welcome to my nephew's wife. May I present my minister, Lord Yoshimitsu."

Amy turned and bowed in his direction.

"And my honorable sister, Lady Haru Akashi."

She hoped with all her heart Lady Haru would at least accept her. With trepidation, Amy stumbled over her Japanese, before finding the courage to look up. In her forties, Toshiro's mother still retained her delicate beauty. There was a calm dignity about her that put Amy instantly at ease.

"I am pleased to make your acquaintance, Amy," Haru said in English. Her dark eyes took a shrewd inventory of her new daughter-in-law.

Food was brought in, but Amy was too nervous to eat more than a few mouthfuls of rice and raw fish with plum sauce. It was tasty and arranged beautifully with special attention paid to color and symmetry. She was especially taken with the shrimp presented in the form of a chrysanthemum flower. Using the ivory sticks as Sumi had taught her, Amy forced herself to eat slowly.

The way the men listened to Haru told Amy of her important position in the Akashi family. There might have been recriminations against her years ago when she rashly wed a Dutch count, but right now her position was clearly that of illustrious sister to the daimyo. Through Akiko, Lady Haru asked Amy to visit her in the morning for a private audience. Amy thanked her and replied she would look forward to it. Well, it was partly true. Amy hadn't come all this way to stay hidden in her room while the council met tomorrow to discuss the Lord Masao Nishikawa matter. She knew the men had discussed it over dinner, but Amy realized she would have to wait and get her information from Toshiro in private rather than ask for an immediate translation. She smiled to herself. All and all, Amy thought, she hadn't done too badly today. From lowered lashes, she studied Haru and found she liked the lady's manner. Haru entered right into the conversation, gesturing one or two times as she spoke rapidly in Japanese. It reminded Amy of her own talks with rival business owners. Yes, she wanted to learn about this interesting member of the Akashi family.

Akiko took Amy to Haru's private apartments the next morning. After a little small talk, Lady Haru thanked Akiko and said she would see that her daughter-in-law returned safely to her rooms. If Akiko was irritated not to be included in the conversation, she did not show it.

Alone with her mother-in-law, Amy waited politely for Lady Haru to begin the conversation. She admired the simple elegance of the light, airy room. There was a delft ware vase on one of the small tables on the side of the room. A small oil painting of a Dutch rural scene hung next to a Japanese brush drawing of a mother and her baby. Because the lady resembled Haru, Amy assumed the laughing little boy in her arms must have been Toshiro.

Sitting across from Amy, the Japanese woman kept her slender hands in the lap of her iris-patterned kimono. "I hope the simple gifts pleased you," she said, eyeing one of the items Amy wore this morning.

Amy smiled and touched the peach silk kimono she wore. "It is exquisite, my Lady. I am humbled by your generosity. Besides, I didn't know how it would go over if I showed up every day in the one kimono I own. After a week, I anticipated walking downwind alone."

Apparently, Amy's blurted admonition did not displease Lady Haru, for she covered her lips with her hand, almost as if she attempted to stifle a laugh. "My son tells me you know the primary reason for this visit," she said, sadness clouding her brown eyes. "Let us hope the council of ministers can end the feud with the Nishikawa family. Lord Masao is a cunning warrior. He waited twenty-eight years to quench his thirst for revenge."

Instantly, Amy reached out and patted Haru's hand. "I am sure Toshiro and Lord Kojiro will be able to convince Masao of the folly of pursuing this vendetta."

Haru shook her head. "It is the method of convincing that concerns me. But let us speak of more pleasant things. Am I what you expected?"

"Well, you are more forceful than I anticipated," Amy blurted out. "I had heard so much about Japanese women that I—"

"You thought," interjected Haru with a soft laugh, "I

would be bowing and full of silent humility. Would it shock you to learn I first met Pieter Valerius because I was climbing a tree? In English you would have called me a tomboy, yet growing up with six older brothers, could I have been anything else?"

For the first time since arriving in Nagasaki, Amy felt she'd met a kindred spirit. "I hope we will be friends, my Lady."

"I believe we already are, Amy-san," said her mother-in-law. "Friend is better than daughter-in-law in my country, for I would not wish to treat you as my drudge."

Sumi had explained how the role of mother-in-law was often the first and only power for a Japanese woman. "I am grateful." And then Amy did find herself chattering away. She didn't even think about Toshiro's meeting with the council until that evening when she and her husband were alone.

From his grim expression, she instantly knew things had not gone well.

Nineteen

"Lord Masao boldly confessed to having one of his retainers smuggled aboard a Chinese ship." Sitting next to his wife on the futon over the tatami on the polished floor, Toshiro shook his head. "With pride Masao told the council he sent that ninja to Amsterdam to kill my father. He has waited patiently to take his revenge." The count took his wife in his arms and held her tightly for a moment. "He vowed I will know what it feels like to have happiness wrenched from my arms as he did when my mother was stolen from him by marrying 'That Western barbarian.' God, I could not get him to back down. My uncle and the council reminded him that they had seen to Pieter's and Lady Haru's punishment. It made no difference to Lord Masao."

"Darling, what will happen now?"

"My uncle and the council have ordered Lord Masao to commit seppuku for having arranged the murder of Count Pieter Valerius and attempting to kill the present count's wife. Nothing less will wipe away the shame he has brought on his own family by such traitorous actions."

Never had she believed this was the way it would end. All during the crossing, she assumed the parties involved would meet and discuss this, with compromises made on both sides. That was the way she solved crises in running her complex business operations. "You mean Lord Masao Nishikawa has been ordered to kill himself?"

"Yes."

"We cannot let this happen. It is so uncivi—"

"You are not in England now," her husband interjected, displeased by the word she'd almost used to describe what would take place in two days. "As my wife you will be expected to attend the ritualistic suicide. My mother and uncle will also be present. Because my uncle's family remained in Edo while he makes his alternate year visit to his province, it will not be such a public spectacle."

Amy searched for something to stop this horrible event. "Why wouldn't Lord Akashi's own family wish to be here? Your mother came."

"Only because she was granted special permission from the Shogun." Toshiro took a deep breath and tried to calm himself. He took Amy's hand. "The Shogun requires his feudal lords to spend every other year in their own province. Thus, the lords must maintain two households: one in Edo, the other in their own province. However, their families must remain in Edo while the daimyos make their provincial visits."

"Why?"

"I knew you would not let it rest there. Well, the Shogun shrewdly realizes that no lord would raise an army against him while the daimyo's wife and family are in his power in Edo."

"You mean the Shogun uses the feudal lord's family as hostages?"

"It is a term I would not have used, but yes, in a manner of speaking, you are correct. And I assure you it has been very effective up to now."

Amy pulled her hand away. "Even though I'm trying, I really do not know if I will ever understand your country, my Lord."

He pulled her back into his arms. After he kissed her smooth cheek, he felt her lean against his bare chest. Playing with the silk ribbons at the shoulders of her sheer nightgown, he said, "I know, *koneko*. Believe me, after living here for ten years, and yearly visits, I am still learning. But I do know this: I would rather see Masao Nishikawa dead than risk losing you from another assassin's attempt on your life."

Amy did not sleep well that night. Some of the old nightmares returned to taunt her. In the morning, she could tell from Toshiro's expression he'd fared no better. He said little to her, and she knew in his mind the matter of Masao was settled or would be in another day.

After Toshiro went to see his uncle, Haru took Amy for a brief tour about the Akashi compound. The stables were immaculate, with polished wooden boards on the floor. The wide-chested horses were pampered by a bevy of servants dressed identically in those simple gray shirts and loose trousers she'd seen so often since her arrival. As Amy was shown the buildings and splendor of the Akashi castle, she was struck by the wealth and status of her in-laws. She learned that currency was measured in *koku,* which equaled five bushels of rice. In his own right Toshiro owned two hundred thousand *koku* worth of rice land here in Japan. How wrong David had been. There wasn't anything peasant-like about the Akashis.

As the afternoon ended and Haru and her daughter-in-law sipped their tea, Amy could remain mute on this topic no longer. She placed the round red bowl on the low lacquered table in front of her. "My Lady, please, may I ask you a question?"

Haru looked pensive. She did not touch the sweet rice cake on her plate. It is about what will take place tomorrow, is it not?"

"Yes." Amy's blue eyes mirrored her worry. "Can you not convince your brother to call off his order for suicide?"

Lady Haru's lovely face contorted with grief. "It is too late. You must understand this is our way of justice. It is an honorable way for Lord Masao to make amends for killing Pieter, and I now realize the anguish my son would have experienced had you been killed that night in Bristol. Amy-san, we can only wait and see what happens tomorrow."

Not about to sit by passively, Amy sought out Akiko. She needed more information.

Amy could not eat the next morning. Everyone went about their duties as if it were an ordinary day. She did not understand the outward calm that pervaded the whole island. The "event," as Amy referred to it, was to take place outside in the open garden behind the Akashi castle. Attuned to the seriousness of the occasion, Toshiro dressed in a white kimono. The golden circle on arms, back, and front contained the sword-shaped leaves of the Akashi crest.

When she heard the sound of a wooden beam hitting the side of a large iron bell, as directed, Amy went and sat next to Haru. Toshiro sat on the raised dais with his uncle and the council of ministers. When a man dressed in white kimono walked proudly into the courtyard, Amy realized this had to be Lord Masao Nishikawa. He had a strong face with a scar on the right cheek. As his family was also in Edo, he had only a few brown-clad retainers with him. Masao walked over to the area where a cushion had been placed on the ground. He knelt down and began tying his legs together.

Amy blanched when she saw that one of his aides began pouring water from a wooden ladle over a long sword. A case carrying the knife for his self-disemboweling lay on a pillow in front of Lord Masao. Amy darted a pleading look at Toshiro, but he did not change his fixed expression. Everything according to custom, each movement carried a special meaning of its own. When she saw Masao pull out the short knife, she stood up immediately.

"Wait!" she shouted in Japanese. "Please allow me to speak."

She saw Lord Kojiro Akashi frown at Toshiro, as if he expected his nephew to control his foreign wife's outbursts. "Please," she repeated, then bowed. She asked humbly that Akiko act as interpreter, not Toshiro.

Toshiro spoke briefly to his uncle and the elderly council members. It was clear to Amy these Japanese men were appalled at her inappropriate behavior during this ritual. Silently, she prayed her husband would forgive her for not being able to act in the proper Japanese manner of a dutiful wife.

Finally, it was Lord Kojiro Akashi who spoke. Akiko was ordered to stand next to Amy. Her request had been granted. Amy had to dig her nails into her palms to keep her voice steady. "My Lord and honorable members of the houses of Akashi and Nishikawa," she began, then waited for Akiko to translate. Evidently some of the Akashi men disliked her politeness with the Nishikawas they saw as their enemy. "Since Lord Masao married shortly after Haru's decision to defy custom and her family by wedding Pieter Valerius, I understand he now has a beautiful wife he loves, seven fine sons, two daughters, and numerous grandchildren." Even Lord Masao nodded with self-importance at the truthfulness of Amy's statement after Akiko translated.

"Lord Masao has many heirs," Amy went on. "Count Valerius is the last of his house in Amsterdam. Lord Masao's death will not bring Pieter Valerius back. Lady Haru has no grandchildren. All have been punished enough. The council ruled twenty-eight years ago that Haru and Pieter must always live apart for their transgression. They did so. Their son lives with difficulty in both East and West cultures, often not accepted in either. Please, let this blood feud end here. Lord Masao's death will cause me much anguish, for I was raised to believe such violence is wrong. If Lord Masao promises not to harm any of the Akashis, including Toshiro or our unborn child, it will be enough to restore harmony to all our houses."

Toshiro wasn't able to hide his astonishment at her last declaration.

"Is this true?" his uncle demanded. "You said the lady confessed to being barren."

Toshiro looked back at Amy.

"My Lords," Amy interceded. "Though I am not with child yet, I am hopeful there will be an heir for the House of Valerius in the future." Inwardly, she knew she could never have children. But she was certain the words might help save a man's life. "I cannot live with the shame that my happiness comes through the death of another." She walked over and knelt down before Lord Masao Nishikawa. The knife he now gripped in his hand, she knew, could be easily used on her at this proximity. Even Toshiro's expert warrior skills could never reach her in time.

"Amy!" Toshiro shouted, showing his fear at his wife's impulsive actions.

Her features set, she placed her hands on the ground and bowed low from her seated position. *"Dansu ni ikimasen ka?"* she asked, her voice carrying to the spectators about them.

Masao looked startled. His cold gaze searched her face and found the amusement in eyes the color of a cloudless sky. Then he realized she knew the preposterous question she had asked at such a time. He bit back a smile, coughed, before it turned into a boisterous roar.

Others around them seemed equally unable to hold back their reactions that this strange foreigner had just loudly asked Lord Masao rather than kill himself, "Wouldn't he rather go dancing?" As far as Amy knew, the minuet hadn't reached here; however, she only hoped her suggestion would relieve the tension for a few moments. It had often worked in negotiating with a quick-tempered rival in business.

She glanced up to see her husband's scowling expression. "This is hardly the time for English buffoonery," he rebuked his wife. "Go back and sit down next to my mother at once." His uncle stopped laughing and demanded a translation of his nephew's censuring English words.

"Has Lord Toshiro married an English clown?" Akiko

translated Masao's question to the council. Nevertheless, he set the knife back down on the white pillow in front of him.

Amy cleared her throat and stood up. "Again I ask that Lord Masao promise not to harm the Akashis anymore, and we can end the bitterness between our families. It is my understanding the Shogun himself is anxious for our two families to end this blood feud."

There were indrawn breaths from the dais when the males wondered how this slip of an English girl had privy to such information. Amy looked up at Haru. The older woman nodded approvingly.

Lord Masao spoke with the council and Toshiro in rapid Japanese for half an hour. Amy stood rooted to the spot waiting for their decision. Finally, she saw Lord Masao shake his head grudgingly. He said something to Toshiro, and Amy was surprised to see her husband nod his head in agreement when he looked back at her.

Lord Kojiro Akashi raised his hand for silence. "It is decided," Akiko translated for Amy. "Lord Masao will return to his family, for he has solemnly vowed never to harm Toshiro, his family, or any member of the Akashi clan again." With little change in the daimyo's expression, he had Akiko translate that his nephew had told him Amy-san was a fragile English rose, biddable and obedient.

"At times, honorable Uncle," Amy answered, then added an appropriate Oriental bow.

Haru smiled at her older brother. "But she is a suitable wife for the panther after all."

"More than suitable," Toshiro added, both in Japanese and English. Pride showed from his eyes as he broke with custom by outwardly praising his wife.

***

Months later when they had nearly reached Bristol, Amy awoke for the third time in one week with that same queasy lurch in her stomach. Glad Toshiro was up earlier and above deck, she barely had time to reach for the basin she now kept near her side of the bunk.

Afterwards, she washed her face and wobbled back to bed. She pressed her hand over her aching head. How ignoble to make it this far and then prove her husband's dire prediction true.

Amy nearly jumped when she felt someone sit down next to her on the narrow bed. She managed to open one eye. "My Lord, I didn't hear you come in," she said and tried to sit up.

"Not feeling well, I see," observed the count.

"All right. You were correct. I am seasick. Now, will you please let me die in peace? Isn't there a sail or hatch you need to batten down in this gale?"

He brushed back a strand of damp hair from her wan face. "The sea is tranquil today," he pointed out, then added, "I've brought you some tea and a plain biscuit from the galley."

She moaned. "Just toss it in the chamber pot to save me the effort later. I know nothing will stay down. I'll never eat again."

"Come, it will help. Trust me, *koneko*. It is the best thing in your condition. It will soon pass in a few weeks."

"Hoping to bury me at sea, are you? Anyway, we'll be home in less than a week," she pointed out, then groaned again. "I'm sure when we reach land I'll be just fine."

"I wouldn't count on it," said her maddeningly calm

husband. He got up and went over to his desk to pick up the tray containing the tea and one warm scone. He reached for a wooden chair and came back to sit next to her. Placing the tray on the small nighttable to his left, he prepared the tea for her. "Try a little," he coaxed again. "It will settle your stomach."

She sat up and cast a dubious scowl at the tea and scone. "I never heard of that as a cure for seasickness."

"No, but it will help with your morning sickness," said the count casually.

"Morning sickness?" Amy's blue eyes rounded to saucers. "I'm seasick."

"I believe not."

"Barnacle balls, it's my ruddy stomach. I know if I'm puking or not."

With the patience of Job, Count Valerius shook his head. "It happens only in the morning, the sea has been placid, and you have not had your monthly flow in two months."

Amy's skin reddened at the casual way he rattled off his reasons why he was right and she was wrong. "I have skipped my cycles before."

Toshiro cut the scone in half for her. "Not since we married, you haven't."

"Do you know how disconcerting it is to be married to a man who studies your bodily functions with such indecent interest?"

"I am always discreet," he said in his own defense before holding out the steaming cup of tea.

She took a sip, then bit into the piece of scone. He wiped her mouth with the edge of a clean linen napkin. As she finished the tea and biscuit, she did admit feeling better. Then the truth of his words soared through her.

She'd found the perfect present for him. "Oh, my, Toshiro, do you realize what this means?"

He took the tea things out of her hand and placed them back on the tray. Gently, he took her into his arms. "Of course, I do, my darling. It's been difficult not to shout my joy since I began suspecting it. However, I did not want to spoil your special moment when you told me. Yet, by the third day of your morning sickness I knew I could not leave you alone to suffer when I could help."

"What a rube you must think me," she said, then laughed at herself. "I was so sure it was seasickness, I wanted to do anything to keep you from finding out that you were right. I never dreamed it was because I'm pregnant." The word sounded wonderful on her tongue. "My Lord, I must be the only woman in the world who had to have her husband tell her the news."

Toshiro could not hold back his own laughter. "Being married to you is truly an adventure, Amy-san."

"Yes," agreed his wife. "English rascals are prone to keeping their husbands on tenterhooks."

That evening at the captain's table, Jan Roonhuysen was the first to congratulate them. "When did you tell your husband the wonderful news?" he asked Amy.

"Actually, it was Toshiro who informed me," the countess stated. "I usually let my husband handle all these domestic duties."

Jan looked back at the count, then stared at the other crewmen about the table, who appeared to be choking in their effort to maintain the same calm expression as their captain.

Toshiro shrugged. "You might as well let it out, lads. Being married to this hoyden for over a year now, I've learned you cannot keep that kind of laughter in. No need to blow your boilers," he said, repeating Amy's often-used phrase.

Amy smiled when toasts went around.

"To the next heir for the House of Valerius," Jan said, raising his glass. "And to the loveliest woman on this ship."

"I'm the *only* woman on this ship," George Stockwell's daughter pointed out, "but I accept the compliment anyway." She looked up at Captain Valerius. "I'm glad I gave into my husband's insistence that I come to Japan with him."

Toshiro looked at his impertinent wife. Ready to come back with a suitable retort, his features changed. "I am pleased you came, too," he admitted. "But if you ever pull such a dangerous stunt again, I'll—"

"Make me walk the plank," she finished, then stood up on tiptoes to kiss his cheek. "You know," she said, stepping back to take in his black attire. "You do look rather like a pirate from this angle."

"Might as well give up, my Lord," advised Jan with a grin. "*Ja,* it's clear the head of Stockwell Enterprises won't always let you have the last word."

"Exasperating woman," said Toshiro, but he leaned over and kissed her inviting lips.

She colored at his unusual public display.

"Well," he said to his amused comrades. "At least that is one way to keep those outrageous English comments at bay for a little while."

Amy remained silent. She was content to be close to

the man she loved, sharing the happiness of their good news with friends.

Two months before the baby was due, Amy sat upstairs in her sitting room with her feet propped up on a comfortable ottoman. Unable to concentrate, she put down the book on Japanese lacquer ware and walked slowly over to that piece of furniture. "To help you during your confinement," Clarice had said yesterday when she left it. Amy ran her hands along the leather arms of her wheelchair. It was unsettling to see this chair again after so many months not needing it. Memories buffeted her.

Months ago, after they'd returned from Japan, her aunt and uncles had been aghast to learn she was pregnant. Clarice nearly fainted. Simon and Henry took the news as if she'd just stated Bristol was about to be overrun by a horde of Tartars. Giles pointed out she was too fragile to bear a child. Dr. Stewart said otherwise. But at Toshiro's insistence, he checked on her often.

Deciding it was too lovely a spring day to stay indoors, Amy headed downstairs, then outside toward the garden. Everyone on the estate took care of her. She had a desire for strawberries, and they materialized. Sumi walked in the garden every day with her if Toshiro was busy running their business. In the warm sunshine Amy felt large and pampered, like an indulged yellow cat.

She greeted Dover on his way with a bale of hay to the barn. Opening the wooden gate, Amy stepped into their Oriental garden. Purple iris, yellow daffodils, green ferns, the carefully raked patches of earth that looked like ripples on a placid sea—Amy always felt safe here.

She walked over and sat down on the wide ledge that surrounded the lotus pond.

Sighing, she willed her body to relax, then concentrated on the rippling water. She thought of how much things had changed since that spring morning when she had visited this pond for the first time. The presence of the wheelchair in her sitting room next to their upstairs bedroom now reminded Amy of her unsettled past. She touched her round stomach when she felt a familiar spasm. The baby probably had hiccups again, the blond-haired woman thought, then smiled. "You are all right, darling," she whispered, then caressed her stomach. Did all mothers talk to their little ones this way before they were born?

Yes, she thought, her mood sobering. Now there was to be an heir for the House of Valerius. While overjoyed at the prospect, Amy still couldn't dismiss her worries about the future. Would this child inherit her mother's illness? How could Amy be certain she was cured, that she wouldn't have a relapse or even harm this child? This last question chilled her. Even if she wanted to go back to that day when she was ten and her life had changed forever, the dark mist blocked her vision. Was it the dragon again? But if the dragon wasn't death as she'd thought the night she tried to drown herself, who was he?

"Amy?"

Startled, Amy looked up to find her husband watching her. Apparently Toshiro had left his workroom early to find his wife. His warm smile engulfed her. "Finish your carpentry for the day?"

"I saw you through the window. You should not be sitting on that cold marble. Here," he added, helping her to stand. He sat down and pulled her gently across the leather apron covering his lap.

"Much better," she admitted, nestling against him. "You make a marvelous chair, even if you are covered with sawdust." She brushed some of the wood shavings from the side of his black hair. He had the sleeves of his tan laborer's shirt rolled up. The scent of varnish clung to him. She sighed with contentment when he kissed her cheek and continued rubbing her back. He kissed and cuddled her a great deal these days.

"Ready to see the wooden elf I made for the garden?"

Amy tried not to damage his artistic temperament. "Yes, of course, but Toshiro, do you think a gnome will . . . ah . . . fit in with the harmony of our Japanese garden?"

He helped her up, then placed his arm around her thickening waist to support her as they walked back toward the small wooden structure that housed his carpentry work. "Oh, I think the six-foot leprechaun will fit right in. I painted his face green to go with the moss and shrubs. Red coat and purple breeches to match the hollyhocks and irises in the garden."

The vision of those jarring colors made her nauseous. She tried again to hide her true reaction at the prospect of such a garish gargoyle right in the center of their peaceful garden. "How . . . unique." During the last few weeks her husband had been working furiously out here whenever he could spare an hour or two from helping her run Stockwell Enterprises. With an eagerness to surprise her, he'd made Amy promise not to step foot in here until it was done.

From weekly hints on this project, Amy wasn't sure she wanted to see the completed project even now. Bracing herself, the countess walked into the room and looked around.

Nothing.

Then she spied the large object that rested on his wide carpentry table. "Oh, Toshiro!" She went over and touched the intricate carvings along the edge of the wooden cradle. At the head was a carved iris with its sword-shaped leaves; next to it a chiseled English rose. "The workmanship could rival the finest cabinetmaker in London." She read the pleasure in his eyes at her praise. "And our children can use this for our grandchildren. It will be in our family for generations."

"I am glad you like it."

His wife gave him a mock look of reproach. "However, sir, I should be very cross with you for teasing me into thinking you were going to bring a gruesome monstrosity into our garden."

He chuckled at her pretended indignation. "Well, if you have your heart set on the elf, I can still—"

She jabbed him playfully in the ribs. "Don't you dare. Barnacle balls, you don't want to scare your son when he takes his first steps and finds such a hideous creature near the goldfish pond, do you?"

"True, might give him nightmares." However, the joviality in his voice faded when he saw Amy look away suddenly at his mention of nightmares. He tipped her face up to his. "Darling, what is it? I've known since our return, especially when your aunt sent over the wheelchair, something troubles you again. You murmured about the green talons of the dragon again in your sleep last night."

For a moment, Amy leaned her head against Toshiro's solidness. Then she stepped back. "I did wonder why you never said anything when I had the wheelchair placed in my sitting room upstairs. I know you are not happy to see it either."

"True, but only you can make that decision of whether to keep it or not." He studied her intently. "You are still haunted by something more than the wheelchair, aren't you?"

She clenched her hands together in front of her and blurted out, "Toshiro, I want you to help me recall what happened the day my parents died."

His reaction was automatic. "No."

"Last year you wanted me to accept your help to remember. You said the past couldn't hurt me."

His features contorted at her suggestion. "Things have changed now. It would be too dangerous, both for you and our unborn child."

Twenty

To keep her husband from turning away, Amy took his hands in hers. "Yes, darling, things have changed. Now I realize I must know and face the truth of that night, otherwise I'll never be able to bury the past and make a new life for us."

As he watched the pleading in her blue eyes, Toshiro knew she was right. But it did nothing to assuage his fear. "When do you want to do it?"

She held on to him, grateful for his compliance, yet still needing his support. "Tomorrow afternoon. I'd like Joshua Rigby to be present."

"And Keith Stewart," the count insisted. He tried to make light of it. "Humor a first-time father."

She reveled in the tenderness of his expression. "Yes, well, just in case you swoon into the lotus pond after working yourself up so, I guess we'd best have Keith there, too."

Toshiro saw her stifle a yawn. "Now, Countess, I think you should take a short nap." They both heard the arrival of their Valerius carriage. Dover was shouting a greeting to Iwao.

"Oh, Iwao is back from London," she chirped, shoving aside her lethargy. "I hope he brought those designs I ordered from Paris. I'm adding a new line in the store and—"

Toshiro placed his finger across her pink mouth. "You can see Iwao later. Besides, I need to find out how our business venture with the king is progressing." The last thing he wanted right now was to have Amy find out who rode in that coach with Iwao. "You just go along now and rest."

She kissed his finger, then gave it a playful nip. "Good thing I'm enormous with child and sleepy, else you'd have a mutiny on your hands. Tell me, Lord Panther, are you going to be this stiff-rumped during all my future pregnancies?"

He kissed her cheek, then patted her hip. "You can depend on it, *koneko.*" He let her see the love in his eyes. "Never did I believe I would find such happiness. Is it any wonder, then, I want to keep you safe always?"

Warmed by his words, Amy reached up and caressed his strong cheek. "As I would see you safe, my Lord." Silently, she prayed she was doing the right thing. When Toshiro had the proof that she was responsible for her parents' deaths, would she lose his love forever? Trying to hide her apprehension, she turned and walked back into the house. Amy knew the dragon would be back in her dreams this afternoon.

As soon as his wife was out of sight, Toshiro raced for his study.

When Iwao knocked and entered, he was ready.

A young man with insolent gray eyes stepped into the room behind the Japanese servant. "Cor, you must be having trouble with that hobby of yours to pay me two hundred pounds to come back here." James Conroy gave the count a self-satisfied smirk. "Your Jappo servant here says you want me advice. You can't rush good workmanship, me Lord. You aristos want everything done in a rush. Bet you tried to force the wood. See it all the time. Now, will you show me the table? I can only stay a few hours. Got to get back to the shop. Old Morton is makin' me a partner, you know."

The count unlocked the middle drawer of his desk and pulled out two pieces of wood. "This shouldn't take long. I want to know what you make of this." He held up the two wooden spokes of the wheel that fit neatly together.

Conroy's eyes widened. "You yellow bast—" He bolted for the door.

A knife in his hand, Iwao blocked the Englishman's path. Panicking, Conroy whirled around to head for the window, but Valerius cut off his exit. The loaded pistol in the Eurasian's hand got the young journeyman's complete attention.

"I would prefer you stay," Toshiro advised calmly. "I believe we should talk. Then I have a job for you. It involves searching for a dragon."

James looked down at the gun. "Dragon? Ya must be daft."

Ignoring Conroy for the moment, Toshiro spoke to his servant. "Iwao, in a few moments I will have a note for you to take to Stockwell Hall. We will have one more guest tomorrow."

Both Keith Stewart and Joshua Rigby looked skeptical when Toshiro told them of his plan for the warm early evening. However, they both agreed to assist Amy and her husband any way they could. Toshiro placed a thick futon on the marble ledge of the lotus pond. Amy sat between her husband and Dr. Stewart. Joshua went next to Toshiro.

"Now, once I begin," the Eurasian told Keith and Joshua, "it would be best if you do not speak."

Grimly, both men nodded.

"Just concentrate on the lotuses moving on the quiet surface of the pond, Amy. Feel the breath moving in and out of you. Experience the gentle lifting and falling of your body."

Toshiro's soothing voice calmed her. Trusting him completely, she did not fight the images that assailed her. She allowed the panther to lead her into a deep trance. Round and round the lotuses made their slow gyrations across the clear surface. She would not be afraid to see the truth. "Yes," she said, her voice faint, "I want to remember."

"Go back to that day, Amy. It began pleasantly. Tell me what you are doing."

A smile transformed her features. This time when she spoke, it was the voice of ten-year-old Amy Stockwell. *"David and I are playing in the garden. Papa brought over a foreign boy to join us. I think he is shy but very well-mannered. I have never seen such striking features. David made an unkind remark about Toshiro, and I told David he was being very rude. I ordered him to say he was sorry, but he told us he never apologizes. David shoved me out of the way. I fell hard on the gray cobblestones of the walkway and scraped my knees. Toshiro is shorter than David, but the black-haired boy tossed David right over his shoulder in a maneuver neither David nor I ever saw before. David landed in the bed of begonias and was furious, but he couldn't do anything because Toshiro's father finished his business and they left."*

"It's late afternoon now, Amy," came Toshiro's voice next to her. "Where are you now?"

Amy worked her lower lip between her teeth. *"It isn't like Timi to wander off. I've been looking all over the house for him. Finally, I skipped out to the flower garden. He was probably burying another soup bone under Mama's yellow rose bush. Oh, oh, no."*

Trying to keep his voice level, despite the anguish he saw on her face, her husband continued. "What do you see, Amy?"

She swiped at her eyes in the gesture of a child fighting tears. *"It's Timi, my spaniel puppy. I picked him up. His neck is broken. Aunt Clarice held me. She told me Mama did it. I tore from Aunt Clarice's arms and ran past my cedar tree to the cliff where my mother and father were arguing again. 'I hate you!' I screamed at Mama, while I clutched Timi's body close to me. She said she never meant to hurt my pet. I don't believe her, and I tell her so. Then the dragon came again. It was dark, and I pushed Mama off the cliff."*

"No, Amy, it did not end that way. It was summer, late afternoon. The sun hadn't set. I've stood on that cliff. It is an open space with nothing to shadow the sun. The cedar tree is on the left of the cliff. Look closer, Amy. Remember. Your father and mother were near the edge and too far away. Who else was there, standing over you and blocking out the sun? Who, Amy?"

Amy began rubbing her hands. *"I'm alone. Nobody is with me."*

"You are not alone, Amy. Do not lie to me. Now tell me the truth."

Her voice rose with agitation. *"I'm alone I tell you. I can't see anyone else. It . . . It's the dragon."*

Purposely, Toshiro made his voice sterner. "There is no dragon, Amy. There never was. The darkness you've always remembered is just a shadow. Someone is standing in front of you. Look closer. Who is with you?"

"Please. I can't see anyone. I'm all alone. I . . . don't want to look. Please don't make me."

"My Lord," Joshua protested, "I really do not think you should continue—"

"Be quiet," Toshiro snapped over his shoulder.

Rigby looked at Keith, shook his head, but said nothing more.

"Who else is with you, Amy? Tell me," the hypnotic voice commanded close to her ear.

"No, please, I—"

"Damn it, you tell me now!"

"It's Aunt Clarice! She is laughing. She told Mama she has everything now, Papa and me. I don't understand. Aunt Clari is patting my shoulder to help me stop crying. She told me I'll be getting the present I want most in a few months."

"And what did you want, Amy?"

"A baby brother. Oh, but what is wrong? Papa looks ashamed. He won't look at Mama. She's started to cry again. Mama called Papa bad names. 'Stop! Please stop fighting.' But Mama keeps screaming at Papa. 'I hate you,' I tell Mama again. 'You killed Timi. You are always shrieking at Papa and me. You keep saying you're too ill to play with me. Aunt Clarice makes time for me. I . . . I wish Aunt Clarice was my Mama.' I shouldn't have said

that. I knew it when I saw the wildness in Mama's eyes as she looked back at me. Then she hurled herself over the edge of the cliff. When Papa tore off his coat to dive in after her, Clarice shouted, 'No, George, let her go. We don't need her.' Papa looked back at Aunt Clarice like he was seeing her for the first time. He wrenched his arm free from her grip and dove into the river. He didn't come back either. I'm frightened. I want to run away, but I can't. 'Come on, Aunt Clarice, we've got to get help.' I want to run for help, but I can't move."

"Why can't you move? Is Timi too heavy?"

"No. I put Timi on the ground."

Behind them they heard the doors that led to the garden open. All three men were too preoccupied to notice the late arrival.

"Then why can't you run for help?" Toshiro watched Amy increase the motions across her wrists. "Why can't you move, Amy?"

"I don't know. I just can't. I'm too afraid. I don't know."

"Yes, you do know. And it isn't your hands you keep rubbing. That day with the rabbit, Clarice said it was your hands. We were all too distracted to really notice. But it's your wrists you keep rubbing when you remember that night, isn't it, Amy? Tell me," he said in a voice that brooked no argument. "Why can't you run away?"

"Because Clarice took Timi's collar and tied my wrists to the low branch of the cedar tree!"

"My God," said Joshua Rigby. He looked at the Scot and could tell from Keith's expression he was just as appalled.

"I'm afraid to stay up here so close to the ledge alone. Aunt Clarice laughed and put my dead puppy in my lap

for company. Then she left. I'm so scared. It's getting dark, and the dragon will come back. He can only survive in the shadows. He watches me when I'm alone. I have to hide in that dark place where he won't ever find me."

Alarmed at Amy's expression, Toshiro got up and stood in front of her.

"They are gone," she whispered in a monotone. "All gone." She stared ahead, not seeing the three men about her.

"Amy?" Terror wrenched the soul from him. He wasn't even aware that Joshua and Keith now stood next to him.

"My God, Toshiro, she can't even hear you." Joshua took out a pocket handkerchief and wiped his sweating brow. "Something's gone wrong here."

Keith went over to her and took her wrist in his hands. "She's in shock."

Clarice Townsend walked slowly over to them. Dressed in a floral-print gown, she matched the warm evening. Taking in her niece's catatonic state, she clapped her hands in front of Amy's face, but there was no reaction. "You've done it, Toshiro. Hah, better than even I could have managed it. Your wife isn't here. I told you she was just like Jane, a weedy, cringing flower."

Automatically, Toshiro placed himself protectively in front of Amy. His expression was less than welcoming to his wife's aunt.

Clarice's dark eyes glinted with pleasure. "My Lord, your note said you needed to see me. I believe your bliss in the marriage bed has just come to an abrupt halt, thanks to your meddling."

Ignoring Clarice, Toshiro focused his attention back on Amy. Keith was checking her. "Amy?" he called again, trying to get her to respond.

"Good to see you, Joshua," Clarice said, acting as if nothing was amiss.

Joshua nodded grimly.

"Well," said Clarice, "Dr. Wakefield and I tried to warn the count about dredging up the past. Oh, Joshua," she said, as an afterthought, "I do want you to remember that Toshiro insisted, even before he wed my niece, Amy's will stands as originally written. If Amy dies or is incapacitated, as she is now, all Stockwell wealth and property become mine."

Mr. Rigby turned a jaundiced eye on Clarice, who was clearly basking in her good fortune. "Got it all planned, Miss Townsend, haven't you?"

Clarice looked pleased with herself. "Yes, either way I couldn't lose. If Amy committed suicide like her weak-minded mother, according to her will all Stockwell fortune becomes mine. If Amy married the Earl of Woodcroft, I knew I could easily control everything through malleable David, just as I did with George Stockwell."

It was Joshua's turn to smirk. "Only you never counted on Toshiro Valerius storming into Amy's life, did you? How disappointed you must have been when David failed to kill the count, after all the trouble you went through to fuel the hotheaded earl into challenging his Lordship. And didn't the count disrupt your plans again when Amy tried to kill herself after you told her she was dying. It seems Valerius is always getting in your way, isn't he?"

Before Clarice could reply, Dr. Stewart touched Toshiro on the shoulder. "It's no use. I'm sorry, my Lord. I can do nothing for her. The shock of learning the truth was apparently too much for her. Perhaps in time she'll. . . ." Appearing helpless, the Scot couldn't finish the sentence.

Toshiro's shoulders slumped, as Keith gently moved him out of the way so he could check Amy again. When the count saw Clarice's look of triumph, he stalked over to her, a cold fury in his green eyes. "Gentlemen," he addressed his two friends, "let me introduce you to the dragon that has haunted my wife's dreams for years. I remembered Clarice's penchant for Chinese jewelry. Putting it together with a few words Amy cried out when she had those nightmares, I tried to ponder how a terrified ten-year-old would describe a dragon with blood-red eyes and green talons. With the threat of prison, James Conroy was quite willing to sneak into Clarice's familiar boudoir and search her jewel case for this brooch." He pulled out the Chinese pin from his inside pocket.

Clarice reached out for the dragon pin with the ruby eyes and green emeralds at the diamond base. "George Stockwell gave me that pin. It's mine."

Toshiro went over and placed the dragon brooch in his wife's lap. "Look at it, Amy. I am certain Clarice wore this pin on her gown that night." When Amy did not respond, Toshiro looked at his two friends. "This . . . creature," he went on, pointing to Clarice, "tied her ten-year-old niece to the low branch of a tree and left her out near the edge of the cliff for five bloody hours. Clarice told the magistrate the sad tale of a frantic aunt searching until midnight for her niece, who had wandered away after witnessing her parents' tragic deaths." He confronted her. "And there never was any baby from your seduction of your sister's husband. You, not Jane or Amy, are the one who is barren, aren't you? Jealous over your elder sister's wealth and position, you became obsessed with getting everything. Dr. Wakefield, inattentive in his practice, only interested in the large fees he collected from you, prescribed laudanum for Amy, as well as her late mother. You administered the opium derivative in their tonic and hot chocolate. Groggy and listless, Amy was asleep by early evening, out of the way for you to have David visit you upstairs. And all the young, inexperienced servants were changed often before they could catch on to what you were really up to."

Clarice shrugged, then glanced back at the unmoving Amy. "You can have your imbecilic wife, Toshiro; she is my gift to you."

"Nooo!" Toshiro shouted, his rage at Clarice's treachery pushing him past the edge of his self-control. He went back to Amy and took her roughly into his arms. "I won't give you up," he cried to his wife. "Amy, listen to me. The truth cannot hurt you. We will face it together. Remember, you carry our child within you. Amy, please do not leave me. I can't live without you. I love you; I need you."

The mist began to clear within her mind. Amy stirred. She heard the anguished voice of her husband. She blinked, then looked up into his tormented face. The tears she saw in his eyes touched something deep within her heart. Slowly, Amy peered over his shoulder at her aunt. "I shared all I had with you, Clarice." Pulling herself away from Toshiro's arms, Amy stood up slowly. Holding the Chinese brooch in her hands, she touched the red ruby eyes. "The dragon," she mused aloud. The truth settled less violently against her. "I remember now. You knew how I blamed myself for my parents' deaths. You could have told me the truth to save me those last four years of torment. Why, Clarice?"

Joshua answered for her. "I was a fool not to have seen it before. Clarice knew you were getting close to your twenty-first birthday, and when you reached your majority you would be sole owner in charge of Stockwell Enterprises. Clarice had to insure her control didn't end."

Toshiro spoke up from behind his wife. "And what better way than to have you awaken from a drugged sleep with your pet rabbit strewn dead across your legs. Clarice knew it would bring back those horrible nightmares. And when you insisted on knowing the truth, wasn't Clarice happy to confirm your suspicions that you'd actually pushed Jane Stockwell off that cliff. The shock to your sensitive mind crushed you, affecting your body so that you needed that wheelchair."

Amy shook her head, hardly able to take it all in. "Clarice, I don't know whether I pity you more than I despise you. I only know I never want to see you again."

It was clear Clarice could not allow Amy to remain all right. "You won't cheat me!" she screamed, her face twisted with outrage. Her hands reached down for Amy's throat.

With an inhuman growl, the snarling panther cut Clarice off. He stood blocking her path. "Be thankful I do not have a sword in my hand, bitch, for I am closer to killing than you will ever imagine. You will never hurt Amy again." When Clarice sprang at him, the count was amazed at her strength. It took Joshua and Keith to pull her away from him.

"George should have married me," Clarice yelled, "not my plain older sister. All that money belongs to me; I'll never rely on the Stockwells for handouts again." Shaking with fury, Clarice couldn't free herself from the two men holding her away from her niece's husband.

The Eurasian never took his eyes off her. "I know you pushed Amy's wheelchair over the edge that day I rescued her. It wasn't an accident. I had a talk with James Conroy this afternoon. I know you paid him with more than money to saw those spokes off Amy's wheelchair."

"It doesn't matter," said Amy's aunt. "No one would believe you."

Toshiro reached into his coat pocket and pulled out the pieces of wood. "The magistrate will believe this proof. And Joshua and Keith have already heard your confession."

"You cunning, despicable—"

"I finally remembered that day you assisted Amy back from the sofa to her wheelchair," Toshiro interjected, his usual control returning. "Later, Iwao told me of the bruises on Sumi's arms after you forcefully ejected her from Stockwell Hall. At first I'd suspected your brothers or David. However, I just felt your hands when you fought me. A woman with such strong hands could easily twist the neck of a puppy, rabbit, or a kitten, something Amy's small, delicate fingers haven't the strength to do, along with my certainty she would never wittingly harm anyone."

"A verra evil woman," said Keith. When he looked at Rigby, both men tightened their hold on their insane charge.

"You idiots," Clarice shouted to her captors. "You can't believe Valerius. He isn't one of us. I sent him away when he came to see Amy after her parents died. Don't you think I'd protect our Amy? I told him she was in Italy. It's Amy you need to put away, not me. She's the crazy one. Just like Jane." Her voice became shriller in her desperation. "Let go of my arms." Her mood changed. Seductively, she rubbed her body against Keith's. "I know many ways to pleasure a man. Just ask

409

David. He's my slave and would do anything for me, just like James Conroy. Men are such fools." Then she laughed, but neither of the men joined her.

Toshiro looked down at his silent wife as Joshua and Keith led Clarice out of the garden. From flirtatious entreaties to raving obscenities, Clarice kept demanding to be have her arms freed.

Amy spoke to her husband. "Please, Toshiro, go with them. Promise me Clarice will be taken to a humane place. Not chained to a wall in those asylums I've heard about. Please, never that."

Toshiro caressed her white cheek with his fingers. "I promise you, darling. Keith knows of a place outside of Bristol where she will be well looked after. Will you be all right until I return?"

"Yes, I'll be all right . . . now. You said you loved me."

"I have loved you since that first time we met when—"

"I was ten and you were thirteen," she finished. "How could I have ever forgotten my wonderful panther?"

He told her about the painting he'd purchased four years ago, partly the instigation for his coming back to England to see her.

"After that incident when I thought I'd killed my mother, I found I couldn't look at that picture of me and Timi. However," she added, smiling up at him, "now I am glad it isn't lost. Perhaps if we have a daughter, we can show her the picture, and she'll understand where she gets her impudence."

When they kissed, it was a promise of love and hope. "Hurry back," she pleaded. "When things are settled, I'll arrange to have my aunt's things sent to her. They meant so much to her. And . . ." she held out the dragon pin.

"Please give this back to Clarice. My father meant it for her, and I have no use for it."

When the carriage was ready, Toshiro ordered Iwao and Sumi to see to their mistress until he returned. He would keep his promise to Amy to see that Clarice was treated compassionately. Nonetheless, the count could not bear to ride in the same coach with that woman. Toshiro rode Kori, while Joshua and Keith stayed inside the Valerius coach with their patient.

It was near midnight when Toshiro made his weary way back home. Sedated by Dr. Stewart with her much-touted laudanum, Clarice proved most cooperative when they took her to a place outside of Bristol. A minister and his wife ran the sanitarium. After a thorough inspection of the premises where Clarice would reside, Toshiro, Keith, and Joshua made the necessary arrangements for her commitment.

As he came up the hill toward his estate, the count tightened his hands on the reins when he saw the orange cast in the night sky. Pressing his knees to Kori's flanks, the exhausted man pushed himself toward Valerius Hall. Terror gripped him when the acrid stench of smoke stung his nostrils. Flames rose into the night sky. He charged to the back of the house, jumped off Kori's saddle, even before the horse had come to a complete halt. Frantically, the count rushed past the open gate to the garden.

He stopped when he saw his wife. Sumi and Iwao were standing behind her like sentinels guarding a precious jewel. He looked down at the burning wood of her wheelchair. Relief swept through him.

Amy turned when she heard his boots crunch on the

gravel path. She smiled after he placed his arms around her shoulders.

Her husband said nothing, for he realized this was Amy's symbolic gesture of giving up her guilt-ridden past. They watched the flames consume the wheelchair until it was just a small mass of cinders. Then he said something in Japanese to Iwao and Sumi. They bowed and left.

"Come, golden lotus." Toshiro turned his wife toward their home. "Sumi and Iwao will make certain the fire is out. Enough adventure for one day." Kissing her tenderly, he ran his fingers through her silky blond hair.

"I hope you do not mind," she said when he freed her lips. "I have decided to turn Stockwell Hall over to my uncles. It was the Townsend family home for generations until Papa saved it from being sold for taxes when he married Mama. I have too many painful memories there. I could never live there again."

"Nor could I," he stated.

"I know I asked a great deal of you tonight in accompanying Joshua and Keith. I am most grateful."

"Amy, when I think of what Clarice did to you, I swear only my love for you kept me from killing that evil bi—"

Amy pressed her fingers to her husband's lips. "We will not speak of it. Forgive it as I have. We have too much to be thankful for to hold on to thoughts of revenge or hatred. My aunt was consumed by such dark feelings."

He hugged her close. "God, I died a thousand times when I thought I'd destroyed you tonight, making you remember the past."

She felt him shudder in her arms. "Darling, I never would have been able to confront the truth if you hadn't shown me the way. I am not afraid of the past or the future because of you," she admitted, her eyes misting.

He claimed her lips. There wasn't an ounce of reserve or holding back in his kiss. "I love you, Amy," he said, after reluctantly freeing her lips. He saw what his blue-black stubble was doing to her smooth little face. "You see, *koneko,* I shall never have my fill of you."

"I find that most acceptable," she said, giving him an Oriental answer.

"Amy-san, you are a delightful scoundrel."

"I do my best." She pressed her body closer to his. "Your son says he is hungry," she murmured, resting her blond head on his chest. "I think there is still some roast beef left from dinner. Let's sleep in the Eastern Wing after we eat."

Toshiro knew she was asking him to make love to her in their private rooms furnished in the Japanese style. Concern overcame his longing. "But is it safe, so close to your time, beloved?"

Amy smiled up at her husband. "Not to worry, for I shall be gentle with the panther," she teased.

Unable to deny her anything, Toshiro allowed his lovely English wife to lead them back up the path to their home.

About The Author

MARY BURKHARDT lives in Southeastern Massachusetts with her husband. She worked as an administrative secretary in the sciences for sixteen years. This year she begins her twentieth year as a nursing home volunteer visitor. Her previous Zebra historicals include *Forbidden Hearts, Midnight Heat,* and *Highland Ecstasy.*

CAPTURE THE GLOW OF
ZEBRA'S *HEARTFIRES!*

CAPTIVE TO HIS KISS (3788, $4.25/$5.50)
by Paige Brantley
Madeleine de Moncelet was determined to avoid an arranged marriage to the Duke of Burgundy. But the tall, stern-looking knight sent to guard her chamber door may thwart her escape plan!

CHEROKEE BRIDE (3761, $4.25/$5.50)
by Patricia Werner
Kit Newcomb found politics to be a dead bore, until she met the proud Indian delegate Red Hawk. Only a lifetime of loving could soothe her desperate desire!

MOONLIGHT REBEL (3707, $4.25/$5.50)
by Marie Ferrarella
Krystyna fled her native Poland only to live in the midst of a revolution in Virginia. Her host may be a spy, but when she looked into his blue eyes she wanted to share her most intimate treasures with him!

PASSION'S CHASE (3862, $4.25/$5.50)
by Ann Lynn
Rose would never heed her Aunt Stephanie's warning about the unscrupulous Mr. Trent Jordan. She knew what she wanted—a long, lingering kiss bound to arouse the passion of a bold and ardent lover!

RENEGADE'S ANGEL (3760, $4.25/$5.50)
by Phoebe Fitzjames
Jenny Templeton had sworn to bring Ace Denton to justice for her father's death, but she hadn't reckoned on the tempting heat of the outlaw's lean, hard frame or her surrendering wantonly to his fiery loving!

TEMPTATION'S FIRE (3786, $4.25/$5.50)
by Millie Criswell
Margaret Parker saw herself as a twenty-six year old spinster. There wasn't much chance for romance in her sleepy town. Nothing could prepare her for the jolt of desire she felt when the new marshal swept her onto the dance floor!

Available wherever paperbacks are sold, or order direct from the Publisher. Send cover price plus 50¢ per copy for mailing and handling to Zebra Books, Dept. 4415, 475 Park Avenue South, New York, N.Y. 10016. Residents of New York and Tennessee must include sales tax. DO NOT SEND CASH. For a free Zebra/Pinnacle catalog please write to the above address.